THE SONG OF THE CYPRESS

GW00400026

CFO

MODERN

THE SONG OF THE CYPRESS

Tonia Parronchi

Sussurro Books

THE SONG OF THE CYPRESS
A SUSSURO BOOK: ISBN 9788890510700

Published by **Sussurro Books**

Second Edition

A catalogue record for this book is available from the British Library

Printed and bound in Great Britain

For my parents, Audrey and Derek, who taught me to dream.
For Guido who shared those dreams and made them his.
For Chris and Andrea, the other dreamers of the family.
For James who made all those dreams come true.

Acknowledgements

I would like to thank all of those who have made this book possible. Any mistakes contained within its pages are mine alone. The hardest thing I found when writing this book was describing the difficult relationships between my protagonists and their parents. These kind of tortured relationships are very common but I am lucky enough to have the most wonderful, stimulating and loving family. They are always there for me whilst giving me my freedom, so that the bonds that tie us never chafe.

Particular thanks go to Caroline Zimmermann, who allowed me to use her beautiful paintings for the cover of this book; www.carolinezimmermann.com.

When I met Scarlett Laroma several years ago and listened to her talks on nature and how we can understand our own souls by looking into the mirror of the elements, I was inspired to begin writing this book. To see Scarlett's beautiful art and words visit her web site: www.bright-threads.com

For all my Italian friends, especially the ladies of my village who have been so generous with their time and memories; Rita, Anna, Elena, Gabriella, Iolanda and Nella.

Special thanks to my friend and agent Abigail Knight and to all those who have read, re-read, corrected and encouraged me each step of the way: Barbara De Mars, Di Blenkinsop, Julia Boone, Maggie Kalnins, Patricia Baldwin, Themah Carrolle-Casey, Vesna Lazarevic-Krebser - you are an amazing group of friends.

SPRING

The Waiting

Spring, season of new beginnings, when all seems possible.
I remember my own beginning as a vague, blind awareness; a subtle
sensation of gritty soil and cool, damp darkness around me. Then a
certainty of something other, a force that could not be ignored. I felt a
swelling within, a desire to expand and push inexorably upwards. I
reached out, snaking thin, vulnerable shoots in the direction that drew me.
At my core, dank coolness enwrapped me but with each surge of energy,
my thinning tips explored new sensations of crumbly earth, pungent with
the scent of leaf mould, moss and spore. At last, the first glimpse of pale
light sent shockwaves through me and triggered a heady spurt of growth,
as I surged to join the miraculous daylight.
After this first frantic scramble for life I settled back, growing slowly in my
sheltered space among the old stones, last relic of the men of Tuscia;
growing accustomed to the rising sun that brought warmth to the day and
the rhythms of the moon as it painted me silver at night. Through a slow,
steady cycle of seasons, I grew ever upward until my girth pushed aside
the stones that had once protected me and I towered above all that
surrounded me and dominated my world.
For the longest time I stood alone, content in my solitude.
Men came and built their dwellings nearby and I watched children play
and grow, age and die. Over time, the homes were abandoned and
rediscovered, the land worked and then forgotten. Soldiers came and with
them came fear but nothing lasts forever:
I was alone once more.
Time and space flowed around me in never-ending circles.
I delighted in each moment of day or year.
I dreamt through centuries yet focused on the intimate second.
I felt my strength grow until it was too great to be constrained by bark and
leaf and then, as I expanded, stretching out toward the universe, I felt the
shock of connection with someone who stopped to rest in my shade. This
was only the first of many such communions with the human soul; so
fragile and yet so brave. Now and then, as centuries passed, a special
soul drew near, one who could hear my song and who, for a short time
sang with me.

1

The old one, who has shared her life with me in this most recent span of time, is tiring now and impatient for her successor to come. When she stops to rest in my shade her once beautiful hands, where they lie on me, are as dark and gnarled as my bark itself.

She has found peace within her heart and now longs to be free of the aching shell of body that holds her in this dimension.

She will not leave me though until she is sure that her true heir is here and so, together, we wait.

Time stretches around me on a chain of circular links, smoothly swirling from one moment to the next.
Certain moments are particularly intense, cutting boldly through the intricate melody of time; as in the instant when I sense a new soul draw near. I feel such a presence now. "She is coming" I whisper to the wind that lazily teases my branches and let it carry my message across the forest to where the old one restlessly waits.

The room was mine: every deep, night-blurred contour was familiar. The faint light from the clock gave the darkness a green tinge as I moved my eyes slowly around the room, focusing on the sharp corners of the wardrobe and the shadowed waves of curtain, unable to understand what it was about the room that was unsettling me. Everything, even the small night-sounds of floorboards settling and the hiss of the radiator, was familiar and yet there was something drastically wrong with my perspective, giving my vision a nightmarish quality. There was a confusion of shapes on the ceiling and a vague, silver glow emanating from it, like a finely spun strand of spider's web hanging down towards me. The feeling of disquiet grew as my eyes began to adjust to the dimness and I suddenly understood what I was looking at. I gasped, fear clawing at my stomach as I realised that there were no weird shapes above me, instead I was looking down from the ceiling at my own body curled up beneath the duvet, a streak of hair across the pillow and one arm flung across the bed.

I jerked in shock and swayed sideways in the air. I turned my head; behind me was the ceiling. Panicked, I felt myself plummet back toward the bed. I was going too fast and drew up my knees to avoid banging my feet painfully against the iron bed frame. I was not quick enough, but to my surprise, instead of hitting the frame, my feet simply slid through it and through the sheets and mattress too. I pulled up again until I was hovering just above the bed staring at my sleeping figure as it breathed regularly, undisturbed by the commotion in my mind. The feeling of panic began to pass as my brain sought solutions to the puzzle.

It had to be a dream, I concluded. I was simply dreaming of being out of my body and floating around my room. There was nothing to fear; actually, the sensation of weightlessness was quite enjoyable. I tried to go upward again and found that I could manoeuvre this dream body with extreme ease. I watched the silver thread, which I had thought to be a spider's web, as it fluctuated behind me, following me as I swept and swerved above the bed. One end of the thread seemed to be attached to my sleeping body's forehead, the other to my dream body. I remembered reading about experiences like this somewhere, where it had been called astral travel or an out-of-body experience and I was quite impressed with my mind's ability to remember such an obscure fact and transform it into this vivid dream.

I smiled and swooped across the room towards the window. There was a slim gap between the thick, velvet drapes. I moved closer, intending to peep through and see what view I could conjure up outside the window, to test just how real I could make this dream, but found that I could not stop. As if my body were made of nothing more substantial than the air itself, I slipped through the curtains, passed effortlessly through the glass and found myself hovering outside my bedroom window. The sudden distance from the ground made me breathless for a moment.

Beneath me lay the gravel drive, between the high, tight hedge that shut the house off from the road. In the light from a street lamp that overhung the hedge the house showed dimly; a squat, brooding shape with tall curtained windows frowning over the bulge of the porch. I felt the usual surge of rebellious distaste as I stared at my home and for once, I did not force myself to swallow the feelings, square my shoulders and put my key in the lock.

4

Instead, I lifted my head toward the streetlamp and drifted through the air towards its hopeful brightness.

As I moved, I was very aware of the pulse of my blood through my veins, even though this insubstantial body should not really possess such physical characteristics. The drumming of my pulse grew louder until it filled my head and underneath it, I heard another sound, my name repeated time and again as a kind of music that reverberated through the air, distant but insistent.

"Ann, Ann", my name was a melody that I was drawn towards, unable to turn back and, no matter how hard I tried, unable to wake up. I flew through the dark, slowly at first, sweeping above well-known houses and roads, then gathering speed until all below me was a blur; shades of dark and flashes of city lights. The air rushed past me, tore through me. I was insubstantial, a veil of spirit made of raw, throbbing emotions; a network of nerve pulses and heartbeats.

The darkness lifted in degrees. I saw brief glimpses of landscape through gaps in the clouds as I roared above them, caught in the grip of the wind or the pull of the stars at my back; an expanse of sea, golden ripples on the purple sheen of deep water; a flash of jagged peaks, white ice shooting blinding sparks at me as it reflected the first rays of the sun. Then the mad rush slowed again and I could make out individual landmarks. I flew between the long blue shadow of a mountain range and the rolling green hills that faced the mountains, down into a valley covered in a patchwork of forests, green fields and olive groves.

I slid effortlessly towards the ground. The early sun shimmered on the dew that collected in droplets on blades of grass and new spring leaves. I had never had a dream of such sensory clarity or one that felt so real. The sounds that I had been following were much stronger now, although the melody itself was not as clear. It had broken into separate notes that were still hauntingly beautiful despite their discordance. My feet touched the ground and sank straight through it. I pulled up, hovering just above the long grass dotted with shivering cobwebs and laughed to find that I really

5

could smell the fresh scent of the morning. The sun was no longer blinding me I realised and looked up to find myself standing in a dark finger of shadow.

A fierce thrill shuddered through my ethereal body as the cool shade enfolded me and I stared up at the tall, verdant column of an ancient cypress tree. The rising sun behind it could not penetrate its thick branches, which spiralled up the tree like many knotted arms, tightly holding secrets within their embrace. The sunlight, unable to pierce the foliage, burst around the tree instead so that it looked as if it were a pillar of fire.

I had the strangest feeling of homecoming. The music in my head had changed to a gentle whisper of morning sounds; birdsong, the dry rustle of a lizard on a stone and a gentle breeze that rippled through the olive grove at my side, raising whip-like branches in undulating, silver-green waves. It was as if time had stopped still and no place, except this one, truly existed. I moved closer to the flaming cypress, its strong, resinous perfume filling my head, until I was close enough to reach out and touch the deeply grooved bark with my outstretched finger.

We connected and a shaft of energy shot through me so powerfully that I jerked away, breaking the connection and then I was falling, falling. Pulled backwards by some opposing force, I cried out to the cypress. I wanted to cling to that place, which had called me to it with a siren's song, did not want to return to my true life and my real body.

I sat up with a jerk, tears damp on my cheeks and the dim light of a grey English dawn filtering through the curtains in my room. I took a few minutes, sitting in my crumpled bed and trying to shake off the hold the dream still had on me until I gradually began to focus on everything that had to be done. It was the funeral today. I had to get the refreshments ready for those who wanted to come back here after the church service and I had to tidy up and clean the house too. I swung my legs heavily out of bed and opened the curtains. It was drizzling. Apt, I thought dryly, making my way to the bathroom, through the oppressive silence of the house. I had

6

lived with this feeling for years but there was a new edge to the suffocating quiet this morning as I absorbed the absence of those habitual, small shuffling noises from my mother's bedroom.

I opened the door to her room and let the mantle of utter solitude slide over me. I observed the room dispassionately. I had automatically remade the bed after the ambulance had taken her body away; sheets and covers precisely folded in layers of blue and grey. Without drawing the curtains, I made my way through the gloom and opened the wardrobe. The clothes Mother had worn, on the rare occasions when I had managed to coax her from the bed, hung in a limp row. I shut the door with a bang, wrinkling my nose as the smell of mothballs chased away the last trace of the fresh, resinous perfume of my dream. The whole house was still full of Mother. The dreary colours were hers, the stale smells were hers, and the rooms were still dimmed with pulled blinds and curtains to sooth Mother's pain, to contain her depression.

Later, at the funeral, I thought that the darkness in my heart seemed to be concentrated into an almost tangible force: the black hearse, the vicar, people's clothes and ties; even the blackbird, sitting silently in the holly bush, as we walked into the graveyard and above it all the sullen, rain-laden sky of England in the spring.

After the funeral, everyone crowded into the small dining room, around the table I had dutifully set with sandwiches and sponge cakes. There were not really many mourners but with them all packed together in the small room, awkwardly holding cups of tea and paper plates, there seemed too many.

My friend Becky suggested wine but I said no, wine might encourage everyone to linger and I wanted them gone. I traipsed in and out of the kitchen with endless pots of tea, filling and refilling the kettle, catching snippets of conversation as I passed. I felt invisible. I noticed that, when they found themselves alone with me, people were uneasy; they tried to be kind but did not know what to say. Although everyone knew what these past years had been like for me, they nevertheless seemed to expect me to fall apart, to be desolate now that I was on my own at last. It was as if

7

they thought I had no life of my own and had existed merely as part of a package marked Mother and Ann.

Finally, people began to leave. As I passed the lounge after saying goodbye to some relatives, I overheard men's voices in the lounge and paused, uncertain whether to offer them more tea or leave them alone. I heard Dave's voice and Jim's soft laugh as he replied. It took me another few seconds before I realised that they were talking about me and by that time, I had already heard too much.

"You should get in there, Jim. She must be worth a bit now."

"Yeah, right, Dave!"

"Why not? She hasn't got anyone else."

"Not my type, is she." Jim laughed again and I imagined his eyes crinkling up around the edges; the way they had when he had sat at my kitchen table, drinking tea before packing away his tools for the night, looking with satisfaction at the new patio he was laying. A wink, a wave, a cheerful "See you tomorrow, doll" and he would leave me every evening feeling warmed by his easy company.

I hurried back to the kitchen. Squeezing past Uncle Harold, I crossed the kitchen, picked up the empty kettle and plunged it under the cold tap. My reflection bulged absurdly in the metal. My nose loomed at me and my face was a flustered moon, blue eyes swimming with unshed tears.

Jim was not my type either, but I enjoyed his friendship and it hurt to be dismissed so casually.

Becky came to find me then, her high heels clacking over the kitchen tiles. Her perfume swirled around us as we hugged. I walked her and Dave to the door, watching them go with enormous relief. Jim touched my shoulder as I stood there, shivering on the doorstep.

"Ok, darlin?" he asked kindly "Give us a bell if you need anything, all right." His boots crunched off down the gravel, the wind blowing his blond hair across his forehead. Thankfully, the last of the relatives followed him when he left, with a chorus of well-meant but insincere exhortations to stay in touch.

"Promise to call."

"You know where we are if you need us, love."

"Come and visit soon, Ann. Ring if you feel lonely."

When they had gone, I carefully cleared everything away and washed up, until the very last trace of them had been wiped out. Then I opened the wine that had been cooling all day, put it into an ice bucket, piled a plate with crackers and cheese and took it into the lounge. I drew the curtains against the streetlamp and the dark drizzle that it illuminated, put on a Percy Sledge CD and sat down on the floor in the middle of the room.

Alone again, I let my mind finally dwell on the images that had been insistently intruding on my thoughts all day. I replayed my dream slowly, until my eyes glazed over. It seemed as if time stretched out around me; future, present and past entwined. Percy sang, I ate. The wine glowed amber as it caught the light. It was over. I was free to be myself again, the way I had been as I spun wildly in the wind of my dream. In the dream, I had been reduced to an ethereal body of pure and absolute self and now that I had glimpsed that spark; the small, fluttering, bird-like thing caught inside the cage that I had built around it; I did not want to lose it again.

Sighing, I considered the fact that I was not sad about my mother's death, felt guilty but not sad. I had looked after her; cooked, cleaned, washed her clothes and urine-stained sheets. I had done everything that a dutiful daughter ought to do, but I had done it without love. I was guilty of not having loved enough, of not being patient enough and that guilt had burnt into me every evening for years, but now I could set myself free of that too. It was as if, in admitting the truth to myself, I had found a kind of absolution.

I poured myself another glass of wine and watched a rainbow curve through the crystal as I brought the glass to my lips. I'm like that, I thought. I'm a transparent glass; an invisible person; an

9

object used every day, automatically but unnoticed. I am a work colleague or an old school friend, someone to be unthinkingly put on the guest list for a party without really being wanted. Yet there was still that spark inside, an inner glow, the only part of me that was real.

For so many years, I had lived in a kind of numb routine. No one knew me, I hardly knew myself anymore. Layer upon layer of self-protection had been added over the years. I looked at the vague reflection of myself in the dark windowpane and assessed myself critically; amorphous, body disguised under baggy clothes, my face hidden behind a sweep of light brown hair.

I twirled my glass by its stem, watching it sparkle and it seemed as if there was a sudden slight scent of cypress in the room. It was time for me to change, seek out the light.

I felt myself opening up to life again, the way I had as a child. I remembered being happier when my father was alive but I had been young then and afterwards the black depression that had closed around my mother had pulled me into its web too. My mother had not noticed anything that went on outside her own head. Because I had been invisible to my mother, I had learnt to ignore myself and hide myself away but that could all change now. My father had left us quite well-off and we had hardly touched the bulk of the money in the bank, since my salary had been enough for our usual expenses. I decided right then that I would put the house, that I hated so much, up for sale and take a year off. I would go travelling and let myself enjoy the freedom of being able to do whatever I decided to do. I raised my glass to my reflection and made a silent toast, to new beginnings.

I was so busy over the next few days, as I cut the threads that tied me to my old life, that time passed with a blur. I resigned from my job over the phone, finding it easier to deflect my boss's well-meant questions without having to look him in the eye. He obviously thought me traumatised by Mother's death and promised that there would always be work for me if I changed my mind. I did not let anyone else know about my plans, not wanting to discuss them, for fear that doing so would spoil the thrill. I booked a flight to Pisa, knowing that I had to start my travels in Tuscany, where my vivid dream had called me. There was a practical motive for starting with Italy too. I had a basic knowledge of the language from some evening classes I had taken and once there I could decide where to go to next.

When it was finally time to leave, I felt as if it was the first moment that I had had to slow down and breathe deeply since deciding to go away. As I stood at the open front door, waiting for a taxi to take me to the airport for my early morning flight I forced myself to take a good, long look at what I was leaving behind. The darkness of the hallway at my back was layered with scents and memories, from my childhood to the present day and few of them were pleasant. The morning air was cold and damp. It clung to my skin, like the clammy touch of a ghost and I shivered and folded my arms more tightly around myself, reluctant to go back inside in spite of the chill. There were no regrets, I could not wait to leave this place behind.

With relief, I heard the throb of an engine and then bright headlights broke up the dark as the taxi swerved into the drive. I slammed the front door behind me and climbed into the taxi, turning just once to look at the house as we drove off. It was already blending into the night, returning to obscurity. I sat back in the taxi, clutching my handbag on my knee, as the repetitive strobe of the streetlamps rushed past outside, sending my reflection in the window into shadow and out again.

"I am heading for the light," I whispered to myself and my reflection smiled back at me, slightly tremulous but resolute.

As I dragged my suitcase, on its clumsy wheels, through the artificial brightness of the airport and checked in my luggage, I wondered once more whether I should ring anyone to tell them where I was heading but my conclusion was the same as it had been before – there was no one that I would miss enough to phone and no one who would miss me. From now on, I was on my own, I thought, and felt my heart lighten.

I arrived in Pisa mid-morning and hired a car at the airport. My Italian was rustier than I had thought but fortunately the girl at the car-hire desk spoke basic English and after that, I got by with much gesticulation and a lot of good will. Once in the car I had to force myself to concentrate on driving on the right and without having any idea of a final destination I found myself on the A1, the "motorway of the sun", that runs the length of Italy. I headed towards Florence, humming to myself as I drove in tuneless contentment. Traffic whizzed past me even though I was only just keeping to the speed limit myself. I had one bad moment when I finally found a car that I needed to overtake and checked my mirror before pulling out. A large silver Mercedes was speeding along the fast lane a fair distance behind and as I began to pull out, it flashed me. Usually I would have taken that as a sign for me to go ahead but the rapid, aggressive flashing was too insistent and I moved back into my lane. Seconds later the car swept past so fast that the hire car shuddered in the gust of displaced air. I drove more cautiously after that and saw that the Italians habitually used a flash of headlights to indicate that they were in a rush, going fast and did not intend to stay behind anything else. I would have to get used to a new road language as well as brushing up my Italian.

As I drew nearer to Florence, I debated whether to stop but was not in the mood for cities or people, so I kept on driving, heading south. The countryside now began to be prettier than the flattish, factory filled land I had driven past so far. Hills rose on either side of the motorway, dotted with cypress trees and impressive villas. This was more the way I had imagined Italy to look and I settled back in the driver's seat and began to relax and enjoy myself.

I only left the motorway at Valdarno because I was beginning to feel hungry and I regretted it straight away when I found myself trapped in the busy roads that wrapped around the town of Montevarchi. I bypassed the town, a little disappointed at the industrial estates and tired looking, dust-engrained houses that lined the road. Even the yellow, ochre and terracotta paint was dulled by traffic fumes and dust although now and then a pretty wrought-iron balcony or show of bright geraniums alleviated the drab scenery. As I drove away from the town, the events of the last week and the early start that morning caught up with me and I felt too tired and hungry to go much further.

I found myself on a road heading towards Arezzo and, as I left the outskirts of Montevarchi behind, I was suddenly immersed in the countryside. Softly rolling hills stretched out, covered in pale vineyards and green fields dotted with farmhouses and beyond the dark green backdrop of thick forests climbing the crests of the hills. On impulse, I turned off the main road onto a tiny lane, little more than a dirt track really, that cut through brushwood and then plunged into a dense woodland of oak trees. I slowed right down and rubbed my tired eyes with one hand as the car bumped over the boulders and lurched across potholes. After about half a mile, the wood thinned and receded until I was driving between tall cypress trees that lined each side of the road in graceful formality.

There was something about that cypress-lined track that drew me to it, tempted me further along it, in spite of the rough road surface that strained the car's suspension to the limit. I began to feel strangely elated, my early tiredness slipping away. I unwound the window to let the dusty air bring the scents of spring woodland to me and I laughed out loud. It was like being on a ride at the fair, bumping over stones and swerving around the torturous bends while breathing in unfamiliar scents and a general air of excitement.

I came to a fork in the road and stopped, unsure which direction to take. As I hesitated, an old woman stepped into view, startling me as she emerged from a half-hidden track in the undergrowth. She stared at me piercingly with clear blue eyes set in a maze of sun-baked wrinkles. She looked such a part of the landscape, in her faded brown dress, her white hair shimmering in the sun like fluffy dandelion seed, and I was so taken aback by her sudden appearance, that I just sat and returned her stare. The sound of the engine idling quietly seemed to echo the beat of my heart. There

13

was no other sound, no birds chirping, not even a soft play of breeze through the leaves. It seemed as if a stillness had descended on the land with the appearance of the old woman and, although she was a stranger to me, there was something so familiar about her that I was utterly transfixed. The moment dragged out, until at last, with a mischievous grin, the old woman raised her arm and pointed a gnarled finger to the right, where the road wound uphill. I thanked her with a nod and drove on. When I checked in the mirror, she had already vanished back into the forest. I was a little unnerved. I knew that I had never seen her before but she had seemed like a part of my past, like a memory that I could glimpse but not quite put into focus. Looking into her remarkable, slightly mocking eyes, I had felt a connection deeper than any I could remember, as if she knew me so well that she could read my thoughts and see deep into my soul.

I carried on driving uphill until the road levelled off and on my right, hidden by a wall studded with caper plants and dried moss, I glimpsed the roofs of several buildings. Around another bend, the road tilted sharply uphill and I changed down to first gear, sympathising as the car whined in protest. It was worth the effort though because as I drove under the arch of a delicate bell tower the sky glowed cobalt blue behind the huge, weathered bell and then the road ended in the cobbled courtyard of a lovely manor, comfortable in its faded, slightly neglected, elegance. Several buildings framed a lawn with an enormous horse-chestnut tree at its centre. The tree's far-reaching branches danced in the breeze that blew, unhindered, through a wide gap between the buildings. Beyond the valley spread out into the distance in myriad shades of green.

The place seemed deserted but, as I got out to take a closer look at the spectacular view, a movement under the tree caught my eye. In the shade, I could now make out two people with several lazy-looking dogs sprawled at their feet. Tails wagged lethargically but the dogs made no move to investigate me. One of the figures came bustling forward; a woman on the wrong side of middle age, her

14

thin, lined face at contrasts with the abundant curves of her body. She burst into speech that was far too rapid for me to be able to understand. I waved my hands in a kind of sign language, hoping that she would speak more slowly so that I would be able to follow her. She laughed, planting her hands on her hips and leant towards me, quivering with suppressed energy as she strained to understand my basic Italian. Close up I could see a thick line of grey roots beneath long hair that had been dyed an improbable shade of dark plum.

I managed to explain to her, stumbling somewhat over the awkward words, that I was looking for a place to stay. The woman clapped her hands when I had finished, which made me laugh. She looked at me consideringly and a slight frown flickered across her features as if she was unsure of something. Then she smiled again and surprised me by cupping my cheek gently with a work-rough hand. She pointed down at the valley

"There, I have a house that might do for you. It is early in the season still and I have no bookings for it yet." She broke off frowning slightly again and then shook her head as if to clear it and continued with a laugh,

"Come, come I will show you the house. My name is Lucia. I will take you there now. Just let me get my car keys and you can follow me down." Lucia chattered on as she walked off toward the garage without seeming to pause for breath. She kept talking even though it was obvious that I could no longer hear what she was saying and I laughed quietly as I looked toward the valley, wondering where the house that she had indicated was.

Beneath the dappled shadow of the horse chestnut, a tall man stood in the circle of dogs, watching me. He wore old jeans and a white T-shirt. His hair was a shiny dark wing that fell across his eyes and as I watched, he shoved it away from his forehead and I saw that his eyes were as dark as his hair. Lucia returned and climbed into her car, gesturing for me to follow her. I let her drive away and then followed her dust cloud at a distance. As I passed the man, I glanced at him again. He was crouched down, petting the dogs and gave a languid wave as I drove away. For the second time that morning, I looked back in the car mirror, disconcerted by something I had seen in the eyes of a stranger. Unlike the old woman in the wood, the man did not disappear. He stood up and stepped out into the sunlight. His gaze was so intense that it made my skin tingle. I checked the mirror again as I turned the bend. He was still there, his lips curved in the slightest of smiles and I watched him, watching me, until he was lost from view.

2

The waiting is over. She came down the road with the woman from the hill; an unprepossessing girl at first sight, long hair shadowing her face and shapeless clothes that made her look disproportioned.
The old one hid behind the girth of my trunk and watched with me, shaking her head and muttering lists of herbs beneath her breath: essence of cypress to sooth the nerves and tone the skin and geranium for woman's self-esteem, to lift the spirit and chase away guilt. She intuitively anticipates what the girl will need most.
As the girl stepped from the car, she turned and looked at me and I felt the shock of connection run through us like hot sap. Here then is my new soul to comfort and watch over. Like a wounded child, she carries her past as a heavy weight but I will take her tears from her and weep away her pain. This is my strength, Apollo's gift.

I threw open the faded wooden shutters, letting the pale morning light flood the room; skimming over my face, chasing the shadows from the whitewashed walls. The shutter brushed over slender tips of lavender beneath the window, then slammed into its rusty latch. Under my fingers, the marble windowsill was smooth and cool and a scent drifted up from the lavender that was ready to bloom any day now.

A month ago, when I arrived, the plants had been smaller; round, velvety-green shrubs growing along the house in the dusty ground. I had known at once that I would be happy here. My eyes had been dazzled by the colours; the yellow stone walls, warm terracotta tiles and a sky the hue of the flowers on the rosemary bushes. I had rented the house without hesitation as soon as Lucia had shown it to me, because of its beauty but mostly because of the cypress.

My eyes sought out the tree at the end of the drive. I had recognised it immediately as the tree from my dream, the one that had called me to it with its strange, enchanted song. I still felt the sense of awe that had shuddered through me at my first sight of the tree. I had never been aware of possessing any kind of sixth sense before but could not deny that I had foreseen this place. Seeing the cypress looming before me, like a dark sentinel as I approached my new home, had sent a thrill though me so that the hairs on my body had risen with a kind of electric response. I found myself extraordinarily drawn to this tree. Its presence never failed to sooth me. It had become a symbol of my new life, of my ability to stand alone and endure everything that life might put in my way. I took comfort from it every day; it made the dark shadows of England seem far away, nothing more than an unpleasant memory that could be easily pushed aside by the scent of lavender and soft sunlight on my skin.

The house itself was charming. Made of old stone, it had been added onto over the years, giving it a charmingly irregular look and rose bushes grew in thick profusion around the sturdy wooden front door. Above the door was a small niche that held the statue of a woman with a secretive smile. Lucia had told me that it was a *madonnina* and that most old houses had a Madonna like that to bring blessing onto the house and those who lived there. To me the statue looked surprisingly real in spite of the years that she had stood outside in all weathers. Instead of the usual style of piously downcast eyes, this statue gazed boldly out, smiling straight at the cypress, as if the two of them shared some secret.

This morning there was a faint misty haze over the valley, moisture caught between yesterday's gentle, evening rain and today's promised heat. I leant out of the window, breathed deeply. The air was still cool with a hint of wild herbs and resinous cypress. The mist was strung out in intriguing patches, dappling fields of green corn and ancient olive groves; rising partly up the hills on the far side of the valley in ghostly swathes. It wrapped

18

around the cypress, softening the grooves in the rough bark and fading the deep green of its spiralling, exclamatory fronds.

Pulling on a T-shirt I went down to make coffee. The worn stone steps and polished terracotta tiles felt pleasantly cool on my bare feet. I hardly bothered with shoes any more. I boiled milk and waited for the coffee to bubble thickly through the small metal pot on the hob. I had stopped drinking tea since coming here too, the taste of it brought back memories of England that I just did not need.

Coffee in hand I wandered outside. The peeling, green paint of the kitchen door rasped against my arm as I passed. My feet made contact with small pebbles in the dust then damp grass that raised a fresh, morning scent. I sat on the edge of the old millstone table, sipped my coffee and put it down. Small birds darted from bush to bush, calling to each other. In the distance, I could hear the faint rumble of a truck labouring its way up the hillside from the sand quarry. Apart from that, there was silence.

Here I found myself aware of every sense, every sensation, in a way I had never known before. It was as if I had been muffled, wrapped up in a chrysalis and only now was able to see and feel properly. Looking down at my legs, I noticed that they were slimmer and lightly tanned, an outward sign of the changes within me.

I focused on a small, childhood scar, just visible in the crease of my knee and smiled, remembering how I had cried while Dad bathed it and rubbed pink ointment onto it. Molly the dog had pulled me over, when the neighbour's cat scared her with a hiss from the branches of the tree above us and I had not had the sense to let the lead go. It was one of the few, clear, memories of my father that I had and I was momentarily overwhelmed by a surge of nostalgia.

There was a stray black cat here too, which came around sometimes, searching for scraps. I could see it now, flat in the long grass by the side of the path, amber eyes fixed on the sparrows and just the tip of its tail in movement. In the past, I would have moved quickly to scare the cat away and save the small birds but here I just watched, my own eyes half closed, holding my breath, waiting for the cat to move. I loved the wildness of this place; the lethal beauty of the cat, the tangle of wildflowers and the profusion of violets creating thick ground coverage as if defying the world to define them as shy.

The cat sprang from the grass, claws outstretched and I leant forward, instinctively copying its movement. In an instant the sparrows flew upwards and the cat landed, gracefully, lifting its head to watch them flutter away, then turned its back on them disdainfully and began to lick its claws with its rough, pink tongue. I smiled, glad that the birds had escaped and amused by the cat's show of contempt.

I finished my coffee and stood, stretching as languorously as the cat, before turning back to the house. It was about nine o'clock. My body clock no longer woke me early, having quickly grown accustomed to my new rhythms. The days when an insistent alarm would shatter my early morning sleep, when I would rise without enthusiasm for a day of work, duty and tedium, were over forever.

Now, as I stepped under the weak trickle of the shower, which was all that the inadequate plumbing of the house allowed, I was aware of the way my body had changed. Although I would never be model-thin the long walks and simple food had certainly made me slimmer and more toned and sunbathing in the garden had given me a light tan.

Stepping from the shower, I dried myself roughly and wound a towel around my hair then rubbed in the body oil that I had been given the day after I arrived. As always, this memory made me laugh. I had been finishing my first breakfast in my new house, a meal provided by Lucia who had taken me under her wing and half an hour after leaving me in my new home had brought down a bag of food supplies for me so that I would not starve before I could get to the shops. She had given me enough food for three people; bread, cheese, ham and wine for supper and her homemade jam for breakfast. As I spread fig jam on my second slice of toast there had been a knock at the kitchen door and before I had had time to stand up the door had opened to reveal the odd, nut-brown woman who had first directed me to the manor. She had come in, smiling broadly whilst bobbing her head, in a strange contrast of deference and self-assurance.

"Ciao, sono Fiammetta," the woman had introduced herself then jabbered on in Italian so thick with local dialect that I could only make out a few words. While speaking she had stared at me with disconcerting intensity. I had had the feeling that she was assessing me carefully and wished I could make more sense of her words. She had pushed a small bottle across the table and with a few words and many gestures indicated that it was an aromatic oil to use after my bath, a gift. Then she had carried on speaking but in a low mumble, as if I were not there. It had sounded to me as if she was reciting a list of flowers or plants for some reason.

Not knowing what to do with the eccentric old woman who stood muttering in the middle of my kitchen and feeling that it would be rude to point out that she was uninvited and unwelcome, especially since she had come bearing gifts, I had indicated my breakfast and asked if she would like something. My voice had sounded coldly polite and unwelcoming to my own ears but she had grinned, the wrinkled skin around her eyes almost hiding the gentle mockery that shone there.

I had had the strangest feeling that she was reading my mind; delving into my thoughts to sift through painful memories, fears and uncertainties; seeing everything that I was in a flash of telepathy. She had grinned mischievously at me, nodding rapidly but not in acceptance of the offer of food because she was already backing towards the door.

"Si, ragazza mia. Puoi andare," she had pronounced and then she had left as quickly as she had come, leaving me to decipher her words, which I had concluded meant; "Yes my girl. You will do".

21

After Fiammetta's visit, I had been somewhat concerned about the safety of my new home. However there had been no other visitors since then and I had not seen the enigmatic old woman near the house again, although I had encountered her now and then in the fields nearby and once or twice she had left small surprise packages on my doorstep, her way of welcoming a stranger, I presumed. I had dutifully used the oil at night after my shower and found it wonderfully soothing, faintly astringent and with a resinous, herby fragrance of cypresses and the garden at dusk.

As I smiled at the memory of Fiammetta's visit, the age-mottled mirror in the bedroom reflected the curve of my lips. I thought that my joyful expression would have been unrecognisable to anyone who had known me in England. I shook my hair free and combed it, frowning at the tangles. The sun had been at work there too, lightening the brown.

I opened the dark-wood wardrobe and peered into its gloom to decide what to wear into the village. Most of the clothes that I had brought with me were shoved, discarded, at the back. They were work-smart; blouses, fitted skirts and trousers suits, or weekend clothes of jeans and loose sweatshirts. I had come unprepared for the heat of the Tuscan spring but had cut off a pair of jeans to make shorts, which, now that I had lost some weight, I wore pulled in with a belt. I so rarely went anywhere, it did not matter what I wore.

Today however, I was going to buy a whole load of new clothes. The bank had finally notified me by letter, since there was no telephone in the house, that my transferred money had arrived and I was free to spend whatever I wanted to. I was also going to buy some art supplies. I used to love art classes at school, although I had not felt like painting for years but now there was a whole different world full of vibrant colour and startling light that made me want to commit it to paper as if to prove that it was real.

Pulling the heavy back door closed behind me and locking it, I slipped the key into the pocket of my shorts, along with the money I had put there earlier. The cat waited in the shade of the cypress tree until I got close then sauntered over and rubbed itself against my legs. I bent and scratched it between its ears. Above me, the cypress loomed, seemingly unperturbed by the heat. I reached a tentative hand out and stroked its bark, enjoying the resinous scent that made the air seem so pure.

As my fingers made contact with the tree, I flinched, remembering how, in my vision the night before the funeral, the power of the connection with the tree had made me fall, jerked back into reality. So far, since moving here, I had been wary of getting too close to the tree and reluctant to touch it, because my memories of the dream were so strong. I was still trying to understand how it had been possible to dream so vividly about a real place that I had never seen before. I had several theories but none of them really convinced me; maybe I had seen a photograph of the valley and it had come into my unconscious mind as a dream or maybe I had just made it up and it was sheer coincidence that this place resembled what I had been searching for. Now, as my fingers traced the rough creases in the cypress's bark, I half expected to be thrown backwards by the force I had dreamt of. I had a sick feeling in my stomach, a fear that I might then wake up in my bed back in England to find that all I had experienced since had in fact been nothing more than a succession of realistic dreams.

My trepidation quickly passed. I did feel a strange sensation shudder through me, almost an electric shock but it was one that left me throbbing pleasantly. When I took my hand away, the sensation stopped and left me feeling peaceful and grateful for whatever mysterious force had brought me here.

I listened for a moment to the soft whisper of the cypress branches then set off along the dusty road. Tall grass grew sporadically among gnarled tree roots. On either side of the road, olive groves and uncultivated fields overflowed with wildflowers, poppies and early wild sunflowers. Beyond the fields and the forest ahead, the distant Apennine Mountains curved along the horizon in blue-grey undulating ripples. I turned onto the track

23

through the forest that led toward the village below, where I could get a train to the market in Montevarchi. I had done this walk every few days, for over a month now and had grown to know every boulder, tree and plant on the way. It took me just under an hour going and a bit longer coming home, when it was all uphill. I had not kept the hire car once I had found my house. I had known at once that I would stay here for a while and, although Lucia had been surprised when I had asked to rent the house for the whole summer, she had agreed, because she had three other cottages to rent on a more lucrative, weekly basis once the tourist season began. Since I had been here, I had rarely seen any other traffic using the road to my house, just one or two shiny cars with German number plates, struggling over the potholes, covered in dust. The cars seemed out of place, as if they belonged to another time, another life. The presence of the hire car had been just as intrusive. Its bright red paintwork jarred with the mellow stone walls; a modern note at odds with the peace of my home. I had driven it into Arezzo, the nearest big city, and left it with the hire firm there, returning by train to the village and walking back up through the forest for the first time. Letting the car go was a decision that I had never regretted in spite of the way my arms ached when I walked home with heavy shopping bags.

As usual, I met no one and was alone with my thoughts. Every time I walked here the way was subtly different; small ferns unfurled overnight, daisies appeared on the mossy banks and the thin canopy of tender new leaves on the oaks grew thicker until they almost hid the valley from view. Once or twice, I had seen deer leaping quickly away into the undergrowth as I drew near and I often saw evidence of wild boar in the holes they left, when rooting in the layer of old, decaying leaves on the forest floor.

I came out of the forest, crossed the busy main road and walked into the village of Montalino itself. It was small and not at all picturesque, grown up around the train station built there about fifty years before. Apart from the station, there was little to draw people to it and few tourists ever stopped there, which suited me fine. I shopped here for food whenever I needed to, preferring to come down often, enjoying the walk, rather than stock up once a week at a big supermarket as I used to back home.

Today I stopped at the newsagents to buy a train ticket, then headed straight down to the station, stamped the ticket in the machine on the platform and stood in the shade, waiting for my train. Pigeons scratched and cooed noisily on the tin roof. A small lizard caught my eye as it scuttled over the hot metal track. Above my head, a bell began its irritating warning that the train had left the previous station and a pre-recorded voice announced its imminent arrival. The train clattered in and braked to a stop with an ear-splitting shriek and a loud hiss.

It was only ten minutes by train, through the green hills to the outskirts of the town. The countryside gave way to allotments and new suburb housing, brick walls and small back yards strung with washing. As the train slowed for the station there was a rush of people along the narrow aisles of the carriage and I joined them, bracing myself against the chair backs as the train braked jerkily. I clambered down to the low platform at Montevarchi and let a group of noisy teenagers rush past me, before making my way through the back streets and into the no-traffic zone of the high street. I window-shopped in the elegant boutiques of Via Roma, smiling to myself at the thought of confronting the frosty stare of the immaculate sales girls inside, knowing that, although I now had the money to buy whatever I wanted, they would judge me by my peculiar cut-off clothes. I was not even tempted by the designer windows though. Everything looked too subdued, the colours too refined and, now that I had found my way into the light, I wanted to surround myself with brightness.

Stopping briefly in the marble coolness of the bank to withdraw some money, I crossed the town square and plunged into the bustle of the market itself. Squeezing my way through a narrow gap between the stalls, I manoeuvred through the crowd. Old women, their bicycle baskets full of vegetables, pushed by, wheeling their ancient machines and young mothers steered bulky

25

pushchairs with little regard for people's legs. I made my way slowly, stopping to examine every clothes stall that I came to, enjoying the easy banter of the stall owners and the impact of linen and cotton garments in vibrant primary colours. The clothes seemed to be competing and clashing with each other, crying out to be noticed. The stalls were a riotous mixture of fashion, soft furnishings and food stalls. Roasting meat and strong cheeses scented the air and the fruit stalls overflowed in improbable piles.

I tried on some clothes in the cramped interior of the market vans, others I just bought anyway, hoping that they would fit well. I had lost the habit of carrying a handbag, loving the feeling of having my hands free and no weight pulling my shoulder down and was grateful for it today, because I was soon laden down with carrier bags of every shape and size.

A sleeveless, red linen dress with a full skirt was so pretty when I tried it on that I did not bother to change back again, just stuffed my money and train ticket into one of the carrier bags and left my old things in the back of the van. My gym shoes looked wrong with the dress though, so I bought strappy sandals to go with it but kept the old shoes with me for the long walk back up the hill later.

After the market, I stopped at a well-stocked art shop and bought the pencils, watercolours and paper that I needed. By the time I got back to the station my arms were aching and I was worn out but so happy I felt like singing. I had a late lunch in the station café while I waited for one of the sporadic trains to take me home. It was a very hot day; sultry and close, the way it gets before a storm. My hair felt lank and heavy and, when the train finally arrived, I piled it up behind me, leaning back against the seat and letting the breeze from the open window dry the perspiration on the back of my neck. I was struck by a sudden, giddy desire to get my hair cut and, as soon as the train pulled into the village, I marched down to the hairdressers at the far end and went in, still not sure what I would ask them to do but thrilled by the idea of changing the last visible sign of my old self.

The young hairdresser looked up with a smile when I went in. He motioned me to wait while he finished curling up the thin, white hair of his present customer. I flicked through magazines, aware that I was an object of curiosity to the other women who were in various phases of preparation, one under a bulky hairdryer, one with a mass of tinfoil on her head waiting for her highlights to be done and a teenager flicking through a magazine. After a while the women lost interest in me and continued their conversation. It was good practise for me to listen to the local accent. I did not catch everything but was bemused to realise that they were discussing the merits of different types of burial. There was some debate on how long bodies should be left buried in the ground before they could be moved into a kind of box in the cemetery wall. The old lady in the curlers then joined in and informed us that she had recently had her parents-in-law dug out of the wall and put into an even smaller container. After all, she said, one must make room for the new inhabitants. The whole thing was completely bizarre and I had to struggle to keep a straight face.

When it was my turn and I was sitting, wrapped in a green cape, staring at my own reflection in the mirror, I still was not sure what to say. The hairdresser swept my hair this way and that, talking to me in careful, easy sentences, unsure how good my Italian was.

"How about a few highlights", he suggested, "or just layer the hair around the face to lighten it up a bit?" I think I stunned both of us when I answered, suddenly certain of what I wanted.

"Cut it all off – short," I said. "Like yours," I emphasised.

He looked unconvinced but I was suddenly determined. I had never had short hair, as a child because my mother liked it long and then because I had found it a useful way to conceal myself so I had just had it trimmed occasionally to keep the heavy fringe out of my eyes.

He began cutting, hesitantly at first, studying my face for signs of regret but then losing himself in concentration. Lock after lock of light-brown waves slipped down the protective cape. I was hot and brought my arms out from beneath the cape so that the lengths of hair now slid down, slipping silkily over my bare skin before falling to the floor.

He skilfully shaped my hair, cropping it short but leaving feathery wisps around my face, framing it in a feminine version of his own short style. As the hair fell, I felt as if I were emerging from some dark, secret place, showing my true face to the world for the first time. My cheekbones were revealed, along with the length of my neck. My nose stood out strongly, my eyes sparkled under arched brows, and my lips seemed to curve more sensuously. It was like having a portrait painted by someone who saw through the mask I wore for the world and stripped it from me with each cut of the scissors. A hitherto unknown sensation of strength flooded through me, as though the very act of cutting my hair had revealed a different person, not your classic beauty maybe but someone who could take on anything the world had to throw at her, someone who was not afraid to live.

I paid the hairdresser and thanked him, accepting his well-worn flattery when he said how good I looked but sensing that, to his surprise, he really meant it; the woman who left his shop was a different person to the one he had first seen.

It wasn't until I closed the door of the hairdresser's behind me that I realised it had grown darker while I was inside and the rain that had been threatening all day was beginning to fall in large drops, speckling the pavement in slow splashes. I gathered my bags together at the tops so that the new clothes would not get too wet but it was even more uncomfortable carrying them this way and, for the first time, I wished that I still had the car to take me home.

The rain held off until I was almost at the entrance to the woods, then, with a loud clap of thunder in the distance, the downpour began. I stood, waiting to cross the busy main road to reach the shelter of the trees, my short hair already plastered to my head, while all around me the rain thudded onto the road so hard

28

and fast that it rebounded, splattering my bare legs with muddy dust and grit.

It was my first taste of a real Italian storm, rather than the gentle rain that sometimes caressed the valley in the evenings. I turned my face up towards the heavens and laughed aloud as the water coursed over my face, stinging and stroking me, running into my hair and dripping down under my dress, along my spine. The rain had cooled the air but only a little. It was still warm enough for the raindrops to feel delicious as they ran down my back; making my skin tingle, making me feel alive, aware, a living statue being cleansed by the greatest sculptor of all. I opened my mouth to taste the freshness on my tongue and flung out my arms in a gesture of abandon.

A horn beeped and startled me. A big, battered looking jeep had stopped and pulled off the road beside me. The window slid down and a man's voice called out to me in English.

"Get in. I'll give you a lift."

I leant in through the open window, debating the offer. The tall man behind the wheel looked slightly familiar and his grin was friendly enough. There was a strange smell in the vehicle and I wrinkled my nose at it. It was a familiar smell and not altogether unpleasant. A noise in the back of the jeep made me turn my head to see a large, wet dog eyeing me curiously.

"We went for a walk near the river and she decided to cool off. Sorry about the smell. "The man laughed, then added,

"You're soaked. Get in. Your house is on my way home anyway."

Another crack of thunder decided me and I pulled open the door and thrust my bags in, piling them on the floor between my legs and on my knees as I muttered thanks. I remembered now. I had seen him with Lucia on the day I arrived, up at the old manor house, standing under the tree, surrounded by dogs.

"The English lady who is my neighbour for the summer." he said teasingly, swinging the big car onto the road and glancing at me sideways with those disturbingly dark eyes.

"You look different," he added.

"I'm wet," I answered, knowing that I sounded sulky; not liking it that he knew who I was and where I lived. He did not sound Italian, not that I cared, but I did not want company and most certainly not that of another foreigner. Any contact I made here should be with local people. I wanted to be immersed in my new country, my new life.

I guessed that he was American, although his accent was not strong and he was dark enough to be Italian. He seemed to realise my reluctance to talk, limiting his response to my brusqueness to a quiet laugh and a slow, appraising look as he turned off the main road into the lane.

"You certainly are soaked but that's not what I meant," he said and then drove on in silence, concentrating on swerving around the wet grooves and holes in the rough road.

I looked down at my legs. They were bare, the red linen of the dress clung wetly to them as it did to the rest of my body, hugging my curves, making me strangely aware of myself and my proximity to him, to his own bare arms and knees.

We passed the row of tall cypresses lining the lane, their tips lost in the dark rain. The rain drummed on the car, harder for a second as we drove past the cypresses. These trees, the epitome of aloneness even when they grew together, offered little shelter. They stood straight, uncompromising, ignoring the rain as they did the sun, as they would be the first to send snow slipping away from them in the winter. Only the wind was allowed to ruffle them, to tug at individual fronds, to make them sing.

"I was sorry to hear about your mother," he ventured and I threw him a surprised look wondering how he knew anything about me. He saw my surprise and grinned, shrugging his shoulders in a very Italian gesture.

"Lucia does like to talk!" he explained, clearly amused by her talent for gossip. I was irritated by the thought of having been discussed and cross with myself for having given in to Lucia's insistent probing. I looked out of the window, struggling to see

30

past the rain that coursed over the glass, feeling cold all of a sudden as unwanted memories stabbed at me.

"It set me free." I said, hearing the flat coldness in my voice. "I expect that sounds hard to you, doesn't it?. . . . . You wouldn't understand." I shrugged too. What did I care about what anyone said or thought about me anyway? He did not reply straight away but as I turned my head back to look out of the windscreen again I could see him from the corner of my eye and saw a momentary tightening of his jaw.

"I understand more than you know," he said quietly and that was the last of the conversation.

He turned off the lane onto the dirt track to my house and, once away from the protective canopy of the trees, the rain came down harder still, pouring over the windscreen as the wipers worked at clearing it. The house came into view, my own dark cypress glowering in the dim light, the flagstones on the path polished by the constant stream of water. He pulled into the driveway stopping just in front of the door, where red roses glistened, budding and bursting open around the stone lintel of the front door; reaching up to wrap around the Madonnina like a halo of red and green.

I flung open the car door, gathered my bags and half turned to him.

"Thank you for the lift," I said stiffly, backing out and slamming the door shut with my elbow.

He surprised me. He did not smile or speak, just gave a small nod of his head. His brown fingers drummed lightly against the steering wheel as he stared at me, his eyes unfathomable sparks of obsidian in the shadows, then he put the car into gear and drove away.

3

The weeks pass. She begins to change. By subtle degrees, she is shedding the weight that binds her. Like a butterfly throwing off its chrysalis, she is discovering her beauty and a lightness of soul. There is still darkness within but she has begun her journey.
The old one watches the girl with me and waits to be needed. We are good at waiting but her time in this place is running out. Now when she leans against me I can feel her age. She tires ever more quickly and admits that she breaths more easily in my shade.
When she is too tired for life she will come to me and I will hold her and sooth her fears until we become one.
First though we must teach the girl.
She must undergo the baptism of spring, be calmed by the mists and washed clean by the rain, until her true essence is revealed.
Only then will she learn to listen and begin to sing life's song with us.

I slammed the front door closed behind me and leant back on it, the smooth wood warm against my bare shoulders, then I kicked off my shoes, ran across the hall and up the stairs and threw my wet bags onto the floor. I flung open the shutters, ignoring the large drips that fell from the window frame onto my hands. The rain was already slowing, the sky above miraculously clear and breathtakingly blue once more, the black storm-front moving away towards the distant hills. The sudden changes in the weather here were disconcerting. As if some capricious deity were playing with the elements.

Over the hedgerows, I could just make out the dark green roof of the jeep as it headed down the dirt track. I had thought that my house was the last one on the road, since I had not come upon any other buildings or tracks when I walked in that direction but he had said my house was on his way home. I wondered where he was going, then I was cross with myself for wondering.

The scent of the garden was overwhelming in its sweetness. Washed free of dust by the downpour it was now gently steaming and releasing all its diverse perfumes into the air. He had not even told me his name, or asked mine for that matter. I was unsettled, unsure of how I felt. I was aware of having been rude, not so much in what I had said but in my posture, my body language. I was not good at socialising, although in the past I had always made an effort at small talk and filling in gaps in awkward conversations but being here had allowed me to forget the rules of society. I rarely met anyone and when I did, could pare the contact down to the barest minimum, using the language barrier as an excuse. I had not needed to be polite for so long that I had found myself unwilling to compromise, even for a short while, today. I wanted to be alone, to wrap myself up in my aloneness, to indulge only myself. I did not want him coming around again, using the excuse of a common language to draw me into a conversation of worthless words that would be forgotten almost as soon as they left the lips that shaped them.

I shrugged, easing the tension in my shoulders. My bags lay scattered around, waiting to be explored again. I opened them all, tossing the multicoloured clothes onto the sheets and the bags onto the floor. I pulled off the red dress and hung it on a hanger to dry, then tried everything on, laughing at my reflection in the mirror as I swirled and posed.

I wondered what expression I would see in his eyes if he could see me now.

I turned sideways to the mirror, to study the back of the green linen shorts that I had tried on with a white vest top. I buttoned the waist, smoothed the fabric over my stomach and surveyed the reflection of the tall woman who still seemed a stranger to me; short, tousled wet hair, aquamarine eyes bright against tanned cheeks.

33

His eyes had been dark, shiny and impenetrable, shutting me out and drawing me in with the same deep gaze.

Suddenly tired of this game of dressing up, I pulled on my gym shoes, which had fortunately been saved a soaking since I had not had to change into them for the long walk home, and went downstairs. I walked down the road, in the opposite direction to the way he had taken, heading back along my usual, familiar path. I flicked the tips of the wet grass with my fingers, sending small showers into the air. The evening was drawing in, the sun sinking lower towards the manor house high on the hill. The sun was gold, turning to bronze and, after the rain, everything sparkled and shone, glinting in the warm light.

I lingered for a while beneath the cypress. The rough bark felt cool and damp and the resinous drops that marked the trunk, like slow-shed tears, were smooth. I felt the unusual tingling, electrical sensation as we connected even stronger than before. I felt soothed by the cypress' sombre beauty, its huge mass and the sense of timelessness that I felt in its shade.

I scraped my heel through the soil at the base of the tree and was suddenly assailed by a torrent of images from my past. The soil was transformed into pebbly sand that gritted satisfyingly between my childishly rounded toes. My parents walked hand in hand along the beach while I crunched through the shallows, enjoying the swirl and suck of the sand beneath my feet. The happy image faded and I was standing in a neighbour's house where I had been sent to play with a girl from my class at school. I watched the girl and her bright, chatty, mother as they made sandwiches for our tea. I was awkward in their presence, quiet because I had no practise in talking. Since my father had died my mother did not see or hear me anymore; I had become a shadow-child. All the many ways that I had developed to escape from the dreariness of my life flooded over me. The solitary walks through the bluebell woods, stopping to throw sticks from the old wooden bridge, while the hoot and whoosh of a fast train on the railway bridge above rumbled and reverberated inside me. Swinging as

34

high as I dared on the wobbly garden swing that my father had put up, believing that if I could swing far enough I would reach another world and find him again.

I opened my eyes on the reality of the cypress bark beneath my hand. I felt strangely healed, as if by letting the memories go I had somehow liberated myself from them. Reluctantly I ran my hands once more across the tears of resin and then, feeling happier, continued my walk.

Rounding a bend, I came upon Fiammetta, her weathered face intent as she gathered clusters of white elderflowers from a bush. She was so short that she could hardly reach to pick the higher flowers.

""Buona sera." My simple greeting was returned, accompanied by the old woman's characteristic mischievous grin. Fiammetta studied me for a moment and then chuckled. She pointed at me and then ruffled her own hair for emphasis.

"Stai bene così," she said with approval. "You look good. Your hair suits you like that, makes you look younger, stronger. It was time to stop hiding yourself away." I smiled back at her, feeling ridiculously pleased at this unexpected endorsement of my new style.

After her surprise visit with the body-oil, Fiammetta had continued to press a collection of unusual gifts on me: eggs from her hens, herbs from her garden and plants picked from the hedgerows, along with rough instructions of how to use them, as tisanes or in salads. I no longer found her presence so disconcerting. It was true that she was a little eccentric and did not follow the polite rules of conversation that most people did but I sensed an innate kindness and wisdom in her. Fiammetta was the only person, apart from Lucia at the manor house, that I came across up here with any regularity and she fascinated me; so tiny and etched by time, her sky-blue eyes like bright marbles hidden amongst her wrinkles. Our conversation was usually limited to one or two words because Fiammetta's thick local accent was so hard to understand but we had formed a bond with smiles. Often she

35

was doubled over beneath a load of freshly cut grass that she carried on her back; walking miles like that, white head bent in front of her load, wide smile ready to dazzle, as she carried the grass home. She fed her rabbits on this lush grass until they were big and fat, then she killed them and skinned them with no regret. They were good to eat. She had given them the best food. That was what rabbits were for.

This evening there was no heavy load for her to carry, just a woven basket filled with damp elderflowers. I picked some of the flowers from higher up on the bush and tucked them into the basket. They had a pleasant, slightly medicinal scent. I wondered what they would be used for.

"Per i conigli?" I asked. For the rabbits?

Fiammetta laughed and shook her head.

"Fiori di sambuco. Da mangiare!" she chuckled, deeply amused that anyone would think of giving elder flowers to rabbits. They were to be eaten, but not by rabbits, she explained. They were good. They were from the plant that gave you its black berries later in the year so that you could make the liqueur, Sambuca. You fried the flowers in batter, sweet or salted, or you made them into omelettes. She laughed again at my bemused expression.

"Ne ho abbastanza," she said, she had gathered enough. She walked away with a small wave of the hand, still slightly bent, as if she was so used to carrying a heavy load on her back that she could no longer stand up straight. I had the feeling that she had something more to say and, sure enough, before she reached the trees Fiammetta turned and shouted out,

"Fanno bene all'intestino ma anche bene al cuore!"

She turned away again chuckling and was soon lost from sight, swallowed up by the shadows of the forest. When she was out of sight, I turned back. The old woman had said, with typical countrywoman's respect for such things, that the sambuco flowers were good for your intestine, to keep you regular. Then she had added that they would be good for my heart.

36

I was still grinning as I walked back through the garden and into the kitchen. I prepared dinner, cooking the kind of flat omelette that Italians call "frittata", with fried onions and courgettes. I took a bottle of water from the fridge and carried my dinner outside to the millstone table. It was almost dark now so I lit candles and took them out too.

The air was still. Small midges danced in the candlelight. Nearby, pale blue irises faded away to white as the light drained from the sky but their perfume remained heavy in the air, seeping through the night to where I sat. I stayed there, unmoving, as still and silent as the flowers until I began to feel chilled, then I took the dinner things in and dumped them in the sink, locked up and went to bed.

It was early, not yet ten o'clock but now I no longer needed to stay up late in order to have some time to myself, I was alone all the time. There was no television and felt no need for one. I followed the news by reading, as well as I could, the local newspapers, buying one when I felt like it. I wanted the silence. I thrived on it.

It had intrigued me that, when he gave me the lift earlier, the American had seemed equally comfortable with silence.

For a second I thought about Becky and Dave. I shuddered to imagine Becky's incessant chatter shattering my peace, or Dave's heavy sarcasm poisoning this pure air. I closed the shutters on the moonless sky, plunging the room into total darkness then made my way through the dark and climbed into the big double bed, where, almost immediately, I slipped into a dreamless sleep.

The next morning I woke unusually early as if some unexpected noise had jerked me from my sleep and I thought I heard footsteps coming from the garden and away down the path. By the time I had got up and opened the shutters there was no sign of anyone but when I opened the kitchen door, I found two brown paper bags on the doorstep. One contained six eggs; the other one was grease stained and fell apart as I opened it. Inside I found sambuco flowers, fried in batter and sprinkled with sugar. They

37

were still slightly warm. I licked the sugar off my fingers, imagining Fiammetta cooking up a batch of sambuco flowers and then walking to bring them to me, leaving them on the doorstep so as not to disturb me. The eggs would be from her own hens. I was deeply touched by the gesture. The simplicity and purity of the old woman's gift seemed to fill the air around me, transforming the morning. It was as if I could feel thin strands of friendship stretching out from my kitchen table, along the garden path, connecting me to Fiammetta's steps.

I quickly washed some strawberries that I had in the fridge and put them in a bowl on the scrubbed-wood table. I laid the greasy paper bag next to the bowl and ate the strawberries with the sambuco flowers, one berry to every sugary soft, delicious mouthful of batter. The flowers were sweet, slightly perfumed. They tasted of hedgerows and rain and kindness. They tasted of life.

For some reason I began to think about the cypress and, taking the last of the fried flowers with me, went out, through the garden and onto the path in front of the house. An early apricot light gleamed on the dewy grass and the sky was striated in icy blue and peach. Between the fields and sky, the hills and the manor house were still dark smudges in the half-light but the cypress cut across them like a bold slash linking earth and air. All at once, I felt the need to commit the scene to memory. I raced inside to get my sketchpad and settled myself on the front steps before the light changed and the magic was lost.

An hour later, the sun had risen fully and was warming my feet while I sat in the shadow of the porch, absorbed in adding a colour wash to my sketch. The cat had arrived and was stretched on the paving stones nearby, like a model in pose. I was struck by the complexity of its colouring. The fur, that at first glance looked black, was in fact a far more subtle mixture of browns and the odd glint of deepest red, which was a real challenge to capture with my paints. I heard a car coming down the lane but until the jeep stopped near the cypress and the American got out, I did not surface from the painting. Looking up and seeing him striding down the path towards me, I felt panicked, like a rabbit caught in a car's headlights. A muffled bark resounded from the jeep and the cat rose, stretched and, with a disdainful glance at the plumed tail wagging frantically in the rear of the jeep, sauntered off into the bushes.

I slid my painting off my knee and stood up to meet the American, not wanting to let him see my work, which seemed too personal. However, I had underestimated the speed with which his long legs propelled him and as I stood up, he was already by my side.

"Good morning." His accent drew the words out and his lips curved teasingly as I instinctively moved back to put some distance between us and stumbled on the step. His big hand grasped my arm firmly, whether to steady me or to make sure I did not run, was uncertain. I found my voice and wished him good morning too, unable to keep the frost from my voice. He let my arm go and when he spoke again his voice was cool too and I regretted the loss of intimacy that my behaviour had once more caused.

For the first time I noticed that he held something in his other hand. He held it out to me now, saying,

"I saw Lucia and Pietro this morning. They came by to bring me some asparagus and I thought it would be a neighbourly gesture to share it with you."

"Thank you." Before I could say more, he turned from me. I saw him look at my unfinished watercolour, then glance at the cypress. His eyes flashed briefly back to my face and then, with a curt goodbye, he walked away.

"Good bye," I muttered, mentally kicking myself for my bad manners and lack of social graces. I still did not know his name and my welcome must have convinced him that neighbourly gestures would not be well received. He drove off without a backward glance and I sat down heavily on the step and looked at the vegetables I was clutching. sambuco flowers and now asparagus, it must be the morning for gifts.

4

Yesterday the old one had a gift. She crept past me at dawn, chuckling as she took a parcel and left it on the girl's doorstep. Then she came and stood with me and munched sugary mouthfuls of fried sambuco flowers in satisfaction. She crumbled a few morsels with arthritic fingers and scattered them at my roots so that I could share the sweetness. The girl found the gift soon after and I felt her emotions flow strongly through the air to me.

It was our deepest connection so far. She was caught deeply in the current of nature, could taste the power all around her, the taste of life itself. Our joined energy flowed through me and I luxuriated in it, stretching it out from my deepest roots to the thinnest tips of my needles high in the clear morning air.

Her mind dwells on the man from the house by the lake and his dwells on her. Instinct tells me that he is as patient as he is strong. Not the lethal patience of the hunter but that of an artist who knows when to move towards a subject and when to wait in the shadows until the light is right, to capture something sublime. Now it would seem that there are three of us waiting for the girl to find herself.

Later, I felt restless and decided to walk up the hill to the manor house. I dressed in new cotton shorts and a striped T-shirt, pushed my feet into the dusty old gym shoes and set off. The sun was already hot, making me more pleased than ever with my haircut, which left my neck bare to the sun's touch. I still wasn't used to my new look and was taken by surprise each time I caught a glimpse of my reflection, as if there were someone else, some ghostly presence that resembled me, living in the house alongside me. I found myself constantly trying to tuck my hair behind my ear, only to find that it was too short to reach. I wished that I had cut it off long ago but accepted that it had never been the right moment before.

As I walked, skirting the edge of the forest where it bordered the fields, steadily climbing up toward the manor that was now hidden from view by a wooded copse, I found my gaze drifting time and again to follow the undulating shape of the dusty track as it snaked its way past my house and on, until it was lost in the woodland lower in the valley. I admitted reluctantly to myself that I was looking to see if I could spot the American's house but I could see no sign of it. I decided to ask Lucia about him when I saw her, pretending that the idea had just come to me, that it hadn't been lurking in my mind ever since his visit that morning.

I enjoyed visiting Lucia, doing so at least once a week to buy wine and the homemade, black olive pâté that she sold. Lucia talked continuously but never expected a reply, so I felt quite comfortable with her. I smiled wryly to myself as I realised that even though I had rarely said much about myself she had been more skilful that I had thought at drawing me out. I would have to watch what I said and remember her radar for intriguing items of gossip. Lucia and her husband, Pietro, did not own the manor, they ran it for a family of minor gentry, who lived in Florence and rarely came to stay.

I could see Pietro now, half way along a row of vines in one of the vineyards that climbed up the hillside in neat, straight lines. He was spraying the vines with copper sulphate to protect them from pests, a job he did every two weeks while the small bunches of grapes were developing and then again if it rained hard, as it had done the previous day. He looked like a strangely shaped, human tortoise as he walked slowly, a large green tank strapped to his back with a pipe at the bottom, the nozzle of which he held in his hand, carefully spraying each plant. The vines grew fast, stretching out with thick branches on each side, as if they were friends, wrapping their arms around each other. I could not see from here but knew that beneath the shade of the large leaves, pale-green grapes would be forming, still as small as pinheads, while delicate new tendrils would have seized hold of and be tenaciously clinging to rusty support wires. Shades of green, from pale tendrils to dark leaves, blended with the tank on Pietro's back and almost hid him from view until he reached the end of each row, when he was revealed again; a silver haired old man with a strange, green hunchback. In the rows behind him, as the sun dried the copper water on the leaves, their colour dulled, taking on the hue of weathered bronze. An occasional breeze stirred the hot air, bringing a faint waft of sulphurous warmth to my nostrils.

As I got closer to the manor, the dogs began to bark their warning. The youngest Labrador came running down the road to greet me, tongue bouncing and tail wagging. The two older dogs, another Labrador and a German Shepherd, were too hot to be bothered, lying still in the shade of the huge horse-chestnut tree. They gave their tails a feeble wag when I entered the courtyard then dropped their big heads back onto their paws. Lucia had been alerted by the dogs and stuck her head out of a window in her apartment on the third floor.

When she saw who it was, she came running down to greet me, wiping floury hands on her apron. She shooed the young dog away and kissed me warmly on both cheeks, chattering on about how glad she was to see me and how good I looked but why had I cut my hair? Oh, no, the men like long hair, not short. Still, it would soon grow back.

She bustled around, waving me into the cool, dim interior of the stairwell and up the flight of narrow steps before her. I trod carefully because the steps were well worn in places and the handrail was absurdly low. At the top I pressed myself against the wall to let her go through the doorway before me.

"Vieni, vieni cara." Lucia welcomed me in, pushing me into the kitchen and settling me down at the table where she had been making pasta. Without asking, she put a pot of espresso coffee on the hob, found cups for it and then turned back to kneading her pasta, while waiting for the coffee.

43

She shaped the pasta into long, thin sausages, then rolled them flat with a rolling pin, chattering gaily all the time, without pausing once to draw breath. I watched her, quietly, glad that no reply was expected. The coffee spluttered and I got up to turn off the gas, pouring it out into the two small cups and adding sugar to my own. I smiled to myself as I heard Lucia telling me, as she did every time, that she never took sugar in her coffee because it was bad for her waistline. Lucia's waist had been buried years ago but she still permitted herself a little vanity.

"I don't know how you can take two sugars and still lose weight, Anna." Lucia chattered on, her speech fast and heavily accented, so that I had to concentrate quite hard to follow her even though my Italian was improving daily.

"You were nice and chubby when you arrived here, now you are too thin. It must be all that walking you do." Lucia tutted disapprovingly at the idea of a young woman walking around the countryside alone every day. It could be dangerous, she warned me, there were snakes, vipers and also the wild boar, which would attack if they had little ones with them and felt threatened. She cast a sly look in my direction and shook her head, saying,

"No man will look at you, you know, unless you put some weight back on, get your curves back again."

All the while that she was talking she was skilfully folding the flat pasta back up into loose rolls and then cutting through them with a sharp knife so that, when she unrolled each thin slice, she was left with a long strand of tagliatelle. When she had a small mound of tagliatelle ready, she rinsed her hands at the sink, then reached up to pull a large, muslin covered plate out of a cupboard above her, setting it on the table between us. Under the muslin was a thick apple cake from which she cut two big slices, pushing one in front of me and taking the other for herself. She did not take sugar in her coffee but that seemed to be the only concession she made to watching her weight.

The cake was delicious, as always. I took another bite and then, when Lucia's mouth was full I said casually,

"I met someone who lives further down the valley yesterday. An American I think. He gave me a lift home because of the rain. "

Lucia's face had taken on the screwed up look of concentration it always did, whenever a foreigner spoke to her, as if she was convinced even before they began that she would not be able to understand a word. When she did understand me, her face cleared and she laughed happily.

"Si, si," she nodded "è americano."

He was indeed American but he was not, as I had presumed, renting one of the manor cottages. His name was Joe and he lived in a house that he had bought from the family some years ago, before they had started doing up the old cottages and renting them out.

"I don't know why such a young, handsome man should want to live so far away," Lucia declared, adding that he was a nice man, a good friend who was always willing to give Pietro a hand with the harvest or anything else he needed. I held my breath, hoping that Lucia would not get distracted and start talking about Pietro's back problems but the American was fortunately more interesting.

"His mother's family was Italian you know. He came here one day and fell in love with that old dilapidated house and bought it. He has made it look really nice. He was a doctor in America but he never talks about that for some reason." Lucia looked disappointed and bewildered as to why the American did not pour out his heart to her and I suppressed a grin. Lucia was the last person to be confided in, unless one wanted one's business spread around the village within hours.

I gathered that people also said it was strange that he was not married and that there was more than one shameless young and not so young woman in the village who had thrown themselves at him but as far as she knew, he was not interested.

"Tu Anna, saresti ideale per lui!" I kept my face expressionless when Lucia pronounced this inevitable verdict, of me being ideal

45

for him, hoping that my lack of enthusiasm would be enough to make Lucia leave this train of thought well alone. I pretended to be looking around, admiring the kitchen. I fingered the homemade, crochet-lace edging the linen tablecloth at my end of the table, which Lucia had rolled up in the middle while she worked the pasta. The house was decorated in typical Tuscan style, exposed dark-wood beams, heavy wooden furniture and plain white walls and curtains, all creating a cool, rather subdued space, an effect heightened by the shadowy light, which was all that was allowed to filter through the half-closed shutters in the rest of the house. Only the kitchen window was opened wide, letting in enough light for Lucia to work.

I was glad of the shadows, they would help me pretend indifference to Lucia's well-meant words but inside me a rebellious anger welled up briefly. I would not be in the least bit ideal for Joe, nor him for me. With a certain bitterness, I remembered Jim's words at the funeral – I was not his type. If I were honest with myself I would have to admit that I was intrigued by Joe, that I had been instantly attracted to him but I still wanted nothing to do with him, or with anyone. I wanted to avoid men, with a man's power to hurt me, crush my feelings and to leave me feeling vulnerable again.

As I had hoped, my silence convinced Lucia that I was uninterested in the subject of the American and the one-way conversation turned back to more prosaic matters; the wine and pâté I needed this week; how many kittens Lucia's cat was likely to have; Pietro's back. As usual, she also quizzed me about the house, asking if I felt comfortable there, making sure there had been no problems. I had noticed that whenever she spoke of the house she would make the sign of the cross surreptitiously and she always seemed both relieved and a little disappointed that my only complaints had been about the ancient plumbing system. For some reason I had never mentioned Fiammetta's visits to Lucia. Both the old woman and the cypress were things I would have kept to myself even if my Italian had been good enough to explain the disconcerting effect they had on me. I left shortly afterwards with a jar of pâté and two bottles of wine swinging from a plastic bag in my fingers. Lucia kissed me exuberantly on both cheeks, smelling of hot perfume and flour, then stood waving and calling,

"Ciao Anna, Ciao Annina," until I was out of sight, around the bend.

Lucia always softened my name, changing the harsh, foreign sounding Ann to the Italian version of Anna. Just one letter made such a difference. I had never had a nickname, never been anything other than plain Ann but I had not corrected Lucia's pronunciation. I liked the way the extra "a" made my name lyrical, made it rhyme with so many other Italian words. Annina was an even softer version of the same name, meaning "little Anna" in the same way that Fiammetta meant "small flame"; such a romantic and passionate name for my tiny, wrinkled friend that it always made me wonder what she had looked like when she was young. These sweet versions of my own name appealed to me, making me think of myself in a way that I had never contemplated before. There was nothing in the word *Anna* to suggest a dull work colleague; nothing to evoke a sterile, unloving home; nothing to make one think of a cold, somewhat frigid woman. I liked being Anna, being softer and more sensual.

My head reeling as it always did after half an hour with Lucia, I took the long way home through the cool shade of the forest, to avoid the midday heat. The cat met me on the drive, basking in the heat of the flagstones. It half raised itself, meowed prettily and patted my ankle with its pink padded paws as I passed. I unlocked the back door and moved through the cool kitchen, opening shutters as I went, so that the sunlight danced in across the floor. Everyone else here kept their shutters closed during the day to keep out the heat and maybe to counterbalance the exuberance of nature outside but I could not bear the dimness, preferring to swelter rather than shut out the light.

Now that I could see, I noticed a letter lying on the floor. The postman shoved any rare mail that I got under the back door if I was out. So far, I had had two letters, one from the bank to say my money had been transferred and one from Mr Forbes, my lawyer, to say he had put my house on the market, as requested. This letter was also from the lawyer I noticed, recognising his office stationary as I ripped it open. It contained an offer for the house, at the price we had agreed on and the documents appertaining to the sale, for me to sign if I still wanted him to go ahead with it. There was another letter enclosed, which he had forwarded for me. I recognised Becky's handwriting and put it aside until I had finished reading the sale documents.

I got myself a drink of fruit juice from the fridge and sat down at the table to read Becky's letter. It was not long, just a note really, asking how I was, where I was and when I was coming home.

You didn't answer your phone so I called you at work and they told me you had left! Why didn't you tell me? They said you just phoned in after the funeral and told them you were going away and to send any further communication via your lawyer. I phoned him and the miserable old sod wouldn't tell me anything, said I should write a letter and he would send it to you. What's going on?!

I crumpled the letter up and threw it in the bin on my way out to the garden. I walked slowly around, shaking off the tension that this small intrusion from my old world had caused. Becky had been a friend for so many years that I had stopped thinking about it; the friendship was just there, like the rest of my life. On Friday nights, I went out with Becky and then I came home again. Looking back on it I realised that in all those years, whilst I had listened to the intimate details of Becky's life, I had never once shared anything of myself or confided one secret yearning. Neither had Becky often enquired about me. All she had needed was someone to listen to her talk about herself. I had advised Becky when she'd sought advice, consoled her when Dave got drunk and treated her badly, walked behind her, in a ridiculously frothy dress, at her wedding but I realised that not even Becky, the person I was ostensibly closest to, would be able to tell anyone exactly why I had run away.

For a while, I considered this coldness within myself, this inability to share my emotions. I was able to do this with the clarity of insight that being here had given me; able to view myself and my life objectively without hiding from the truth, out of guilt or fear. The sadness gradually faded away as I walked, bare feet stepping lightly through the grass, crushing the wild thyme that grew in flat, pink, patches. I lay down, resting my head on a cushion of thyme, feeling the faint prickling of grass stalks on my back and breathed in the scent of my new world, until peace was restored. I was not the same person at all, I realised. The person I used to be had needed a cloak of distance and coldness, in order to survive in a bleak and dreary world whereas now I was happy. Being alone right now, I felt less lonely in my aloneness than I had ever done in my previous life. Enjoying being alone did not mean that I would want the same isolation forever; just that it was what I needed now.

I felt alive here. My senses cried out for attention. I was warmed by the sun, coloured by it and intensely aware of every second of every joyous day. I was no longer cold, I was no longer pleasant and polite when I really wanted to scream, I was no longer dutiful; now I was myself, just that and nothing more.

5

This morning a faint breeze stirred me and I began to hum to its rhythm as the dew evaporated quickly from my branches in the first heat of the day. The heat will burn into my needles throughout the day but deep in the ground, beneath the hardened crust, the recent rain gently cools my roots. My roots go deep and they are strong enough to hold me and sustain me throughout the endless cycle of the seasons.
The wounded girl is like a young sapling, still buffeted by every change in her world but now she too has begun to form a network of roots and spread them deep and wide.
I love spring, its abundance, its unruly, joyful quest for life; breaking free from the cold grip of winter to become part of life again, to join in the riot and tumble of grasses and plants all around me. I surge ever upwards, new tender shoots reaching for the sunlight that peeps through hazy clouds. The heat of the day is balanced by the cool of the night. The delicate scents of garden and field waft over me on the light breeze.
I watch the girl with deep compassion, as she struggles to break free of the personal winter that binds her.

I had never before been so aware of the tremendous life force all around me. In the garden, as one plant finished flowering another was ready to burst open in its place. The straggling hedges of pyracanthus lost their frothy whiteness. As the flowers died; turning rusty brown, then falling, small green berries began to swell in their place. There was a riot of growth everywhere, tumbling and shooting in thick, tangled hedgerows. The wisteria and honeysuckle sent out tentative, curling tendrils, looking for support, then exploded into leaf and bud so fast that I sometimes believed I could see them growing. I spent hours in the garden sitting in the shade, sketching and painting this abundance of life.

The jasmine, which twirled and tangled all around the garden on fences and railings, became decorated with delicate star-shaped blossom. I cut some, marvelling at the sticky white sap that oozed from the wounds and coated my fingers in milky glue. I arranged the long, twisted strands in vases where they draped across surfaces in intricate patterns and filled the house with their perfume.

In the first week of June, on my shopping trips to the village, I saw posters showing pictures of pure-white Chianina bulls, advertising the village animal fair the following weekend. Mara from the newsagents was helping to organise the fair and exhorted me to come along, whenever I popped into the shop. It seemed like a fun idea, a glimpse of local folklore and I found I was quite looking forward to a bit of socialising.

The weather was still a little temperamental when the fair began, far hotter than England in the spring but with the odd cloudy or rainy day. It was Saturday afternoon when I finally decided to walk down the hill to the fair. Knowing that all events in Italy started late to avoid the midday heat, I waited until around 5pm to set off. Even so, I could feel the heat from the ground through my old shoes, as I made my way past the undulating, golden-blond fields of wheat and grass. It was a relief to enter the shade of the trees and I was glad of the shelter the forest gave me as I made my way down the footpath to the village.

Montalino was dressed up for the fair. I mingled with the groups of people strolling along the high street towards the playing fields, all wearing their Sunday-best clothes. People greeted me with friendly smiles and curious looks as I passed them and then, before I was out of earshot, enjoyed a bit of gossip about the "foreigner". I was mostly thought to be English but a few people happily argued that I was American or even German. I was amused to be considered interesting enough to be local colour and glad that I had bothered to put on a dress instead of shorts so as not to draw more attention to myself. Even the gardens seemed to have put on a show in honour of the event, boasting red, pink and yellow roses everywhere.

Seen above the moss-stained roofs of the houses, the church's brick bell tower dominated the village and as I neared it the bell sounded the hour, clanging six times so loudly that it drowned out the sounds coming from the fair behind it; of children's excited voices and a crackling loudspeaker announcing the events. The fair was held in the playing fields that backed on to the church, in the welcome shade of huge fir and lime trees. There were a few stands set up around the edge of the field selling local produce; wines, cheeses, ornaments made from olive wood and knickknacks. Further in the shade there were wire cages for the animals; massive Chianina cows and bulls, pigs, goats, sheep and ponies. The village children ran around, chasing each other through the crowds, spinning on the roundabout, wriggling down the rather un-slippery slide and swinging wildly on the swings. Their parents gathered in groups to chatter, keeping a vague eye out for the little ones and occasionally wiping noses and rubbing skinned knees. In the car park behind, a marquee was set up with trestle tables for the evening and a large, handmade poster hung limply in front with a basic menu printed on it.

I walked slowly round, stopping to stroke the soft nose of a white calf and to look at some grubby kids with extremely long, floppy black ears, suckling enthusiastically from their tired-looking mother goat. I had changed into sandals when I left the wood and now my feet slipped a little in the dry pine needles and straw that covered the dusty ground and my feet felt gritty and dirty. I had brought a handbag with me to carry my walking shoes and its unfamiliar weight was rubbing my shoulder. I did not think I would stay long. The fair was quaint but its bucolic joys were limited. I could see no one there that I knew well enough to stop and chat to. Just as I thought that I saw someone waving madly at me and spotted a blur of plum coloured hair bobbing up and down as Lucia struggled to make herself visible through a group of people surrounding her stall. She had told me that she was going

52

to be there, selling her homemade jam, pâté, oil and wine. I wandered over to say hello. Lucia appeared a bit flustered. She found time to grab me and kiss my cheeks and admire my dress before turning back to serve. I stood by the stall for a while, helping myself to the small squares of toast with green olive pâté and accepting a plastic beaker of Pietro's wine that Lucia thrust at me, enjoying watching her enthusiastic sales patter.

"Where is Pietro? Isn't he helping you today?" I asked when the crowd thinned temporarily. Lucia laughed good-naturedly and shook her head. Her hair was looking quite spectacular today. She had obviously been to the hairdresser that morning and the result was a gleaming, dark-plum coloured mass of teased up waves.

"That man!" Lucia moaned fondly, "He brought me down and helped me set up then said he had things to do and would pick me up later." She leant forward and added in a stage whisper,

"Much better this way. He is too slow, puts people off buying. You need to be quick to make a sale." She demonstrated her technique by honing in on a new potential customer with a calculating gleam in her eye. I finished the wine, realising that I could already feel my cheeks flushing slightly. The beaker has been almost overflowing and, without meaning to I had somehow finished it and only eaten a couple of squares of toast to counterbalance the effects. Waving goodbye to Lucia I moved on. The next stall was selling cheese and the air was ripe with them. I picked up a piece of strong pecorino and munched it hungrily.

It occurred to me as I surveyed the crowd that although the people looked undeniably Italian, this had more to do with their attire and mannerisms than their colouring. Their body language was so completely free from English restraint. People stood close to one another, teenagers sat casually on each other's knees on the park benches, men hugged other men and everyone gesticulated wildly and raised their voices to shout over the top of anyone else in the vicinity. If I had not heard that they were only discussing the weather or the football I might have thought they were arguing with each other. Before moving here I had imagined most Italians would be dark haired and swarthy but that was not the case, there were quite a few fair-haired people too. While some of these looked natural the majority of the older women obviously obtained their golden locks from the hairdresser. The most popular hair colour was a close tie between unsubtle highlights and the odd purple that Lucia also favoured. I smiled happily to myself, soaking in the atmosphere.

Just then I saw another face that I recognised, an elderly woman with thinning, sandy-white hair and freckles. Here was another anomaly. Her family were all redheads and, apart from her, extremely tall. I crossed over to her and touched her arm.

"Rita!" I bent to kiss her papery cheek with genuine pleasure as she turned and smiled up at me. A widow in her seventies Rita was the friendliest woman that I had met in Montalino village. We bumped into each other frequently because Rita ran errands to the village shop all day long. She never walked slowly, instead she had a light, half-running gait that made her look constantly in a rush, although she always took the time to stop and chat with me whenever our paths crossed.

As we hugged now, Rita felt so tiny that her bones seemed insubstantial. It was almost impossible to believe that she could have born four children, three of them now tall, strapping men. As was often the way in Italy, Rita's family still lived with her or near her and she was kept busy all day long, cooking and cleaning for them and her numerous grandchildren. Her family turned up for lunch at varying hours, from midday till three o'clock, as the factory, office or schools finished for lunch and she often made different meals for each one of them, depending on their individual tastes. It was no surprise that she looked quite worn out with so much to do at home and I was surprised to see her at the fair, because I knew that she would usually have stayed at home, preparing dinner for her family.

"Ciao Rita. Che bello vederti qui." I said how lovely it was to see her and added that I was surprised that she had found time to come. Normally she wouldn't have but she had been invited out

54

for dinner today, she explained, looking a little surprised herself at this unusual situation. As far as I knew her family took her pretty much for granted so I was pleased by the idea that they were treating her today. At that moment, the old woman looked over my shoulder and smiled widely. Glancing behind me, I saw the youngest of Rita's sons sauntering towards us and next to him the American, Joe.

The men were both taller than most of the other people around them but otherwise complete opposites in looks. Luca, with his easy, blue-eyed smile, strawberry-blond hair and lanky frame, resembled his mother but Joe was darker than most Italians. He was the same height as Luca but his broad shoulders seemed to expand into the space around him and his eyes flashed darkly from under a lock of black hair that flopped over his forehead.

Joe said hello quietly and stood back, while Luca greeted me with an Italian kiss on both cheeks. When I looked at Joe again I was surprised to see him standing with his arm around Rita, who was gazing up at him delightedly, looking almost girlish. He was obviously on very good terms with the local people and I felt myself blushing, as I remembered how I had been worried that he might force his company on me because of the bond of a common language. I had been completely mistaken. He had made no new effort to contact me since I had brushed him off rudely when he had brought me the asparagus. Now I realised that he spoke Italian almost perfectly and had good friendships here in the village whenever he wanted company. I felt foolish and presumptuous and was glad of Luca's lively chatter to distract me as we strolled across the park. Joe seemed to know everyone, casually greeting people as they passed by. He stayed close to Rita, treating her as if she was his special ward and, a little later on, I realised why when he rubbed his stomach and said teasingly,

"If I don't eat something soon, I'm going to fade away. Shall we go and get that pizza now, Rita?" Rita blushed and looked flustered. Now I understood that her presence at the fair was due to Joe's insistence. I also realised that she felt a bit out of place and it was this moment of sympathy for Rita that allowed me to say yes, when Joe turned and asked me if I would join them.

Rita beamed gratefully up at me and linked her arm through both of ours as we walked across to the tent for dinner. Luca shouted goodbye from behind us and I turned in surprise to see him wave and set off for home.

"Isn't Luca coming?" I asked.

"Are you disappointed?" Joe's expression was unfathomable. I was saved from having to answer him as Rita began explaining, excitedly, about how Joe had arrived at her house that afternoon to see Luca and then, when he realised that for once she would be on her own for the evening because everyone else was going out, he had insisted that she keep him company at the fair. Joe's eyes met mine over Rita's head.

"I hate eating out alone," he said, his face softening into a gentle smile that made me catch my breath. I turned away from him, pretending to study the menu. To my annoyance, my heart was beating fast.

Rita debated the simple menu, with the relish of someone who rarely goes out and was clearly getting so much pleasure out of this little outing that soon I felt myself relax and fell into discussing the merits of pizza over pasta, red wine or white, then escorted Rita into the tent and settled her at a trestle table. We sat looking out from beneath the dingy marquee at the crowded playing field, while Joe gave our orders to the cashier, at a till set up outside. While we were waiting for Joe to return Rita and I chatted. I had seen everyone that I had ever met in Montalino at the fair, except for Fiammetta and mentioned it to Rita. Her reaction surprised me. She frowned and shook her head.

"Ann, you shouldn't have too much to do with Fiammetta. I have known her all my life, well enough to know that most of what is said about her is untrue but you are alone here and do not need to be tarnished by her reputation." I questioned her some more but her answers were brief and reluctant and she was obviously relieved to change the subject when Joe came back and straddled the bench next to me.

The meal was a very casual affair. Once the orders were placed and the money paid, the food was cooked and brought to the tables by local volunteers. From the snatches of conversation that I could overhear it seemed that people rarely ended up with exactly what they had ordered and an inordinate number of things were spilt by the unprofessional waiters, most of whom were youngsters, but that all added to the charm of the evening.

Joe stretched his long legs out, looking cramped at the low table. I made a concerted effort not to shift away from him, very aware of his knee as it brushed my thigh. To cover my confusion I asked him how much I owed him but he waved my question away with a grin and when I would have insisted, he said to me in English,

"It is my treat. Don't spoil this evening for Rita, please Ann. She'll sense the disharmony, so please if you have to fight me, can you save it till later?"

Rita's head bobbed merrily as she listened to us, then she clapped her tiny hands and said,

"Ah, l'inglese! Come mi piacerebbe parlarlo." How she would love to speak English. Joe laughed and said he would teach her. He began getting her to repeat simple words until she exclaimed,

"Basta!" She'd had enough, her head was spinning.

The pizzas arrived and some local red wine, served in old water bottles. The pizzas were on plastic plates and we had to cut them with plastic cutlery. I broke my flimsy knife almost immediately and Joe stood up to get me another but Rita pulled him down again and explained how pizza should really be eaten, folded into a fan shape, picked up and bitten into.

We wrapped our pizzas in paper napkins, so that the sauce did not run over our hands and burn them and we laughed at the juicy mess around each other's mouths. Rita could not finish her pizza so Joe took what was left, saying that he was grateful, because his had not filled him up. Rita watched him with warm eyes and said in a quiet undertone,

"What a good man he is, so gentle and kind."

Across the playing field, lights went on, shining on a small stage that had been haphazardly rigged up. Members of a band began settling themselves there, tuning up for the dancing later. I studied Joe while he was distracted by the band. I had thought of him in many ways these last few days, intrigued by him, finding him mysterious with his dark gaze and unpredictable manner. I had not considered him as a simple, kind man but, I realised, these were indeed the qualities he had demonstrated tonight.

Memories, triggered by the English words that she had just heard being spoken, surfaced in Rita's mind, bittersweet and urgent. Staring unseeingly into the dusk, Rita began to talk about her life during the war and Joe and I listened in silence. An indomitable spirit shone in her old eyes as she talked about things that had happened long ago, reliving them for a brief moment.

She told of how she had been young and pretty then, with long, red hair that hung in curls down her back. Her parents had run the small village shop that sold everything from food, to clothes and shoes. During the war, she said, the Germans were everywhere, because there was an airfield in the valley, below where Joe lived now. In a nearby village, a concentration camp had been set up but quite often allied soldiers managed to escape from it. They hid in the forest, where I so often walked. Rita's parents used to send her off every few days, with as much food as she could hide in her bicycle basket and she would cycle along the footpath until the escaped soldiers showed themselves and then give them the food.

Even the harsh glow from the overhead bulb that illuminated Rita's face so honestly could not dim the magic that these memories wrought on her old face, blurring her features, softening her mouth from its usual thin line.

"I remember one man; he was English – a gentleman. He could not speak Italian but he always helped me off the bicycle and propped it up for me. He seemed quiet and shy. He had a soft smile. He walked with a limp although he tried to hide it.

He realised the danger I was running by bringing supplies to them, more than I did myself then. I sensed that he was ashamed to be living like that. He was a real gentleman. One day he asked me to bring him something special. How he struggled with gestures to make me understand what he wanted. Finally, I understood that he was ashamed of his appearance, of his unkempt hands. He wanted a pair of nail scissors. The next time I went, I took him some and he thanked me so sweetly. The others were so hungry that they only thought about quickly unloading the food I'd brought for them but he sat, leaning against the trunk of a huge oak and carefully cut his fingernails. When he gave the scissors back to me he raised my hand and kissed it."

Rita sighed, coming back to the present with a jerk.

"I wonder what happened to him," she whispered. The hand that she had raised, when she remembered his kiss, trembled slightly.

Joe reached over and took her hand in his. He nodded towards the improvised dance floor where a few older couples were already waltzing and asked her to dance. At first, Rita made a fuss. She hadn't danced in years, she protested, had probably forgotten how to, but she was happy to allow Joe to persuade her and soon they joined the others, swirling slowly round to the music.

Joe was the youngest person dancing. Only the elderly danced the *liscio* ballroom style now. A group of small boys kicked a football around at the edge of the dance floor, young couples strolled around holding hands or stood in lively, laughing groups. I noticed that Luca had returned, his arm around a pretty, dark-haired girl. He called something out to his mother and Joe as they passed him, incongruously matched in height and age, yet flowing smoothly to the rhythm, joined by tenderness.

The night seemed to swirl around me, keeping tempo with the music, seeping into the light. Suddenly I needed to leave, while I could, before Joe found it necessary to offer me a lift home. I pushed back my chair, startled by its loud rasp as it scraped over the ground. I caught Rita's eye, forced a smile onto my face and waved at her merrily, indicating with gestures that I was leaving to walk home.

The night closed in on me as soon as I left the playing fields, held at bay by the street lamps until I got close to the forest. I was not worried about finding my way, knowing from past experience that my eyes would soon adjust to the absence of artificial light, allowing me to see perfectly well, even in the depths of the wood, by the starlight.

I walked over the railway bridge, crossed the empty main road and started up the familiar path into the trees. I pulled my walking shoes out of my handbag and swapped my sandals for them, before beginning to climb up the steeply rutted footpath. I made more noise than usual, stomping harder with my feet than necessary in order to frighten away any nocturnal animals or snakes that might have been sleeping in my path. It was the first time that I had walked the forest path at night; usually I kept to the road if I felt drawn to wander around at night but I did not find the dark disturbing.

I was so preoccupied with my own emotions that I hardly noticed my surroundings. I pushed myself harder than usual, taking advantage of the cool of the night to lengthen my stride, so that soon my breath was coming fast. Occasional strands of spider's web caught on me and I brushed them away. Far off an owl hooted. My feet crunched on dry mud and loose stones and in the undergrowth some nocturnal animal scuttled over dry leaves. I sincerely hoped that the only animals I encountered would be small ones but Lucia's warning about wild boar made me push on even faster.

As I walked I thought of Rita and her English prisoner-of-war and of how sweet Joe had been with her. I had been wrong about Joe, I acknowledged, realising how my past had still been moulding my thoughts, making me cynical and judgemental, instead of allowing me to open up and see the truth in people. I had been projecting my own ideas onto Joe, viewing him suspiciously but now I recognised his innate kindness. He genuinely liked Rita. When he had asked her to dance I had seen him look beyond the surface to the pretty red-haired girl that still laughed within her. I wondered what he saw when he looked at me.

In the indifferent dark; turning all to shadow, muffling sounds and hiding secrets; I walked on. The dark curved around me and soft starlight guided my steps. I slowly allowed myself to admit how much I liked Joe and wanted him to like me. Well, I had changed such a lot in the last few months and now it was time to see just how deep those changes really went, to open up and risk a little. I had been rejected before, knew that kind of hurt too well. However I thought I had glimpsed attraction in Joe's eyes tonight and if I was right then it would be worth the risk.

6

Spring for me is water. The sap runs fast through me, the morning mists and dew bathe me, my roots stretch in cool dampness. When the rain forms a shallow puddle beneath me, I can see a reflection of myself; a small, distorted image reaching toward the sky.
The image offers but a glimpse of truth. If I drop a cone to the surface of the puddle, the image will shatter then gradually reform. Our reflection in water shows us, briefly, what we are and allows us to challenge it, to believe that we are stronger, more substantial than that delicate image, which evaporates with the kiss of the sun.
The girl can sense freedom now. She is almost ready to join the old one and link her spirit to ours. Then we will flow like water, free as rain, following deeply gouged rivers, or swelling and tumbling out to forge new streams; flowing as emotions do, wild and deep, changeable, mercurial.

I came to the end of the forest footpath, where it joined the side road. The cypresses lining the road loomed tall, stretching towards the stars above. A gentle breeze blew here, as the forest opened out, sighing and singing through the cypress branches, welcoming me. For a second I stopped, lost in reverie, dwarfed by the giant trunks. I ran a finger lightly over the rough bark of the nearest tree, tracing the intricate patterns, still lost in contemplation of my emotions.

As my breathing adjusted to its usual rhythm after the exertion of the climb up the hill, I had the unsettling feeling that I was being observed. A breeze swept down the valley, rustling dry music from the leaves as it passed. In the silence of the night, the ragged whisper from the forest sounded almost human and I shivered, the clammy heat on my skin from the climb suddenly cooling. I rubbed at the goose-bumps that prickled my arms and took a deep, calming breath, trying to recapture the sense of belonging and being at one with the night that had accompanied me until now.

My eyes had long since adapted to the dark of the night but now, as I carefully studied the shapeless realms of undergrowth and forest where the shadows swallowed the starlight, I felt exposed. Taking a step back away from the cypresses, into the centre of the road, I searched the gloom for a glimpse of whom or what I sensed there. Then suddenly a flash of silver appeared in the space between two gargantuan trunks. My breath caught in my throat as I fought back the wave of fear that washed through me, leaving my limbs feeling heavy and weak. An eerie cackling laugh rang out and I sighed with relief as the rest of the person beneath the shock of silver hair became clear.

"Fiammetta!" I said weakly. She laughed again, moving forward slightly so that I could see her more clearly.

"Ciao ragazza," she whispered, her sun-hardened skin and dark clothing still blending so well with the shadows that only her ghostly halo of hair was clearly visible. I took a deep breath and forced my feet to cross the short distance between us. Fiammetta grinned and I had the impression that she was enjoying her dramatic entrance and the effect it had had on me. I remembered Rita's comments about Fiammetta earlier that evening. Rita's disapproval had seemed to stem from the fact that Fiammetta had not been to church in recent years. As a non-catholic, I was not expected to go to mass every Sunday but for the old women in the village not to do so was unthinkable. Rita had reluctantly hinted that Fiammetta was an embarrassment to her family because she had chosen to live away from the village and far from the accepted rules of society. I had sympathised with Fiammetta and felt a natural empathy with her. She seemed to be unafraid of being different, defiantly content to go her own way and live life by her own interior rules. She struck me as being a deeply spiritual person, in tune with the natural world and with herself and I felt instinctively that she would confront her own life with brutal honesty.

63

The old woman also possessed a very black sense of humour I thought wryly, the corners of my mouth curling into a smile as my heartbeat slowed back to normal. There was something childlike and wild about the old woman. Her sudden appearances were well timed to startle and she played up her reputation to the full.

"Guarda qua," she ordered me to look, digging deep into the oversized pocket of her shapeless dress. The pocket bulged strangely and emitted a high-pitched sound of fear. Immediately the old woman's demeanour changed from prepotence to gentleness and she made a soft, soothing sound deep in her throat. The wriggling in her pocket stilled and she pulled her hand out and held it up to show me. Nestled in her palm was a tiny, tabby kitten. I ran a finger down its bony spine, smiling as it quivered, hissed bravely and twitched its spiky little tail.

"Abbandonata," Fiammetta informed me. The litter had been abandoned in a plastic bag, thrown from a car probably.

"Only this one survived. It shows her will to live is strong." I was touched by the unexpected tenderness in Fiammetta's voice. Then her mood changed once more to a kind of sly teasing.

"So, what were you dreaming of girl? You made so much noise coming up that path that you woke the whole forest." I had not thought of it until now but we had been speaking in a kind of quiet undertone, as if talking any louder would disturb the night. I waved my hand vaguely in the air, unwilling to reply. I felt as if Fiammetta already understood far too much of my private thoughts without being told. She crowed with laughter and walked back into the forest.

"Hide your thoughts while you can, girl," she called back softly and disappeared into the night.

She was gone so quickly that it was disconcerting. I reached for the cypress trunk beside me, suddenly needing to feel its solidity grounding me but the ancient bark reminded me of Fiammetta's rough skin.

A sudden, soft, footfall behind me made me spin round, my heart pounding with the unsettling awareness that there was someone else there. Only then did I see the outline of his jeep parked by the side of the road. Joe must have been there when I reached the road because otherwise I would have heard him drive up. I wondered if he had seen Fiammetta. Probably not, from where he was parked she would have been hidden from view. That was all I needed I thought, cursing Fiammetta under my breath. Joe must have thought that I was standing by the side of the road talking to myself like a crazy woman.

"It's me," Joe spoke gently, reassuringly as he walked towards me.

"I didn't mean to scare you, just wanted to make sure that you got home safely. Rita was worried about you walking through the forest at night."

Something in his tone told me that it was not only Rita who had been worried. I fought back my instinctive, caustic, remark about being old enough to look after myself and my embarrassment over having been seen talking to the shadows. Joe had cared enough about me to make sure that I got home safely. Now was the time to act on the decision I had made while walking through the forest; to open myself up, allow myself to feel emotions and live with them. Biting back my defensive retort I took a deep breath, surprised to find myself trembling a little and, still touching the cypress for strength, I forced a smile,

"I didn't mean to worry anyone," I replied, "I needed the walk, the peace. I'm not very good around people sometimes. I don't know how to behave the way that they expect me to."

My heart was hammering as I stood, as still and straight as the cypress I touched. I felt him smile in the shadows, then he stepped closer and I could see his face, dimly lit by the stars. He reached out and touched the bark close to my hand, so that I could feel the heat emanating from his fingers.

"Maybe people don't expect you to behave in any particular way. Maybe they just want to get to know you."

Joe moved his fingers a fraction closer to mine. He looked up at the dark branches above them and whispered,

65

Folded like a dark thought
For which the language is lost,
Tuscan cypresses

At the feather-light touch of his fingers, as his voice curled sensuously around his words, my long established reflexes took over,

"Don't quote poetry at me!" I snapped at him.

He laughed softly and said mockingly,

"The underlying darkness of Lawrence seemed to suit you rather well."

"I'm sorry," I mumbled feeling ridiculously close to tears.

Joe moved his hand until his fingers covered mine, pressing them against the rough bark.

"Tell me what you feel," he asked. He did not let go of my hand but neither did he step any closer. After a while, I managed to look up at him but I could not make out his expression in the dim light, just see his tall outline close to me, looming over me.

"I love these trees. They are so straight and strong," My voice was scratchy and I cleared my throat then plunged on, desperate to touch him with my words, to make contact with him, let him know this one small part of who I was.

"They reach for the heavens, as if they want to paint them with their tips. They stand alone without being lonely, or in groups without compromising their individual integrity. They are simple and intricate. Sometimes, they even seem to sing to me."

He stood in silence when I finished speaking, looking down at me, smoothing the soft flesh of my thumb with his slightly calloused one. Then he said, in a voice as gentle as the night breeze,

"May I take you home now, Annie?"

When I nodded, all at once unable to speak, he let go of my hand, walked me to the jeep and settled me inside.

He flipped on the jeep's lights, starkly illuminating the forest. Moths fluttered unsteadily into the beams. The stars withdrew their magic. As he drove off the air rushed through the jeep from the open windows, fanning our skin. I did not feel the need to speak, this time the silence between us was comfortable, although charged with an energy I was ill-equipped to read. As we neared my house Joe glanced at me, searching my face with a smile and I smiled back.

He did not turn into the drive this time but stopped alongside my own cypress tree. He got out and started poking around on the ground by its roots. I joined him, puzzled but intrigued. Joe stood up as I walked over to him and held something out to me. The cone that he slipped into my hand was smooth, with a faintly resinous scent.

"Do you know how the cypress got its name?" he asked. I shook my head.

"It comes from a Greek legend. It seems that Apollo loved a man called Cyparissus, who accidentally killed his beloved pet stag. Cyparissus begged Apollo to let him grieve forever for his loss and the god turned him into a tree that could weep."

Joe ran his thumb over the drops of resin that did indeed look like tears running down the trunk.

"If you soak the cone and then leave it in the sun until it opens, you can save the seeds to plant in the autumn. That way you can surround yourself with cypresses."

He kissed me lightly on my cheek then drove away; leaving me clutching the cone as if it was the most precious gift I had ever been given.

I watched the jeep's lights zigzagging down the road until they were lost from view and only then did I stir, breathing in deeply the heady scent of jasmine mingled with cypress that I had been unaware of until then. In the kitchen, I pulled open cupboards to find a small plastic bowl that I filled from the tap, then I carefully placed the cypress cone in the cool water.

I carried the bowl up the stairs with me, slopping cool drips onto the stone under my dusty feet. I showered quickly and then, naked and still damp, crossed my bedroom to open the shutters wide. A warm night breeze played over my damp skin, the

67

perfumed night invaded the room. In the garden below pinpricks of light danced in and out of the bushes as the fireflies played. The night was a deep, velvety purple. I climbed into bed, draping the mosquito net, a recent acquisition, around me, leaving me safe to stretch out on the cool cotton sheets without dreading a whining drone near my ear. Thinking of mosquitoes, the image of John Donne's clever lovers came into my mind, discussing a flea that sucked blood from one and then the other and I found the idea strangely erotic then laughed at myself.

From the open window, cool air drifted sensuously across my naked body. The swathes of netting around the bed shone faintly as the starlight played upon it, so that, lying within, I felt as if I were inside a net, fathoms deep in a dark sea.

Joe had called me Annie, the softest, sweetest version of my name that I had heard yet and I had felt at home with that name. An *Annie* could lie in a ghost net in a deep-velvet-sea of a night. An *Annie* could feel a soft breeze caress her skin and wish that it was his fingers tracing intricate patterns over her body.

The bowl with the cypress cone was on my bedside table. My mind was full of his subtle scent, which had filled my head when he stood close; a salty warmth of skin under freshly laundered clothes. My cheek still throbbed from the gentlest touch of his lips against it and my hand seemed to have the sensation of his larger and rougher one, burnt into it.

As I slipped into dreams I knew that all my defences were down, that I was truly myself for the first time in years, free to love and be loved, or not, whichever turning my life took. As I opened up to pleasure, so I also accepted the possibility of pain. I could no longer hide myself away, become invisible to keep my distance from life. I would take what life could give me and live it day by day; feel it, taste it, experience it in all its exquisite ways. I would shake free from the past. That last thought brought me a feeling of utter peace as I slept, silvered by the starlight's impartial glow.

7

*When the girl is near me and I reach out to her, she breaths deeply of life.
I absorb her wild emotions, calm her anger and give her my strength. This
I will do, until she learns to stand alone.
She feels her way, at first not trusting the glimpses of truth her instincts
reveal but nevertheless drawn along the path that she is destined to
follow. Trust is not immediate, rather must be built, one step at a time.
The man from the house by the lake knows this well. He waits patiently
for her to take each tentative step along the difficult, at times painful, path
of self-discovery that he already treads.
The lake reveals truth veiled in mystery. True reflections of sky and self
turn to prophecy in wind-forged images.
Future, past and present are equally clear to those who seek to see.*

I passed the next few days in a kind of a dream state. I walked to the village for supplies, sunbathed, ate dinner in the garden, just as I had done before and these things still gave me enormous pleasure but underlying everything else was my constant awareness of Joe. I did not see him but I knew he existed and knew that he was aware of me too. Each day I checked the cypress cone, waiting until it gradually opened up in the sun. When the seeds showered out as I tapped the cone, I carefully collected each one and wrapped half of them in paper, placing them in a kitchen drawer until autumn. The other seeds I lay on the scrubbed-wood table and stirred them thoughtfully with my fingers. Inside these tiny seeds was a new life patiently waiting to begin, life that I could almost sense through my fingertips.

It was a glorious afternoon, blazingly hot outside, warm and sultry even in the kitchen with the cool flagstones beneath my feet. It was time to test myself. I wrapped the seeds, slipped them into the pocket of my beige shorts along with the back door key and, without giving myself time to think again, without brushing my hair or changing my wilted green T-shirt, I began to walk down the road towards Joe's house.

The olive groves were older here. The gnarled trunks twisted into contorted shapes, silvery leaves shimmering in the heat. After a while, the olives gave way to a shady tunnel of oaks and evergreen Holm oaks, which gave welcome relief from the heat of the sun. Along the roadside fragrant yellow broom brightened the shade and prickly junipers filled the undergrowth. At the end of the tunnel, the countryside opened out a little. The road was bordered by crumbling stone walls; man's efforts to tame nature already half reclaimed by moss and ivy. The ivy also twined around the sprawling oaks but they, massive and proud, wore it imperviously.

As I rounded a bend, the wood ended abruptly and the valley spread out below me, a distant road winding through it, flanked by fields of pale wheat and spiky green corn. On the other side of the valley, wooded hills, dotted with small villages, rose gently again towards the startling blue of the sky. Now I had my first glimpse of Joe's house, its pale stone back towards me, nestled into a hollow below a copse. In front of the house was a field of blazing sunflowers, their huge faces upturned towards the sun they mirrored. There was a narrow footpath cutting through them leading to the house, while the gravel road that I was on followed the outer curve of the field.

I took the footpath, stepping between the huge flowers, feeling a little like Alice in Wonderland as I walked through the sea of tough green stalks, leaves wilted to their sides under the punishing sun. Around my head the bright yellow petals glowed and I felt as if I was swimming through sultry heat where no breeze penetrated below the surface of gold.

I heard a dog barking but the sound was muffled by the sunflowers. The house that I could see, framed in yellow at the end of the path, was built of weathered stone and as I drew closer, I noticed that it was kept in perfect condition. The wooden shutters were newly varnished. The old lamps fixed to the walls with intricate wrought-iron brackets, showed no sign of rust. Terracotta pots stood along the stone path that ran around the house, filled with earthy-smelling geraniums that tumbled and spilled from them in a profusion of red and pink.

A low growl made me stop, eyes searching, coming to rest on the shape of a large dog that was half hidden by the thick stalks of the sunflowers. As soon as I looked at it, the dog began to bark, never taking its gaze from me but coming no closer either. After my first fright I could see that, in spite of its noisy barking, there was no real anger in the dog's stance, in fact the sunflowers by it began to dance as the dog's tail thumped against them. I stood still, undecided about whether to go on now or turn back but then I heard Joe's voice calling out to the dog and knew that it was too late for flight.

"Luna, stop barking at the birds!" Joe was grinning good-naturedly as he came round the side of the house. The dog ran to him, jumping up until he pushed her down and crouched by her, ruffling fur and talking to her quietly, wiping away wetness with the back of his hand, as she licked his cheek. Then he noticed me and stood slowly, the dog quieting down immediately as it sensed his mood, standing close to his leg, its tail moving in a gentle rhythm, once more eying the intruder in the field.

Joe's expression was unreadable. He wore an old pair of leather sandals and faded blue shorts. His tanned chest and arms glistened with sweat and his face was streaked with dirt. As he pushed his hair away from his face I saw that his hands were dirty too and I quickly leapt at the escape route they offered, already half turning to go as I said, in a voice that sounded harsh and breathless,

"Sorry to disturb you, you are obviously busy . . . " I didn't get any further because he had covered the distance between us in a few long strides and touched my shoulder gently, turning me back round to him. I looked up. His head was higher than the sunflowers, their gold throwing light on his face while the sun streaked his sleek black hair, illuminating him so clearly that it was impossible to look away, impossible not to see the goodness there in his strong face or to avoid responding to his wide smile.

"I'm so glad you've come, Annie." Joe propelled me forward with a light touch on my shoulders and now that the dog knew I was a welcome visitor, she greeted me with proper enthusiasm, jumping up at me, almost knocking me over with the solid weight of her. Joe laughed and clapped his hands once, sending Luna running off ahead of us only to come tearing back towards us then off again, madly leading the way out of the field.

"She's not a puppy any more but she still behaves like one." The warmth in Joe's voice was echoed in the dog's adoring gaze. Joe chatted on, his words allowing me time to get some kind of a hold on my emotions.

"I've had her for three years now, got her from Pietro and Lucia. She's half German Shepherd and half Labrador and although she barks a lot I don't think she would be any good as a real guard dog, she's just too soft."

"She's lovely but she made me think twice about coming closer so I think she does her job well."

"Yes," he laughed, "until you get closer and then she just licks you to death."

We had walked around the side of the house, planted with lavender and rosemary. At the front was an expanse of sparse, yellowing lawn, broken by large firs, mulberries and persimmon trees and to the right were a couple of small stone barns, one set half into the hill. Beyond them a screen of willow leaves and rushes grew around a small lake where the lawn ended. The clear water of the lake reflected the pure blue above, the earth gazing back at the sky, balanced and harmonious.

"How beautiful," I said, taking in the view slowly, feeling the peace of the place pervade me so that, when I next looked up at Joe, it was with a real smile lighting my face and he drew a quick breath at the naked emotion shown there. He stood so close to me that I could smell the salty scent of the sweat that glistened on his skin and my fingers burned with a desire to touch him.

72

"What were you doing before I got here?" I asked, the sound of my voice breaking the spell that had held us and he looked at his hands as if only just aware of the dirt on them. He shrugged and shook his head,

"Just working on something in the barn. I guess I'm pretty dirty," he said ruefully. "Give me a few moments to get cleaned up and then I will show you round, ok." He waved towards a bench beneath a mulberry tree.

"It's nice and cool there," he said, already walking towards the house. "I'll be right back." he called over his shoulder. The dog made to follow him but he stopped her with a gesture and said, "Stay Luna,"

Luna sat, head on one side, pink tongue hanging out, watching him go, then she followed me into the shade and flopped down at my feet, head on paws, watching the house. I leant down, rubbing the soft fur. We were, I realised, both concentrated on Joe's hidden movements behind the walls, waiting.

The key in my pocket that jabbed me as I leant forward reminded me of the excuse I had planned, to justify coming here. When Joe emerged from the house soon after, I had the small packet of cypress seeds in my hand, fiddling with it like a talisman as I watched him stride across the grass towards me. Luna had run to greet him as soon as he appeared and now frolicked excitedly at his side. He had changed into clean shorts and a white T-shirt, with the same scuffed leather sandals on his feet. His hair was wet from the shower and combed straight back from his face, probably the only moment when it would stay like that instead of flopping forward over his forehead. Somehow, his appearance made me think of a young boy, freshly washed and dressed, his hair carefully slicked into place by his mother and that image made it suddenly easy for me to hold out my childish offering with a grin.

"Here," I said, "I collected the cypress seeds like you told me and I thought I would bring you some."

I held the packet up to him and stood, becoming aware as I did so of my own crumpled clothes and dusty state. He took the packet

I offered, the light touch of his fingertips on mine creating a raw thrill of pleasure. He opened the packet with a smile, rubbed the seeds thoughtfully and then wrapped them up again, putting them carefully in his pocket.

"Thank you." His voice was warm, a low deep timbre with its trace of an American accent. I looked down at my feet as I cast around for something to say. My comfortable gym shoes were more grey than white now and the walk had added a fresh coat of dust to them that streaked up my left ankle too.

"Lucia said that you're a doctor. That you were a doctor – in America." I tailed off under his unsettling gaze, wondering if I had said the wrong thing, if I had stepped too close by asking him about his past when I knew next to nothing about him or the life he lived here. However, Joe did not seem to mind, although his expression, as he looked at me, was thoughtful. He smiled, a kind of one-sided grin that looked slightly sad, then took my hand lightly in his, leading me across the lawn towards the small, stone barns.

"That was a long time ago, Annie." He sighed, looking ahead now but even though his eyes were no longer disconcertingly upon me, his hand wrapped around mine made my heart thud loudly.

"Come on. I'll show you what I do now," he continued, "I've found something I enjoy far more."

He let me go when we reached the biggest barn, tugging up the heavy metal latch on a wooden door and leading me inside. The contrast with the timeless, surroundings could not have been greater. The barn was full of modern machines, lathes and tools and the floor was covered in fresh wood-shavings and dust. The smell took me back to when I was very small and was allowed to help my grandfather in his shed, while he painstakingly planed away thin layers of wood from underneath a sticky, swollen, door. That memory and a jumble of others, triggered off by the scent of wood shavings, made me shut my eyes for a second, as time seemed to merge and fuse. When I opened them again Joe was pulling dustsheets from bulky objects at the end of the barn and I

74

moved closer to see several, beautifully crafted, pieces of furniture; small tables, chairs and chests.

"You make furniture!" My voice sounded incredulous but he did not take offence, just laughingly asked me what I had imagined him doing. I had no reply to that but throughout the time that I had been striving not to consciously think about him and also, in more recent days, when I had not been able to avoid doing so, I had never once imagined him as a carpenter. Seeing him now, surrounded by his work, it seemed at once the only thing that I could imagine him doing, so easily did he carry himself in this space. He touched a table, running his fingers over the polished grain then he showed me how the lathe worked, spinning tiny whorls of pale wood and sweeping them away onto the floor.

"I have a contract with a shop in Arezzo that specialises in homemade furniture. Sometimes I make what I want to but more often I get commissioned to make something. See that chest over there?" He pointed to a small sturdy chest with a brass lock hanging from it. I walked closer and saw that there was a narrow frieze carved around the box with simple scenes of ships, pirates and parrots.

"I'm doing that for an old lady as a birthday present for her grandson. A real pirate's treasure chest!"

I laughed, crouching down and touching the carved figures.

"What wood is this? Is it cypress?" I asked, seeming to recognise the resinous fragrance that emanated from the chest.

"Yes. Cypress is a hard, durable wood. It is ideal for cabinets and wardrobes because it keeps its scent and that seems to repel moths and woodworm." When I looked up, he was watching me closely and I had the impression that he had been debating something within himself.

"Is this what you were working on when I arrived?" I asked.

"No." Again, I saw the shuttered, hidden look flash across his face but then he seemed to make up his mind about something and he called to me to follow him.

After the dim interior of the barn, the sunlight was quite blinding and for a second, as I stood outside the door, I could not see where he had gone. Then Luna, her plume of a tail wagging in the air, came to round me up, taking me to the smaller building that was half set into the grassy hill behind it. A twisted fig tree wrapped around one side, blunting the corner with its huge, overlapping leaves. The unripe figs were about the size of walnuts, tender green and full of promise.

Joe was inside, his back to me when I entered. He was just finishing wrapping something in a piece of old sheeting, which he had torn up to use elsewhere as rags and dustsheets. There was a large table in the centre of the room, which took up nearly all the space. It was covered in small tools: files and chisels and rasps. Joe lifted the object that he had been working on from the table and put it on a high shelf, which ran along the rear of the room, next to various pieces of wood of all shapes and sizes.

"Here," he indicated a lower shelf, standing back to let me press past him. I held my breath as I felt the heat of his body radiate onto mine, then forgot his presence for the first time in days as I gazed, spellbound at the objects in front of me.

"I found a better use for my scalpel," he joked, then seeing my hesitation, said, "They won't break – you can hold them if you want."

Some of Joe's carvings were simplistic ones, like his work on the child's treasure chest; wooden cooking utensils decorated with fruit, small ashtrays with geometric designs. They were probably meant for the tourists in the shop in Arezzo too, pretty souvenirs to remind people of a special holiday. It was the other carvings that had me mesmerised, the ones where all of Joe's art flowed freely through the grain of the wood. For these pieces, he had mainly used olive wood. He explained to me that, although it was harder than some woods to carve, he liked the added surprises that the complex wood grain brought, adding an extra dimension to his work, as if the wood itself was participating. I could see exactly what he meant; the delicate animals, birds and figures seemed to

76

be alive, the grain adding movement to them, as if capturing them at the precise moment when they stopped to rest.

By far the most beautiful sculpture was a large one of an old man. At first I thought that it was unfinished but when I looked closer I saw that it had been left that way for a purpose, so that a third of the figure was still in the thick trunk that Joe had carved it from. I thought of Ariel, set free from his leafy prison by the magician, Prospero. There was indeed magic here. As I studied the sculpture, I realised that the old man was Pietro, his head and one arm free, the rest of him still part of the wood that held him. He was looking down, concentrating as I had so often seen him do, on the delicate vine leaf that he held between his thumb and fingers. A slender tendril of vine curled up around his hand so that man, vine and tree were forever joined as one.

"Oh, Joe." I could not find the words that I wanted to tell him how I felt. I gently placed the carving back on its shelf and then turned, reached up and kissed Joe's cheek then pushed past him and went back into the sunlight.

The spell was broken, the moment of magic past and the day was beginning to cool into evening. I was about to say that I must leave but he spoke first, from behind me, where he was closing up the barn door.

"Do you know what today is, Annie?" When I looked at him blankly he continued, "It's the summer solstice, the longest day of the year. Since it's also the first time that you've visited me here, I think that deserves to be celebrated, what do you think?"

He carried on quickly, not giving me time to reply, or refuse.

"Use my bathroom to freshen up while I get the barbecue set up and we'll have dinner out here. How does that sound?"

This time he did wait for me to reply, his dark eyes daring me to accept, the doubtful set of his mouth showing that he expected me to refuse. When I said yes, his lips curved into a slow smile and he nodded in that inscrutable way of his, then showed me into the house.

Inside was as well kept as outside, all polished wood and mellow stone, with oriental rugs to add splashes of colour and landscapes in oils and watercolour, which brought the countryside into the house too. I asked him if he painted but he said no, the paintings were done by different local artists. He could not draw at all, his fingers only worked when they could get straight into the wood, feel it, model it and shape it.

He handed me a clean towel and left me in the bathroom on the first floor, thudding noisily back down the stairs. Through the open window, I heard him whistle to Luna and then the sounds of clattering as he began to set up the iron grate to cook our dinner.

The bathroom was a large, cool room with pale blue tiles and old-fashioned ceramic fittings. It smelt of the same soap that I had noticed on his skin. I showered quickly, drying myself, not on the clean towel that he had given me but on the damp one that he had hung behind the door after using it earlier. I wrapped myself up in the scent of him; pondering on the insight his work had given me into him.

I thought about the different facets of Joe I had seen. He was a mystery that I wanted to slowly unravel, layer by layer. There was Rita's "kind" Joe; there was Lucia's friendly loner with an unknown past; there was the Joe I had first seen with his unsettling, unfathomable eyes and now there was the artist who could see deep into things, to the underlying truth in people. Joe had revealed Pietro to me, through his carving, as a man at peace with nature, part of it, revelling in it. Before, I had just thought of him as Lucia's husband who worked in the fields and had a bad back; now I saw the essence of him. I wondered, somewhat uncomfortably, as I pulled on my limp clothes again, what truths Joe could glimpse inside of me.

I did not bother to put my shoes back on, slipping silently downstairs in my bare feet. At the bottom of the stairs, I glanced into a room I had not noticed on my way in. It was a study with a sturdy desk, a computer and a couple of comfortable chairs. What stood out for me though were the books that lined the shelves, were piled up on the desk and overflowed onto the floor. The only things I missed about England were my books and now I was overcome with a fierce hunger to read again.

Through the window, I could see Joe and had a moment to study him without his being aware of me; his T-shirt stretched taut across his broad shoulders as he bent across the grill, blowing life into the tinder and charcoal; before Luna's frantic wagging made him turn and see me. He waved and leant in through the window. I felt stupidly as though I had been caught peeping at things I had no right to see and spoke quickly to justify myself.

"I saw the books and since the door was open I just came to have a look." He smiled as I babbled on, telling him that I had not realised until now how much I missed my own books. When I had finished he said,

"Borrow whatever you want. Have a look around and then come and give me a hand out here."

He turned back to the grill and I looked around the room, searching for something that would leap out at me and let me leave without further prying but his eclectic choice was such fun that I lingered in spite of myself. Books always give a glimpse into the soul of their owners and the enigma of Joe was heightened for me as I saw that he had something of every genre, from factual manuals and local guidebooks to novels and classics and even poetry. The books were well used but not so well dusted and it was easy to see which ones he consulted most frequently from the amount of dust they had collected. I flicked through a few, surprised and slightly horrified to see the broken spines and folded pages so contrary to my own way of carefully handling each book I read. One book, that I vaguely remembered having tried but being thoroughly bored with, was less bent than others. It opened to a page where Joe had scrawled "Load of crap. I'm giving up!" I laughed. This irreverent attitude was alien to me but demonstrated a living relationship with each book he read.

In the end, I settled on a well-worn copy by an American author who I had always meant to try and reluctantly left the other treasures to join Joe and Luna outside.

He put me to work at once, sending me around to his small vegetable plot to pick salad. I pulled up a lettuce and a few handfuls of pungent rocket and basil, and then picked some beef tomatoes, feeling the sun's warmth radiating from them as I buried my nose in the plants, breathing in their muskiness. I made myself at home in his kitchen, rinsing and slicing, opening cupboards to find plates, olive oil and salt. The smell of the meat on the barbecue wafted in from the doorway, making my mouth water. I carried my salad out to find that the patio in front of the house had been transformed. The sun had now sunk low on the horizon and Joe had laid a table with a duck-patterned tablecloth that made me smile and placed citronella candles everywhere to ward off the ubiquitous mosquitoes. It was entrancing. I placed my things on the table and went back to fetch the crockery. Joe lifted the meat from the grill, laying it in a long dish and handed it to me, going back to the kitchen for a big, half-round of country bread and some red wine.

The raucous chorus of the cicadas, that had strummed the hot air all day, faded then died away with one lone insect's final rasp. The silence of evening slid around us as we ate ravenously, conversation flowing easily between us. We discussed books and art, our homes here in Montalino and why we loved them, the colours of the Tuscan earth. I could not remember ever feeling so at ease. I was not tongue-tied. I did not feel unwanted. In fact, I was holding the attention of someone I wanted to be interesting for.

The phone rang once and Joe excused himself leaving Luna to entertain me. As soon as he had gone she got up from where she had been lying at our feet beneath the table and fetched me a filthy old tennis ball. Dropping it in my lap she gazed up at me beseechingly until I threw it for her. A few delightful minutes passed in this way and when Joe came back out he found me giggling at her antics as Luna struggled to retrieve the ball from under a bush, going so far under that all I could see was her tail spiralling wildly around. I stopped laughing when I saw Joe's serious expression and asked him if something was wrong.

"Not really," he said shoving his hair back and giving me a slightly tired grin. He slumped down in his chair and stretched his legs out, taking the ball that Luna presented to him absentmindedly and lopping it far down the garden for her.

"That was my sister Molly," he explained. "My father had a small stroke a few weeks ago, nothing too serious and he is recovering well but Molly is having to cope with it all alone. Dad can be a bit cantankerous." He looked across at me as he spoke and I saw a mixture of irritation and guilt in his frown. So much for me thinking that he would not have understood me when I had said that my mother's death had set me free. It was obvious that I was not the only one who had troubled family relationships.

Joe's good humour soon came back as he talked fondly about his sister and about his mother who had died some years previously and whom he had obviously loved a lot. He confirmed what Lucia had told me about his mother being from an Italian family.

"She was born and bred in Boston but she felt Italian. She always spoke the language with my grandparents, so I grew up almost bi-lingual. Then when she died I decided to take some time to travel and discover my roots. I spent some time in Umbria and it was fun to meet distant relatives although most of the close family had emigrated with my grandparents to America after the war. There was nothing special to keep me there though so I was on my way back to the States and I stopped at the Manor for the night. This was before the family started redoing the houses and renting them out. Lucia ran a small bed and breakfast for them. Pietro showed me around the place and when we drove past this house he mentioned that the old Count was thinking of selling it. That was all it took."

81

Joe lent back and stretched his arms wide, so that I worried that the chair might break beneath him. I wondered a little at the similarities between our stories. We had both been drawn here and known as soon as we arrived that it was the right place for us.

Luna settled down again and I held up my hands.

"Thank you Luna, that was a lovely game," I told her. Her ears swivelled towards the sound of her name. "It was also very mucky." I added and Joe laughed

"Nothing like a bit of dog slobber to make you feel right at home," he declared then pointed me to an old stone basin and pump set in a wall. We washed our hands together, arms touching and I did not know if the delicious shivers I felt came from the cool water splashing onto me or his proximity.

The sun on this, the longest day of the year, was reluctant to leave but finally it faded away from the sky, leaving it a cool, pale blue that darkened to grey over the distant Apennines. The sun slid behind fir fronds and foliage, illuminating thin wisps of cloud from below.

When the candles began to be necessary instead of just pretty, Joe brought out a quarter of a huge watermelon, cut lengthways. He sliced off fat, triangular wedges and we finished our meal with their fresh sweetness. The air cooled around us as the sky darkened. I looked into the candle on the table as its amber flame danced for us, attracting moths and patterning our faces in ever-changing ripples of light. Under my feet the stone slabs of the patio still held on to the sun's warmth while above me the first dim stars showed in the heavens, waiting for the light to fade away completely and let them burn in their full glory.

"Walk with me down to the lake?" Joe's voice cut through my silent reverie, bringing me back to the present. He pushed back his chair and took my arm, fingers curling around the smooth flesh above my elbow. Luna trotted alongside then darted off to investigate the rustle of a lizard in the bushes. In the dark, the spreading mulberry and firs reached wide into the encroaching night, as if wrapping themselves in its velvet. The willows leaning over the lake swayed to the music of night insects and frogs.

The water of the lake was black, seeming far deeper than it had during the day. I stood close to Joe on the grassy bank, contemplating the smooth surface, until a thin sliver of crescent moon escaped from the cloud that had shrouded it and turned the ripples on the water into intricate, silver filigree. Our elongated shadows, like twin cypresses, stretched out; close but separate. Then, a slight breeze stirred the water and my shadow danced into his in the ripples. I stood still, hardly daring to breath, as my shadow reflected my desire so that, although we stood apart on the bank, in the water we merged, waltzed, blended into each other and became one.

SUMMER

The Burning

Summer, season of fire, when the power of the sun is omnipotent. Heat scorches the land, blanching out the vibrancy of life. Animals hide in the shadows, waiting for dusk. Fires catch quickly in the dry undergrowth and flash through the woods, destroying everything in their path. Nature holds its breath, nurturing its strength deep within, striving to survive, yearning for rain.

I am the shape of the flame, symbol of eternal life; a cool green flame resisting the summer heat. As fire is an agent of transformation, a forge for the creation of the radiant, astral body, so I will help the girl create her own wings till she can fly.

At my roots, there is still moisture. Deep down in crevasses of mineral and stone that lie beneath the dry, cracked soil, secret springs well up to where my roots sought them centuries ago.

I will survive but the fiery sun beats down on me and makes me tired. I endure.

I pull my energy deep inside during the day, focus it on the coolness at my roots then, when darkness brings relief, let it flow free again.

8

My girl glows like a summer fire, passion bursting from her in sparks. Her emotions rage out of control. She wastes her energy, showering it around in futile excess when she is alone, then clamping down to make it invisible whenever anyone draws near.
Like an animal she goes dashing off to lick her wounds. She must learn that there is no point in fighting nature, one must simply endure and know that after the searing heat of summer will come autumn's gentle rain, just as the icy grip of winter will melt at the touch of spring.

He didn't kiss me. Why didn't he kiss me? The thought twirled around in my brain all day. Every time I thought that I had pushed it aside it would resurface, making me stand still wherever I was, mulling it over until I got fed up with myself and shoved the thought away again for a while. I had wanted his kiss, had been almost sure that he was going to reach out for me when we had stood by the lake, watching our moon shadows entwine but he hadn't and neither had he kissed me when he drove me home, except for a light touch of his lips to my cheek. I had been so sure that he was attracted to me too. Now I wondered if maybe I had been presumptuous, so overwhelmed by my own desire that I had supposed he would feel the same. If the passion I felt was one-sided, I must have embarrassed him because surely he must have been aware of my yearning; to me it had felt like an almost palpable force.

As I walked around the house or through the wood to the village, I began to doubt myself once more. I was so inexperienced in these things. Although not a virgin, my few, clumsy attempts at loving were so long ago they were almost forgotten. Never before had I known such all-consuming passion, such an infinite desire to know someone intimately, to be inside his head, to have him inside my body.

Now that summer had officially arrived, it seemed as if the weather wanted to prove it, as the days became hotter and hotter. The thermometer showed a constant high of around 35–40 degrees, day and night and I finally turned native by closing my house up to the midday sun in order to keep it a little cooler. The hot, sultry nights made it hard to sleep, which in turn left me unable to escape the emotions that pressed ever more insistently on me. In that emotive moment between day and night, the ache of desire within me and the frustration and bewilderment that had replaced it, as each day passed with no word from Joe, confused me. I had replayed every second of that evening again and again, searching for clues. For me everything had been so perfect. I could find no moment that jarred, no awkward words. I had felt relaxed in his company, at home with him and also with myself. How could I have misread things so much?

The heat drove me to the village earlier every day that I needed supplies and I finally came to realise that I needed a car after all. I mentioned it to Rita one morning and the next time I bumped into her in the greengrocer's, she had a surprise for me. Luca knew of a car that was for sale, right there in the village. We left the grocer's together and Rita hurried me along the road and into a side street by the bar. She searched the brass nameplate outside an apartment block, finally finding the name she wanted and buzzing. She spoke quickly to the disembodied voice that answered and soon after an old man appeared. He had a thin ring of snowy white hair around a brown bald patch. Tufts of hair sprouted from unruly eyebrows and from inside his ears. There was a vague filminess to his eyes no doubt caused by cataracts but his expression was shrewd and a little wary. Rita introduced him as Armando and we solemnly shook hands then he led us further down the street to where a dilapidated looking Fiat Panda was parked, somewhat crookedly, on the pavement. The car had once been white but was now decorated with small scratches and patches of rust.

87

"It is old, like me," Armando said, shaking his head ruefully. "It has been a good companion but now the doctor says that I cannot drive anymore. He says my eyes are not what they were – bah, what do doctors know, eh? But still, now my wife nags me if I take the car keys and my children are cross with me all the time." He scratched at his bald head, jangling the car keys in his pocket as if reluctant to hand them over, then brought them out with such force that he shot loose change over the pavement too. I bent to pick up the change and hide a smile. When I handed the money to Armando he shoved the keys at me.

"Try it. It will start first time," he declared, and I tugged open the driver's door while he stood close, mumbling to himself about how the car had never once let him down in all these years.

Rita was asking how much Armando wanted for the car. When he told her she screeched that it was impossible, far too much, robbery. They bargained noisily, while I turned the key in the ignition. As promised, it started first time. That was the good part. The bad part was the smell. Armando had obviously used the car for transporting his ducks and chickens to market. The back seat was filthy with a mixture of straw and excrement and the stench, heightened by the heat, was powerful. I laughed. This would do me fine. The seats would wash, the smell would fade and the car was small enough for me to park behind the jasmine bushes, where it would not be too obvious or look out of place. I climbed back out, squeakily slamming the door, to find Rita grinning and Armando sulking over the deal that had been made.

I promised to bring Armando's money down later and pick the car up then but, when Armando realised that I was on foot, he insisted that I take the car immediately. Soon it was agreed that I would drive with him into Montevarchi to register the sale and sort out the documentation. Armando insisted that I should not pay him until the next time I came to the village, demonstrating once again the warm and trusting nature of my new neighbours.

As we drove out of the village, I saw Fiammetta by the railway bridge. I waved at her and she raised a hand in greeting but she looked at Armando, not at me. The old man looked back at her and made a swift sign of the cross. In the mirror, Fiammetta's eyes followed the car and her smile was mocking. I glanced at Armando but decided not to ask him why he had crossed himself when he saw Fiammetta. I had seen others do the same thing when I mentioned Fiammetta's name and was aware that even normally sensible people like Lucia and Rita seemed to be superstitious about the old woman. Fiammetta herself was well aware of her effect on the villagers and I sensed that she played on her reputation, drawing a certain vindictive satisfaction by toying with people, staring them out and smirking craftily, as if she knew their innermost secrets.

I spent the morning with Armando, happy to let him handle the seemingly endless discussions that accompanied the relevant paperwork. It was quite fascinating to watch him work his way through the offices, browbeating the clerks into submission like the military man he told me he had once been. He was magnificently cantankerous, gesticulating widely, shrugging his shoulders wearily, thrusting out his lower lip in a petulant way and generally making things so uncomfortable for everyone that I was sure they rushed the paperwork through in order to get rid of us as quickly as they could. Once the car had been officially transferred into my name Armando insisted on taking me for coffee. We sat in the shade of the portico, outside the bar in the main square where he could nod curt greetings to anyone he knew, enjoying the speculative looks his friends gave me. He did not introduce me to anyone. I was a secret; a subject for future conversations, to be lingered over and dissected at his leisure for the next few months. He mentioned that he had been to England, in Surrey and laughed when I asked if he had enjoyed his holiday. I winced when he told me that he had been a prisoner of war there. Patting my hand he said,

"No need for that face girl, I have no regrets. I didn't want to join up anyway but in those days, if you did not join the army the Black Shirts made your family suffer and I had a wife and two young sons. My brother had no family. He joined the partisans and lived in the mountains for years but I could not risk my family like that so I joined up and tried to survive for them. When I was caught, I was just glad to be alive. Very few of the men from my village who went away ever came back. At least they treated us ok in the camp. The English weather was dreadful but they had us working outside mostly, helping out on the local farms." As he spoke, Armando's eyes glazed with memories.

"I remember one day we were being marched home in the early evening. It had been a hot day for once and we were walking near the place they called the Golden Valley. It was a very beautiful place. All of a sudden, I saw this little girl at the side of the road. She was a tiny mite with hair so pale it almost looked white. She was pushing her bike because it had lost a peddle and when she saw us coming she pulled it off the road as far away from us as she could, pressing her back into the hedge and staring at us with such fear that it broke my heart. She looked about the same age as my youngest. I called out and our guards stopped and had a cigarette while I mended her bike. I tried to talk to her but she just stared at me with those terrified blue eyes and as soon as the peddle was back on the bike she rode off as fast as she could."

He finished the coffee in his cup and the sadness drained from his face as he became aware of his surroundings once more. I was finding echoes of the war here in Italy, in the memories of the old people, that I had never been aware of before. For the first time I considered the fact that my own grandfather had fought a war against the people that I had chosen to live amongst and yet I had never encountered anger or prejudice over my nationality. Armando had spoken with hatred of the Fascists and Rita had been terrified of the Germans but both of them had seemed grateful to the allies for having liberated them. It was unsettling though to think about the harsh realities of living in occupied territory, fighting a war that you did not want to in order to protect your loved ones from your own neighbours.

Driving home after dropping Armando off in Montalino again, I pushed all thoughts of the past away and concentrated on the pleasure of having a car again. I was beginning to learn the intricate workings of the grating gears and know the severe limitations of the car's suspension. I sang to myself as my shopping bounced merrily around in the back. Hot, dusty air poured in through the open windows carrying wafts of broom and hot earth to alleviate the stink of chickens. Then my good mood vanished as I reached the wood, where I was assailed by a sharp memory of Joe driving me home after our summer solstice dinner.

We had been standing by the lake when Joe had suddenly said that he would take me home and strode off to get the Jeep. I had been surprised by this abrupt end to the evening but once in the Jeep, he had seemed quite normal, pointing out the constellation of Scorpio, shining above us as we drove. I had leant my head out of the window for a better view. In the open countryside, with no man-made lights to dim their splendour, except the twinkling pinpricks from the village in the valley, the whole sky had seemed spread out over us like a great velvet cloth studded with diamonds.

"The heavens' embroidered cloths" I said, the words from the half-remembered poem coming to me, although I could not recall the rest.

"What did you say?" Joe had asked, driving into the wooded tunnel of oaks but before I had been able to reply, he had gasped and braked so suddenly that I had been thrown forwards. Trapped for a second in the jeep's headlights, a small deer had stared at us with startled eyes, caught between curiosity and fear. The fear won out and the deer whirled, plunging back through the undergrowth of juniper bushes, leaving us spellbound.

Now, as I drove up the familiar road in my ancient car, I wrestled again with the enigma of Joe; what did he think about me, why hadn't he contacted me, how could I get the damn man out of my mind? I parked the car behind the jasmine bush, grabbed my shopping and slammed the door, far harder than I needed to, determinedly forcing thoughts of Joe out of my mind once more.

I was hot, sweaty and probably smelt of poultry. The first thing I needed to do was wash the car thoroughly, then I would jump in a shower and let the water smooth my tension away. I turned round with my arms full of shopping and saw with horror that I had a visitor. Luca unfolded himself from my back doorstep, where he had been sheltering from the sun. I had been so caught up in my thoughts of Joe that I had not even noticed Luca's car parked a short way down the lane.

Luca kissed my cheeks, laughing when I remarked on the unpleasant odours in the car and excused myself if I smelt the same.

"Mama told me that you'd bought the car," he said, "I wondered if you knew how to go about getting it insured, or if you could do with a bit of help."

"Thanks Luca. You're a darling. Yes, I need help. Come into the kitchen and I'll get us a cold drink, then you can explain it all to me."

Luca grabbed my bags and followed me inside. I got fruit juice for us and we sat at the table while he explained about the insurance and offered to go into Arezzo with me the next day, since he had a good friend with an office there. I accepted with relief. After dealing with the Italian bureaucracy involved with the registration of the car sale today, I was exhausted and had been dreading trying to make myself understood with the insurance people.

I walked Luca back to his car and laughingly refused his half-hearted offer to give me a hand at cleaning out the car. As he walked away I remembered something and called out to him,

"What time do you want to go tomorrow?"

He turned, ran a hand through his red curls and grinned,

"Not early! Joe and I are taking our girls out to a concert tonight and we'll be late. I'll pick you up at about 11am. Ok?"

I nodded. I smiled. I waved. Luca drove away raising a cloud of dust behind him.

I turned and fetched soapy water from the kitchen. I scrubbed and scrubbed and scrubbed until the car was spotless and my knuckles were sore. I left the car with all doors open to dry off and walked, for hours, without knowing where I was going, until I was so tired that I did not think I could go another step then I went home, showered and fell into bed without eating.

I had no appetite; there was a sick ache inside me. I wished that I had no mind either, that I could just switch off my thoughts and shut away my emotions but that old trick of mine no longer worked. I had discovered how to feel again and now I was going to have to learn to live with the pain.

Joe was going out that night with his girl. He had a girlfriend. It was no longer a mystery why he had not kissed me. All the time I had been falling for him he was just being nice to me.

Somehow, I fell asleep and when I woke in the morning, I knew what I needed to do. I used the trip to Arezzo with Luca to book a flight to England, after we had sorted out my car insurance. I got the first flight available for that same evening. Luca dropped me back home, somewhat puzzled by my sudden departure, which I had explained to him as an urgent need to sort some things out at home. Then I threw myself into the task of packing a small bag and closing up the house. I drove the tatty old car along the motorway to Pisa and parked it in a side street close to the airport, certain that no one would ever want to steal it, then squared my shoulders and made my way towards the terminal.

Running away had been a spontaneous reaction, a flight from pain. I had realised even while I was driving to the airport that I was probably making a mistake but, unlike the olden days, I did not berate myself. I conceded that a short break would do me no harm and would without doubt help me to view things more clearly. It was not the end of the world if Joe did not want me, it was a shame for me but in the long run it would not alter my life.

I felt a sudden stab of nostalgia for home. I would breathe some fresh air in England; it would at least be a relief from the heat of recent weeks. I would sort out the last details of the house sale myself and clear up any other outstanding matters that Mr Forbes had for me. I would see a few friends, and then I would come back.

Once I got to England, I had to decide where to stay. I did not want to go home and did not feel like staying with Becky. Anyway, it was too late to just turn up out of the blue, so I got a taxi to a motel on the outskirts of Burntwood and checked in for a few days.

When I had first decided to return to England, it had been the gently rounded countryside that I had pictured and a cool wind blowing my hair. I had day-dreamed of the windswept cliffs of Cornwall when I was on the plane, toying with the idea of spending a few days down there; walking the coast, smelling the salt in the air where seagulls keened and swooped. However, once I was actually back, all my plans seemed wrong. I was there; ordering tea and toast in the motel, walking down the busy high-street to the lawyer's office, meeting Becky at lunchtime for a sandwich and fending off her irritating probing into every detail of my new life; but all the time I was aware that my heart was elsewhere.

Back in my old house, as I packed a few personal items and my favourite books in my bedroom, I felt strangely detached, as if someone else was inhabiting my body. The inner peace that I had become used to was eluding me here. I would have to find a way to live with my feelings for Joe, without allowing them to hurt me anymore. Being here in this house had confirmed to me that I could not come back to live in England. An idea of how to begin this transformation of my way of thinking occurred to me and I began to sort through my books until I found a slim volume of Yeat's poetry. Opening the book, I flicked through the pages until I came to the poem I wanted. As I read the beautiful description, of the heavens being like a magical cloth that the poet would like to spread beneath his lover's feet, I was struck anew by the poignancy of the last lines: *I have spread my dreams under your feet; Tread softly because you tread on my dreams.*

I took a pen out of my handbag and found a sheet of writing paper amongst the things on my desk then sat on the floor, leaning against my old bed while I pondered exactly what to write. I would copy out the poem and add a note to Joe as a way of marking the change, for me, from desire to friendship. I hoped I would be strong enough to be able to enjoy Joe's company from now on, however infrequent, without losing my head. I would somehow manage to remould my emotions and subdue them into an acceptable warmth. In the end I wrote,

"Dear Joe,
I've just got back from a flying visit to England and I thought you might enjoy reading this poem. I quoted part of it the other night, just before we saw the deer. I am sure you will understand now why I referred to that beautiful sky as the "heavens' embroidered cloths". Every day and night that I spend in this beautiful place, where we have both chosen to live, I feel as if I am treading on those exquisitely woven cloths, made of all the myriad hues of light and dark and all the subtle shades in between. I hope you like the poem too.
Your friend,
Annie."

The note sounded stilted and formal as I read it, over elaborate, trying too hard. Words were such clumsy tools for expressing emotions. While I had been writing my thoughts had curled around memories throwing the shadowy image of Joe's face onto the page but the words just sat coldly there. Still, it would have to do. I looked around me. There was nothing else for me here. How could I regret selling the house when there were warm stone walls, sunflowers burning fire along the hills and cypresses waiting for me.

I had agreed to meet Becky in our local pub that night, to catch up properly, so at eight o'clock I reluctantly took a taxi to our old haunt. The Tudor-style pub looked just the same, its thatched roof at odds with the busy, traffic-laden road thundering past its door. Inside the air was redolent with an acrid mixture of smoke and beer over an older, engrained and stale smell of the same elements. Becky saw me come in and stood up, waving me over to a corner table. I wove my way through groups of people I vaguely recognised. The ceiling pressed close, smoke curling round the low beams. Becky was still standing, dressed in tight jeans and a low cut T-shirt. To my dismay, I saw that Dave and Jim were there too. I fixed a smile on my face and forced myself forward to greet them.

Becky kissed my cheek, Jim rose courteously, his back still towards me and Dave, who had already seen me, stumbled clumsily to his feet. The look of amazement on Dave's face gave me a start. I could see attraction where once there had been distain. I greeted him with a cool peck on his cheek before turning to Jim.

"Bloody hell, Ann, you look different," Jim spluttered, his good-looking face split by a grin of genuine appreciation. I held out my hand, feeling the same easy pleasure I had always found in his company. As he had said to Dave, on the day of the funeral, I was not his type and he wasn't mine either but I had always found him attractive and enjoyed his good-natured quips and warm cockney vowels.

"Do I?" I grinned back at him, realising that there had been a subtle shift in the way we all related to each other. I was no longer Becky's plain friend, an almost invisible addition to their group. Becky was aware of the shift too and reacted to it. With a sharp glance at me she said loudly,

"It's Italy that's done it – all that sun. We should go there Dave, go and visit Ann and get a tan ourselves."

"Whatever it is, you look great," Jim struggled on, an unfamiliar light in his eye. He still held the hand I had given him to shake and showed no sign of letting go so I squeezed it gently and let my own arm drop. He lowered his gaze in quick

96

embarrassment, then looked up at me again and, encouraged by my bemused smile asked,

"Where is it you have been staying exactly then, darlin?"

"Tuscany."

"Whereabouts exactly?" Dave butted in, his sarcastic drawl just as irritating as it had always been. I hid my dislike with a pleasant smile and told a blatant lie.

"Near Lucca," I said, the lie tripping easily from my tongue. Anyway, it was true really, I thought, I did live near Luca, just not the city that Dave would think I meant.

The rest of the evening was spent in this vein with me turning conversation away from myself, avoiding their questions. Becky began to pout as Dave drank more than he should and began to leer at me openly. Jim did not drink much; he seemed content to watch, looking at me as if I was some strange treasure that he had just uncovered.

When it was my time to buy a round I elbowed my way up to the bar and waited to catch the barmaid's eye and give her the order.

"Hello, little Ann," Dave's voice close to my ear made me jump. I could smell the beer on his breath. The bar was crowded but he was deliberately pressing himself against me.

"I'll give Ann a hand with the drinks, Dave. You'd better get back to Becky before she walks out on you. She's about to blow her top, mate." I looked behind Dave with relief, as Jim came to my rescue. Dave shrugged and went and Jim took his place next to me. He kept his distance and I slowly relaxed. The barmaid noticed Jim immediately and I could understand why. With his easy smile, his blond good looks and his stocky, muscular build, he was not just attractive but looked like a nice person too. He ordered the drinks for me and turned round with a smile.

I met his gaze, thoughtfully. He was not as tall as Joe, just a bit taller than I was. I did not desire him but there was a pleasant warmth in my stomach as he looked at me admiringly. In that moment I understood just how much my life had changed. I

97

thought of my cypress, unyielding but strong, its roots holding deeply to the land while its tips reached for the heavens and an unmistakable scent of resin momentarily overcame the scent of beer and smoke. I had fallen in love with a place and Joe was part of it but, even without him, I could be happy there, live my own life and be myself.

My unsmiling assessment of him had wiped the friendly grin from Jim's face and now he touched my cheek with a tentative finger and said,

"I can give you a lift home tonight, if you'd like."

I nodded, debating.

"It depends on how late you want to stay."

"I'm ready to leave when you are."

We carried the drinks to the table, stayed a few more minutes and then I stood up, hugged Becky quickly and said Jim was giving me a lift. He was already on his feet and placing a hand under my elbow, he steered me through the crowd; avoiding further questions or the making of plans, whisking me away before the others could react properly.

Out in the car park the air was cold and it was raining; a hard, stinging rain.

"All right?" Jim questioned me and I knew he was not just asking me about the rain or the episode in the pub with Dave. I looked into his eyes, smiled calmly and took his hand. I was fine, more than that, I was glad that I had come here now. I had needed someone to want me, needed to learn that I could make someone desire me. As our feet crunched across the gravel, I looked up. The stars were muffled by clouds, the sky lit by the orange glow of city lights. It was not home any more but it was right for now, for this brief moment in time.

9

I know myself, my limitations and my strengths. My wood has always been used by man to build things that will last through time. It endures, does not rot or wear easily. In my physical entity, I am strong and although I am rooted in one place, my spirit soars where it will.
My girl is beginning to redefine her own limitations now, to be whole again. She is no longer a prisoner to duty, cut off from herself and her emotions. Nor is she in the self-imposed exile that was necessary, while she licked her wounds and regained knowledge of self.
Only when she learns that she has all she will ever need within herself, will she be able to find room in her heart for others. We wait; the old one, the man from the lake and me. I am content with the fleeting moments when we all connect. She must come to me at her own pace.
I am never lonely. When I am alone, I listen to the whisper of the wind, the slow growth of the plants, the soft passage of a cloud.
What others call silence I call song and the strength built on the silent passage of time is what I offer.

I was in a plane again, cocooned in the impersonal tube as it sliced through the sky. Chin cupped in hand I surveyed the vast, ever-changing, cloudscape from the rounded window, glad that I had been allocated a seat by myself so that I could gaze out, without distractions; catching the occasional glimpse of a world turned to miniature before the bulging cumulus wrapped the world up in cotton-wool again. In this safe no-man's-land between earth and space, I was free to review my life in peaceful solitude.

Last night I had known, from the moment that Jim had joined me at the bar, where I was going to take things. I had invited him up to my room in the motel, glad of the anonymity of the surroundings, feeling even then a sense of timelessness, of stepping back from my life and taking a moment for myself alone, with no need for guilt or explanations or sentiment. Not that I did not like Jim, I had always liked him but I did not care about him beyond that particular moment.

Making love with him had been everything that I had needed, at least on a physical level; the gentle touch of a skilled lover, excitement and release, then a deep calm afterwards. It had been pleasantly unhurried, rendered more tender by the odd awkward moment; the snagging of unfamiliar clothing, the hastily pulled on condom breaking our rhythm.

I had felt absolute control of my body, thrilled by the unfamiliar power I had over him as I took exactly what I wanted. When he had left, I had been glad. I had been grateful to him for the tenderness he had given me and pleased by his promise to call me later, although I had known even then that, when he did, I would not be there. That part of my life was over, finished. Thanks to Jim, I had rid myself of any lingering self-doubts. I was attractive. No long, lonely future stretched ahead of me. If I wanted companionship, I would be able to find it. I still ached to think that my partner wouldn't be Joe but, in the end, it didn't really matter: What was truly important was that I'd found myself again. I did not have to live alone. I could choose the path my life would take and if I desired solitude, then that was my choice and not something inflicted upon me by life or other people. I turned my attention back to the window where the clouds had been replaced by a breathtaking swoop of nothingness, plummeting down to jagged Alps. Sunlight glinted off snow and I smiled.

The car was where I had left it. It had acquired an extra layer of dust in the few days that I had been away but it started first time and I thought of old Armando with a fond smile. It was already dark so the air was bearable. I set off, feeling my home calling to me, hurrying me along the now familiar road. Under the scent of soap, a faint smell of chickens lingered. The engine chugged faithfully and the suspension squeaked complainingly.

I unwound the stiff windows completely when I turned onto my road, letting the odours of broom, dust and resinous cypresses in, to whirl around my head, making me feel almost giddy with pleasure. I slowed down, almost stopping when I drew alongside my home but something urged me on, and instead I drove straight towards Joe's place.

This time I followed the road as it swerved around the field of sunflowers, their great heads bowed as if resting for the night; waiting with a primordial patience for their god to rise again from the east. Joe's house was in darkness except for the light from one room, which shone a welcoming beacon out across the lawn. I turned the car around then ran quickly to the front door, posted the note into the letterbox and ran back to the car. I heard Luna's muffled bark from behind the thick stone walls as I drove off again but I did not look back.

The moonlight on the olive trees, as they waved in the soft night breeze, transformed them into a swaying sea, undulating in silver ripples over the ancient land. I could feel the vast force of history that lay buried beneath the surrounding fields and burnt in the stars above, illuminating the earth with the light of long ago. I felt time warp, bending around me. The past enclosed me, the future beckoned and I was here, in the middle of this infinite universe; alive, so very alive.

Home again. The jasmine had lost most of its flowers but still scented the air subtly as I parked the car. The dry grass looked pale in the moonlight. Fireflies sparked nearby as I walked towards the house, my fingers touching and discarding objects in my bag as I searched for my key. I swore under my breath as I almost tripped over something that lay in my path. Stepping round it, I found the key and opened the door. Flicking the light switch I blinked at the sudden glare then kicked off my shoes and crossed the kitchen to dump my bags by the big table. Then I went back to see what had been left for me, spreading my toes in pleasure on the smooth, cool tiles. I thought that maybe Fiammetta had been again to bring me some eggs, or that Lucia had left me some wine but now, in the clear pool of light around the doorway, I saw a

101

small bundle of rags that I recognised from Joe's workshop, and I ran to pick it up.

I kicked the door closed behind me and placed the bundle on the table, forcing myself to relax when I realised that I had been holding my breath. My fingers were trembling as I unwrapped the cloth to reveal a small, exquisite carving. I pushed the rags away, ignoring them as they fell to the floor and sank down onto a chair, transfixed by Joe's gift.

From a rough base, where the olive bark was still in place, grew two cypresses. Between the trees, a delicate fawn stood poised in that instant before flight, inquisitive, fearful and poignantly beautiful. The pale wood was highly polished with a darker grain running fluidly through it giving the impression of movement, as if a light breeze was ruffling the branches. There was no note but, when I picked it up to look more closely, underneath he had carved the word **Annie**.

10

The man is as patient as I thought he would be, content to watch and wait. He observes the girl struggling to conquer her unfamiliar emotions with infinite tenderness.
He has made his own difficult decisions and fought to carve his own path through life, to find the inner peace that she is beginning to glimpse. Now he moves slowly closer. He invites her to look with him into the infinity of time and space, to feel the insignificance of their individual lives and yet know that the spark, called soul, can burn as fiercely as a dying sun.
When he has shown her the flame, he will feed the fire between them with simple everyday pleasures until she is drawn into the reality of his world.
The old one is less patient.
She feels her strength ebbing away and knows that she must reach out to the girl now while she still can. She chooses this most magical of nights and I will form the bridge between them.

I was too restless to sleep. I unpacked my travel bag and changed into loose trousers and a T-shirt then padded back downstairs and poured myself a glass of Pietro's red wine. I revelled in being barefoot again and at the taste of the strong wine in my mouth. I swirled the wine around my glass creating a ruby coloured vortex and breathed in the heady, musky aroma.

Taking the wine outside I sat on the millstone, sipping slowly, swinging my legs gently. The garden was at once familiar and strange. In the few days since I had left there had been subtle changes and as I searched out each new shape and scent, I felt peace seeping back into me along with a sense of bewildered excitement caused by Joe's exquisite gift. I had spent so much energy trying to find a way to think of him as nothing more than a friend and now all that careful planning had been blown apart by the message I sensed in Joe's carving.

The sudden crunch of stones under heavy tires, made me jump. It was Joe. I could just make out his shadowy shape as he slammed the jeep door shut and turned round, carrying something bulky in his arms. He saw me then, as I leant forward and stopped a short distance away, his eyes blacker than the night. A silence stretched between us, charged with some emotion I could not define until he finally broke it, saying gently,

"Welcome back Annie."

I moved slowly towards him. The long grass brushed my calves, raising goose bumps on my skin. I could see him more clearly now in the faint light; the strong, straight line of his nose, the curve of his jaw. We stood close enough to touch, absorbing each other's heat and scent and my senses were so heightened that I was aware of an infinite number of images in an instant, as if time had slowed. I saw Joe in minute detail; his skin and hair daubed with starlight, the weave of his white linen shirt, the dark stubble on his chin. The cool ground beneath my feet was slightly damp with dew. A spider's web stretched between loops of jasmine, quivering delicately. The night insects fluttered and whirred.

"Thank you for the poem," he said at last.

"You're welcome," I answered. The words sounded so banal, so cold, that to cover them up I added quickly,

"Thank you for the carving of the deer. It is beautiful, so delicate it seems almost real."

"I'm glad you liked it." He took a step away from me and shook open the bundle he was holding, spreading a blanket out, flattening an oblong of long grass.

"Today they celebrate St Lorenzo here. Every 10th August people lie out at night and watch for shooting stars," he said, lying down on his back as if he belonged here, in my own space.

The coarse wool blanket felt scratchy on my bare thighs and arms as I lay beside him, examining the stars sprinkled across the dark sky, trying to pretend that lying with Joe in my garden at night was a completely normal thing to do. How was I supposed to make myself think of him as a friend when just being close to him had this effect on me? I felt so tense that he surely must sense it. However, when he spoke he sounded quite normal,

"It's the night when the largest number of meteoroids are supposed to fall to earth," Joe continued, "Although to be honest it isn't quite as precise as that, just that there is more chance of seeing shooting stars around this time of year, because as the Earth turns it passes closer to certain constellations, where there is a higher concentration of meteoroids." He laughed and turned his head to look at me, adding

"Listen to me. I sound like a professor. Actually I only know all that because I looked it up on the internet today but it's traditional to stay up on the night of St Lorenzo and make wishes on the shooting stars that you see."

I kept my gaze on the sky, uncertain of how to react but my lips twitched slightly in response.

"I read the poem," he continued after a while, "Must I tread softly, so as not to hurt you?"

He did not laugh, just let the question lie there between us but I did not know what answer to give him. In spite of the gift he had left for me, which seemed to indicate that he felt something for me, he already had a girlfriend. I had promised myself that I would learn to treat him as a friend and yet I wanted him to touch me. I felt confused again, all my self-composure abandoning me.

The silence had drawn out and become uncomfortable as I hesitated over my reply. Joe muttered under his breath and sat up abruptly. I sat too, feeling cold all of a sudden. Moving apart to put more distance between us I wrapped my arms around my knees as I surveyed him.

I could think of nothing to say that was not charged with a thousand unspoken emotions. I was afraid to break the silence, had to keep holding on to my resolve not to impose my own feelings onto him, not to misunderstand him or exaggerate his meanings

105

and I was just too tired to do that. The events of the past days were catching up with me. All I wanted right now was to sleep and shut out this unwanted bombardment of my senses.

Just then, Joe shouted, pointing upwards. I followed the arc of his arm and saw a shooting star as it streaked across the sky. A flash of light, bringing hope, granting wishes.

Joe sighed and sank back down on the blanket again and after a while, I did too. I wanted to say something but my mind was blank and Joe seemed very distant as he lay next to me, withdrawn from me. Long seconds stretched between us until, shifting slightly on the blanket Joe cleared his throat and began to speak again. His voice was patient, almost hypnotic.

"Legend has it," he said, "that shooting stars are actually tears shed by Saint Lorenzo, the martyr, as he was tortured. Those tears were destined to roam the heavens for all eternity. Each year some are supposed to fall to earth, on the day that the saint died, bringing magic and hope with them."

Joe had turned his head to look at me again. I felt his gaze sink into me, felt it as a warm breath across my cheek. Although I still stared rigidly up I was aware of his lips curving into a half smile and his next words were full of tenderness,

"They say that on this night all those who have suffered, or who are in pain should make a wish and that the saint, remembering his own pain will make those wishes come true."

After that, suddenly the tension inside me was gone. I made no conscious wish but some pressure within me was released. Silence settled around us again, not an absolute silence, rather a calm quiet filled with soft, night sounds; an insect in the dry grass, a mosquito near my ear that I swished my hand at, Joe's gentle breathing. I searched the sky for the magical shooting stars and a thought suddenly struck me with great force.

I am.

"I am," I repeated and that one idea was so simple, so deep and complete that I was filled with the force of my own identity. I was aware of myself, of the fact that I existed within this vast universe,

106

part of it but individual. I was just as real as the meteor that had streaked through the sky above us moments before, turning into dust as it fell. I was whole, a unique amalgamation of flesh, blood and bone, of emotions, quirks, fears and desires. I was more real even than the stars that shone so brightly in the firmament, for who could know if the sun that had produced such powerful light was burning still, or if it had died years ago.

Joe moved his hand, slid it over the rough blanket until it lay beside my own; the lightest of touches.

He is, I thought. I am and he is. If he moves his hand any closer then the whole equation will change and will become *we are*.

My eyes blurred with unshed tears and I closed them for a moment. I was so very, very tired. Behind my eyelids, I could still see the stars in the blood drumming in my head and then I felt the world moving slowly beneath me, as the stars spun faster in the sky. I felt, rather than heard, a faint humming in the air and turned my head instinctively to look at the cypress. A slight breeze rippled its branches and it seemed to beckon me.

I moved towards the cypress and became aware that I was dreaming when, instead of lifting my feet and walking, I floated through the night effortlessly. It was a strangely real dream though. The kind of vision I had had the night before my mother's funeral. I could see my real body lying close to Joe, two dark shadows in the grass and I could smell the garden and feel the cool air on my skin. Bound to my body by a thin silver cord I was free to explore the night.

When I reached the cypress, I stopped. In the night, all was shadow but there were myriad shades of dark; hues of purple and blue streaked with slithers of silver. I looked up then to see a shooting star blaze across the sky but instead of fading away to nothing, it changed course and streaked toward the forest. I felt myself torn from the shelter of the cypress, caught in the fiery wake of the light, which zigzagged through the trees ahead. I surged through the forest, along a path that I did not recognise, a deer track that twisted torturously between the oaks and beeches.

Even though I knew I was dreaming, I instinctively ducked under low branches, swerved to avoid the tangle of brambles that invaded the path and felt the silken threads of cobwebs cling to my face and bare limbs. The scent of wild mint wafted up as if trodden beneath my feet as I skimmed the path. The shooting star streaked ahead and I saw the woods lit up in its ethereal beam. The path followed the dried-out bed of a stream, sometimes running alongside it and sometimes rising up and along the edge of deep, secret gullies. Then the light slowed down and I drew near enough to see it take on a form that was vaguely human, a silver shape ringed with an aura of sky blue.

Fiammetta, I thought. The colour of the old woman's eyes. The shape moved and seemed to point deeper into the forest. I floated past the figure and looked where it was pointing. Lit by the ghostly glow I saw a thin bridge of earth across the dry gully and at the far end a huge oak tree with a split trunk. I looked through the gap but the light was too faint for me to make out what lay beyond the oak. I glanced down into a pool of water glittering between the two parts of the trunk. The numinous light faded. As I stared into the still, dark water I felt the dream begin to dissolve and the forest fade away.

11

The old one chuckles to herself as she waits for the girl to come to her. She picks sweet smelling camomile as she watches the girl sleep in the garden under a rough blanket.
Her first lesson will be about simple plants, spoken in simple language but soon, now that the connection has been made, all barriers formed by language, time and place will be smoothly cleared away.
The girl is healing, as the old one grows weak. Her eyes are fully open. She can see life flow around her, feel it in her veins. Her heart is slowly opening too, pushing out unneeded fears, recognising the beauty of love. She is ready. Now the song can begin.

When I woke, it was still dark. Joe was gone but he had wrapped his half of the blanket around me before he left. I turned my head at a movement nearby and saw the cat crouched beneath the jasmine bush. Its eyes flashed at me. The air was not cold but I shivered slightly as I unwrapped myself from the blanket, damp with dew and stiff from my night on the hard ground. I shook the blanket out and folded it, then carried it under my arm as I made my way to the house. The kitchen door was still open. I dropped the blanket on a chair and sat at the table, staring at a piece of paper; stark white with bold black writing scrawled over it; that lay at the centre, held in place with a small, smooth stone.

I left the note there while I prepared coffee and toast, casting frequent glances at it but hesitant to read it. Finally, when I could put it off no longer, I sat down, sipped my coffee, pulled Joe's note toward me and read;

"Hi Annie,
I am having some friends over for lunch on 15th, for Ferragosto. I hope you will join us.
Joe."

Ferragosto, I knew, was a public holiday in Italy. Ostensibly the day when Catholics celebrated the assumption of the Virgin Mary into heaven, in actual fact the day was celebrated in a style that seemed more of a reflection of its pagan roots. No one worked that day and all those who could drove to the countryside for hours of feasting, with picnic lunches or elaborate barbeques. Joe's note was simple but I read a challenge in it. I wondered who would be going. Luca and his girlfriend maybe. Joe's own girlfriend obviously. What exactly did the man want from me? I had been prepared to be his friend but all that romantic talk of shooting stars last night and the carving that he had obviously done especially for me indicated that he wanted more than that. He did not seem to be the kind of man who casually tried to seduce every woman he met but how was I supposed to judge his actions?

I crumpled the note in my hand and deliberately threw it into the bin, tipping coffee grains in on top. I felt suddenly restless. I needed to get out, to walk in the relative cool of the dawn before the oppressive heat of the summer could push me inside again. I slammed the door shut behind me and strode out along the path trying to outpace my confusion. I glanced in the direction of Joe's place, letting my eyes adjust to the half-light, hesitating under the cypress tree, trying to get my thoughts in order and decide where to go.

"Buongiorno ragazza!" A voice nearby made me jump. Fiammetta was standing in the long grass to my left, waving at me. I was reminded of the weird dream that I'd had the night before and how I had imagined that the shooting star which I had followed through the forest was actually the old woman, leading me to some mysterious place; a place of great importance for me. Then I shook my head at my ridiculous fantasy. She was just a tiny old lady with an unsettling capacity to appear out of nowhere, no matter what everyone else seemed to think. I smiled at her and, seeing a couple of bulging plastic bags on the ground, asked her what she was picking.

"Vieni" Fiammetta beckoned to me and I stepped off the road. By the time I reached her, my legs were wet with dew. Fiammetta opened a bag and shoved her hand inside, pulling out what looked like clumps of weeds.

"Insalata dei campi" she explained "più buona di quella che si compra nei negozi." The wild salad was much better than the salad sold in shops she said, her lip curling in contempt. I looked in the other bag, which was half-full with what appeared to be daisies.

"La camomilla," Fiammetta said and reached down, pulling the heads off a clump of tall camomile at her feet. "senti," she said, holding the crushed flowers under my nose for me to smell them.

I began to help, filling the camomile bag while Fiammetta wandered around looking for her wild salad plants. Every now and then, she would stop and dig a plant out with her nails. She would show it to me, tell me its name and let me taste the leaves. Some were sweet, some bitter and others rough and spiky and unpleasant in my mouth. The plants had to be gathered at dawn when they were at their freshest, she explained. I knew that I would never remember all of them or be able to recognise them by myself but I enjoyed the lesson and as I picked the camomile heads and breathed in their apple-like scent, I became so intent on my task that my previous bad mood slipped away.

The sun rose higher as we worked. Every now and then, we would catch each other's eye and smile. When her bag was full, Fiammetta came over to stand near me in the shade of the cypress. Her bright eyes gleamed darkly amid the crinkles of her brown cheeks. She explained how she would spread the flowers out to dry in the sun when she got home. Then they would last her through the year. She liked a drink of hot camomile before going to bed. It helped her sleep. A crafty look came into her eyes then and she added that she would bring some that she had already dried and give it to me.

"Ne hai bisogno" she said firmly, you need it. Camomile helps you to sleep. It helps you relax. She cackled then, her old woman's laugh and I thought that she looked like a good witch in a fairy tale. To change the subject I pointed to the pretty, bright blue flowers growing on long stalks at the edge of the field and asked what they were. Fiammetta gazed at me shrewdly for a second, letting me know that she was not going to be side-tracked, then chuckled and said,

"Cicoria." It was chicory. During the war when there was nothing to eat people made coffee from the chicory roots in autumn. But, she said, returning stubbornly to the subject that interested her, it is camomile that you need. You drink my camomile before you go to bed. Then you will sleep better. You will have no dark smudges beneath your eyes. You will relax. Then you will be fine. She nodded to herself as she spoke, gathered up her plastic bags and walked away across the field. I sat and leant against the trunk of the cypress, listening to the old woman chuckling to herself as she went down the lane. I looked up, following the grooves in the trunk and the spiralling branches that seemed to point towards a cloudless sky the colour of chicory petals. Fiammetta was right. All I needed was to catch up on my sleep and I would be able to put everything into its proper perspective again. I smiled and laid my head back against the rough bark of the cypress and let the special feeling of peace that emanated from it seep through me.

I stayed there most of the morning, observing the small movements of insects among the flowers and the heat shimmer from the ground. The humming of the cicadas throbbed around me and I contemplated how life must appear to the ancient, giant cypress. Small problems of life and love would be no more than a blink in time. Death itself would be seen as a part of the never-ending cycle of life. I found the thought of my own insignificance, in the infinity of time, rather reassuring.

That evening I heard a motor scooter coughing up the drive and went out to see a teenager climbing off his dusty bike. He shook out his long, curly hair and retied it with a band at his neck. He wore no helmet in spite of the new law that made it obligatory. A small silver stud glinted in his eyebrow. When he saw me he grinned, a young boy's wide, easy grin that brought an answering one to my own mouth. He unhooked a bag from his handlebars and waved it at me then swaggered across and handed it to me.

"Ciao" I greeted him, guessing who he was, from his eyes, even before he told me that his grandmother had sent him. He thrust the bag of dried camomile at me, gave a vague explanation of how to make the tea, then waved an arm, said "ciao" and got back on his bike. He pushed it round and started it with a sputter, then revved up and sped off, leaving clouds of dust at each bend in the road.

Before I went to bed that night, following the precise instructions that Fiammetta had put inside the bag, I boiled some water and put a pinch of camomile in to steep for five minutes then poured it into a mug, added a spoonful of honey, a generous squirt of lemon and sat at the kitchen table to drink it. The instructions had been written in scratchy handwriting on a scrap of paper that looked as if it had been torn from a school exercise book and I imagined Fiammetta dictating the words to her bright-eyed grandson. Or, maybe she had written it herself; the erratic script went well with her air of mischief. I knew so little about anyone, I thought. People's real lives were a mystery. With each small contact, one touched the surface of another's life but the rest remained hidden. I was still wondering about Fiammetta; whether she was married and if so what was her husband like, how many children and grandchildren did she have, whether she was really a witch?; when I fell into a deep dreamless sleep.

The next day I felt truly rested for the first time in ages. I spent a girly day, shaving my legs and conditioning my hair. I was inspired by the leftover camomile tea which I used to rinse my hair and then on cotton-wool pads over my eyes. All the time I was pampering myself my mind was on the picnic the next day, trying to decide whether to go or not. However after a while I realised that I had already decided. I could not resist the temptation to be with Joe and I wanted to see for myself what his girlfriend was like. I remembered Fiammetta's crafty look as she

113

had told me that I needed the camomile and I had to grin. With all the camomile I had used that day, I could not be anything but relaxed. I laughed out loud. Life was good. With or without Joe, life was good.

Since I did not want to be the first person to arrive at the picnic I waited until midday on 15th and decided that I would drive to Joe's, to avoid walking in the hottest time of the day. As I bumped over the potholes, I rehearsed a few bits of Italian small talk in my mind and tried to keep calm. The hot air that came through the window did not cool me at all. Summer had truly arrived in all its sultry power and it was like a force field pressing down, making me feel as dry inside as the grass along the roadside. The oppressive atmosphere was accentuated by the incessant throbbing song of the cicadas in the trees and I felt my doubts about coming today return with a vengeance.

Parked in front of Joe's house were three other cars and I did not know whether to be relieved that I would not have to cope with any further intimacy with Joe or annoyed that there would be a big party of people that I did not know. Luna bounded up to me and swiped her tongue along my bare leg as I swung out of the car. She raced off barking and Joe and Luca came around the corner of the house and waved to me. The two of them descended on me and swept me with them towards the noise coming from the patio. I handed Joe the bottle of wine that I had brought and let Luca take my arm and pull me toward the group of people gathered around the long table. To my relief I recognised Rita, Lucia and Pietro. Luca's girlfriend was there too. I remembered seeing her at the village fair. She gave me the small, tight smile that Italian women reserve for any female who is talking to their man and then turned back to continue her animated discussion with the only person I had not seen before; a pretty, petite girl with long black hair and a very tight t-shirt. Luca casually introduced his girlfriend as Giulia and her friend as Carlotta but I was saved from having to say anything myself because I was surrounded by the others and

114

hugged warmly by Rita and Lucia while Pietro clasped my hand and then pinched my cheek roughly.

It was a joy to see Lucia. There was no need to say anything, all I had to do was keep my attention focussed on her and pretend to be listening while she chattered away. Pietro handed me a glass of wine and then slipped away to join the other men. Lucia and Rita then decided that it was time to bring out the food and I was roped into fetching plate after plate from the kitchen. The two older women had brought most of the food themselves and there was a gentle sort of competition going on between them as they extolled the virtues of each dish, agreeing that if left to a man the picnic would have consisted of nothing but beer and salami. I unwrapped containers of warm lasagne, frittata and platters of roasted meats and carried them out.

The two younger women had joined the men and showed no sign of wanting to help out in the kitchen. I watched as Carlotta twirled a lock of glossy dark hair around her finger as she smiled up at Joe and I ignored the impulse to dump the lasagne on her head. I swung back to the kitchen and began to deal with the plates of cold food and salads.

I popped a piece of fennel from the salad into my mouth and crunched. The cool aromatic flavour woke up my taste buds and I began to feel really hungry. As I chewed, the bustle of activity and conversation outside was pleasantly dimmed and I fell into a kind of daydream about the Greek myth of creation, which I half remembered from somewhere. Prometheus had mixed earth and water to model man's body, Athena breathed air into the body to create the spirit and Prometheus then reaped the displeasure of the gods by taking fire from the wheel of the sun, in the shape of a giant fennel stalk, to give mankind the gift of fire to create a higher soul. I surveyed the innocuous looking fennel in the salad bowl and laughed to myself. It was quite amazing how the mind could surprise you now and then with pieces of information once read and long since forgotten.

115

I kept myself busy in the kitchen, passing plates to the others until the last dish had disappeared and I no longer had an excuse to hide there. The table was laden with food. The patio was in the shade of the house at that time of day but Joe had also set up a couple of big canvas umbrellas to keep the sun off us, as it made its way around the house later on. Rita was calling to everyone to sit down while Lucia bustled around distributing plastic plates. I grabbed the first chair that I came to and sat down.

Pietro sat next to me and began to ask me about my garden. Usually a man of few words, Pietro came alive whenever he spoke about things that grew in the earth and I was grateful for his company. I expected Lucia to sit on the other side of me but she had joined Rita. The two older women had stopped urging everyone to eat and were now exclaiming over the blouse Giulia was wearing. To me it was a fairly nondescript white cotton one although I had to admit that it showed off her tan well. It crossed my mind that Lucia and Rita were keeping the girls talking until everyone else was seated. Just as I was wondering about that Joe pulled out the chair next to mine and plonked into it, swiping his hair away from his eyes and grinning at me as he reached past me for a hunk of bread.

"I'm starving." he said and then everyone else sat down and began reaching across the table, passing plates and shouting for others to be passed along to them. I sat quietly, listening to the loud chatter and banter around me. Carlotta had sat opposite us. She refused the glass of wine that Pietro handed her saying that she never drank alcohol and then talked animatedly about the concert that she had been to with Joe, Luca and Giulia a few days before, removing any last doubts that I might have had, about her status, from my mind.

Vivacious, pretty and very self-confident, she was so different from me in every way that I found to my surprise that I did not resent her too much. I understood why Joe was attracted to her and laughed inwardly at my arrogance in thinking that there could ever be anything between him and me. Once I resigned myself to the

116

idea that I had no chance of winning Joe's affection, I actually relaxed and began to enjoy myself. I stumbled a bit at first, as I joined in the varied conversations around the table in my inadequate Italian but it got easier the more I tried, easier still after a second glass of wine and soon I felt part of the gathering in a way that I would never have thought possible. Rita asked me about the car and I made everyone laugh as I told them how long it had taken to wash away the smell of chickens. Lucia tried to get everyone to tell me that I must put on some more weight again and grow my hair longer to be more feminine but I found to my surprise that I had two unexpected champions. Pietro, in a rare moment of rebellion, told his wife to stop interfering and added that I looked just fine to him.

"Come una rosa che sta sbocciando adesso." he said and blushed the colour of his wine. I was so amazed to be referred to poetically as *a rose that is just beginning to unfurl* that I almost choked. Joe clapped me on the back, which did not help much. He laughed at my expression and teased Lucia about being married to a poet without knowing it. While Lucia shouted that she expected Pietro to say things like that about her when they got home, Joe looked at me darkly and said,

"Annie e sempre stata bella per me, ma adesso sembra più felice, e così si nota di più."

The food disappeared remarkably fast and then Joe brought a rubbish bag and we all dropped our plastic plates in and threw away the leftovers. The men waved the women away, when they would have got up to clear the table and they brought out the fruit and cakes themselves. Then Joe made coffee for everyone and Pietro produced a bottle of his vinsanto after-dinner wine that he had been saving for a special occasion. I sipped the sweet, amber liquid and realised that I had drunk far too much but I was not sure whether the warm glow inside me was caused by the wine or by Joe's words. He had said that I had always been beautiful to him but now I looked happier and so it was more noticeable. Carlotta had sent me a sharp look across the table when he had said that and then she had pouted a bit and been magnificently sulky for the rest of the meal.

By about five o'clock, the party began to break up. Pietro and Lucia left first and then Rita began to gather her things together. I gave her a hand to wash up the plates that she had brought with her, although Joe forbade her to wash anything else. Luca and Giulia loaded Rita and all her things into his car and after much hugging and kissing they drove off. I suddenly realised that I was alone with Joe and Carlotta and was obviously one too many but the problem was, that I really did not think I ought to drive. I felt quite tipsy and even on the tiny back road, where you hardly ever met another car, I did not think that it would be a good idea to get behind the wheel. I turned to face Joe and laughed, saying,

"I am afraid that I have had a bit too much of Pietro's wine, Joe. I will walk home and get the car tomorrow if that is ok with you." I was about to say thanks and leave, ignoring the look of disgust that Carlotta threw my way but Joe stopped me.

"Stay awhile Annie," he said, then he smiled at Carlotta and thanked her for coming. He walked her to her car and opened the door for her, thanking her for her offer of help with clearing up but saying that I would give him a hand. She had no alternative but to leave at that point, although she made her feelings clear by the way she revved off down the drive and screeched around the corner.

Joe looked at my face and laughed at the look of confusion he saw there.

"Right, washing up time" I said and turned towards the house.

"We will think about that later." Joe declared, taking my arm and leading me towards the lake. "I am too hot to do anything else now," he continued, sitting me down in the shade of the willow. Joe took off his sandals and sat next to me, plunging his feet into the water.

"Oh, bliss." he murmured, leaning back on his hands. It looked too good to resist so I dangled my own feet over the bank. The

118

water was shockingly cold after the heat of the day but it felt wonderful. Joe looked sideways at me.

"I would suggest a swim but think that maybe we had better wait until we are completely sober for that." When I looked at him, he smiled and I felt my own lips curve up in response. He held my gaze until I felt uncomfortable and had to look away. I heard him sigh and suddenly felt cross with him. What did he think he was doing, sending his girlfriend home and then taking me paddling as if I was some child that needed to be placated?

"How long have you been going out with Carlotta?" I asked in a cold voice feeling suddenly very sober indeed. There was a slight pause before Joe spoke, while I kept my eyes firmly on the ripples of the lake.

"Carlotta has not ever been my girlfriend," he said and I could hear the smile in his voice, "She's a friend of Luca's girlfriend, that's all. We've all been out a few times together but that's it, no romance."

"Oh" I said lamely and then when he did not say anything else I added "Good" and dared another glance at him. He was watching me, his expression calm, his eyes deceptively blank, but for the first time I understood that this was a mask he wore when he did not want his thoughts to be read. He cleared his throat and spoke softly,

"Annie, when Luca told me you had gone back to England for a while, I didn't understand why you had gone so suddenly, without telling me."

I started to explain but he interrupted me,

"Let me finish, please. It's not easy to find the right words, I'm always so damn scared that I'm going to frighten you away somehow. From the first moment that I saw you, you reminded me of a fawn, like the one I carved for you, poised for flight. You were talking to Lucia and your smile was the prettiest I had ever seen but then you saw me and you shut yourself away. The next time I saw you, when you were caught in the storm, you were so different. You looked stronger, more sure of yourself but, again as

119

soon as you saw me, you shut off and made it very clear that you didn't want anything to do with me. I've been trying to reach out and get to know you, without scaring you away, ever since. That's what I tried to carve, that wildness in you, and your beloved cypresses." He smiled, then added

"I didn't even come close."

"Joe," I breathed, but again he stopped me, with a light touch of his finger on my lips.

"Do I scare you?" he asked and all of a sudden the answer was no and he read it in my face. He put his arm around me, drew me close to him and kissed my hair.

"Well, I'm a bit scared myself," he confessed with a wry grin. He took my chin between his fingers and kissed me properly, very gently.

"So, let's take it slow. Ok?" he asked and I nodded.

"I'll take you home now and tomorrow I will pick you up and take you for a drive and then you can get your car when we come home." He stood up and gave me his hand. He pulled me to my feet and hesitated. I was not sure if he would pull me close and kiss me again or step away and I did not know what I wanted him to do. The warmth caused by the wine had long since melted into the exhilaration of being so close to him but I was glad when he stepped away. I needed a little time to readjust and he instinctively knew it. He really could read people. Now I knew how he saw me; as someone easily hurt and easily scared away and he was so right. However, he had given me a precious gift by letting me know that we had all the time in the world, I thought, as he helped me up the bank and held my hand across the lawn.

12

The old one comes to me in the early dawn when my energy is at its greatest..She leans on me, absorbing all that I can give her but we both know it is not enough and that death rides at her shoulder.
Often men shudder in my shadow. They find me dark and threatening. In their minds, cypresses line up along the cemetery road, beckoning them towards their end. They think of our branches used for funeral wreaths and coffins made of our wood. Those few who know that wreaths at first represented eternal life in the service of Hades seldom remember that he was not only god of the underworld but of earthly riches too; a god both stern and just. Men look at me, enduring through time, and tremble to contemplate their own mortality. They fear me especially in the summer, that time of passion, of fire and the oppressing awareness of our own vulnerability in the face of such heat.

I did not sleep well, of course I didn't. When I got into bed, my brain would not stop trying to analyse every word that Joe had said to me and suggesting clever things that I should have said, if I hadn't been such a tongue-tied twit. Then, when I finally did fall asleep, the wine I had drunk woke me up in the early hours with a raging thirst that just would not go away. I stomped blearily down to the kitchen and drank orange juice from the carton. I did not turn on any lights and tried to keep my eyes half closed, in the vain hope that I might be able to get to sleep again afterwards. Back in bed, the sheets felt lumpy where I had tossed and turned too much and the faint light coming through the shutters was falling on my pillow, exactly where my head lay. I stayed still for another few minutes with my eyes screwed tightly shut, because I really did not want to look tired today. It was no good though; I gave up and went to make coffee. Maybe some breakfast would help calm the butterflies in my tummy.

It was ten past six according to the bedside clock as I opened the shutters wide and scent of lavender rushed past me. The morning was beautiful, already heating up enough to evaporate the dew. As always my eyes were drawn to the cypress; dark sentinel dominating the landscape. In the shadowy half-light near the massive trunk, I saw a movement and lent across the cool windowsill for a better view. The movement came again, a glimmer of white, moving in a rhythm that sent alarm bells ringing in my head, even before I had worked out what I was looking at. Slowly the shape clarified itself as Fiammetta, white hair catching the light even though her brown skin and black dress were almost invisible in the shadows. I grabbed the clothes I had worn the day before and ran downstairs, disturbed by the way the old woman had been standing, bent over as if struggling to stay upright.

I ran down the path barefoot, ignoring the stones that dug sharply into my soles and called Fiammetta's name as I came closer. She was gripping her chest with one hand and leaning all her weight against the cypress. Her face looked white beneath the tan and her breathing was rough. I touched her shoulder gently, unsure if she had heard me calling her and not wanting to shock her but she nodded and gasped,

"Sto bene. Sto bene," She did not look or sound ok and I told her so, then put my arm around her and tried to lead her towards the house.

"Ti preparo qualcosa da bere," I'll make you something to drink, I suggested but she laughed hoarsely and stood straighter, refusing to come with me. Her blue eyes sparkling with her customary dry humour as she shook her head.

"Non ho niente, è solo la vecchiaia." There is nothing wrong, just old age, she assured me and for that there was no cure that she knew of. She turned and patted the cypress' trunk in a gesture that was almost a caress.

"Maybe he knows of a cure?" she suggested then laughed again and shook her head. "No, not even this old friend of mine can stop

122

time. How much time he has seen go past, how many lives have begun and ended in his shade."

I was not sure if she was speaking to me or to herself but then she looked at me again and reached up to touch my cheek. I put my own hand over hers as she said,

"Our time will come, yours and mine and still he will go on. There is magic here. Can you feel it? Oh yes, girl, I know you can." As she said this she let her fingers drop from my face but kept hold of my hand. I felt a little off balance myself and reached for the tree trunk to steady myself. Fiammetta laughed; that familiar cackle; then repeated,

"Yes, you can feel it. Let yourself listen, child. Don't fight things so much. Our friend can be strong for you, let him help. Feel the magic in your veins – it will be all yours soon."

The rough bark beneath my fingers and Fiammetta's calloused hand in mine felt almost the same and there was a strange energy in the air that seemed to run through us all as if we were part of a single entity. I closed my eyes and leant back, feeling the connection surge within me. Blood and sap flowing together. The power was incredibly strong and beneath it a sound like a low hum, a sound that could have been a small insect buzzing in the grass, or the breeze among dry needles, or the clouds gathering in the sky. It could even have been time itself, humming as it glided inexorably within our cells.

I gasped and backed away, breaking the circle. The cypress stretched above, immobile yet somehow more alive than ever. I looked at Fiammetta and saw her grinning wryly at the shock on my face. She seemed to have recovered her strength at the same time as I had lost mine. My knees felt incredibly weak and I needed to sit down.

"Vai, vai," she waved me home gently and then turned herself and began to walk slowly away. I watched her go, unwilling to leave the shadow of the cypress, wanting to understand what had just happened between us. After a short while, she looked back at me, the way I had known she would.

123

"Soon" she said, and walked on, nodding to herself.

In the end, I kept Joe waiting in spite of my early start. I showered and ate breakfast in a kind of dream state as I struggled to find a practical explanation for what I had felt with the cypress and Fiammetta. I tried but could not quite convince myself that my tiredness and concern for the old woman had created the weird sensation that I had felt. At least I would be too preoccupied to worry about going out with Joe, I thought.

Fat chance. Ten minutes later I had several different choices of clothes laid out on the bed and still no idea which ones to put on. I heard the jeep pull up, which galvanised me into grabbing the first pair of shorts and t-shirt that I had put out on the bed and pulling them on. I grabbed my sandals and checked myself in the mirror quickly. I ran my fingers through my hair once more then went to close the shutters. Joe had parked in the shade of the cypress and was getting out. I called to him and he waved at me and smiled. In the back of the jeep, I heard Luna's muffled barking.

"Bring a pair of walking shoes." Joe called and I nodded and pulled the shutters in behind me. I tossed my gym shoes into a large bag and, with a last deep calming breath, left the house.

I had run through several scenarios to prepare myself for this morning. In one, Joe was friendly but cool, regretting what had passed between us the day before. In another, I made a witty comment to make him smile. I had even considered the possibility of him not turning up at all, so I thought myself prepared. The sun was already hot, running over my body and hair like solid fingers. Joe looked cool in the shade. He wore a white linen shirt hanging out of a pair of well-worn beige shorts but in place of the usual sandals he had a pair of equally worn trainers. He waited for me to come to him, leaning back against the tree, his eyes seeming darker than ever in the shadows.

Part of me was reluctant to get close to the cypress, in case I felt the strange pull of its energy again. As I reached the car, Joe pushed himself away from the tree and came to meet me. My "good morning" was lost in his lips. His arms pulled me unresistingly closer until I was moulded against him. He kissed and I melted into him, the fire that had been simmering inside for so long flaring up fiercely. For the second time that morning, my knees felt weak. Joe's lips were so firm and warm, his hands stroked down me, flowing over me; sculptor's hands shaping me, making me aware of every curve. He lifted his mouth from mine, raised an eyebrow and a slow smile spread across his face.

"Maybe we should just stay right here?" Dark eyes glittered. The corner of his mouth curved up. He smelt clean, with undertones of male. The low hum of the cypress began to ring in my head. I reached up and kissed Joe, letting my lips explore his mouth, enjoying his sharp intake of breath and the way his arms tightened around me. I felt like metal, heated to the point where I began to liquefy inside, began to take on the very form of the man who held me. The humming was within my body, running through my veins.

Joe pulled away. The humming receded and I began to be aware of the real sounds of the morning and Luna barking madly in the back of the jeep. Joe stroked my face and nodded at the dog.

"She's worried that she's going to miss her walk." The word *walk* produced another manic burst of barking. I laughed shakily and disentangled myself, smoothing out my t-shirt, which seemed to have absorbed Joe's scent. He opened the door of the jeep for me. I got in and turned round to rub Luna's nose that was sticking between the bars at the back. Joe ran his fingers down my spine and I felt breathless all over again. He started the engine and I patted Luna once more then struggled with my seat belt. My hands were trembling. This was quite ridiculous, I thought. I was sure that I had never felt like this, not even when I was a teenager.

The jeep bumped over the potholes, down the lane and onto the asphalt, heading towards Montalino. We drove through the village and down the hill that curved steeply toward the Arno River. The poplars lining the road were turning prematurely yellow from lack of rain. Dust from the roadside whirled up behind us as we passed. At the bottom of the hill, I turned my head to the right to get a

125

glimpse of the river as we crossed the bridge. The water was a sluggish yellow, flowing under the ruined arch of the Roman bridge downstream. The river was reduced to a third of its usual size, the mud banks grey and cracked. The summer that had begun in such a passionate feast of colour was now burning all to dust.

"Everything is so dry!"

"Yeah, we could do with some rain. Summer isn't my favourite time here." Joe laid a hand on my knee, rubbed it gently. "It will all change when the rains come. Every year it seems as if everything is dying and then it rains and life starts again. The storms are really something too. They are so intense." He grinned at me and put his hand back on the wheel as we started to climb into the mountains. The silence sat easily between us. I gazed out at the scenery that changed so swiftly as we drove up the twisting mountain road. The beeches and oaks gave way to huge chestnuts and then the conifers took over. On our right, as we circled up, I had glimpses of breathtaking views where the valley dropped away below, while on the nearside the forest was thick and the shade was cool. Now the road began to cut through huge slabs of rock, some with small streams trickling over them and a short while later Joe pulled the jeep off the road into a small parking area.

I got out with him and stretched, luxuriating in the slight breeze. Joe opened the boot and Luna jumped out and charged me. Once she had licked me thoroughly and therefore given me what she obviously considered to be a proper welcome, she ran ahead into the forest. Joe handed me a couple of empty water bottles and nodded at a sign hanging crookedly from a nearby tree. *Fontana delle Lucciole* I read, following Joe up rough-hewn steps in the rock.

"Fontana means fountain but what does Lucciole mean?" I asked.

"Firefly. Actually, it doesn't exactly mean a fountain in this case. The best way to translate it would be *the spring of the fireflies.* I always fill a few bottles when I come here. The water is wonderful."

It was too, sweet and clear as it trickled from an old pipe that had been hammered into the rock to make it easier to fill a bottle. It was also icy cold, which was surprising after the heat of the day. I cupped my hands beneath the water and drank then stood back while Joe filled the bottles and Luna explored the undergrowth nearby. I imagined the winter snow slowly seeping down into the earth on the mountain top and working its way through the rocks, finding cracks and fissures to travel along, or gradually eroding new ones, absorbing the hidden minerals as it went and finally reappearing on the surface again, enriched with the hidden treasures of the earth.

Luna needed a bit of encouragement to make her get back into the jeep. She reluctantly put up one paw at a time and in the end Joe had to hoist her rump on board. She lay down and eyed him reproachfully as he shut the door and I had to laugh. Joe shook his head.

"It is always like this. She knows that it isn't much further but she would rather walk now. We are going to a small village where there is a shop run by an old lady who makes her own bread and wine and sells local cheeses and prosciutto. It will take us about ten minutes now."

"Good. I'm hungry." I had not thought about it before but now that Joe had mentioned food I was suddenly very hungry. Joe pointed up through the trees as we rounded the next bend and I had a glimpse of stone houses before we plunged back into the trees.

A few miles later, we reached the village. Joe drove off the road and parked by a small church. He clipped Luna's collar onto a lead and we walked along the road, up a small flight of steps and found ourselves in the tiny village that nestled into the rocks above the road. What few houses there were climbed steeply along the hillside and ended in the forest. There was a small shop at the top of the steps with a tatty bead curtain across the door and a few

127

rickety tables set on the cobblestones in front. There was an assortment of seating, various ancient chairs and some thick chunks of tree trunk.

Inside, the shop was quite dark. A tough looking woman with steel grey hair pulled back into a bun greeted Joe and began preparing the food that he ordered. She sliced prosciutto and a kind of thick, crumbly salami made with fennel seeds called *finocchiona*, cut a huge chunk from a cheese round and then disappeared into a room at the back and returned with two flat loaves of bread. Joe handed me the bread and asked me to take it and the paper-wrapped meat and cheese outside. I found a table in the shade thrown by the church tower on the opposite side of the road. A rough fence made of wooden poles acted as a rustic barrier, separating the edge of the terrace from the road a few metres below. I sat with my back to the drop and looked at the village houses. Small, wrought-iron balconies softened the severe stone facades and the odd pot of bright geraniums added colour. On some of the walls, caper plants clung improbably in the cracks, flowing down in small-leaved cascades, their frilly flowers glowing among the greenery.

The bread was still warm. I unwrapped everything and laid it out across the table. Joe joined me, carrying a bottle of wine, plastic cups and a knife for the cheese. Everything smelt so good. It tasted even better. Joe poured the wine and laughed when I said I was not sure, after yesterday, if I should have any.

"One glass won't hurt." he reassured me, breaking off a large piece of the flat bread and passing it to me. The bread, covered in olive oil and salt, was called *schiacciata* he told me, which meant squashed bread, due to the shape. It was delicious, as was everything, or maybe the surge of lust that ran through me each time I caught Joe's eye had given me an appetite.

Over the meal, we talked and this time we began to probe deeper beneath the surface of each other's lives. We broke off bread with our hands and folded slices of finocchiona and prosciutto around it. Joe cut himself a piece of the creamy cheese then held it out across the table for me to bite into, his eyes holding mine all the time so that my heart flipped over. Luna lay at our feet, patiently waiting for scraps of fat and cheese rind.

I found myself telling Joe about the time before coming to Italy, about my mother and our life together, or rather the lack of it. I had never opened up to anyone like this but it felt strangely right. Joe listened, asking the occasional question, not letting me change the subject when I would have avoided talking about the things that had hurt so much. When there was no more left to say he half stood, leant across the table and kissed me gently, with lips that tasted of salt and wine. He did not offer any trite remark to make light of my words, just let the outpouring of emotion lie between us. Luna huffed a deep sigh from under the table and Joe smiled, kissed me again and then bent down to ruffle her fur.

"Time to have that walk, girl" he told her, then ducked his head to avoid the swipe of her tongue, her reward for the magic word. This time she was less reluctant to get back in the car, she obviously knew that her part of the day was about to begin. We drove further still along the mountain road until it branched in two and we took the sharp left-hand fork that zigzaged steeply upwards. The main forest was behind us, the few remaining trees a sparse reminder of its shade. The sun was bright up here and although the air was a few degrees cooler than in the valley, I was glad that I had rubbed in my sun-protection cream that morning. The tarmac gave way to a packed dirt road as we neared the top and then Joe pulled into a large, deserted car park. We got out and released Luna, who shot off like a bullet across the gravel and onto a grassy track that led along the bare crest of the mountains for as far as I could see. Joe caught hold of my hand as we followed the happy plume of Luna's tail. The view was spectacular and the going was relatively easy, the track a well-trodden one.

"Why did you decide to stay here Joe?" Now that I had told him about my past, I felt entitled to ask a few questions myself. His grip tightened on mine for a moment but he did not answer and I thought he was going to ignore the question. Then he whistled to

129

Luna and, walking over to a small copse of trees, plonked himself down beneath them and patted the grass beside him.

"It's too hot to walk and talk. Come and sit with me and I will tell you all the juicy secrets of my life." We laughed but I was aware that beneath the banter there was a reluctance to talk about his past that I empathised with.

"I'm like you, I guess, don't talk about my past much. You once told me that the gossip in the village was that I had been a doctor in the States. That's true. I don't really know why, except that my father was a surgeon and I suppose I just did what he wanted me to do and followed in his footsteps.

Dad was proud of me and I quite enjoyed it, although I never had the passion that he did. Then my Mum got ill with cancer and no amount of treatment helped. I watched other doctors trying different chemicals on her and trying to cut the cancer away but nothing worked and Mum just shrank away before our eyes and within a year of being diagnosed, she was dead. It was the last straw for me. I realised that I did not want to carry on with that life. For every thrill of a life saved or an operation done well there is the counter side of the people you cannot help, the ones who die while you are trying to save them.

Dad can cope with that, put it into a separate compartment and concentrate on the positive side of his work. I couldn't."

I touched his hand and he turned it over, wove his fingers through mine.

"I had what they call *burn out* back home. I just couldn't take any more and I threw in my job and left home to come travelling through Italy, looking up those distant relatives I told you about." He smiled at me, "I found I didn't miss my old life in the least and it was a relief to be away from my father's disappointment. When I found the house, I knew that it was somewhere that I could be happy. I bought it on impulse really. It was pretty tumbledown and I did most of the rebuilding work myself and found that I really loved working with my hands and living in a way that was in tune with nature.

130

My dad is still angry with me. He thinks that I dropped out and maybe he feels that I abandoned him too, I don't know exactly because he hasn't spoken to me for a good few years now."

"I'm sorry."

"Yeah, so am I. I keep waiting for him to come round. My sister keeps in touch, lets me know how things are going there but she says that every time my name is mentioned Dad leaves the room or gets angry. I can't help that. I love living here. This is the life that I should have been living all along and I am much happier. I just wish that Dad could understand that too."

I moved closer to him and Joe put his arm around me and kissed my hair. We stayed like that for a while and then Luna began to get restless so we set off along the track again and gradually began to talk of small, inconsequential things but with a new knowledge between us that allowed us to feel more comfortable together.

This feeling of closeness lasted as we drove back down the mountain in the early evening and stopped in another pretty mountain village. I bought us ice creams, three flavours each and then we walked along a path that skirted the village and overlooked a sheer ravine. I felt dizzy when I peered down along the vicious looking rocks to the froth of water that boiled among them at the bottom. Joe finished his ice cream before I had got half way through mine and gave the end of his cone to Luna, who had not taken her eyes off it once. I licked a bit more lemon and yoghurt flavoured sweetness and then gave up.

"Do you want it?" I asked Joe and he eyed it, clearly tempted and then shook his head and indicated the dog,

"No, but I know someone who does."

When I had given the ice cream to Luna, Joe pulled me back until I was leaning on him. His breath was warm on my hair, his body felt so solid against my back. I touched the soft hairs on his forearms and felt something new underlying the excitement that poured through me as always at his touch. I looked at Luna,

131

contentedly rubbing traces of ice cream from her nose on a patch of grass and realised that this new feeling was peace.

Later, as the jeep bumped once more along our rough road, Joe made plans for dinner.

"How can you think of eating again?"

"Well, there is more of me than there is of you and anyway the mountain air always makes me hungry. I have some great pasta sauce that Rita gave me."

"Cheat" I interrupted, grinning.

"Not so" he defended himself "I can cook but if Rita feels sorry for me, living all alone without a woman to look after me, I would be a fool to refuse her offerings."

We parked alongside my battered car in front of Joe's house and, although my stomach was full to bursting, I was not going to turn down dinner and the chance of a bit longer with Joe, so I followed him into the house. Inside the door, the red light on his answer machine was blinking and he pushed me towards the kitchen.

"I'll just check the messages. Make yourself at home," He passed me the bottle of wine that we had begun at lunch. "You can pour us a glass of wine if you like. The glasses are in the cupboard over the sink."

I took out two balloon glasses, put them on the table and began to pour the wine, only half-aware of Lucia's tinny sounding voice on the answer machine, thanking Joe for the Ferragosto picnic. I had never felt so happy. Luna thumped her tail on the stone floor as if in agreement. A new voice came on the machine, a woman's voice that caught my attention because it sounded ragged and desperate.

"Joe. It's Molly. Dad had another stroke last night. He's in the hospital. They won't tell me how bad it is: They keep telling me they won't know anything until he comes round but he won't come round. Oh Joe." She broke off, obviously trying to choke back sobs.

132

"Shit" Joe hit the cancel button and came into the kitchen. His face had gone white. I went to him and put my arms round his waist.

"You will have to go home, Joe."

"I know," he stroked my hair distractedly, his thoughts already elsewhere. All I could do was offer some kind of practical help.

"Do you want me to look after Luna?"

"Would you? Please. I don't know for how long …. "

"It's ok, I'm not going anywhere."

He looked at me then, really looked at me and whatever he saw there made him smile just a little.

"I'll be back Annie," he said, kissing my forehead "I promise."

13

Since antiquity men have come to us, gathered our branches and cones for their medicines and their perfumes. The stones at my base whisper many stories to me; of the Etruscan men who enjoyed the aromatic scent of my oil and the Romans who cut my bark to obtain resin that they used on slow-healing wounds and burnt as offerings to their gods.

The old one knows the secrets of nature too. She uses my essence and that of other plants. She talks to me as she gathers what she needs, muttering that I am astringent, I help to stop haemorrhage, tone the body and ease the mind of nervous tension. Even though I cannot offer a cure for what ails her now, I sense no fear in her; regret maybe, and a certain dry, defiant humour, as she prepares for the next step, death.

My girl has finally breached the gap between us and has felt the power of the connection that will flow from now on, growing stronger and stronger until we can stand as one and listen to time as it ebbs and flows.

Joe had been gone for two weeks. He had driven to the airport about an hour after hearing from his sister and now I had a whole load of complications that I had not wanted in my new life. The biggest of these complications was lying at my feet now, looking as woebegone as only an abandoned dog can. I rubbed Luna's golden fur with my toes. She raised her head, looked at me with sad, brown eyes and laid it back on her paws.

"He'll be back Luna, he promised." Her ears twitched at the sound of her name but that was her only reaction. I got up from the millstone table and walked aimlessly around the garden, pulling up a few straggling weeds here and there. Luna fell in behind me. She had become my shadow since Joe had left, for which I was grateful, because I had been scared that she might have tried to run away to find him. Instead, she had obviously taken his instructions to stay with me to heart, but she was missing him badly. She was not the only one either. Joe had insisted that I take his mobile phone so that he could contact me and had rung every evening since arriving home to give me an update on his father's health. So far, there had been little change. Joe was staying with his sister and her family and they were taking it in turns to sit with their father, hoping for a miracle. For now, Joe had no idea how long he would have to stay.

It was strange having a phone again but I loved hearing Joe's voice in the evening and was glad he had insisted on me taking it because it kept the connection between us alive. I had promised to keep an eye on his house, water the plants when they needed it and take in any post that arrived for him. Joe had also asked me to treat it as a second home, to borrow books or music and to make use of the computer whenever I liked.

At first, it had felt wrong being in his empty home but after a while, I had begun to get used to the space, to find my own places within it. I liked to curl up in one corner of the old settee in his study, drinking coffee and reading. I loved walking with Luna down to the lake and looking at the sky reflected there, remembering the way our shadows had danced together at the summer solstice. I moved around his house, exploring it for signs of Joe in every object; delving into his life, without him there to defend his choices, to justify or explain them. Luna's frayed rope-toy forgotten behind the settee, clothes that carried the essential scent of Joe, his music, the food stored in his cupboards, were all clues to the essential Joe that I yearned to know.

Luna and I had just come back from Joe's this evening, laden down with a bag of tomatoes from his garden and another with my art supplies. I had been gradually reacquainting myself with rusty techniques I had learnt at school and now had quite a collection of sketches and watercolours. My attempts to draw Joe, from memory or from the old photos in his study, showing him and his family before his mother became ill, were not very satisfactory but I had done a few that I liked of Luna. What pleased me most were my recent watercolours. At first, I had been hesitant, trying to

135

follow rules that I only half remembered my art teacher explaining and my efforts had been clumsy and child-like. Gradually though, I let myself relax and use the paint the way I instinctively wanted to and the results were very different. My favourites were the ones that I had done of the cypress, its dark, exclamatory spirals stark against different backdrops of sky, as each time of the day wrought subtle changes.

The summer was dragging on. Maybe I felt time moving so slowly because I was missing Joe or maybe I was like the rest of nature, withdrawing my reserves of strength, hiding away from the searing heat of the days, wondering if this dryness would ever end. I walked in the morning or the early evening and during the day kept inside with the shutters closed against the sun; something I had not thought I would ever do but I had not taken into consideration the omnipotent force of summer.

This evening, after watering Joe's plants and picking some ripe tomatoes, I had finished a painting of the lake at dusk and then Luna and I had walked back through the field of sunflowers. The once brazen flowers now hung their heads, as if ashamed of their dull-brown, dried-out age. They stood sadly, defeated by their sun god, waiting to be cut down. Seeing them looking so tired and old I was reminded of the way Fiammetta had looked the last time that I had seen her.

I had not encountered Fiammetta since the morning when I had seen her leaning against the cypress for support, fighting to catch her breath. Yesterday, when I bought my usual supplies at the manor house, I had asked Lucia about her and had been shocked by the reaction I got. Lucia had stopped in the middle of pouring out our coffee and looked at me sharply.

"Fiammetta! How do you know that woman Anna?" As usual, an answer had not been necessary. Lucia had frowned as she finished pouring coffee and handed me a cup. She had sat down and pushed a plate of biscuits towards me, shaking her head as she talked.

""That woman. Don't you get involved with her. You know me, I don't like to gossip but people say that she is a witch." She had mistaken my attempt to hide a snigger, at her conviction of not being a gossip, for an exclamation of surprise.

"Si, una strega. A witch. She has a nice house in the village with her son and his family but she refuses to live with them. Instead, she lives alone in the woods in an old house that is almost falling down and has no electricity. She gets her water from a well and keeps warm in front of a fire in the winter. She makes potions too. I know because once, when Pietro delivered some wood for her fire, I went with him and I saw her. She had a big pot over the fire and she was stirring it just like a witch. I told Pietro that he shouldn't go there anymore but he never listens to me, that man, when does he ever listen to me. Carrying that heavy wood and him with his bad back."

I had stopped listening when Lucia started on about Pietro's back but later, as I had been leaving with my wine and a large slice of homemade jam tart that Lucia had pressed upon me, I had seen the man himself. Pietro had been putting away his tools in a garage. When I had called to him, he had straightened up and come over to kiss my cheek. He was not a man for small talk so I had asked him outright if he had seen Fiammetta recently.

"I saw her a while ago," I told him "and she did not seem very well, I wondered if she is ok."

"Oh, Fiammetta is getting older, like the rest of us but she seemed fine when I drove past last week." He had understood the quizzical look I gave him. Jerking his head towards his apartment, he had sighed,

"Don't go listening to my Lucia. She means well but ...... the old woman is no witch. She just likes her own company. I make an excuse to drive past now and then, just in case she needs anything but she is fine by herself. Her grandson goes up to see her often too. Don't you worry about her." He spoke about Fiammetta fondly and the warmth in his voice surprised me. Pietro was a good few years older than his wife but definitely younger than

Fiammetta. I wondered once more about how Fiammetta had looked when she was younger. She would have been pretty, striking even. Maybe jealousy was behind Lucia's violent dislike of the older woman.

I had been concerned enough about Fiammetta to ask Pietro for directions to her house anyway. Tomorrow I might take a walk up there. Luna would enjoy a run in the woods too, it might cheer her up a bit.

Thinking about something to make the dog happy, I remembered the jam tart that Lucia had given me and went into the kitchen to get it. I was not really hungry this evening. Jam tart and a glass of iced tea would do fine and if most of the crust found its way to the dog at my feet, she would not mind at all.

Just as Luna and I were finishing our improvised snack, the phone rang, as I had expected it to. It was just after nine, which meant that it was afternoon in Boston, the time Joe usually checked in. As always, the sound of his voice made me smile. Luna pricked her ears up and sidled closer. I stroked her absentmindedly as I listened to Joe's news and then recounted my own day. There was never much to say really but somehow we managed to talk for ages, telling each other details that, if we had been living close by we would have not thought of mentioning. Somehow, these small details conjured a different kind of intimacy and after the phone call I could sleep better, replaying the conversation in my mind, until sleep overtook me.

The next day I set off with Luna along the path through the wood that Pietro had told me about. I had waited until five before setting off to find Fiammetta's home. I estimated that it would take me about an hour to get there and a bit less coming back. It would not be fully dark until about half past eight so I had plenty of time. The ground was packed earth, deeply rutted by tractor tyres to begin with, which I could imagine turning into tiny streams when it rained. It was dry and dusty now, like everything else but at least the thick shade was cooler than it was at home. As I walked further along the unfamiliar path, past rackety wooden huts and empty, mesh pheasant cages, I was glad that the hunting season had not started yet. Pietro had told me when I first moved here that hunting was allowed from 16th September until the end of January and had warned me to be careful when walking at that time, to keep to the main footpaths and wear bright clothing so that I would not be mistaken for a target. I took his ominous warning more seriously than I had done Lucia's earlier, well-meant advice about the dangers of the forest, because Pietro was the last person to exaggerate or dramatise. However, Lucia had been right too, as a recent experience had proved.

On our way home from Joe's one day I had been caught up in my thoughts, watching Luna shining bright in the sun as she trotted a few paces ahead. Suddenly she had skittered sideways on the path, stopped and growled. In the dry glass that straggled along the middle of the lane, I had seen movement and called Luna away urgently. In the grass, there had been a squirm of baby vipers, five or six of them, zigzag patterned. They had curled around each other, a tangle of tiny, grey-brown, venomous bodies. I had taken Luna by the collar and pulled her around them, extremely thankful that she had warned me before I put my foot onto them.

I clambered on up the hill along the path that got smaller and wilder the further I went. I waved away another vicious horsefly and wondered, once more, whether to turn back. I was unsure of my welcome. Fiammetta was such an enigma and I would be descending upon her uninvited. Luna was not bothered by the horseflies, running in and out of the undergrowth, covering at least twice the distance that I did. We topped the hill and the path began to meander downhill again. Surely we would come across Fiammetta's house soon. There was no sound except the dry rustling produced by Luna as she scrambled up a bank and the irritating buzz of the horseflies. I scratched my thigh where one had managed to bite me and then became aware of a faint scent in the air. Luna had smelt it too. She raced back to me, barking. Smoke. All at once, I was scared at the possibility of a forest fire. We had walked far further than I had anticipated and I was not sure we would be able to escape from the forest if a fire took hold. Then we turned a corner and I heaved a sigh of relief as I saw a thin plume of smoke coming from the chimney of an old cottage.

A few chickens were pecking in the yard and I called Luna to me and clipped on her lead before she decided to run and play with them. The house was old and small, built partly of stone with a newer section of whitewashed brick added on. Pots of herbs and bushes of lavender and rosemary grew in the open space in front of the house. Several rabbit hutches sagged in the shade, their inhabitant's whiskery noses pointing curiously at me. There was also a rather cross-looking sheep, tied by a long rope to a tree near the rabbit hutches. The sheep glared at us and Luna retreated behind my legs. The front door was shut and I wondered whether Fiammetta was out somewhere and my visit would be in vain after all. Then I heard a noise nearby and followed it around the house, calling out as I went.

Some movement in the woods made me stop. Luna's ears pricked up and she quivered at my side. A second later two shapes appeared. One was the stray black cat that often hung around my house, eating my scraps. The other was a well-fed tabby kitten. I smiled as I recognised it as the kitten Fiammetta had rescued on the evening of the village fair. Both cats haughtily ignored Luna and sat provocatively, one licking its fur, the other showing sharp little teeth in a pink-tongued yawn. Luna surprised me. She did not bark, just bristled and continued at my side in stiff-legged superiority. I should have known that the black cat belonged to Fiammetta, I thought. They both possessed the same air of mystery and mocking distain.

The house stood in a clearing and on this side of it was a large vegetable patch. I recognised the greenery of onions, frilly carrot tops, courgettes and potatoes. Tall plants of beans were growing up the wall of the house and several orange pumpkins swelled, large already, among their creeping vines. I turned the corner and came to the back of the house, where Fiammetta was sitting on a rickety chair by the kitchen door, a basket on her knee and a sack by her feet. She looked up and beckoned me toward the house with a movement of her head, without stopping her rhythmic movements. She picked a handful of cannelini beans from the sack, ran her fingers along the dry, white and pink pods then dropped the beans into the basket and let the empty pods fall loose on the ground.

"Sorry to come uninvited." I began but she just tutted.

"I knew you would come," she said with a grin, handing me the basket of beans and pushing herself upright.

"Leave those in the sun to dry." I put the basket on the ground where she had indicated, then Fiammetta took my arm and ushered me into a cramped kitchen.

"Let the dog go. She won't bother the chickens. Anyway, they have the sheep to defend them and the cats can take care of themselves!" She chuckled, dusting off a chair and indicating that I should sit.

From the low beams above my head hung bundles of drying plants and herbs and platted lengths of onions and garlic. In spite of the summer heat, a small fire burnt in a fireplace that stretched the length of one side of the room, with a tarnished copper pot bubbling over it. A tube curled from a spout in the pot lid, down to a bowl on the floor nearby and after a few seconds of incomprehension, I suddenly realised that I was looking at a makeshift still. I shot a look at Fiammetta, trying to imagine her distilling illegal grappa. The room smelt of nothing more sinister than herbs and chicken soup, although the still made the room unpleasantly hot. Fiammetta was observing me curiously.

"At my age I suffer more from the cold than the heat." She said. Then she laughed out loud, her face crinkling with genuine amusement. She jerked her chin in the direction of the still

"What do you think it is, grappa?" she laughed even more when I nodded, hugging her stomach with glee and rocking back and forth on her chair.

141

"Not grappa, no. On a cold evening in winter, grappa can be good maybe but I don't make it. That is for the oils from the plants."

"Essential oils." I said, my face warm from the heat and from being the object of such mirth. I smiled back at her, realising that the strongest of the many scents in the kitchen was of roses.

"Rose oil?" I asked and she looked pleased.

"From the petals. Good for the skin. I will give you some – It is too late for me child!" She laughed again then nodded at me approvingly.

"Stai meglio, ragazza." She set about making tea, putting another small pan of water over the fire and adding two pinches of some herb to a teapot.

"Yes, you look much better, girl. We'll have malva tea. Digestive, good for coughs, sooths the throat, helps the breathing." Fiammetta had turned her back on me, muttering about the therapeutic properties of the pink-flowered mallow plant under her breath. She seemed to have forgotten that I was there, completely caught up in the preparation of her tisane. Watching the old woman bent over the pot, mumbling to herself, it was not hard to see why Lucia thought her a witch.

Spread across an ancient wooden table were several small reed baskets, covered in fern leaves. On a dresser at the far side of the room were other baskets of various shapes and sizes, some of which were unfinished. I could imagine Fiammetta working on them in the evenings. The room had no electrical appliances, not even a fridge but I supposed she must have a pantry somewhere, maybe dug underground, where she would be able to keep things cool. I looked up to find Fiammetta staring at me. Her direct gaze was disconcerting. I had the feeling that she could see inside me, to places that even I did not know existed. Then she smiled, her skin splitting into deep wrinkled patterns. She handed me a chipped mug, pushed a jar of honey towards me and then pinched my cheek.

142

Cheek pinching is such a uniquely Italian gesture, a rough expression of affection that is usually reserved for children. Pietro did it to me sometimes too. Maybe they both thought of me as a child. Certainly, I always felt that I was learning something when I was in their company; learning about the rhythms of nature that I had never encountered in my life in England, where vegetables and meat came from supermarkets, pre-wrapped in cellophane, sterile and uninteresting.

"What are these?" I indicated the reed containers.

"Ricotta moulds. See. I make cheese with the sheep's milk then I heat the whey a second time and scoop out the ricotta, the word means *cooked again* did you know? Then I line the moulds with fern and fill them with ricotta." She lifted the ferns covering one of the moulds, showing the smooth whiteness within, decorated by the leaf's distinctive pattern.

"Prendine una. Take one and some honey too. I have a few hives in the woods. The bees make honey from the woodland trees and aromatic herbs, so their honey contains the essence of all the medicinal plants. It is very good." She got a plastic bag from a drawer and put a fern-wrapped ricotta and a jar of honey in for me then sat next to me and picked up her own tea. I thought it was time to explain my visit.

"How do you feel? I was concerned about you." I indicated the mallow tea, that she had said was good for breathing difficulties, thinking about the way she had seemed to struggle for breath as she leant against the cypress.

"Do you feel better now?"

"Si, si. I'm fine. I know how to take care of myself, girl. You on the other hand, you are just learning, but there is still time." She sipped her tea and raised her penetrating gaze to me again. The heat in the room suddenly seemed oppressive. A sharp pain shot through my skull and I pressed my fingers to my temples.

"He will come back. In the season of the hunter, when the Blood Moon shines, he will return. New life will begin when another ends. Every end is a beginning and every beginning a little

143

death. A life will quicken in a womb when another soul flees its shell. This I know."

Her voice had taken on a strange, almost hypnotic quality and her eyes, although fixed on mine, looked inwards at something only she could see. I touched her hand and she shuddered briefly. She looked suddenly very old and tired. Standing up abruptly, she held out the bag with her ricotta and honey in it and walked me to the door. I was glad to get back outside and feel Luna rub against my legs. I turned to say goodbye but Fiammetta had gone back indoors already. She had said all that there was to say.

I had been inside far longer than it had seemed. The light was already fading from the sky and the shadows stretched long across the forest floor. I hurried down the path, anxious to get home and felt relieved when I stepped onto the familiar dirt road, where I could see my house and the cypress standing guard over it. Luna ran ahead, her energy seemingly boundless. Dusk was settling over the landscape. Up on the hill the manor house and the cypresses by the cemetery created a jagged silhouette against a sky of faded blue. Far away, on the other side of the valley the mountains were covered by a false horizon of cloud peaks in pastel shades of apricot, rose and grey. As I watched, the clouds slowly deflated to reveal a sliver of pale moon, like the blade of a sickle. I shuddered, remembering Fiammetta's prophetic words. I did not understand what her words had meant but when I had touched her hand and brought her out of her trance-like state, the look in her eyes had been one of sad resignation.

I stopped beneath my cypress and ran my fingers over the trail of resinous bumps that ran down the trunk like amber teardrops. All was very still and very quiet. I felt the humming in the air, seeming to filter up from the ground at my feet, from the roots of the cypress, along its trunk and into me. This time I was prepared for the sensation and I did not jerk free. There was nothing to fear. I felt the energy throbbing through me until gradually the hum separated into many small, soft melodies. The melodies shaped the dusk, turning objects into sound and I began to hear a message in

144

this strange song. Life; a series of circles within time, beginnings and endings, a dance, a symphony. To flow within these cycles, accepting them without fear, was harmony.

I stood there for a long time, until night had overtaken day, until I could sing the melody of the cypress in my own head. Only then, did I move my hand from the smooth tears and walk away with a heart full of peace, leaving my fears and sadness behind.

14

Throughout the long, searingly, hot days of summer I gather my strength. I reach out towards the girl, call her to me and teach her to listen to the world with me. She begins to feel the universe flex its power, to sense the riches that await discovery for those who choose to look.
The old one knows that the time has come to share all of her own knowledge. Step by step, she will show the girl how to look deep into herself, until she can hear the song of life, within the silences of the world, without flinching.
Soon she will be able to free her soul from the weight of her body and shine in the air, like a sultry heat-haze on the rain-parched path.

The clouds that had blocked the mountains from view last night had been building up in the sky all day and the air was thick with the threat of rain. As Luna and I walked along the lane towards Joe's house, I noticed that a remarkable change had come over the land. In spite of the sultry heat, cloud cover had given enough respite for the plants to lift their heads and everywhere the land seemed to vibrate with its longing for water. I wondered whether we would have time to get back home again before the downpour began and doubted that there was any need to water Joe's plants today. It would not matter though, getting caught in the rain would seem like heaven and I longed for it with the same urgency as the rest of nature did.

My real reason for walking through this sticky heat was the parcel that the postman had brought this morning. It had been obvious, when I saw the American postmark, whom the parcel was from and I ripped it open in the hallway as soon as I had shut the door behind the postman. The rattle of the post van's exhaust had been hidden by Luna's appreciative barking, as she smelt the dog chew that Joe had sent her. I had tossed it to her and she had snatched it from the air, scrabbled, claws skidding on the tiles, for the kitchen, slid to a halt under the table and proceeded to attack the chew. I had followed her and finished unwrapping the parcel at the table with her. Inside had been a note in Joe's bold, black scrawl, which had said only **Missing you!** There had also been an MP3 loaded with music for me to try and a book.

Whenever he called in the evenings, Joe and I had been discussing each new artist and author that I had discovered among his varied collection, most of which I had enjoyed, although some I had found too hard going. I had been getting a glimpse of a different culture, one that shared the same language but offered startling variations. William Faulkner's complex and rather macabre images stayed with me long after I had read them but I found his books disturbing. The jazz albums were challenging and not always pleasant but there were beautiful classical pieces that I had never heard, which drew me into their musical intrigue. Then there was the small section of punk rock, which I had teased Joe about, although I had actually found the image of Joe as a teenager with an "angry young man" defiance rather touching, given what I knew about his later career choice in order to please his father.

The book was by Steinbeck, another American author who had been new to me before I dipped into Joe's shelves but whose prose style I found more accessible than Faulkner's. My trip to Joe's house today was to choose some more music and load it onto the MP3 player so that I could listen to it at home. It seemed as if Joe was determined to drag me back into contact with the technological world, first a telephone and now music but I also knew he was right. My time as a voluntary hermit was coming to an end.

Luna flew off ahead of me when we reached the path through the sad looking sunflowers. She always stayed fairly close to me until we got here and then the hope that she might find her master at home lent her wings. I knew I would find her by the kitchen door, head flopped on her paws in disappointment. I wiped my forehead with the back of my hand. The humidity was unbearable

147

today. I thought about Joe's gift and smiled. He was in the middle of a family tragedy and even so had found the time to think about me. Once again, I found myself confronted with the kindness that lay at the core of this man I loved.

Love it was, I no longer had any doubts about that. The last few weeks had made my feelings very clear. It was not just the physical rush, the fire that flared within me at the thought of Joe, or the loneliness that I felt without his presence nearby. More than anything, it was the tenderness that I felt when we spoke and I heard the underlying sadness in his voice. His father had not recovered consciousness and Joe now accepted that it was very unlikely he ever would. Joe had not had a chance to talk things through with his father and he did not know if the conciliatory words he spoke could be heard or understood. The fact that Joe made no effort to hide his feelings from me when we talked at night had let me get to know him in a way that might have taken us years otherwise. I had changed in the last few weeks too, opening up to let Joe get behind my protective shield and now I was discovering the consequences. Whereas before I had thrived in my aloneness, now it was full of lonely corners that only thoughts of Joe seemed to fill.

I reached the end of the tunnel through the burnt sunflowers and made my way along the side of the house. I broke off a sprig of lavender and crumbled it between my fingers for the pleasure of its scent as I shook off my sad mood. I would soon have to tackle the job of cutting off the dried shoots, here and under my window at home. Maybe I could make lavender bags to use in the wardrobes, because it seemed a shame to just throw the flowers away.

I was surprised to see that Luna was not in her usual place by the kitchen door and looked around for her. I called her name and in response heard a man's voice call out. For one heart-stopping moment, I thought it must be Joe but then I saw Pietro pushing himself up from where he had been kneeling among the tomato plants. Pietro waved and then bent to massage his knees.

148

"I'm getting too old for this. My knees don't like it any more, Annina. No, no!" he exclaimed as I leant forward to kiss his cheeks. He held out both hands, covered in earth, "Look at me. I don't want to get you dirty too."

"What are you doing?"

"I'm getting this plot sorted out for Joe. When he comes home, he will be glad to see it all in order. I have to throw these tomato plants away. There is no strength left in them and Joe put them too far in the shade, see. Those others down there against the house, they are still full of flowers because they get the sun all afternoon."

"Can I do something to help?"

"Well, I wouldn't say no to a coffee, if you will join me. Then you can watch me put these winter vegetables in."

"That sounds like a good idea," I assured him and went to fill the espresso pot. I put the pot on the gas and found two white china cups. I opened the window over the sink and watched Pietro at work while I waited for the coffee to bubble through. In spite of his silver hair and old man's stiffness, Pietro was a strong man, sturdy and square. With streaks of earth on his face and clothes, and pieces of dried tomato leaf caught in his hair, he blended with the garden in the same way that he did with his vineyard. His clothes had been washed so many times that they had lost their original hues of browns and greens and become a sort of camouflage smudge. I found myself considering the aptness of names once again and wondered whether Pietro would have come to resemble the rock he was named after, if he had been christened differently. He and Lucia seemed very happy and were obviously fond of each other, despite their opposing characters. In company, it was rare to hear him speak and if his wife was around, he regressed to a series of grunts and nods, which she interpreted as she wanted but I had found that he could be quite voluble if you found him immersed in the earth, his true element.

I poured the coffee, placed the sugar bowl, cups and a few biscuits on a small tray and put it on the kitchen windowsill, then

149

tossed a biscuit to Luna who had been patiently guarding the tin for me and went back outside. Pietro straightened when he saw me and wiping his hands on his trousers, came to join us. His thick, brown fingers seemed clumsy with the sugar spoon and yet he handled the tender young nursery plants with great delicacy. This was something that he and Joe had in common. They managed to create beautiful things in spite of the size of their hands. Pietro broke a biscuit in two and fed one half to Luna who had transferred her guard duty to his feet. I smiled.

It was easy to see why the two men got on so well and to imagine them working alongside each other in harmony. Lucia had said that Joe was always ready to give Pietro a hand with the harvest or any other jobs that needed doing and I imagined that they would work all day without speaking more than a few words. Words were unnecessary. I remembered the beautiful carving of Pietro that Joe had shown me, evidence of a bond between them of deep respect and understanding.

The water of the lake mirrored the grey swirls of cloud in the sky. The air felt like a second skin pressing wetly against me. Pietro chewed his half of biscuit then jerked his chin at the sky.

"Rain. Maybe tonight, maybe tomorrow. The end of summer."

"Good, I cannot wait for it to cool down a bit."

"Oh, it won't get much colder for a while but once the big storms have come, the air feels different, you can breathe properly again. Maybe this year we will have a proper mushroom year. I can't remember now how long it has been since we have had the right conditions for porcini mushrooms. Recently it seems that either it doesn't rain enough or it gets too hot after the rain, or else it gets too cold at night and they don't grow. This year, if we are lucky, might be just right." His eyes took on a rapt, far-away look as he continued,

"I remember once when I was courting Lucia. We met up in the woods early one morning. I was searching under the big oak where my father always found porcini but Lucia, she was a bit fed up with me for bothering about mushrooms when we were alone

150

together for once, so she stomped off and sat down in a clearing nearby. Then she let out a screech and I went running to her. I thought maybe there was a boar or a snake but instead I saw my Lucia holding the biggest porcino I'd ever seen. It was as big as my head, smooth and firm and she had almost sat on it. When I joined her we found enough mushrooms right there in that spot to fill both our baskets." Pietro chuckled, blushing a little at the memory, which made me think that mushrooms were not all that he and his Lucia had discovered in that wood so long ago.

Pietro turned back to the vegetables he had been planting. I followed him over to the carefully dug rows and watched while he showed me what to grow for a good winter crop and how and where to plant it. He sowed seeds of fennel, lettuce and spinach in the rows, breaking up the hardened soil first with a trowel and then crumbling it between his fingers. Then he started to transplant the seedlings that he had brought with him; two types of cabbage, cauliflower, broccoli and leeks. Each delicate plant was handled with the same care as Pietro's gnarled, dirt-stained fingers prised them gently from their nursery pot and settled them into their new home.

I left Pietro among the plants and washed up the coffee things then went into Joe's study to choose some music. I picked out a variety of classical, blues and Latin American music, something for every mood, then closed up the house again and went to say goodbye to Pietro.

"Ciao Annina." Pietro kissed my cheek this time although he was very careful not to get me dirty. He gave me a plastic bag with melons, cucumbers and courgettes from the garden.

"The grapes will be ready for the harvest in a couple of weeks, by the end of September definitely. Would you like to help?" he asked as Luna and I set off along the path. I assured him that I would and he promised to let me know the date.

"Just hope that we won't get any hail. Rain is fine, we need it, but hail will damage the grapes." Pietro cast a speculative look at the sky as if calculating the probabilities that the dark cloud mountains over our heads would have ice in their hearts. I sent my love to Lucia and left him, still gazing at the sky, lost in thought.

The humidity descended around me again as soon as I left the shade of the house. It was almost 7 pm but the heat still felt like a physical force. Huge cumulus seemed to swell as I watched them. The clouds, which had been almost nonexistent all summer, now dominated the landscape and the sky in the distance was as dark as night. I saw an occasional flash of lightening split the blackness as the front moved steadily towards the mountains. I hoped that it would rain here and not pass by. The trees and wildflowers in the olive groves seemed to quiver as they sensed the promise of rain.

I thought about Pietro again. He had been looking after Joe's garden, even though he had not been asked to do so. It was a kind act and one that reassured me, because Pietro obviously had no doubt that Joe was coming home. I acknowledged to myself then that I had been worrying about the fact that Joe might decide to stay in America, that maybe he would rediscover the good side of life there and enjoy being close to his sister and his old friends. I was glad that I had met Pietro today.

I considered the way that Pietro had explained planting up the winter crops to me. He was a quiet, patient teacher and I found it easy to understand him when he spoke. I was not sure if my Italian was really that much better or whether it was the slow way that he spoke that made him easy to follow. Maybe it was a mixture of the two things. Italian was definitely becoming much easier for me. I had even dreamt in that language a few times recently, mostly dreams about not being able to find the right word but nevertheless proof of my growing fluency

Back home, I was confronted by evidence of Luna's presence in my life as soon as I opened the kitchen door. There was a new smell in the house, the scent of dog, which was not exactly unpleasant but was not perfumed either. I grabbed the broom from the kitchen cupboard and began to sweep up the fur balls that rolled around on the tiled floor. Luna sneezed in disgust and left me to work, taking herself out into the garden and plonking down to finish off the chew Joe had sent that morning, which was already reduced to a piece of soggy hide.

I have always hated housework but, as always, once I started to clean one thing I suddenly noticed all the other jobs that needed doing. Sighing I went to find a duster and then remembered my new CD player. With the Gypsy Kings blaring out, dusting was much more fun and I even tackled the bathroom, singing along to the music as I scoured the sink and toilet. It was only when the music finished that I became aware that what had seemed to be part of the percussion was actually the drumming of rain on the roof.

I ran downstairs, past Luna who had taken refuge under the kitchen table and into the garden. I stood barefoot in the grass, letting the rain soak into me as it soaked into the ground. I felt as if I was absorbing the water into my skin the way a tree draws it from its roots. The air was heady with the scent of wet plants and grass. Leaves that had looked dusty and dry for weeks were suddenly slick and gleaming. The weight of the raindrops bent the dry lavender shoots almost to the ground but freed their scent and the pyracanthus berries glowed bright orange in the half-light.

I looked across the garden to the dark cypress against a darker sky. Lightening lit the tree from behind, illuminating it in such detail that the image seemed burnt into my retina. I stretched up my own arms in an unconscious echo of the cypress; letting the rain run through my fingers, plaster my clothes to my body. The grass was oozing muddily under my feet, the rain too heavy for the sun-hardened ground to accept immediately. A wind had sprung up from nowhere and although the temperature was still warm, the wind on my wet skin chilled me. Thunder rumbled, sending a shockwave of sound through me and lightening flashed again. Luna began barking madly from the kitchen and I decided that maybe she was right to have preferred the safety of the house. The lightening seemed too near and too frequent to make staying in the rain appealing, so I went to join her. As I walked across the lawn, something hit my arm and I yelped. Hailstones as big as marbles began to whiz through the air and rebound off the ground and I broke into a run. The wind was blowing the rain and hail in through the kitchen window and I wiped my muddy feet quickly then dashed round the house closing windows and shutters against the storm.

The hail did not last more than a few minutes but it rained for hours, drumming incessantly on roof and windows in a primitive rhythm, interspersed with the occasional violent crash of thunder. I sliced up the small, sweet melon that Pietro had given me and put it on a plate with some of the strong-flavoured local prosciutto ham and a thick slab of bread. I poured a glass of wine, put the whole lot on a tray and took it into the lounge. I searched through Joe's music until I found what I wanted and then sat on the rug on the floor with Luna curled by my side, waiting to share my meal.

Thunder crashed. Nina Simone sang *my baby just cares for me*, in her extraordinarily complex voice. The wine, in its plain glass, smelt of berries. For a moment, I remembered sitting on the floor like this, listening to Percy Sledge with rain streaming down the windowpane, the night after my mother's funeral. How different I had felt then; how sad and lonely. Now, although the scene was almost the same, everything had changed. Luna felt warm against me. The rain outside was natural, elemental and longed for.

Pietro had said earlier, about the grape harvest,

"It all depends on the rains. Too much and the grapes will be big but not so sweet, not enough and the wine will be too strong and very little of it. I judge the date for the *Vendemmia* by the rainfall and the sun."

The elements, harsh or gentle, made themselves felt so powerfully here. The real difference between the person I had been and the one I had become was that now I was in tune with myself and consequently with nature, which had become such an important part of my world. Before, the rain had merely been a nuisance and the sun never enough to lighten my mood. Now there was a reason for everything that nature gave. The way I felt with the cypress's music humming in my veins; of being connected to

154

the universe, to the elements and the cycles of life; had let me feel at peace with myself. It was true that I was alone now but soon Joe would call and we would talk. I was safe in my home of cool terracotta tiles and weathered stone walls, warmed by thoughts of a man I loved, listening to Nina and the cleansing, rejuvenating rain.

The sun was just rising when Luna's excited barking woke me the next morning. As I staggered downstairs to see what had upset her I heard someone rapping on the kitchen door. There was only one person I knew who was up and about so early so I was not surprised to see Fiammetta when I opened up. Luna stopped barking, sniffed at Fiammetta's shapeless brown dress then dashed off into the garden to play in the muddy puddles.

I invited Fiammetta in and quickly closed the door so that Luna would not come back and shake dirty water all over us. Fiammetta pulled out a chair and sat down, looking quite at home. Her bright eyes sparkled with mischief as she accepted my offer of coffee and toast. This was the first time I had seen her since my spontaneous visit to her home and it seemed as if there was a new intimacy between us. She seemed completely at ease in my home, whereas she usually refused my invitations to come in. As I set the table for two, made coffee and toasted bread, Fiammetta leant back comfortably in her chair and looked around her. She did not say anything until I put the honey she had given me next to her then she grinned at me and asked me to make her a milky coffee in a big cup,

"At my age you cannot eat toast without softening it." She confided with a rueful chuckle.

"Brava ragazza, I'm glad you are using the honey. You won't get any colds or flu this winter if you eat it. Did you know that there are substances in honey that the scientists haven't identified yet, or that it is the only food that can generate heat? That is why it helps to warm us in winter. You can use it as a salve for wounds and it kills off harmful bacteria inside and out. My grandson bought me a book about bee keeping. He likes to help me out with the hives. Sometimes he sits with me for a while and reads to me from that book. He's a kind boy." She dipped a teaspoon into the honey and put a dollop into her coffee.

"The rain was good last night, wasn't it? Did it sing you to sleep?"

"Yes it did. You're right the sound was like a kind of music."

"If you know how to listen, everything in life is music. You know that now. You have heard the song of the cypress, the way I heard it for the first time and the way that all of the cypress' companions have heard it throughout the centuries." She smiled enigmatically and dunked her toast into her coffee until it was soft enough for her to chew on safely.

"Today I am going to teach you. There is much you need to know and not as much time as I had hoped." Her face darkened for a moment but then she pushed herself up and brushed crumbs from her skirt before setting off briskly towards the door.

"Wear jeans and a long-sleeved shirt. We will not be sticking to the path and there are snakes around. They know not to bother me," she informed me and I did not doubt it. Not even a snake would have the temerity to take on Fiammetta when she was in this mood. It was a good job I had not planned anything else for the day.

Fiammetta opened the door before I thought to warn her about the filthy state Luna would doubtless be in but, as the dog leapt up from where she had been waiting on the doorstep and made to lunge inside, Fiammetta raised one hand and murmured something that I did not catch. Luna sat back on her haunches with a look of surprise. I ran upstairs to get dressed in the clothes that Fiammetta had told me to wear and when I got back down the dog had not moved an inch.

Fiammetta had brought two reed baskets with her and we each took one. It fit easily over my arm, swinging with the rhythm of my stride as I joined her. We walked together into the long, thin shadow of the cypress until we reached the tree itself. Luna flopped down at a distance as if wary about getting too close.

Fiammetta put her basket down and touched the tree trunk with one hand, indicating that I should do the same. When I put my right hand on the rough bark, she took hold of the other and closed her eyes. Once again I felt the strange humming in the air and let it roll through me, closing my own eyes and giving myself up to the sound. Fiammetta's hand was as cool and rough as the bark. I felt the way I did as a child when my father took me on a ride at the funfair. The same sensation of spinning wildly, whilst being held safely in place. It seemed as though the whole universe was spinning, with me at its centre; future and past merging as time spread outwards in infinite circles. After a while, I felt Fiammetta's grip on my hand lessen and I opened my eyes. She held my gaze for a second, blue eyes unsmiling and yet immeasurably kind. She released me and walked away in silence leaving me to relish the absolute peace our communion had created.

We went first to the olive grove, placing our feet carefully to avoid slipping in the patches of slick mud between the long grass and weeds. Once again Fiammetta showed me various plants; some to pick for use in salads, others for medicinal use. She dug her fingers into the wet soil around each plant and held it up to me. As she named each plant and its particular qualities she seemed to forget that I was there and her speech became almost a chant. It was as if she was singing an enchantment or retelling a story from long ago that had been passed on, by word of mouth, from generation to generation. This time though, I found that it was easy to follow her meaning. It was as if the effect of the cypress was still with us, making us one, so that as she spoke of chicory and dandelion, of camomile and wild mint, I knew almost before she spoke the words what they were to be used for.

"Gather chicory leaves before the flowers appear and the roots in autumn; good for anaemia, the liver, loss of appetite and constipation. Dandelion for cholesterol, cellulite and obesity and for the gout. Camomile to relax, to help you sleep, treats burns and

157

calms infections. Wild mint for ringing in the ears, spots, hiccoughs and nervous spasms."

I fingered the wild mint that Fiammetta called *nepetella*. When I crushed the leaf between my fingers I identified the perfume that I had noticed often on my walks, so evocative of childhood; my Father's favourites, roast lamb with mint sauce and the small white sweeties, like little pebbles, that he had kept in his pocket.

Fiammetta's voice had a hypnotic quality to it. I listened as I followed her around the field and then into the forest, in a trance-like state. My head began to feel swollen with the amount of new information that I was absorbing, as she continued to list ingredients for ointments, salves and tisanes. The sun had now risen and the day was hot, with moisture steaming off the ground that was wet from last night's rain. We were quite a way into the forest now, following an overgrown animal track and my head had begun to throb badly.

I recognised the track we were on. It was the one from my dream on the night of St Lorenzo, only this time I was not floating above the ground but really had to duck to avoid the low hanging branches and wipe the cobwebs from my face. The brambles caught at my jeans and the scent of wild mint rose from the ground. Fiammetta must have sensed my discomfort because she stopped and turned back to me, rubbed my arm and pinched my cheek.

"Enough for today child," she said and her voice was normal once more, although a little hoarse from talking so much. She delved in the large side pocket of her dress and brought out a pinch of lavender, which she rubbed between her fingers to release its perfume. Then she smoothed her fingers gently around my temples, increasing the pressure gradually, until it was almost too much to bear. She stood back then and smiled,

"The headache will soon go. Come on, just a bit further. I have a treat for you." She was right, the headache had lessened as soon as I smelt the lavender and breathing in the scent of the rain-washed forest as it gradually heated up, the pain went completely.

158

I walked behind Fiammetta alongside the deep, dry gully I had dreamt of. Luna plunged ahead, impervious to the energy I felt in the air, a sense of something predestined and mysterious.

We came down a sloping bank and there was the moss-covered earth bridge across the gully and the oak with the split trunk guarding the far end. Fiammetta stood exactly where the ghostly figure of light had in the dream and indicated me to go ahead of her.

Il Ponte delle Fate Fiammetta whispered. A fairy bridge she called it and as I walked across the crumbly red earth; stepping carefully over huge roots, very aware that if I slipped I would have a long way to fall into the dry bed of the stream; it did indeed seem like an enchanted place from a fairytale.

"See the oak, split but not dead. Its spirit is strong. All life possesses a spirit, some stronger than others. When you have learnt the Cypress' lessons you will be able to feel the living force in the plants instinctively, know how to use them." I put my fingers on the oak trunk for balance and turned my head to look at Fiammetta. She grinned at me and bent down, fingers grubbing in the soil at the side of the path to uncover the roots of a tiny oak sapling. The light was dim but when she pointed it out to me, I could see the acorn still there between plant and roots. Fiammetta gently pushed the earth back around the miniature oak and straightened up, pointing with her grubby fingers at the huge tree at my side. The oak blocked my path and to get past it I had to hold onto the trunk and swing round it, out over the gully and onto the grassy bank at the other side. As I did so the old woman spoke close behind me, her voice once again laced with mesmeric echoes,

"The old ones believed that oaks are the gateways between worlds."

My feet found a firm foothold on the far side of the tree. Although I was convinced that Fiammetta was just being dramatic, with her talk of gateways between worlds, still I found that my mouth was dry as I turned to give Fiammetta a hand. She did not need my help though, swinging round the trunk with the ease of someone who had done it often. Her hair caught the sunlight, a fluffy halo of white. Her grin was childlike but her eyes were knowing, glinting with suppressed mirth, well aware of the atmosphere she had conjured up.

Ahead was a large clearing, the ground dappled with leafy shadows and warm sunlight. A force did indeed emanate from the clearing and as I walked alongside Fiammetta into the hollow, I felt a shiver of prescience shoot through me and I knew that my future was tied in some way to this bewitched place. Fiammetta was studying me closely and now she nodded briefly, as if pleased by my reaction. I saw my reflection in her dark pupils and with a jolt realised that my own expression was an echo of Fiammetta's; feral and possessed of some mystic knowledge that, as yet, I had not put to the test.

Lichen-stained rocks pushed out from the grass here and there. A tangle of blackberry bushes took advantage of the sunshine on the left side of the clearing, their prickles snaring onto the lower branches of the beech trees to form a thick screen. As we came out of the shade of the forest and into the sunshine, I could see that the hollow was the home to three big trees, their bulk testimony of the extra light and rain that they received away from the rest of the forest. There was a mighty walnut tree on the far side of the clearing and on the right a chestnut tree with immature, prickly fruit hiding amongst the long serrated leaves. Closest to us was a wild fig tree, its huge, strangely twisted branches spreading wide. Swollen fruit hung beneath the enormous leaves. Fiammetta reached up and picked a fig. She handed it to me and picked another for herself. I pulled off the thick green top of the fig, revealing grainy flesh that shaded from pale green to rich pink. We looked at each other as we bit into the sweet, warm stickiness then grinned in satisfaction.

"When you get home, wash them and split them in half, then lay them on a large board to dry out. Put them in the sunshine in the morning and the late afternoon but be careful not to leave them in the midday sun or they will burn. When they have dried out you can put them away in a box, with layers of paper between them and then at Christmas you stuff them with walnuts and eat them as dessert." Fiammetta instructed, between mouthfuls.

We ate as many figs as we put into our baskets, our fingers and mouths sticky with sap and juice. Then we turned our attention to the blackberries. Most of the blackberry bushes that I went past on my walks looked tired, their berries already picked by people and birds. The bushes in this clearing, being so far off the footpaths, were still full of fruit. The berries were smaller and less succulent than the ones I used to pick in England, since they did not get the same amount of rain to help them to swell but they were sweet and before long, our baskets were full to overflowing and our sticky fingers stained red.

It was almost dark when Fiammetta led me back along the track and indicated the direction for home, then kissed my cheek in an unusual show of affection and left us. Luna and I walked home, tired but satisfied. I felt as if I had learnt so much in the last few days. Pietro had taught me about planting the garden crops for winter and Fiammetta had shared some of the secrets of the plants.

Once, Fiammetta had asked me if I could sense the magic in the air as we stood by the cypress. Now she had shown me the hollow and there was magic there too. A sense of ripeness and fertility, a hidden place, in the heart of the dark forest, filled with sunlight and fruit, where the simple gesture of picking a sun-ripened fig; tasting the sun in its warm flesh, the rain in its succulence and the earth in its sweetness; was in itself a kind of enchantment.

AUTUMN

The Quickening

The seasons flow on, in cycles, ever repeating circles. Now autumn, season of fertility and harvest, is here and the fire and dust of summer fades. Nothing is ever absolute, all is in perpetual motion and what appears to be contrary is actually continuity. Swollen fruit slowly ripen to perfection before the harvest; fecundity is the sister of death, which is nothing more than the harvest of the soul.

Like spring, this season is a buffer between the harsh extremes of summer heat and winter ice.

Throughout the centuries, pagan ceremonies have been held to give thanks for the plentiful gifts of autumn and poets have honoured its fruitfulness. On the eve of All Hallows, however, only the brave walked abroad and fearful jack-o-lanterns glared before each home to scare the demons away. A beautiful paradox, autumn.

The old one uses her remaining time to pass on her wisdom to the girl. Calling on the last reserves of strength and wisdom, she pushes away the spectre that haunts her and takes the girl with her, to hidden places where the magic flows strong along the ley lines. She weaves her gentle magic and the girl absorbs it all, opening up to the universe.

Our girl is truly beautiful now. She glows with life and love. Alone again, as the weeks pass she will ripen like the fruit of the wild fig and when at last the quiet man returns to her she will be ready to concentrate all that she is on him. The girl will move in one direction, the old one in another. I will not be able to alleviate the pain when the old one is too weak to make her daily journey to me. We both know what the future holds for her. There will be no endings though, we will still be connected, us three, our thoughts flowing together easily through the autumn mists.

15

*The girl slips through time with me. Time has no meaning when we join.
I hold her as she floats above the ever-changing land; catch her as she
swoops towards the far-flung stars. She says that I seem to stretch up,
like a brush ready to paint the canvas of the sky.
She seeps into the ground, following the curve of my great roots and
stretches herself out in the womb of the world with me.
Soon she will begin to explore a new universe of love, blessed by the
gentle shimmer of starlight and the soft breath of autumn. While I stay
immobile, here by the Etruscan stones, she roams both the physical and
the spiritual realms and, where our souls meet, we are one.*

Luna and I drove down to do some shopping in Montalino. The
day was warm but Pietro had been right when he had told me that
after the rain the air would no longer seem suffocating. With all
the windows open, the wind was whipping around the car, sending
up the fur that Luna was still shedding, so that my navy trousers
were covered. The wheels drummed over the bumpy road, Luna
panted noisily and the jam jars on the back seat added to the usual
cacophony of car noise. I was so used to the car's eccentric
rhythms now that changing its stiff gears was as easy as breathing.
The jam in the back was what I had made from the blackberries I
had picked with Fiammetta a few days before. I had decided to
take a couple of jars down for Rita and stock up with a few
essential items at the same time. My hands and arms, I noticed
ruefully, were still covered in scratches from the brambles. It had
been worth it though, because the jam had turned out really well
and I had managed to make two blackberry and apple pies and put
them in the freezer and still have enough fruit left over to stew
some for my breakfast. I had also been putting the figs out to dry
as Fiammetta instructed me, although I did not know how many

would make it through to the winter because the temptation to eat one when I passed was irresistible.

Along the roadside the bushes and grasses were flourishing again after the much needed rain and there were patches of fresh green among the older dry leaves. Hints of autumn were already showing though, in yellow beech leaves and the brown seedpods speckling the thorny acacia trees.

As I parked the car opposite the small parade of shops in the village, I saw Rita bustling from the butcher's and into the general store. I left the car windows open and ordered Luna to stay, then crossed the road to intercept Rita. As usual, the general store was crowded with people queuing at the counter and others waiting for advice on clothes or choosing toiletry items. Rita was the last in the queue and she gave me a hug when I joined her. We chatted while we waited then Rita gave her complicated order, of something different for every member of her family and I got some fresh bread, ham and cheese.

"Have you got time for a coffee, Ann?" Rita wondered and I said that I would love one and told her about the jam that I had brought for her.

"I've never made jam before but it turned out really well, although you can see that I got quite scratched picking the berries." I showed her my arms and she tutted at the sight.

"Blackberries so late. Wherever did you find them?" I told her vaguely about the clearing in the woods but did not mention Fiammetta, partly because I remembered Rita being disapproving of her and how Lucia had gone on about her being a witch, but mostly because there was a secret bond between Fiammetta and myself now that I was reluctant to discuss. Whenever I thought about the hollow I felt my skin raise in bumps as a sense of foresight came over me and I knew, without understanding why that the hollow held the key to part of my future. The cypress too was something I could not discuss with anyone because I would not have been able to find the words to explain our relationship. Since going to the hollow I had spent many moments with the tree,

165

testing our connection. Whenever we touched my actual surroundings would fade and I would be caught up in a reverie that drew me ever deeper.

I fetched Luna from the car and Rita made a fuss of her, then we walked the short distance to Rita's house and let Luna get reacquainted with Chicca, Rita's small mongrel. The two dogs scampered happily around the yard and I followed Rita up the outside staircase to the upper flat that she shared with Luca. Her eldest son and his family lived on the ground floor and her other son a few doors away so it was rare to find Rita alone. I offered to give her a hand to put away the shopping but she waved me off and instead insisted that I sit on a high-backed chair at the formal table in the lounge, while she made us coffee.

A small table near the window glinted as the sun caught the gold chains that covered it. I had been surprised when I moved here to discover that behind the normal looking facades of the houses were many artisan gold-workshops and small factories. Rita worked late into the night, after she had finished all the housework, cooked and cleared away, to finish off the chains that she then took to the factory around the corner. She was paid a pittance for her work but it helped to augment her pension and she could not stay still without having something to do. Even if there was no gold for her to work, she would sit at the little table, where the light was better for her eyes and work on delicate embroidery instead.

From my uncomfortable seat, I watched Rita darting about in her cramped kitchen, which was really no more than an alcove separated from the lounge by a thin partition. She stuck her head around the wall and asked,

"How is Joe? Have you heard from him?" before disappearing from view again. Rita did not know how close Joe and I had become but I could see from the gleam in her brown eyes that, with infallible women's intuition, she suspected. I fingered the tablecloth that Rita had crocheted as my mind returned to the phone call I had had from Joe yesterday. No one had rung for Joe

166

on his mobile since he had been away and he usually phoned me in the evening, so I was surprised to hear ringing as I stepped out of the shower in the morning. I had rushed, dripping and found the phone on the bedside table where I had left it the night before, having taken it to bed with me when Joe had failed to ring for the first time since he had left.

"Joe's father died yesterday," I told Rita, remembering the way his voice had choked as he held back his tears. "He phoned to tell me," I added, thinking about how tired he had sounded. He and his sister had been by their father's bedside all day, watching him slip away and then Joe had stayed awake until the early hours of the morning, wandering around the house, besieged by memories, until he thought I would be awake.

Rita stuck her head around the partition again, head on one side, more bird-like than ever.

"Madonna! I am so sorry for Joe." Rita shook her head and crossed herself. I smiled at her mild imprecation and then decided that, given her profound religious beliefs, she had probably been calling on the Madonna in prayer. She seemed to have an intimate relationship with all the saints, calling on the right one to help her in any aspect of her life, as if they were old friends.

Pulling out another heavy chair Rita sat down and took my hand in her tiny one.

"Ann, cara, I am sorry for Joe but it will be a relief too. If there was no chance of his father recovering then it is better to die quickly, I think. When will Joe be coming home?"

"I am not sure. There will be a lot of things to sort out now. I don't expect he will be able to come home for another couple of weeks yet." Joe had told me that he and Molly would need that time to sort out their father's affairs and the thought that he was still not close to coming home made me sad and then guilty at my selfishness.

Rita patted my hand and went back to the kitchen. After much clinking and rattling, she returned carrying a silver tray. She had obviously used her best things because it was the first time that

167

she had ever offered me coffee from the ornate tray and the delicate china cups decorated with butterflies. She put the tray on the table and I marvelled once again at how deceptive appearances can be. The tray was very heavy and yet Rita had carried it easily. There was a core of steel inside her delicate frame. I went to pick up a cup but Rita stopped me. She opened a glass-fronted dresser and pulled out a bottle.

"Today we will have caffè corretto." Seeing my look of confusion, she laughed and explained. No, the coffee did not need to be corrected, it was just the way coffee was referred to when you laced it with a liquor of some type. She poured us both a generous measure of clear liquid from a green glass bottle with no label.

"Ecco la grappa. My cousin's homemade grappa this is. Try it," she urged. I sipped my coffee then swallowed fast and choked. It was far stronger than I had anticipated and the grappa had burnt my throat. Rita giggled. If not for the wrinkles and thin sandy hair she could have almost been a child as she sat, dwarfed by her elaborate furniture. I grinned and took another sip. The coffee was undoubtedly the most potent that I had ever sampled but, once I got used to it, it was really quite pleasant.

Rita leant forward and touched my hand again,

"There are some moments in life when a touch of grappa is needed. You looked so sad Ann, that I thought this was one of those moments."

"I don't know whether to thank you or not," I teased, "This stuff is strong enough to blow one's head off, and it seems to me," I added, seeing that she was still nursing her own cup, "that you are not drinking yours!" Rita put her cup back on the table and pushed it away from her with a grin.

"Oh, I don't drink Ann but I thought I would keep you company."

I finished my coffee and leant back, feeling the heat course through my body and tinge my cheeks with pink. Rita began to laugh again. She gestured to the green glass bottle with less than two inches missing from the top;

"Do you know how long I have had that grappa?"

"Not long, I should think, because there is hardly any missing."

"Seven years. It is seven years since my cousin came to stay and brought it for us. He and Luca tried it after dinner that day and it hasn't been touched since. Luca choked like you did, only he was drinking it neat and he had to get up and rush to the kitchen for some water. He said it almost took the lining off his tongue. My cousin; he was already in his eighties but still driving and doing everything for himself, looking after his vineyard, making his wine and grappa; he knocked back his drink and then finished off Luca's. He said that a glass of wine with lunch, another with dinner and a grappa in his coffee at breakfast before he set off for the vineyard, was what kept him so strong till such a great age. When he left, Luca said that he would rather die young and he put the bottle in there and hasn't touched it since."

Driving home an hour later I felt much better. My visit to Rita, not to mention her cousin's grappa, had made me warm and happy again. Two weeks was not really very long and then Joe would be back. In the meantime, I had friends here, like Rita, Lucia and Pietro, who really cared about me. I had Luna's constant devotion and most of all I had Fiammetta and the cypress.

In the end, the two weeks that had seemed so long flew by and now I found myself wishing that I could make time stand still. Joe was due home this evening. He had told me he would be here at around 9 o'clock to pick up Luna, so of course I had invited him for dinner. I'd had days to prepare everything but at this precise moment, I felt as if I would never be ready in time. I was nervous, that was the problem. Tasks that I usually managed without thinking about were suddenly difficult. I had already broken a plate and two glasses when tidying the kitchen. My fingers felt so clumsy that I had cut myself on the knife I was using to skin the pumpkin for a risotto. I wanted to get all the ingredients chopped and as much prepared as possible before I had a shower, so that I would not smell of onions and garlic. I glanced at the clock. It was only seven so I had all the time in the world. I really must stop panicking like this.

I rinsed my hands and dried them on a tea towel, told Luna to stay where she was, on her rug by the door, then went upstairs to shower quickly. It wasn't cold enough yet to wish that the house had central heating but over the last few weeks the evenings had grown cooler and standing under the lukewarm shower was no longer pleasurable. I wrapped myself in a towel and rubbed my hair dry. I'd had it trimmed two days before so that it fell into place around my face. I had spent ages trying to decide what to wear. Joe would have been travelling all day and would be tired and jetlagged. He would probably just want to eat something and then go home, so getting all dressed up would be out of place. At the same time, I wanted to look nice for him and show him that I did sometimes wear clothes other than shorts and T-shirts.

I had bought some more new clothes recently as the shops got in their autumn stock. Now I stared into the dark-wood wardrobe and sifted through jeans, cords, long-sleeved tops and cotton jumpers while I waited for inspiration to strike. In the mirror on the back of the wardrobe door my bedroom was reflected; sloping beamed ceilings, a few of my favourite paintings on the white walls, flaking green shutters framing distant purple-velvet mountains with the silhouette of the cypress cutting through them like a sword. The mirror also reflected the bed. The bed was made up with crisp, pale blue sheets, matching pillowcases and a thin quilt with a patchwork of stars and moons, which I had found on the market and fallen in love with. My cheeks suddenly felt hot as my gaze slipped to the bedside cabinet where I had put the condoms that I had bought at the chemist yesterday. Oh yes, I thought wryly, I had prepared just about everything.

I pressed the damp towel against my cheeks to cool them down and then quickly dressed in a black-jersey top, cut low at the neck and a long, loose skirt patterned with flowers. I shoved my feet into black leather sandals with a small heel and ran back downstairs before I could change my mind again. In the kitchen, I pulled a small packet from my handbag, where it had been lying forgotten all week and slipped the cool hoops of earrings through my lobes. The crystal drops glittered as I checked my reflection in the windowpane.

Luna did not care for my dinner preparations so far. Onions, garlic, pumpkin and rice did not interest her in the least. However, as soon as I opened the fridge she appeared by my side in the hopes that something more tasty would be coming her way. I checked that the bottle of Berlucchi spumante, that rivalled the best French champagnes, was cold enough. Luna sat back on her haunches, disappointed when I closed the door again having taken out nothing more interesting than the butter dish. I stroked her soft ears and she thumped her tail on the floor, telling me she loved me even if I had not given her a titbit. I bent down and kissed her head. She would be so happy to see Joe but I was going to miss having her under my feet all day, tripping me up and covering the house in dog hair. I opened the fridge again, took out the cheese and cut off a large slice. One fluffy paw lifted up hesitantly and two enormous eyes informed me that she was genuinely starving. I tossed the cheese in the air and she caught it, then high-tailed it under the table in case I tried to take it back.

I checked the clock – it was almost eight, still too early to start cooking but too late for me to go out for a walk to calm down. For a moment, I considered going to the cypress but although I needed the peace of mind that our communion brought, I was never quite able to control time when we connected. Sometimes it lasted mere minutes but there had been other moments recently when I had lost hours; spinning in space with the stars or floating, cloud slow through the autumn sky.

171

I had washed up everything earlier, the table in the lounge was set and the room studded with candles to create the right atmosphere, dinner was ready to start and would only take twenty minutes. I was too wound up to sit and read and the music that I had chosen earlier was already playing as the MP3 player ran through the music at random. What the heck could I do! Then my eyes lit on the coffee pot and I remembered Rita's words when she gave me grappa in my coffee. This was definitely one of those moments that called for a caffè corretto.

I filled the coffee pot and put sugar in a cup then very carefully measured out one small capful of the grappa that I had bought, with this kind of emergency in mind. The caffè corretto was not nearly as potent as the one Rita had given me but its heat and the ritual of preparing it calmed me. I opened the kitchen door and leant against the scratchy frame, sipping slowly as I let my eyes adjust to the near-dark. A few thin clouds split the silver crescent of the moon, which hung suspended above the tip of the cypress. It looked as if the cypress had just finished painting the curve of a C, as if it was writing its own name across the dark sky. It called to me and I closed my eyes and reached out with my mind, letting my thoughts slip through the cool of the night.

The paint against my shoulder was rough through my sleeve. The tiny handle of my cup was smooth between my fingers. The garden scents rose up and mingled with the sharpness of the coffee and spirit. Then gradually my awareness of my surroundings lessened until only the cypress existed.

The air around me seemed so light that I felt as if I were floating; across the garden, down the path and then up along the great length of trunk into the spiral of branches and on, upwards to the very tip of the tree. It would take just a small stretch of my soul to reach up and paint the moon with my fingertips, to lie across a dark cloud and ride the sky. I changed direction and moved fluidly back down through the resinous branches and into autumn-soft earth. Snaking down through the network of roots, I spread out, like the roots, into an intricate web. I thrust through

172

damp darkness, blindly sensing the moisture, the rich nutrients and then down again to rocks and gemstones, and the pulse and heat of lava at the core of the world.

Luna's tail whipped my legs and I opened my eyes, finding it hard to come back fully into my body and shaken by the strength of the hold my vision had on me. This had been the first time I had connected with the cypress without actually touching it and it had felt astonishingly powerful. Then I saw headlights flash on the drive and realised that Joe's jeep was here. Luna raced towards it barking and whining, then jumped up scratching and scrabbling at the door in her desperation to get to Joe. I ran out after the dog and pulled her off by her collar while Joe got the door open. Joe flashed a grin at me then bent down to Luna and the next few minutes were spent in chaos as she licked and jumped and yelped, trying to cover every part of her master with her scent.

When Joe finally stood up and took me in his arms, Luna butted her head in between us and we broke off, laughing. I led him back to the kitchen. Light spilled from the window and the open door, golden and welcoming. As I crossed the threshold, I kicked something with my foot and glancing down saw that it was my coffee cup, which I must have dropped earlier. I picked it up and placed it in the sink feeling momentarily unsettled at the idea of having been so far away from reality that I had not noticed the cup slipping from my fingers.

I took down two tall glasses and opened the fridge to get the spumante.

"Would you like a glass?" I turned round as I spoke to find that Joe was not near the table as I had thought but standing behind me and as I turned he took the bottle from me, returned it to the fridge and pushed the door shut. He put his hands on my shoulders and pushed me back, pressing me against the door. He cradled the back of my head in one hand and brushed his thumb across my cheek. He kissed me then and I wrapped my arms around his neck and hung on. My senses were spinning the way they did with the cypress. I could smell Joe beneath the stale odours of aeroplane. I

173

had forgotten how big he was. I stood on tiptoe to reach his lips and his body was wide and hard, like a wall of warmth.

There were no words in my head, just sensation. I led Joe in silence along the hallway and up the worn stone steps to my room. From the lounge a saxophone wailed; a long pure note that matched the ache of longing in my heart. Joe pushed the bedroom door closed behind us and we shared a smile at the sound of Luna's resigned huff as she flopped down outside, body pressed close to the door, waiting.

Without turning on the lamp or lighting the candles I had so carefully placed, we undressed each other. In the wardrobe mirror, the cypress was reflected; a shadow frosted by the moon's cold breath. The same light shone on us, highlighting the curve of a cheek, the sharp plane of a shoulder blade. Joe lifted me and laid me back onto the quilt so that I was suspended between the patchwork sky beneath and the infinite reach of the heavens outside.

Touch upon touch, my hands echoed Joe's as he explored me with strong, sensitive fingers. All was profoundly new; the dark hair that curled on his chest; the smooth tautness of his collarbone; the quiver of muscle beneath the surface of his skin as my fingers slid across his ribs to his stomach. When he had shed his clothes and their stale odour of travel, I could smell Joe himself again. I buried my nose in his chest and breathed deeply, filling my senses with him. I ran my tongue along his shoulder and up the side of his neck tasting sweet saltiness and an undertone of aftershave.

All my senses were focused on us. With our limbs entwined, we were close enough to seem one yet still remained separate. The few sounds that broke the silence, the chords of music welling up from the floor below, a dull bump against the door as Luna shifted position, were muffled by the thudding of my heart.

The way Joe's breath caught in his throat echoed the rhythm of my jumping pulse. My body had never felt so real. I closed my eyes and let myself move with him, blend into him until I dissolved inside, the way I had earlier with the cypress. My soul floated free in the air and my body was the earth, clay being moulded. I ached deep within, burning then melting into a river that flowed throughout my body. Wave upon wave of sensation swept through me until I cried out, a primordial note that rang in my head, blocking out all else.

"Annie." His voice, a rough whisper seemed to come from far away. He pulled me back into the curve of his arm, buried his lips in my hair and settled his hands possessively on me, one flat along my spine, the other curving across my hip. We were so close that we breathed each other's breath. We smelt of each other, were each other and in Joe's dark eyes I saw my own reflection as my lips curled into a smile.

16

How she can fly, my girl, on the wings of love. She learns so quickly. She feels the elements, the pulse of life and delves into it with the same passion that she is beginning to colour her life with. Now is the time to let her leave the shelter of my gaze. Our connection is solid and she understands that it is unlimited by time and space.
To set someone free is to bind them to you forever with invisible threads as fine and strong as gossamer.

"You cannot still be hungry!" I exclaimed. Joe winked at me in reply and popped another fig into his mouth. I looked ruefully at the fig board, which lay across the kitchen table, and the meagre handful of half-dried fruit left on it. I had not got round to putting it outside in the sun yet this morning and at the rate that Joe was eating the figs, it would not be worth it.

"I knew they wouldn't all last until winter, Joe, but I thought some of them would make it." I laughed and picked up a fig myself. I bit into it; sticky, honeyed and granular; then offered the other part to Joe. He wrapped his long fingers around my wrist, slipped the fig into his mouth and then slowly licked my fingertips. His eyes narrowed slightly. The air between us crackled with energy and I caught my breath. Joe was so beautiful. He released me and leant back in his chair, long legs in faded jeans stretching below the table, bare feet tickling Luna's tummy. His blue shirt was unbuttoned, the sleeves rolled up and at that moment the sun slid out from its veil of cloud and varnished his skin in mellow autumnal light. He gleamed like bronze at sunset, molten streaks highlighting the dark wing of hair that fell across his forehead.

"You make me hungry." Joe teased and I felt the heat rush to my cheeks. His dark eyes held mine and I was suddenly unsettled by his proximity in my home. He was just so big. He filled up a room with his physical presence and when he was near, I felt like a helpless moth drawn to him. I stood up intending to tidy up or wash the plates, do something inconsequential to avoid the magnetic pull of his gaze. His hand gripped my arm to stop me and he pulled me down onto his knee.

"Don't run from me anymore, Annie." He sounded serious all at once. I flicked a look at him, saw the doubt in his expression, the vulnerability that he allowed himself to reveal and I realised that once more I had been backing away from him. I was still fearful of being hurt but until now had been unaware of my own ability to inflict harm. Instead of trying to distance myself, I sank down in his lap.

"Ok." I said, resting my forehead on his. This feeling of being loved was so unfamiliar to me. I did not know how to behave as part of a couple but if I wanted Joe, I would have to learn. This was a junction, a joining or turning point in my life and I had to make sure that I took the right direction.

Last night after we had made love we had dozed and then loved again until finally I had let the night swallow me and slept properly, only to be woken shortly afterwards when Joe had announced that he was starving. So, we had relieved Luna of her guard duty and gone downstairs to the kitchen where we had cooked the risotto together, then eaten in the lounge by candlelight and talked for hours, catching up on each other's lives, while Luna sprawled happily between our feet.

We had slept until dawn when the light from the open window woke me. I had opened my eyes to find my bed shrunken, diminished by Joe's bulk as he lay in a tangle of covers. When I slipped out of bed to go to the bathroom he'd stirred then settled once more but when I got back into bed after pulling the shutters closed he had woken, rolled over and taken me in his arms again, moving rapidly from sleepy cuddles to passion.

Now we were having breakfast at lunchtime and my whole world felt out of kilter, warped and wonderful.

"Annie," Joe spoke into my hair. I got up, gave him another fig - we might as well finish them at this point - sat back in my chair and smiled at him.

"Joe," I teased, using his same, solemn tone of voice, which made the side of his mouth twitch.

"I'm trying to be serious here, give me a break." His accent had strengthened during the weeks back in his homeland. I loved the sound of his voice, the twang of accent, the depth and resonance.

"Come home with me now. Come and live with me." My mouth fell open. I had not anticipated this. I had not thought beyond the shower I had planned on having when he left, the tidying up that I would do and then a long walk; actions I could use to regain control of the rhythms of my life.

Joe was watching me. The sun on his face illuminated him so honestly, shadowing the small lines around his eyes and glinting off the few threads of grey in the dark gloss of his hair.

"I don't want to be alone anymore." He read my hesitancy and lent forward to give emphasis to his words.

"Keep this house, Annie. Keep it as your special place if you feel like you need your own space but ..... give us a chance. We have both been alone so long that I know it won't be easy. Letting someone else into our lives, learning to accommodate another person's needs." He pushed himself up from the chair and stroked his fingers along a deep groove in the table.

"Nothing worthwhile is ever easy, honey." He smiled gently then clicked his tongue to call Luna. I stood too and followed him to the door.

"Joe, I don't know what to say. I didn't expect this."

"It's ok. There is no rush." He touched my neck just below my ear, the tenderest of touches. I shivered as I watched him drive away, Luna gazing imploringly at me from the back of the jeep as it bumped off down the lane.

I went back into the house and began to tidy up but the sudden silence, with only my own noise echoing hollowly around the kitchen, was unbearable. The house, my home, was nothing without Joe and Luna to fill it.

I left everything and ran outside and down the drive to the cypress. The cypress stood as it always did, alone, aloof and impervious to life as it changed around it. The cypress was not lonely but neither was it human. It could not feel this icy void inside, this sudden vortex of emptiness. I began to cry. Hot tears washed down my face, welling up deep within me and spilling to the ground, splashing the half-buried stones at the base of the tree.

I touched the rough bark and jerked free. My body stood straight and rigid, fingers splayed across the trunk but my spirit soared up, plunging through the branches and out, into a sky of mottled blue and grey. I lay in the breeze and watched the jeep driving along the road, past silver-green clouds of undulating olives, past the mighty oaks and the stubble in the harvested sunflower field. Warm thermals wafted me up. The breeze tugged me down. Above the clouds the sky stretched, azure pure into the stratosphere. I soared up until I was so high that I could see the sea on both sides of the country, with the Apennines curving through it like the backbone of a sleeping dragon. I stretched out and spun through the air, whirling with gulls then plunged into the waves that curled towards the shore. I rolled within the waves, snatching at pebbles, tugging at the rocks. Then I felt some subtle force pull me and tumbled back along threads of silver to hover above the cypress once more. I have suffered "a sea-change, into something rich and strange" I repeated Ariel's song in my mind, luxuriating in this exquisite freedom.

The cypress called and I began my decent towards it then jerked as another force reached me and spun me wildly across the forest. Fiammetta was bent over in the herb garden by her house. She was picking rosemary. I smelt it, sharp and aromatic as she snipped off tender tips. She was muttering;

"Rose of the sea; digestive, antiseptic, fights depression, calms the nerves ....." She broke off in mid sentence, straightened up, rubbing rosemary between her fingers.

179

"Ciao, ragazza!" she chuckled, and then the world began to spin so fast that I no longer knew which way was up and which was down and the song in my head turned discordant and all went black.

I came to at dusk, the scent of rosemary and resin in my nose, in my pores. I rose stiffly from the cool ground and walked down the shadow of the cypress toward the house. I had gone too far, too fast. I would have to be more careful from now on. However, the exhilaration of my mind's journey was still strong and it squashed any latent fears that otherwise might have cautioned me.

In my bedroom, I took down my suitcase from the top of the wardrobe and began packing a few things, enough for a day or two. I added toiletries from the bathroom and took the time to shower and change into jeans and a pale blue cotton jumper. On my way out of the house I paused, opened a kitchen drawer and took out my packet of cypress seeds, remembering, with a smile, how Joe had given me the cone on that spring night, so that I could surround myself with cypresses. Then I closed up the house and got into the car. As always, it started first time. I smiled and drove down the drive. I stopped beneath the cypress but there was no sense of saying farewell. It would be here whenever I needed it. We were connected in ways that went beyond the physical.

When I reached the entrance to Joe's property, I was surprised to see Luna sitting in the middle of the road, as if she had been waiting for me. When I pulled up and opened the passenger door she clambered in, tongue lolling, oozing happiness. I buried my face in her buttery-soft fur. She licked me passionately and then sat back against the seat in a strangely human-like way and let me drive her the last few metres to the house.

I carried my case around to the back door and left it there, following Luna down the lawn to the lake. It was dark by now and at first I could not make out where Joe stood but then as I drew closer his shadow gradually separated from the others. He heard me coming and turned round.

"Hi." I said.

"I didn't expect you to come today. Actually I was afraid you wouldn't come at all."

"So was I."

Joe folded my hands into his and pulled me closer. The clouds muffled the stars and the water of the lake was a deep black hole at his back. I shivered as the chill of the night settled into me and Joe tucked his arm around my waist and walked me across the grass to where the house glowed, warm and welcoming. Welcoming me home.

17

This is the season where life and death are most inexorably linked. Small animals rustle in the undergrowth, hiding seeds and nuts in secret stores and fattening themselves for hibernation.
Men busily harvest before the frosts can ruin the crops. The fruit is picked, the acorns buried but these are, in effect, yet more beginnings. The acorn that the squirrel forgets and the seeds spilt as the harvest is brought in are covered by a rainbow of falling leaves. Nestling in their rich bed, among the scent of musty spore and decay, they will wait out the harsh embrace of winter, safe in autumn's warm cloak.

It was one of those marvellous autumn afternoons where the sultry heat, fed by the frequent rain showers had built cumulus castles in the sky and the Apennines shimmered behind the heat haze. This morning it had been cold enough for me to need a woollen jumper for my walk and the evenings were becoming fresh too but this afternoon there was a lazy warmth in the air, reminiscent of summer, as we dangled our feet into the cool water of the lake.

In the weeks since moving in with Joe everything had changed. My life before already seemed remote and dreamlike. We followed diverse rhythms each day. Sometimes we got up at dawn and sometimes we lay in bed until late. Occasionally we talked late into the night but most evenings we could not wait to fall into bed and each other's arms. Usually Joe worked in his workshop after breakfast while Luna and I walked the woods around his house but at other times we lingered so long over breakfast that it merged into lunch. Most days Joe joined me for a short stroll with the dog in the evening but he left me my space in the mornings. We fitted together with easy harmony, which came as a surprise to both of us, so convinced had we been that we were embarking on a difficult phase of transition, from the life of a single person to that of a couple.

The sun was uncomfortably warm on my neck now and the temptation of the water too great. I stood up, slipped off my clothes and dived, naked, into the still water. The reflection of the clouds shattered as I dived in and then gradually the ripples slowed and the image formed on the surface again. Joe and Luna watched me from the bank. Luna was flopped in the shade of the bushes but Joe did not ever seem to burn. He had regained the tan that had faded while he was in America and looked darker than most Italians again. He wore only his old work shorts, white with wood dust and his hair had grown a little longer so that it flopped constantly down across his eyes. He shoved it away and grinned at me.

There was a strange intimacy in sharing my life with another. Even boring chores like housework were less tedious when someone else helped, in fact, it was almost fun. I dusted, Joe hoovered. I washed, he dried up. I weeded the garden, he mowed the grass. The house fitted me too. It was warm and noisy, full of doggy smells and Joe's presence. I had got to know every creak that the rafters made as the house settled for the night. I luxuriated in having a shower that supplied a powerful torrent of hot water and made coffee in the noisy percolator that Joe preferred to espresso in the morning, served in his favourite mug with the chip in the handle. I knew what clothes Joe kept in his closets, which ones he loved and those he never wore. I knew the way he dressed; first pulling on shorts or jeans, then his T-shirt on his way down the stairs. I knew the way he sliced onions and the way he whistled between his teeth when he worked.

On the day after I moved in, Joe had taken me to the shed and together we had potted up the cypress seeds that I had brought with me, along with the ones that I had given him. He had promised me that, when the seedlings came through in the spring, we would choose the two strongest ones and plant them at the end of the drive, so that I could watch them grow older alongside us.

His faith in our relationship, even at that early stage, had been incredible to me but I knew him well enough by now to know that he did not waste words and could see in his face the unwavering conviction that we would grow old together.

I did not walk down to the village much anymore because there was so much to buy. Joe ate like a horse and so did Luna, so once a week we all drove down to Montevarchi and shopped in the big supermarket there. Eating had taken on an importance that it had not had before. Joe loved food and, fortunately for me, he loved to cook too. One of the nicest things about living together was being in the kitchen, chatting and sipping a glass of wine, while we chopped ingredients and cooked. Joe cooked with the same passion, intensity and tenderness that he showed when we made love and I was constantly reminded of his sculptor's capacity to bring things to life with his hands.

I hadn't known that it was possible to love like this. To want someone every second of the day and miss them as soon as they were out of sight. The novelty of having someone look after me still thrilled me. Joe had bought me my own mobile phone and insisted that I take it with me when I walked, in case I needed him. He had also bought me proper walking boots to keep my feet warm and dry, now that it was often wet and muddy in the woods. When we walked together, he took my hand and helped me down crumbling woodland banks or over slippery shale and even though it was unnecessary it demonstrated how much he cared about me.

Above me bulky clouds rolled down from the mountains, unfurling like smoke at the edges. I looked at Joe looking at me. The desire I felt was mirrored in his eyes. I kicked my legs out and cool water surged between my thighs. I stretched and slowly stroked my arms through the liquid sky as I swam back to him.

I had dreamt nearly every night since being here, vivid images of the cypress and the hollow. Each night I soared through the dark to the cypress and then followed the route that the shooting star showed me to the hollow. Every time that I woke up it was with the same sense of prescience, of being inevitably linked to the place. It was never exactly the same but there was always a pervading sense of ripe, primitive fecundity. At times it resembled my first dream, cloaked in night and shadows. At other times it was dawn or dusk or mellow daylight and I could see everything in extraordinary detail; the small lizard basking on the fig tree, surrounded by fruit that was swollen and burstingly ripe; the star-shaped moss growing in thick clumps on the lichen-scarred rocks.

I was hesitant to talk to Joe at first about the recurring dreams and about my strange experiences with the cypress and with Fiammetta, but when I did he had not teased or mocked me. He had said that it sounded rather like astral travelling, as if the cypress was the key that let my mind explore the world without being encumbered by my body.

"Don't let it worry you, Annie" he had said, ruffling my hair. "There is more to the mind than has yet been discovered. Think about the kind of sixth sense that animals possess or the way that mothers instinctively know when their babies need something. When I was working as a doctor I heard quite a few stories about those types of experiences, people who believed that they had been out of their bodies for moments in time."

I was glad that I had spoken to Joe about it. His way of rationalising the experience, without belittling it, of seeing it as just another facet of my complexity, was very comforting.

The next morning we woke early because Pietro had asked Joe to help him with the *vendemmia*, the grape harvest. I nibbled toast and watched Joe as he concentrated on doing justice to bacon and eggs. He was on his third slice of toast, thick with butter, with which he scooped up the runny egg. He became aware of my scrutiny and grinned at me,

"Want some?"

"No thank you. If I ate the way you do I would be huge. What time did Pietro say to get there?"

"As soon as possible. He's concerned about the rain forecast for the next few days. He said the grapes were just perfect for harvesting now but that more rain would make them start to rot. "

185

He finished his last bite of breakfast, fed the crunchy bacon rind to Luna who was lying under his chair waiting for this moment and pushed back his chair. Outside the air was cool and damp. Yesterday's cloud castles had evened out to a thin, grey, layer and patches of mist still hovered over the forest. I was wearing an old green jumper of Joe's that he had shrunk in the wash. It was still too big for me and I had it rolled up several times at the wrists but I loved the scent of Joe, which inexplicably lingered in the wool. I had put on my oldest jeans because Joe had warned me that the vendemmia was a dirty job and was wearing a t-shirt beneath the jumper in case the sun broke through the clouds later and it turned out to be as hot as yesterday. We pulled on our muddy walking boots at the kitchen door and Luna ran out and scratched at the back of the jeep, eager to be off. Joe spoke to her sharply and she laid her ears even flatter to her head and looked sheepish. She had been thoroughly told off yesterday and she was being careful to keep on the good side of her master today.

On our morning walk yesterday Luna and I had surprised two deer. They had leapt away in alarm and, to my horror, Luna had taken off after them. She had bounded through the undergrowth in pursuit while I shouted her name in vain, until I was hoarse. We had been on one of the established public footpaths but all the paths ran close to the hunting reserves and I had already heard a few shots cracking out from the direction in which Luna had run. I'd shouted so loudly that I was breathless and my throat hurt. The animals had gone so quickly that there was no way I would have been able to follow them. Finally, the dishevelled dog had reappeared a little further up the path and trotted back to me looking highly satisfied with herself. I'd snapped on her lead and taken her straight back home, my legs trembling at the thought of what could have happened. Joe had heard us coming back and stuck his head out of the workshop. He'd taken one look at my face and known that something was wrong. When I'd explained he had spoken sharply to Luna and ordered her to lie down outside

186

while he took me into the kitchen and made me drink a strong, sweet coffee.

"I should have thought that you don't know all of Luna's commands. I'm sorry, honey. If she ever takes off again just shout *Qui* and slap your trouser leg," he told me. I had been able to see the funny side of the situation, once the shock had passed and gave him a wobbly smile over my coffee cup.

"Qui! Luna speaks Italian too?" I'd joked and Joe had looked relieved.

"She's a bi-lingual dog, all right. When I got her from Pietro and Lucia she had already learnt a few basic commands. She also knows *giu* instead of down and *basta* instead of enough."

Looking at her now; huge, sorrowful brown eyes and a woebegone expression as she fixed on Joe's fingers tying the last of his laces; I had to laugh. I loved that adorable dog and could not image life without her now.

When we arrived at the big vineyard on the slopes below the manor house, Pietro and Lucia were already hard at work. Lucia bustled over to say hello but Pietro just raised his arm in laconic welcome and carried on. Lucia was wearing a similarly scruffy outfit to mine but with the odd addition of purple Wellington boots covered in small pink hearts and she had tied her hair into tight plaits at each side of her head. Joe kissed her cheeks and grabbed a pair of secateurs and a large red plastic basket, disappearing through the rows of vines towards Pietro. I saw his shoulders shaking as he suppressed his laughter at Lucia's appearance, incongruously girlish for a woman of her age and I hid my own amusement by giving her an extra long hug. I wondered how long it would take Lucia to get round to asking about Joe and me. Pietro had tactfully asked Joe to mention the grape harvest to me when he had phoned but I knew that news of our cohabitation was already common knowledge. It took less time than I had anticipated. Lucia gave me a pair of gardening gloves, some secateurs and a wicker basket and told me to start work cutting the grapes on the other side of her own row so that we could talk. She showed me what to do and then, without even stopping to draw breath, plunged in,

"So, Annina, you are living with Joe. I knew it would happen right from the beginning. I told you that he was perfect for you, do you remember? I said to Pietro that it was only a question of time. Are you happy?" She gave me no time to reply. "Of course you are, I can see it in your eyes. Your skin is glowing and you look prettier. I think you have put a bit of weight back on too. That is good. Men like something to get hold of in a woman. Now you need to let your hair grow long again or else you will not be able to wear it up for the wedding." She was shouting by now because, being more used to the work, she was quicker than me and had moved down about three vines ahead of me. She did not see my astounded face or the furious colour that rose in my cheeks at her casual assumption that there was a wedding for her to look forward to. Fortunately, Joe and Pietro were too far away to hear. I let Lucia get even further away from me until she finally stopped gossiping and then I began cutting the grapes again.

The black bunches were surprisingly heavy and they made a very satisfying squelch when they hit the other bunches in the basket. Dozy wasps droned, moving drunkenly away from the grapes they were gorging on when I wafted at them with my gloved hand. My gloves were soon covered in juice and my fingers were damp and sticky inside. I filled my basket and bent to pick it up then grunted in surprise at its weight and put it quickly back down. Joe passed by at the end of my row, on his way to tip his basket into the tractor-trailer and saw me struggling. He called to me to leave it and when he came back he joined me, kissed me thoroughly, then swung my heavy basket up and off, as though it weighed nothing. While I waited for him to come back with the empty basket I picked another bunch and began eating the sweet grapes, spitting the pips out at my feet. The vines were heavy with fruit and smelt divine, sweet and occasionally slightly alcoholic when the grapes were over ripe and swarming with wasps. Joe brought the basket back and I held up my bunch for him to bite

188

into. Juice ran down his chin and I reached up and licked it off. Joe grasped my hips and pulled me close. He nuzzled my bare neck and when I shuddered he sunk his teeth into the tender flesh at my collar bone, not hard enough to hurt but enough to make me gasp.

"I love your hair short like this," he growled "but if you ever let it grow again I want to see you wear it like Lucia's. I've always had a thing about that little Dutch girl look." I shoved him away with a smile, then I thought of something else and called him back,

"Joe. What do we do about a toilet?" I asked. He snorted and pointed to the trees at the edge of the vineyard.

"Oh, no!" I said and he nodded and went away laughing.

The cloud layer thinned enough to let the sun through in patches as I made my way back from the improvised toilet. Luna had found my mission very interesting and made me giggle when she crouched down alongside me and, in the way of women all the world over, we went to the toilet together. I had begun to feel hot, so I pulled off my jumper and tied it around my waist. After a while, my fingers began to be a bit sore, in spite of the protective gloves, and I was glad when Lucia came to get me for a break. The tractor-trailer was parked under a walnut tree and Lucia had spread a blanket on the ground in its shade. I plonked myself down next to Joe and peeled off my gloves. We had only finished half the vineyard and the other plants stretched out in long rows, heavy with black bunches that threatened to reduce my hands to a mess of sore blisters that afternoon.

Although Pietro looked after all the manor house's vines during the year, the harvest itself was handled by temporary workers who were brought in especially for the job. The overseer had been to the manor a couple of days previously and had decided to wait one more week before beginning the harvest but Pietro thought that it would rain and did not want to risk the grapes in his personal vineyard being spoilt. He did not have a lot of faith in the overseer's worth. Years before, when Pietro had first asked Joe to help out with his harvest Joe had refused payment but accepted the wine that Pietro had insisted on giving him. Over the years they had developed a kind of ritual of harvesting the field together and having a harvest picnic at the same time.

I was surprised to find that it was already one thirty. I also discovered that I was starving and when Lucia unpacked a hamper she had brought, full of Tuscan bread, sliced ham and salami and thick wedges of cheese, I tucked in, almost matching Joe with my enthusiasm. Pietro opened a bottle of wine and we drank from plastic beakers. We ate and drank and chatted, lolling on the ground in bacchanal revelry, until every last crumb had been eaten. To finish with, Pietro cut bunches of red uva-fragola which he grew especially as table fruit; tiny, seed-filled pods of strawberry-flavoured grapes. I lay with my head on Joe's lap, watching patterns of sky behind the walnut leaves, only half listening as Pietro explained that a classic Chianti wine was made with a blend of red Canaiolo and white Malvasia and Albana grapes. The red colour of the wine had little to do with the colour of the grapes but was determined by the tannin found in the stalks and skins of the crushed grapes.

"I use the same equipment that my father used and his father before him,"

"Yes!" broke in Lucia in irritation and jerked me awake again, "and you shouldn't. It is backbreaking work and you could use the machinery that the manor house uses, or better still add our grapes to theirs and let them pay you with bottles of their wine, the way they suggested. It is ridiculous to go on doing the wine ourselves like this."

Pietro looked at his wife's exasperated face and sighed. I had never seen him get annoyed with Lucia, he seemed to realise that her frequent attacks on him were caused by concern; a caustic demonstration of her love for him. He did not let himself be browbeaten either, though. He locked eyes with her and said stubbornly,

190

"Their wine does not taste as good as ours. They put too many chemicals in so that it always tastes the same. When I drink my wine I want to remember each individual summer - how the grapes grew and how I judged their sweetness. I want to remember what the vineyard was like in that particular year. I will do it the traditional way until I am too old to do it at all and then I will drink up every bottle that I have stored away and hope that I die before it runs out." Lucia tutted under her breath but relented when Pietro pulled one of her girlish plaits and she shrugged and patted his hand.

After lunch Pietro and Joe drove the tractor up the hill to unload the grapes at the manor, while Lucia and I began to work again. The alcoholic rush from the wine kept me going for a while but by the time Joe and Pietro came back with the empty trailer, I was flagging. My fingers had blisters on them and my shoulders and back were throbbing. I tried cutting with my left hand for a while but it was awkward and soon those fingers were hurting too. I wasn't the only one to feel this way. At the end of the row I was working I came upon Lucia sitting on the ground, looking quite exhausted. She gave a small smile when she saw me but for the first time since I had known her, she was too tired to speak.

We didn't finish the vineyard until late afternoon and then Joe and I drove up to the manor in the jeep while Lucia sat slumped next to Pietro on the tractor. Luna wasn't at all tired of course and as soon as we reached the manor she bounded off to play around with the other dogs. I envied her energy. It was all I could do to keep from groaning when I realised that we hadn't finished yet. I thought longingly of the hot shower I would have as soon as I got home, following Joe into Pietro's large garage where he began shovelling the grapes into a mangle on top of a huge wooden barrel. My stride faltered as I reached the doorway and a sudden thought hit me. Joe looked up at me and I smiled at him to reassure him that I was fine. He turned back to the mangle, arm muscles bulging as he swung a heavy shovelful of dripping grapes up and tipped them into the machine. I had suddenly realised that I

191

thought of Joe's house as home. It was my home more completely than any other place had ever been and it was so because I belonged with Joe.

Joe worked with a quiet concentration that told me that he too was at the limit of his force. He measured each swing of the shovel until the mangle was full, then he tossed the shovel onto the pile of grapes on the floor and wiped his hands on his jeans. He shoved his hair out of his eyes and then stepped up onto a metal crate and began to turn the mangle handle. His white t-shirt was stained with purple-blue juice and wet with sweat. His hair was wet too and clung damply to his face.

"I want to get as much done as I can so that I spare Pietro a bit," he explained, his voice echoing slightly around the stone walls. He finished with the mangle, stepped down and picked up the shovel again. I sank down on the old manger built into the wall and rested, since there was nothing I could do to help. Outside the dogs began to bark joyously and I heard the tractor rumble across the cobbled stones. Pietro reversed the trailer into the garage and Lucia and I gave him a hand to tip it up and let the rest of the grapes tumble onto the ground. Pietro picked up another shovel and joined Joe by the mangle. They shovelled alternatively until the mangle was full then took it in turns to wind the handle, crushing the grapes that fell with a splashy, squishy noise into the barrel.

"Come on Anna. We will get them a drink and a snack. They will need it." Lucia took me by the arm and I followed her up to the apartment. I washed my hands and used the toilet thankfully, then I went into the kitchen and helped Lucia get some food ready. Once back in her kitchen, she seemed less tired and I was dreading a new onslaught of *Joe* questions but luckily, she was too caught up in the food preparation. We whisked eggs and fried onions for a thick frittata. Lucia cut slabs of bread and gave me a bottle of wine and one of water to carry down while she brought the food on a tray.

In the barn the men had almost finished with the mangle but they refused the food until they had finished, I think because they knew that once they stopped they would be too tired to carry on. Joe heaved the last of the grapes up and Pietro gave a vigorous twist of the mangle handle then they straightened up and grinned wearily at each other.

Lucia wet an old towel she got from a shelf and tenderly wiped Pietro's face with it. He was too tired to protest. He sat down on a broken old chair and let her take care of him. I found the tenderness between them overwhelmingly touching and looked over at Joe to see if he had noticed them. I found him looking at me instead. His mouth twitched into a tired smile. I crossed over to him and wiped his face with my filthy t-shirt, which made him laugh. I bent down and kissed his damp hair.

"Come and eat something, love. You look so tired." I took his hand and led him over to where Lucia had laid out the food on a battered wooden bench. Joe made a sandwich from two slabs of bread and a huge slice of frittata, sat back on the rim of the manger and pulled me down onto his knee. I reached out and took a piece of frittata too. Lucia and Pietro were watching us fondly. Pietro poured the wine and Lucia brought us two glasses and we toasted each other, munching in peaceful harmony.

"E fatto" It is done, Pietro said in quiet satisfaction. "Grazie."

Joe waved away the thanks with a tired roll of his hand. A faint noise, like the crackle of static caught my attention. I looked outside. The dogs scampered across the courtyard towards the garage and joined us, shaking themselves vigorously.

Pietro slapped his hand on his trouser leg, triumphant at being proved right, as the rain that he had been so concerned about fell outside in a cool, scented drizzle that slowly darkened the cobbles.

18

There is a mellowness to autumn that I revel in, aware that winter is not far behind. Wind tugs leaves from the branches and they swirl and dance like multi-coloured butterflies. Rain seeps deep into summer-hardened earth, swelling streams and bursting rivers, which, flooding, feed the earth again. Moisture rises up to shroud the land in mist, or soften the frosty dawn. Drowsy wasps move drunkenly from grape to grape. Rain patters on dry leaves. Bonfires crackle, insects drone, small creatures scuttle in the hedgerows. Warm days and frosty nights. The scent of wood fires and roasting chestnuts. Sticky fallen fruit fermenting on the ground. Odours of moss and fungi and leaf mould.
All this autumn offers; rich as an artist's pallet, a sensual feast.

Pietro's weather forecast had indeed been correct. We had a week of intermittent drizzle and warm sunshine. The nights were not as cold as they had been before the rain but everywhere I looked the countryside was changing. Hidden by mild, misty mornings the trees suddenly bloomed into bright shades of yellow, orange and red. Gentle breezes teased and tugged among the branches, then tossed the dry leaves into the air. Where they fell, they formed a colourful carpet for Luna to dash through; scattering the leaves once more and ploughing sodden paths across the ground, grinding the rich palette prematurely to streaks of slick brown. The misty air, when I opened the shutters in the morning, was saturated with the musty, muddy scent of wet grass and leaf mould. I was reminded daily of Keats's description of autumn as a *season of mist and mellow fruitfulness.*

Joe and I had ached for days after the grape harvest and Lucia had phoned to tell us that Pietro was in bed with a bad back, or to use her colourful expression *il colpo della strega*, the witch's blow. He was remarkably resilient though and a few days later he called us himself. I was in the kitchen when Joe answered the phone. He beckoned to me and I joined him and stood close enough to hear. Joe's end of the conversation had already given me a clue to the identity of the caller, consisting as it did of a series of monosyllabic replies and meaningful grunts. Now I could hear a background bubble of lament as Lucia raged at her husband at the other end of the line. Pietro ignored her stoically.

"When?" Joe asked, running his hand up my spine. I snuggled closer to him.

"I will come past your place at six tomorrow morning."

"You are a stupid, stubborn man." Lucia shrieked, "You can only just manage to sit to pull on your own underpants again, let alone tie up your shoes and you expect to go ... "

"Fine." Joe replied. They both said goodbye together and Pietro put down the phone.

"Poor Pietro. Lucia sounded really cross." I turned to face Joe, wrapped my arms around him and leant back to look up at his face.

"I expect that is why he wants to get out of the house." His eyes narrowed to dark slits as I wriggled my hips teasingly against him.

"Good job he didn't want to go this morning," I said. Joe answered with one of those meaningful, manly grunts he had just been practising with Pietro and, to my delight, carried me back up the stairs.

At six thirty the following morning, I wondered why I had agreed to come mushrooming. I had revised my opinion about it not being so cold at night. At this time of the morning, with fingers of fog sliding into the gaps in my clothes, the very air that we breathed seemed to be unpleasantly wet and cool. I could not recognise the path that we were on, although I knew it was one I had walked frequently. Trees loomed out of the fog, limiting our consciousness to a dim circle of dark trunks within an eerie wall of white. The earthen path was broken by rivulets formed by last night's rain and slippery underfoot. The only sounds were the sporadic patter of water dripping from above and the harsh "caw" as rooks cried a warning of our approach.

Pietro however knew exactly where we were, leading us forward at an excruciatingly slow pace, stopping every few seconds to poke at the leaf mould with his stick and then exclaim in frustration. So far the mushroom hunting expedition had not been a great success. I wished that I had stayed in bed but kept quiet, walking a few paces behind the two men so that their bulk at least rid the path of cobweb strands and I did not have to keep brushing them off my face but could leave my hands jammed in the relative warmth of my pockets.

Usually, when I walked, the ground was the place that I paid the least attention to. My eyes were more naturally drawn to the patterns of green and blue in the canopy above, or to the ever-changing beauty of the trees themselves. However, today Pietro was like a truffle dog, with all his attention focussed on the ground and Joe and I obediently followed suit. I really wouldn't have minded if we did not find porcini. I enjoyed their flavour in sauces but on the few occasions that I had eaten them fried, the way the locals raved about, they had left me cold. There was something about the softness of the flesh inside the crisp, oily batter that turned my stomach. They had an odour of decay and I was always extremely aware that only an expert could tell the difference between an innocuous porcino and a poisonous *malefico*.

"Ah." A gasp of awe made me catch up with the men. They were both crouched around a raised bump of dried leaves between exposed oak roots.

"Guarda! Che bellezza, Annina." Pietro's tone was reverent. "What a beauty," he declared, smoothing away the leaves to reveal the dark brown back of a large mushroom. A porcino. Thank goodness, I thought, maybe we could go home now. My feet were freezing and my nose felt as if it was dripping. I caught Joe's sardonic glance and ignored it. He knew my sentiments about mushrooms very well. I did not want to upset Pietro though, so I made all the right noises of pleasure as he gently prised it from the ground and placed it in his basket. Pietro was transformed. His granite face split into the deep crevasses of a happy smile. Under thick silver brows, damp with mist, his eyes shone with the thrill of the chase. He was on a quest. Renewed by his discovery he set off once more, basket clutched tight in his fist.

Joe bent and kissed me lightly on my cheek.

"Are you ok?" he asked with a smile. I gave him a wry look then nodded. Strangely enough, seeing Pietro's pleasure had cheered me up a bit and now, to encourage me further, the fog was beginning to clear as the sun burnt through, evaporating it.

Watching the ground had its advantages. I spotted some beautiful wild cyclamens in the undergrowth and delicate ferns unravelling their fronds on muddy banks. A snail slimed a trail across a tree stump. Cushions of star-shaped moss glowed a green so bright that it was almost luminescent. Clumps of lichen; miniature, silver-green, tree skeletons; were fresh and surprisingly spongy to the touch and the moss was dew-wet and soft as velvet.

As the morning drew on the sun got warmer until the last lingering patches of mist cleared and I was able to take off my red rain-jacket and tie it around my hips. I was wearing red and Joe had on a yellow fleece top because of Pietro's warning about hunters. Pietro himself was wearing his usual muddy colours but had tied a jaunty red scarf at the neck. I suppressed a giggle at the thought of him wearing a camouflage outfit so that he could sneak up on unsuspecting fungi.

He had reassured us that we should be safe today. He knew most of the local people, had been hunting with them all his life and regularly met up with them at the village bar in the evenings. Over a coffee and the occasional grappa he and his cronies would gently probe each other for information on where to find the best mushrooms and plan their game hunting trips. Joe, I knew, had never become involved in the local passion for hunting. He had refused Pietro's efforts to teach him years ago and the old man had accepted that without trying to convince him, settling instead on teaching him the rudiments of mushrooming.

I found it hard to reconcile the thought of Pietro, the quiet man of the earth that I knew, with my image of a bloodthirsty hunter. I was frequently having to revise my old opinions here, in this world where nature was so real, so vital, that it was almost a protagonist in one's daily life. I was forever aware, not just of the picture postcard beauty that the tourists saw but also of the wilder, often vicious side of life. Earlier we had walked past the carcass of a fox lying by the side of the path next to the wire fence that demarked the territory of the hunting reserve. It had been recognisable only by the colour of the few tufts of rotting fur left among the cleanly picked bones. There had been no smell of death, in fact Luna had not even paused to sniff at the skeleton. Pietro had said that it had probably died of natural causes; old age maybe, or it might have somehow got caught in the wire fence and been unable to escape. It was a macabre reminder of the primitive, untameable side of nature. Through the wire I had been able to make out the green mesh of hunting hides, nesting in the trees like dark deformities.

I knew I would never be able to enjoy hunting myself, shuddered at the proximity of it here and yet I was no longer sure that it was something to be condemned. I had eaten the game that Lucia sometimes gave me, knowing that Pietro had killed it himself. I had watched Fiammetta carry home huge bundles of the best wild grasses for her rabbits, so that they would be well fed and therefore taste better when she killed them. Animals were made for eating but alongside the practicality there was also respect, an awareness of the way the animal lived and of its death, which was totally missing in the pre-packaged, cellophane-wrapped meat found in a supermarket.

Joe stopped sharply in front of me and if we had been walking any faster I would have bumped into him. I thought he must have seen a mushroom. I hoped he had, because since Pietro had found the first one hours ago, we had seen no sign of other edible fungi, although Pietro had pointed out many species of toadstool to us. I walked around Joe. He was examining a fallen branch that lay

198

across a rock at the side of the path. He bent and ran his fingers slowly over the bark. Mottled with lichen crust, the rock supported a sinuous curve of moss-furred wood. Joe shook his head. He looked up at me and said,

"No matter how hard I try, Annie, I won't ever be able to create anything half as beautiful as this." I held his hand as we walked on and thought how lucky I was to be loved by this man.

Half an hour later Pietro found a mushroom field. We came out of the trees into a newly cleared section of forest. In the summer he had cut the saplings here for firewood and now, among the stumps, leaves and grass we found about twenty *bubbole*, otherwise known as drumstick mushrooms, which they resembled as they grew, before the tips opened out wide and they took on the appearance of small umbrellas. These tall mushrooms were so easy to spot that even I would have found them. Luna got sworn at because, infected by the general excitement, she crashed right through the bubbole that Pietro had been stooping to pick. I took her by her collar and we sat on a tree stump and watched the men pick the others. Pietro was not satisfied with what he considered to be inferior mushrooms but his expression of pain as he straightened up indicated that his back could no longer be ignored and he decided to call it a day. He produced a plastic bag from a pocket and divided up the mushrooms.

"Plastic bags are no good for collecting mushrooms really," he explained "a reed basket is best because it allows the spore to fall through the holes. You must always try to give back to the forest that which it gives to you." Joe assured him that he would acquire a basket and then insisted that Pietro take the precious porcino back for Lucia. Pietro gave a satisfied grin and didn't protest at all.

Our way home lay in the opposite direction and as we set off down the narrow track that Pietro indicated for us to follow, I thought I recognised this part of the forest from my dreams. Joe's stomach had begun to rumble ominously; he was probably imagining ways of cooking the bubbole, but he was very noble and accepted a detour when I suggested it. At first the going was easy. The temperature was perfect for walking and the fog a mere memory. It was warm enough not to need our jackets and specks of sunlight penetrated the russets and greens of the foliage, dappling our faces.

I was sure now that this path was the same one that I followed relentlessly in my dreams that led to Fiammetta's hollow. The deer track was wide enough here for us to walk side by side, although I knew that soon it would narrow out as it began to twist along the gully. Ahead the track led uphill where the tips of cypresses topped the rounded canopy of the forest in jagged protrusions. On either side of the path, between the trees, the undergrowth was a thick tangle of bushes; junipers, hiding misty green and purple berries amongst their spines; rosehips glowing bright on leafless briars and the occasional *corbezzolo*.

Something crunched beneath my boot. I was treading acorns into the soft earth and in an instant I flashed back through time and was standing between the long, tweedy legs of my father and my mother's nylons and sturdy walking shoes. Mother was holding something out to me; a knobbly acorn cup with a smooth, shiny inside. Mother laughed down at me and then up at my father. Her cheeks were pink from the exertion of walking and she was happy as she explained that the fairies used the acorn cups to drink from.

I snapped back to the present. Joe was looking at me quizzically. I picked up an acorn, popped it from its cup and handed to him.

"I just remembered something nice about my mother, about her showing me acorn cups like these." Joe squeezed my hand in understanding. As we carried on I realised that this one, small memory had helped to ease the bitterness I harboured for my mother in my heart.

We reached the side of the gully. I looked through the beech trees that straggled down the steep banks to the riverbed below. It was no longer dry. A small trickle of water seeped along the bottom, stirring leaves, gurgling over rotten branches. I felt a sudden, unexpected chill run through me. I began to lead the way alongside the gully but the track no longer seemed familiar. I pushed on but with less conviction. All of a sudden it seemed wrong to bring Joe here. It had become inexplicably cold as if the thick forest had cut out the sunlight. It was almost as if some force had closed off the path, putting obstacles in our way. I looked behind me. Even Luna seemed to be effected by the surroundings and was pressed close to Joe's legs. Fine threads of web caught on my face and brambles clung to my jeans. I tripped and the thorns snagged along my hand, raising tiny bubbles of blood. I stopped, sucked my hand and decided to turn back.

"I can't remember the way." I lied and I think Joe saw the lie but left it unchallenged; the spooky atmosphere had got to him too. We retraced our steps and I felt the weight that had been pressing on me ever since we reached the gully lessen. The forest had forgiven us again now that we were heading away from the hollow.

There was a rustle in the undergrowth. Luna pricked up her ears but stayed by Joe's legs. The thought of meeting wild boar on this narrow path was unnerving. The noise came again and then I gave a sigh of relief as Fiammetta stepped onto the track in front of us.

"Ciao ragazza." She took in our bedraggled appearance with a dry look and began to walk towards us. She did not look well. She walked slowly, stooped, with an old woman's gait. She looked too small for her shapeless clothes; an ancient polyester dress with a knotty brown cardigan over it, done up to the neck for warmth. Her white hair was unkempt and had lost its shine. Only her eyes were the same, sky blue and mocking. Luna ran to her and sniffed excitedly at her saggy cardigan pockets. Fiammetta gave the dog a sharp glance and mumbled something. Luna sank down onto her haunches, nostrils quivering at the scent coming from the pocket but well behaved again. What a handy knack she had for calming the dog.

I introduced Joe and he took Fiammetta's hand and kissed it. I was as surprised by his gallant gesture as I was by Fiammetta's reaction to it. She became quite girlish, looking up at Joe

201

coquettishly and nodding her approval but when she spoke she addressed her remarks to me as if Joe was not there, or as if he could not understand her.

"Hai scelto bene, vedo. You chose well, I see," she informed me then took me by the elbow and led me back up the path in the direction of the hollow, so that Joe could not hear.

"Girl, this is not the place for him, not yet. The hollow is our place, our secret place, do you understand?" She rubbed my cheek and her fingers were cold and papery rough. She jerked her head toward the gully.

La Radura delle Driade, the old people called it. Do you know what I mean?" I shook my head. "Radura" meant a clear space in a forest but I did not know the other word.

"Driade – the spirits that live in the trees – the nymphs of the forest." Of course. What a fitting name for the place, Dryad's hollow. I nodded and she cackled and poked at me with her bony finger.

"It is the secret place for the daughters of the cypress. The ancient ones thought it was a sacred place. Men were allowed there only for their fertility rituals – they were very welcome then, believe me," she cackled again and broke off in a fit of coughing that left her clinging to me, breathless.

"Fiammetta, come and sit down until you feel stronger. Joe and I will take you home. You don't look at all well." I looked for Joe and saw that he was already making his way up the path, a concerned expression creasing his brow. Fiammetta heard him and waved him away with a tired movement of her arm until he stopped, reluctantly. The old woman straightened up with an effort. Her eyes blazed feverishly showing a desperate force of will that kept her going, in spite of her weakness.

"It is a place where the energy of the earth is at its peak. That is why the old ones worshiped the Earth Mother there. They gave the force many names, Demeter, Cybele, Hera, all names to symbolise the force of continuity." Her eyes had lost their focus the way they had done when I had visited her home and she had spoken to me of Joe's return and the blood moon.

"The cycle of life. That is what we seek to understand, it is what the cypress teaches. The quiet man will be welcome in the hollow only at the time of the blood moon. When it is time you will know." She paused, drew a deep, tremulous breath. Her eyes, still locked into a trance stared right through me.

"Do not mistake conception for a beginning, nor death for an end. These limitations do not apply. Fly beyond them, girl. Fly free. If you are lost, swirl within the cypress and you will find me."

Joe crunched through the leaves towards us. His face was set in a stubborn expression and when he spoke it was with a gentle firmness that broached no argument.

"You are not well Signora. Why don't you lean on me and we will take you home?" Fiammetta shook her head and smiled at him. She patted his hand and I noticed that her fingers were filthy, nails dark with mud. She spoke to Joe for the first time;

"Thank you. I told the girl that she had chosen well. I don't need your help though. I will be fine, I feel much better now." Surprisingly she did sound better. Her voice was strong again and her eyes were bright and even slightly flirtatious. Once again I wondered what she had looked like when she was young. She gave me a grin of complicity as though she had read my mind.

"Come here dog." Fiammetta commanded and Luna jumped up at once. She sniffed madly at Fiammetta's pocket again but stopped immediately when the old woman lifted her hand. She chuckled, flashed a look from me to Joe and grinned craftily,

"There is something that you can do for me, if you will." Joe nodded hesitantly. He was aware that he had been trapped into something but was too polite to refuse whatever favour she had in mind.

"You can give this to Pietro. I won't be seeing him again to thank him, for the firewood that he never let me pay for and the

203

other odd jobs he's done for me." She dipped her grimy hand into her cardigan pocket and pulled out a handful of small acorns.

"For the rabbits," she smiled at me, rummaged again and produced a small, brownish ball. Joe and I peered at it. I wrinkled my nose. Whatever it was had a pungent odour which wasn't unpleasant but was extremely strong.

"A truffle." Joe identified the ball and took it between his own fingers, peering at it interestedly "I didn't know you could find them around here."

"If you know where to look." Fiammetta slid her eyes sideways at me and I had a sudden image of her kneeling in front of the giant oak that guarded the hollow, delving her fingers deep into the soft ground. She nodded, looking pleased with me. She rummaged once more in her pocket and produced another, slightly smaller truffle that she dropped into my hand and folded my fingers around. She pressed my fingers for a second and I knew that she wanted to say something more but instead she blinked away the moisture in her eyes, dropped my hand and began to walk away.

"Let us accompany you," Joe went to follow her but she waved him back. She took a long, hard look at us, her gaze moving slowly from my face up to Joe's. I had a horrible feeling all of a sudden that she was going away, that I would never see her again, which was ridiculous. As if she had read my mind, her eyes began to twinkle with suppressed mirth. She nodded at the truffles.

"They are aphrodisiacal you know. I don't suppose you two care about that but Lucia might be surprised." She threw back her head, cackled suggestively and walked away without a backward glance.

Joe watched Fiammetta until she was out of sight then turned his dark gaze on me. "Interesting lady," was all he said.

19

Autumn, season of Cybele. Goddess of the earth and the moon. Ruler of the natural world, goddess of fertility and magic. Throughout the centuries men have linked the cypress with Cybele, representing life after death and comfort from grief.
They call us the tree of the blood moon, October's hunter moon.
I observe the frantic movement and blur of colour around me with contentment. My roots luxuriate in water, warm and abundant. My evergreen tips sway to the rhythm of the playful wind as it tugs and tumbles my swollen cones to the ground.
In the soil at my base, the last green grass of the year grows between the moss-patterned Etruscan stones. In this small hollow the old one will lie, head resting on the earth's soft pillow. Earth to earth.
She will turn her sky-blue eyes to me one last time and I will look back at her, until her soul soars free and her new journey begins.

I stayed at home when Joe drove up to take the truffle to Pietro that evening. I needed some time alone and withdrew from the thought of Lucia's incessant chatter. Thoughts of Fiammetta had stayed with me all that day, hovering in my mind as soon as I lost focus of the everyday business of changing my clothes, preparing lunch and chatting to Joe. Her spirit seemed as strong as her body had appeared weak, another one of those contradictions that I was always encountering in the old woman. I could feel her presence in my head, hear her voice intoning the words *blood moon* and *Dryads Hollow*. The warm blue sky through the kitchen window was the exact colour of her eyes, glazed over as if in a trance, in communion with the elements.

At dinner I managed to shake off the strange mood that had gripped me as I stood by the oven and watched Joe flipping and flattening the bubbole heads with a wooden spoon as he cooked them. The scent of mushrooms and garlic filled the room, mingling with steam from the pasta pan and the berry-sharp tang of wine as I raised my glass.

Joe was laughingly recounting Lucia's reaction to the truffle gift. I could imagine all too well her indignant tutting as Pietro unwrapped the unassuming looking, warty ball and filled her immaculate kitchen with its overpowering odour. Joe described Pietro as being quieter than usual when Joe had told him about Fiammetta, how she had said that she would not see him to thank him herself. Joe had omitted to mention in front of Lucia that Pietro had been giving the old woman free firewood.

I had been pondering her prophetic words and they had left me with a cold, hollow feeling inside. It was as if Fiammetta knew she was dying, could predict exactly when and where. I sensed that she was already so weak that any other person would have been lying immobile in a hospital bed but she was striving to keep going, by sheer force of will, until the moment she had designated to be the right one.

I sipped my wine and watched Joe as he concentrated on the frying pan. His shoulders were so broad that they blocked my view of the pan. He wore jeans and an old grey sweatshirt with a pair of comfortable, old-man style slippers without socks, as a concession to the autumn chill that permeated the terracotta tiles. He had pushed up the sweatshirt sleeves and his tanned arms were sinewy and strong. He smiled at me over his shoulder, reflected light glittering in his dark eyes so that they looked a tawny gold, then quickly turned back to the pan. He slid three bubbole onto each plate and passed them to me as he checked the pasta once more. The mushrooms had shrunk quite a lot in cooking but each one still measured about 10cm across. I tried a bite and was pleasantly surprised to find them deliciously firm, garlicky and hot. I could taste the forest in them. Joe cut slabs of bread and began to mop up the juices on his plate. He raised an eyebrow at me to ask if I wanted bread but I smiled and shook my head. The first few minutes of a meal were nearly always silent as Joe

206

concentrated on filling the aching gap in his stomach. Once the first hunger pangs were stilled he would relax, push back slightly in his chair and begin to talk.

I found myself thinking about Pietro and Fiammetta again. Fiammetta was probably about ten years older than Pietro and I had a sudden flash of knowledge, as vivid as a memory, although it could not possibly have been a memory of mine, and again I felt Fiammetta's presence nearby.

I saw Pietro as a teenager riding a bike that seemed far too small for him, dismounting and propping it against a hedge in the village. He was already tall and square, his young face sculpted into sharp planes of solid bone. His hair was a wild, curly mass, rebelliously defying the fashion edicts of that time. His clean white shirt was pulled tightly around his wide neck by a formal tie and he now took a grey suit jacket from the back of his bicycle and shrugged it on. People walked past heading for the church and shouted greetings at him but he seemed distracted, as if waiting for someone. Then all at once a dull red flush spread up his neck and across his cheeks and I saw his eyes light up as he watched a woman swing towards the church from the opposite end of the village. He had stopped in the best place to observe her without seeming to do so but the woman knew he was there. She was tiny but shapely, in a tight-waisted red dress patterned with blue flowers. Her hair curled and swung around her shoulders as she moved, glinting deep chestnut where the sun stroked her. She walked alone and although the other people around her nodded politely there was no warmth in their greeting. As she passed a group of older women and men she bobbed quickly, a gesture that was half respectful bow and half mischief but she kept her eyes on the ground, so that no one could read her expression. Now that she was closer I could see that her dress was old, faded at the seams and frayed a little at the collar but she wore it as a flower wears its petals, with the wild audacity of a woman comfortable with her own beauty. When she was near the church she stopped. Tossing back her hair she looked directly across at Pietro and she smiled.

In the knowing, mocking smile, I recognised Fiammetta. Her eyes were brighter than the sky and they saw straight through the youth who stood immobilised by desire in the shadows of the persimmon tree. Then she spun on her heels, was swallowed by the gloom of the church and Pietro was free to move again; drawn from the shade and across the square towards Fiammetta, his *little flame*.

Joe scraped the last of the mushroom juice onto his crust and carried it across the kitchen with him as he checked on the pasta. He judged it cooked, crammed the bread into his mouth and chewed while he strained the pasta and tossed it in butter. He carried the pan to the table and dished it up then unwrapped the truffle from the damp paper we had put it in earlier and grated it on top of the pasta.

The truffle was exquisite. Joe and I made appreciative noises simultaneously and we both laughed. Joe pushed back his chair a little and chewed more slowly.

"You know what you asked me about the hunter's moon?" he asked and I nodded. I had told him a bit of what Fiammetta had said to me and asked him if he knew what the hunter's moon was. Joe had told me that it referred to the full moon in October when, in the olden days, it was considered the perfect time to hunt, although nowadays most of the hunters preferred to get out early in the morning and spend the nights in the warmth of their homes rather than running around in the forest in the dark. He had also had an explanation for it being known as the blood moon; something technical to do with a lunar eclipse that turned the pale moon to orange and red, although not every October full moon coincided with a lunar eclipse. Instead of becoming totally dark when the earth blocked the sun's reflection, the earth's atmosphere scattered the light spectrum and bent the red hues toward the moon.

Joe glanced up at the calendar on the wall. His dark scribble covered the page, with important dates highlighted in red, which almost covered the printed graphics showing the phases of the moon.

"It is tomorrow actually." Joe said and I felt as though I had been punched in the stomach. I pushed my plate away, not hungry anymore and folded my arms across myself as icy fingers of foreboding gripped me from inside.

That night was the first time since moving in with Joe that I did not dream and that was more disturbing than any dream could have been. In the dreamless void of the night I shivered, in spite of the warm covers that I pulled up around me and Joe's body radiating heat alongside. My head began to throb, my whole body to vibrate until I finally jerked awake with the noise of the cypress screaming in my head.

I stumbled from the bed, feeling my way through the grey dawn that slipped around the shutters and grabbed my clothes from the chair where I had thrown them the night before. In the bathroom, I found that I had dropped my bra and one sock but the call of the cypress was too urgent to go back and search for them so I pulled on my jeans, jumper and shoes, ignoring the unfamiliar rasp of wool and leather on my bare skin.

I ran downstairs, grabbed my car keys from the hall table and pushed Luna back inside when she tried to leave the house with me. The wind flipped my hair across my face and tossed a shower of leaves across the car. My fingers felt clumsy as I groped for the lock. The sky was the glowering pewter of the pre-dawn. I drove carefully down the drive, trying not to wake Joe with the noise then as soon as I judged that I was far enough away I pressed my foot hard on the accelerator. I was hardly aware of my surroundings. The noise that summoned me was overpowering, discordant and unrelenting. I drove too fast, skidding a little on the bends, desperate to reach the cypress. My old house came into view, a dim shadow hunched below the strip of dark cloud that cut the tops off the mountains and furled down the lower slopes like a ragged fringe. A tiny speck of gold slid from behind the cloud and the landscape began to glow as the sun coloured the day. I slammed the car to a halt next to the jasmine bush and got out. The air was cold and I wished that I had brought a coat. I noticed in

209

passing that the garden already looked unkempt and abandoned. Wild twists of wisteria snaked through the hedge and across the path, pointing towards the cypress.

The noise in my head had diminished now that I was near the cypress. I moved along the path, staring up at it, trying to understand why I had been summoned. Then I saw a streak of blue at the foot of the tree and broke into a run. Fiammetta lay, as she had planned, in the grassy gap between the old stones. She was wearing her best clothes; a blue silk blouse under a navy suit and impractical black patent leather shoes that were ruined with mud.

"Hello girl," she croaked when she saw me. She looked as though she was dead already, cold and white, lying in a stone coffin. A gold crucifix that I hadn't noticed before lay across her neck. I sank to my knees next to her and tried to take her head into my lap but she stopped me. She grasped my hand with her frozen claw and spoke so softly that I could hardly hear. She was fighting for breath and her voice was hoarse and weak but her eyes fixed mine in intense, blue supplication.

"Let me be. I am where I want to be ...... I want to smell the earth once more; let it cradle me." The rising sun smoothed away the last shadows and gleamed gold into her white hair, slid over her face in a warm caress. Fiammetta smiled, then the light in her eyes faded.

I saw her soul rise from her body; a clear silver light. I felt her wrap around me and then rise up and slip among the dark branches of the cypress. I did not want her to go. I felt bereft without her. I was drawn after her and looking down, saw myself kneeling by her body, gripping her hand tightly but neither of us were really there.

I followed her as she spiralled upwards. The cypress was singing now, a sweetly poignant melody; a hymn of remembrance; a gentle invocation of blessing as she passed. At the tip of the tree Fiammetta streaked upward along a slender ray of sunlight that cut through the clouds and I reached out towards her but the cypress held me back. It held me gently, tenderly in its branches; rocked

210

me as I cried, crooned to me as I struggled. Trapped like a dryad in its loving embrace, I surrendered. I lay enclosed within the cypress, gazing up at the infinite blue stretching above the clouds.

Joe was calling my name, fear making his voice harsh. I heard Luna's crazed barking and frantic scratching as she tried to get out of the jeep. I was warmer and I realised that Joe had draped his jacket around my shoulders. It smelt of him. I could smell Joe, the cypress, the damp grass. I opened my eyes and found that I was still kneeling with Fiammetta's hand clasped in mine but the hand was cold and lifeless. She was no longer there.

I looked at Joe. He clasped my face between his hands and said my name over and over like a prayer. I had never seen Joe look scared. I looked up and realised that the sun had fully risen and that I must have been kneeling there for a long time.

"I'm ok." My voice sounded strange, distant and hollow. I slid my fingers away from Fiammetta's, stroked her blue silk collar.

"She's dead, Annie."

"Yes, I know." I smiled at him, tried to move and realised that I was too stiff. Joe helped me stand and then pulled me roughly into his arms and held me tight, rubbing my neck to release the tension there. I buried my face in his shoulder; hot tears soaking into his shirt as I stood in his clumsy embrace. His lips pressed into my hair, his heart beat close to mine. Beneath the sorrow that I felt for Fiammetta, came the joyful realisation that, for the first time since I was a young child, I could cry and there would be someone there to hold me while I did.

"I'm all right." I mumbled into his chest and I was. Joe was the one who needed looking after, I realised. He'd had a shock, finding me like that and not being able to make me respond when he spoke to me. At that moment I heard a siren and turned inside Joe's arms to watch an ambulance race along the road, bouncing and bumping towards us. Joe must have called them I realised.

I let Joe deal with the ambulance crew, while I climbed into the backseat of the jeep and rubbed Luna's nose. She thrust her head as far as she could between the bars and I lay mine on the seat back and let her lick my face clean of tears. When she was certain that I was unhurt she rested her nose next to my head and with a huge sigh, studied me with her warm, brown, eyes.

Joe glanced at me every few seconds while he showed the ambulance men Fiammetta's body and explained how he had found her. He hadn't dressed properly either, I noticed. He was wearing slippers with his jeans and his hair wasn't brushed. Two men brought a stretcher from the ambulance but Joe stood in front of them and said something that I could not hear, then he bent down and picked Fiammetta up in his arms. She looked as small as a child, shrunken and misshapen but even in death there was something rebellious about her. She had chosen when and where to die, she had even chosen what to wear. The blaze of her silk blouse was a defiant statement, shouting out to the world that she had not been afraid.

I looked at the cypress standing aloof, casting a shadow across Fiammetta's body as Joe carried her to the ambulance.

Do not mistake conception for a beginning nor death for an end. These limitations do not apply. Fly beyond them, girl. Fly free. If you are lost, swirl within the cypress and you will find me. I do not know whether I just remembered her words or whether the cypress whispered them to me but I did not feel sad any more. Fiammetta was not lost, she had just moved on to a new kind of existence and the cypress had held me back because it had been her time to leave, not mine.

The ambulance drove off, in silence now that there was no need for haste. I got out of the jeep and went to Joe. Sun warmed my face and I had never felt so alive or so aware of the proximity of death. Joe took my hand, pulled me closer. His dark eyes scrutinized me and I smiled reassurance.

A shadow played across my face. I looked down; saw the shadow of the cypress stretch away from where we stood then sway very slightly in the wind, stroking back across us like an obscure caress. All around us the landscape was bright with drifting dappled leaves and autumnal berries. Only the cypress remained unchanged by the season, its intrinsic secrecy inviolate. No shafts of sunshine penetrated its density. The light, unable to pass through its armour of needles, enfolded the whole, creating a glowing aureole around the tree; an aura of calm. The wind pushed against the cypress until it bent just a little, its upper branches leaning towards us, making the shape of a bow. Air filled the bow and ruffled the needles. The resin scented air wafted coolly around my face and in my ears I heard the last, faint strains of the cypress's eulogistic song.

20

There are places and moments in time that are steeped in magic.
Moments where the divine reaches through all barriers: places that have
been recognised as holy since the first man gazed upon them.
You cannot seek this magic out but must wait for it to reveal itself to you.
As a lake is an eye in the earth, reflecting the heavens and hiding
beneath its surface the mysteries of the depths, so the eye of the hollow
also joins all worlds.
Below the surface lie hidden mysteries; the gentle flow of water, the
fertility of the earth, the passion of fire and the purity of air.
All the elements are wedded in such a place and the force of life is
overwhelming.

Joe would not let me drive home. He bundled me into the jeep and drove with one hand on my knee, as if to reassure himself that I was still there. Once back in the comforting familiarity of the kitchen, he busied himself making coffee and toast, treating me like a convalescent. I accepted the coffee but the toast tasted like sawdust and I pushed it away. For once Joe wasn't hungry either so I fed it to Luna with his approval.

"Luna warned me that something was wrong this morning. When you left, she came upstairs and jumped on the bed and would not leave me alone, even when I shouted at her, so I followed her downstairs." Joe rubbed a foot over the dog's back absentmindedly, his mind focused on the events of the morning. "She kept scratching at the door so I thought that she needed to have a wee. You weren't in the kitchen and I began to get worried and then I followed Luna out and I realised that your car was gone."

"Good girl, Luna." I fondled her silky ears and fed her the last piece of toast. The kitchen smelt of home. Last night's garlic and truffle scent lingered still and blended with the rich aroma of our coffee and Luna's warm fur. Thinking about last night reminded me of the vivid image I'd had, of Fiammetta and Pietro when they were young. I turned to Joe.

"Maybe you should go and tell Pietro what happened."

"We'll go together. I don't want to leave you."

"I'll be fine, Joe. I don't want Pietro to hear about it in the village." Joe nodded slowly and then agreed. He was aware of the friendship between the Fiammetta and Pietro too.

I watched him drive off, then called Luna to me and, coffee in hand, walked down to the lake. I sat on the bank and watched the wind play on the water. The willow branches whipped in and out of the water, churning it up. The bushes that edged the lake were reflected in its choppy surface; shades of amber and rust around a centre of blue. Gusts of wind ruffled the water too, sending ripples shimmering right across the lake. In the distorted reflection of sky there was rhythm in chaos. The wind gusted and ripples shivered across the water like a sudden tremor across an animal's flanks.

Fiammetta had chosen her day well. The warmth and beauty of a sunny autumn day and the underlying hint of wildness in the teasing wind. I would miss the old woman. Miss her physical presence in my life. Suddenly I knew what I wanted to do. Fiammetta had said that the hollow was our special place. She had also said that I could take Joe there on the day of the blood moon; well, that was today and it was there that I needed to go. I lifted my head, let the wind flip my hair back from my brow and turned towards the house with a new sense of purpose.

When Joe returned I was packing the picnic I had prepared into an old rucksack that I had found in his wardrobe. He put a bag down on the table and eyed the rucksack.

"Going somewhere?" he asked, a note of tension in his voice as if he thought that I was running away. I went over and kissed him.

"We both are." I reassured him and explained my need to celebrate Fiammetta in my own way.

215

Joe emptied a bag that he had brought back with him. Imagining how shocked I must feel to find someone dying, even though she was unaware of how close I had become to Fiammetta, Lucia had packed up the leftovers from their Sunday lunch for us. It was typical of her to imagine that every problem could be solved by food but I found it quite touching too. I had forgotten that it was Sunday and until now I'd had no idea how the time had flown and that it was early afternoon already. We put cold roast chicken and homemade apple cake into the rucksack along with the bread, cheese and wine that I had already gathered together. At the door I hesitated. Luna was all aquiver at the thought of a walk but I was reluctant to take her to the hollow. Joe understood my hesitance and, going to the cupboard where he kept all of the dog's food and treats, crouched down.

At once Luna's attention shifted to her master. She raced to him and took up the position of a pointer that has caught a scent. Joe rummaged. Luna's ears pricked up and swivelled with every noise. She dribbled on the tiles and licked her chops. Joe sat back and closed the cupboard. He was holding one of the special hide chews, shaped like a bone, which usually kept her happy for an hour or two. Luna daintily raised one paw in the air and then quickly swapped to the other, in case that one was more pleasing. Joe laughed and gave her the chew. She dashed under the table with it and paid us no more attention as we left the house.

We parked the jeep as close to the forest path as we could, pulling it off the road and into a gap between the junipers. Joe shrugged the rucksack onto his shoulders and I led the way into the trees. The atmosphere was so different today. The trail was easy to find, as if the forest was opening up to us. The wind was less powerful here, sheltered as we were by the mighty trees. Unseen birds chattered and scolded, then flew away with a whirr of wings. A breeze ruffled the canopy and disturbed the leaves sending them falling around us, like small yellow butterflies. I saw a puffball mushroom by the side of the path, its whiteness tinged with grey. I touched it with my boot and it collapsed, firing spore across my foot and into the fertile leaf mould.

You see girl, a beginning within an ending. No one spoke the words but I heard Fiammetta's voice in my head as clearly as if she was walking alongside me and I smiled.

We reached the gully. Joe took my hand as we looked down the steep slope to the slow trickling water. This was where, only yesterday, we had been forced to turn back by the hostility in the air around us. My eyes followed the path that edged the gully. There were no cobwebs catching the sunlight and the brambles that lined the path seemed as though they had been draped back to clear the way. A harsh, screeching call in the branches made me look up sharply as a big bird flapped its wings and soared low; swooping along the path, the way I had done when I followed the shooting star in my first dream of the hollow. It was a jay, the reddish brown plumage and distinctive striped wing briefly visible before it was swallowed up in the shadows. I shivered as it screamed again, a ghostly form among the tree tops, banking sharply then fluttering back to land a short distance from us. It seemed to stare straight at me before pecking at something on the ground, turning side on as it did, so that a ray of sun flickered across its wing. The patch of blue wing-feathers shone for an instant, like the gleam of Fiammetta's silk blouse. The jay selected an acorn, cocked its head almost mockingly then flew away low, following the footpath. I smiled to myself, knowing now that I was indeed on the right path and that Fiammetta wanted me to bring Joe to the hollow today.

We walked carefully. The trail was narrow and we had to clamber over tree roots and duck under low-hanging branches. The slow murmur of rainwater seeping through the fallen leaves in the gully accompanied us, at times fainter as the path meandered away then gradually growing louder again. Finally I saw the fairy bridge that crossed the gully. I swung around the guardian oak with the split trunk then turned to watch Joe cross the mossy bridge. He grabbed the oak trunk and swung round after me, the pack on his back thumping against him. He smiled at me and we walked together into the warm, sunlit clearing.

The huge fig leaves were yellow, curling at the edges, mottled with brown. The figs had all fallen and as we passed the tree a faint whiff of fermenting fruit rose from the grass. The late afternoon sun seemed to illuminate everything with heightened clarity so that even the tiny dust motes sparkled in the air. The wind was absent here, the air warm and sunny. Brambles and creepers hung around the hollow; an intricate pink and red tapestry. Chestnuts littered the ground beneath the tree's spreading branches, bursting from their prickly protective shells, while further on, ripe walnuts in their blackened cases clung stubbornly to their tree.

Joe looked around him slowly. I could see the artist in him absorbing the beauty; the shapes of the branches, the symmetry of the hollow. I was pleased when he did not speak, didn't feel the need to define the place with inadequate words. He smiled at me, swung the rucksack to the ground and walked across the hollow. He began pacing carefully around the boundary with his eyes fixed on the ground. I sat on a cushion of star-moss on a flat slab of rock and leant my head back. I gazed up at the eye of sky above and filled myself with thoughts of Fiammetta.

The sky was the exact colour of her eyes. The very air in this place seemed permeated with the essence of her. It had been right to come here. I closed my eyes, breathed deeply of nature; sweet fermenting figs, leaf mould, spore and dampness below the surface of the soft earth. No church service could have brought me this sense of peace. Here, in our secret place, I could finally believe that her death had been merely the beginning of her journeys and that she was at peace.

I felt a sudden coolness on my shoulder as Joe sat next to me and blocked out the sunlight.

"Do you know?" he said, "This clearing looks as if it's a perfect circle and yet I cannot see any signs of it having been cleared. I expected to see some sign of trees having been cut down, even if it

218

was done years ago but there is nothing." I opened my eyes and turned my head a little. His face was in shadow, eyes deep black holes, dark hair streaked with chestnut where the sun lingered. I kissed him, cupping his face in my hands and pulling him down to me. I wanted him more than I had ever done, knew that he felt the same but something made me pull back. There was some small thing missing that marred the perfection of the moment for me. Joe masked his disappointment quickly. I knew him so well now that I could tell exactly what he was thinking. He was berating himself for being an idiot, thinking that I had just suffered a huge shock and the last thing I would feel like doing was making love.

"Let's collect some of those chestnuts," he said, busying himself in practicality once more. I watched him through half-open eyes as he shook food from a plastic bag onto a rock then took the bag and began to pick up the chestnuts. Using a stone he bashed them open, with more force than was absolutely necessary.

How wrong he was, I thought. I wanted him to touch me so much that I ached. I felt the blood in my veins, racing, pounding. My lips where I had kissed him were burning. So what was it that had made me pull away? Joe gave up with the chestnuts and turned his attention to the walnut tree. He found a broken branch in the undergrowth and began to whack the tree with it. The stubborn walnuts clung desperately for a moment and then gave up the struggle, tumbling to the ground at his feet. I got up and stretched, then went to help. If he could release his sexual tension by bashing a tree, so could I. Joe surrendered his branch and watched as I attacked the walnut. It felt good, swinging the heavy wood, feeling it shudder as it connected with the tree and sent the nuts tumbling down. Joe watched, one eyebrow arched in amusement then burst out laughing as one nut fell on my head. I laughed too and dropped the branch. Together we collected walnuts, using our sweatshirts as containers and then dumping the load into the plastic bag. When the bag was full, Joe unwrapped the picnic and we settled down on the rocks to eat.

219

The sun began to set and the light turned thick and golden. The night that slowly enveloped us was cool. I untied my jacket from my waist and pulled it on. Above the hollow the sky changed moment by moment, fading to grey, streaked vivid pink and peach. When the half-light grew so dim that the outline of the trees began to blur, Joe lit a few small, nightlight candles that he had thought to bring. He had also anticipated finding our way home in the dark and brought along a torch. I loved his practical streak but right now, as he placed the candles around the hollow, carefully wedging them on the rocks so that they would not fall, I realised that he had just supplied the magic that had been missing before. I cleared away the remains of the food, poured the last of the wine into our glasses and stood up. I took Joe's glass to him and raised mine in a toast.

"Thank you Fiammetta, for all that you taught me, for your friendship and your wisdom. I will not say that I will miss you because I can still feel you with me wherever I go."

Joe touched his glass to mine and we drank. The hollow was alive with flickering flames and dancing shadows. Moths whirred around the candles. Small animals rustled in the undergrowth. The moon edged into the clearing. Bit by bit it slid through the sky, silhouetting the intricate pattern of branches until it was free and slipped across the hollow, pale and pure, a perfect orb. The hollow was bathed in subtle moonlight, transmuting all from the gold of day to silver night. The slab of rock where we had eaten our picnic was transformed as it reflected the light. A huge oblong of white rock, stained dark at the centre where the soft moss grew, it resembled a pagan altar.

I crossed over to the rock then turned and reached for Joe. He lifted me and laid me down on the cold rock. The moss cushioned my head. I remembered Fiammetta asking me to leave her where she lay, so that she could smell the earth and feel its caress and I understood her now. Joe's hands slid beneath the layers of my clothes. I arched my back so that he could unhook my bra, felt his fingers on my breast, then a sudden chill as he jerked my sweatshirt up roughly and took my nipple in his lips. We struggled out of our clothes, ignoring the cold air, aware only of the fire raging beneath our skin. When he thrust inside me, trapping me between his weight and the ungiving rock, I stared over his shoulder at the moon. I was wild, alive. Joe moaned and I turned my head, nipped his ear lobe with my teeth. My whole body felt torn in two, cold outside but flowing like lava within. I strained against Joe, rising up to meet him as he pushed into me. Our breath mingled, clouding as it chilled.

There was something elemental in our lovemaking, something that was as old and relentless as time. Feelings flooded through me with the insistent force of a river, turning my body slick with desire. The night air that I inhaled in deep gasps shrouded me like a cool second skin. The ground beneath my toes and the rock that scraped my back, as I thrust my hips towards Joe's, held me connected to the earth, while the moonlight tinged our bodies with white heat. Joe's eyes locked onto mine, blurring as he climaxed and my body shuddered violently with him.

After a few seconds Joe rolled to one side, freeing me. He fumbled behind him and pulled his jacket across us for warmth as we lay exhausted by the passion that had gripped us so completely. Finally, the cold forced us to move. We struggled back into our clothes, shivering. Joe sat on the rock, pulled me onto his lap and nuzzled my neck. Then, as we watched, the moon began to change colour. An orange light suffused its surface as the earth's shadow glided across it. Orange deepened eerily to red. The blood moon dominated the night.

21

My disciples never leave me completely. We are connected in a way that transcends the banalities of time and place. I am the bridge between this world and the shadow-lands. In the misty mornings of autumn, if you look beyond what you think you can see, you might glimpse the shapes of their spirits lazily swirling in vaporous folds around me.
The girl is learning fast now. She already accepts that her preconceived boundaries belong to her past and that she is free to wander where she will. If she listens to her true self, she will find the door within, which opens on eternity.

It rained for the funeral. I woke to it drumming on the roof and shutters. As we drove toward the village, with the fan on full blast to clear the condensation and the windscreen wipers straining to clear the rivulets from the glass, the noise on the metal roof was a percussion that drowned speech. We had left Luna behind once more but the air was still thick with doggy-damp smell.

Joe edged the jeep carefully around the waterlogged potholes, at times forced off the road so that the tires left flattened arcs of grass in our wake. Pockets of mist lingered below the tree line under a sullen grey sky. The foliage that remained on the deciduous trees hung wetly limp as the rain dripped off them in huge droplets.

We reached the village and I fingered the fold in my black trousers, worrying again about the bad impression I was going to give, when I turned up at a funeral wearing a bright red jacket but I had not had time to buy anything more suitable and the red one was the only coat which would keep out the rain. We parked opposite the garden with the persimmon tree. It was much larger now than when I had seen it in my vision, its orange fruit hung like miniature Halloween lanterns among slick leaves. I half expected to see Pietro standing underneath it but there was no one there.

Joe reached into the back for the umbrella and then came round to my side, holding it over me as I got out. He was so tall that the rain slanted beneath it and splattered against me but I didn't care. My smart shoes were slippery on the pavement and soaked before we had gone more than a few metres. I held onto Joe's arm and enjoyed the spray misting my skin.

The small red-brick church was crowded, villagers spilling out onto the paved space in front, where the black hearse was parked. I stopped worrying about my attire when we reached the church. Some people, mostly the family and friends, were more formally dressed but most of the people crammed into the church had come in what they had been wearing at home. Everyone turned up out of respect for the deceased but no one bothered about changing their clothes. One old woman was still wearing an apron, which peeped from under her coat.

We squeezed inside and stood at the back of the church. A buzz ran through the congregation when we entered, people turning towards us, taking in the fact that we had arrived together. Heads bent toward each other and whispers echoed around the walls. I saw Lucia and Pietro sitting near the front, shoulder to shoulder. Pietro turned his head as if aware of my scrutiny and I caught his eye. He nodded solemnly. Lucia turned in the pew to see who he was acknowledging and waved merrily before rearranging her face into a more fitting expression. The priest entered from the vestry, followed by the altar boys in their long white robes. Everyone settled down with a final shuffling of shoes and clearing of throats. The priest began to intone the formal words of his service that were taken up by the congregation in a ritual echo.

In the front row I could see Fiammetta's family. I recognised her grandson's long hair, tied back with a black band. He sat slightly apart from his parents staring fixedly at the coffin. His mother huddled into her husband's arm. The coffin gleamed in the central aisle, bright flowers spilling over it from an intricate

223

wreath. The priest led the altar boys around the coffin, swaying incense, murmuring in Latin. The powerful smell made me feel light-headed all at once and a moment of claustrophobia struck me. I pushed my way towards the door and back into the open air where I immediately felt better.

I wondered what Fiammetta would have thought of this ritual. Rita had implied that Fiammetta hardly ever went to church but in my vision I had seen her entering this very church as a young woman and when I had found her dying she had been wearing a cross at her neck. Personally, I found the church oppressive but I was not sure if the feeling came from me or from Fiammetta, whose presence had been with me so strongly since her death.

My own feelings about religion were ambivalent. Spirituality was very important to me but I had never been comfortable in a church. Whenever I was inside one I felt as if all those desperate prayers, which never seemed to be answered, hung stale in the air, like old smoke in a pub. Too many times, I had experienced the pious turn petty and spiteful as soon as they exited the church, envious of another's car or dress, angry at some supposed slight. I often saw religion as a refuge for the lonely, the desperate and the deluded. I respected Rita's beliefs and was conscious that she was that rarity – a person who genuinely tried to fill every corner of her life with goodness and kindness. However, I believed that there had been as much spirituality and intrinsic goodness in Fiammetta, who seemed to have found her illumination in nature. She had taught me the importance of creating one's own spiritual depths, in a way that had nothing to do with the recognised rules and regulations of religious dogma. She had shown me that to seek out a higher way, to undertake a personal spiritual journey in life, was of the utmost importance. She had taught me that, in order to love one must first learn to love oneself and that the more love one has inside, the more one's capacity for love grows.

I sat on a low brick wall in the shelter of the church porch until the bells began to ring their three-toned mourning toll and people poured out of the heavy wooden doors again, gathering around me in groups, chattering in hushed voices. Umbrellas whooshed open as the porch became too crowded. A few men pulled up their jacket collars and made a dash for the comfort of the bar across the road. I was too cramped in the porch so I went out and stood in the rain to wait for Joe to find me. This action was clearly considered the height of madness judging from the muttering and appalled glances I was getting.

A group of men carried the heavy coffin out and slid it into the open hearse. Fiammetta's son came out, still comforting his wife and behind them her grandson held an umbrella over them all. He saw me standing in the rain and a smile lit up his features. He had his grandmother's eyes, the same chestnut coloured hair that she had had when young and the same way of indicating equal amounts of warmth and mockery with a smile. I smiled back at him and thought how proud Fiammetta would have been to see him today, already a head taller than his father, a hint of strength to come in the width of his shoulders. His silver eyebrow ring glinted as he turned his head and I knew that Fiammetta would have enjoyed this small sign of rebellion too. Behind him I saw Joe pause for a second in the doorway while he searched the crowd for me. When he saw me his shook his head in exasperation and brought the umbrella over to cover me. He kissed my wet hair and muttered, "What am I going to do with you?" with a laugh.

The hearse set off, people forming a procession behind it as it moved slowly down the high street. The traffic had been stopped by the police and now queues of cars were building up at either end of the village as the long procession wove its way past the shops and houses. People filled the whole road, walking slowly in twos and threes, crowded together under bright, multicoloured umbrellas. I grinned to myself as I imagined Fiammetta's gleeful appreciation of this scene; friends and enemies alike, all marching behind the hearse in the pouring rain; stockings and trousers splattered with muddy water, drips trickling down collars from umbrella spokes.

Walking by Joe's side, I was struck by the difference between this funeral and my mother's in England. There was genuine sadness on some of the faces around me but at the same time, there was a sense of acceptance. Life and death were as natural as the changing seasons. This death had been more dramatic than others but Fiammetta had been old, eccentric and even feared in life; there was no sense of tragedy. In fact most of the crowd seemed to have been drawn more by curiosity than by friendship. Some old women nearby hooted with merriment as they remembered going to dances with Fiammetta when they had all been young. Before she went crazy, I heard one say, automatically making the sign of the cross that I associated with any mention of Fiammetta. Two men behind them were unrepentantly talking about football. People complained about the rain, saying that it was a terrible time of year for a funeral, moaning about the long walk. I eavesdropped on people as we walked past them, wondering if anyone would have the temerity to call Fiammetta a witch or whether the solemnity of the occasion would stop any gossip. So far, it seemed that a sense of propriety prevailed.

We had reached the outskirts of the village now. Tall, yellow-tipped spikes of corn leant drunkenly in the fields. In small, family vineyards leaves shone yellow and red in defiance of the weather and the allotments near the roadside were full of sturdy black cabbages and waterlogged lettuces.

The procession turned into the winding lane that led to the cemetery and the cars on the main road, released from their long wait, sped off toward the high street. I had not been to the cemetery before and was surprised at its neatness. Gravel pathways led between precise rows of graves, each one neatly tended and adorned with fresh flowers and faded photographs of the person resting there. Older remains had been moved into tidy wall-graves that lined the cemetery, the upper rows reached by steps, also decorated with photos and flowers. On one tiny grave, a white-marble angel cried across the inscription, which showed a date of birth the same as that of the baby's death.

At the far end of the graveyard reddish brown soil was piled in crumbling, soggy heaps around the sides of a newly dug grave. A big crowd gathered around it as the priest said his final words and the coffin was lowered into its resting place. I shuddered as I heard it squelch into place. I could detect no warmth in the priest's words, no sense of his having known Fiammetta and I wondered again how many times she had gone to church in the last years of her life.

Fiammetta's son bent and threw a handful of earth into the grave then wiped his muddy hands on a tissue his wife offered him. The priest murmured something to them and hurried off. When he left, people followed him, eager to get home and out of the rain. After a while the family also walked slowly away, back towards the village. The grandson said something to his parents and they stopped, while the boy ducked out from beneath the umbrella and made his way through the departing crowd to my side. Joe covered him with our umbrella and we all stood, watching the rain puddling on the wooden coffin and seeping around the flowers left on the muddy graveside.

Pietro and Lucia left. As they passed us Lucia called goodbye loudly. She had paid her respects to a woman she had never liked, of whom she had been slightly jealous and now she was anxious to put it all behind her and get home. She did not notice Pietro slip something from his pocket and throw it into the grave before putting his arm around Lucia's waist again and leading her away.

"Signora," the boy spoke. I turned my attention back to him, noticing for the first time that his eyes were red-rimmed and he had a small scab on his chin as though he had cut himself that morning, shaving away his sparse beard in an effort to look his best.

"I am so sorry. " I said. He shrugged, cast a look down at the coffin and then back at me.

"She knew that she was dying. She made all the arrangements she needed to. She even made me promise to look after her rabbits

227

and that awful sheep." The humour was back in his eyes now, as he remembered promises made and already regretted.

"She asked me to give you something. May I bring it up to you this afternoon?" I nodded in surprise and he took off, running across the graveyard to where his parents were waiting by the gate.

"Let's go" Joe said and I nodded. I had brought something in my pocket to leave for Fiammetta and now I pulled out a small posy made from cypress twigs and things I had collected from the hollow; sprigs of chestnut, walnut and fig. As I dropped the posy a chestnut broke free. It bounced once then rolled down the coffin to rest alongside a rose; just a tightly curled bud cut from the stem so that it would fit unnoticed into Pietro's pocket, as red as the flame that Fiammetta was named after.

Fiammetta's grandson came late that afternoon. The rain had ceased and the sun was shining again. The capricious weather brought a smile to my lips. If Fiammetta could have planned her funeral, she would have wanted it like this; dramatic and uncomfortable to make the burial unforgettable and then a glorious and benign end to the day. I had not expected the boy to come today. The road was boggy and full of deep puddles, which would have been impossible for him to negotiate on his small motorbike. Instead he had borrowed his father's car and, when I saw it turn up the drive with mud splattered right up the sides, I hoped that he had promised to wash it for him too.

I opened the door to welcome him but did not manage to get hold of Luna's collar in time. She flew down the path and leapt up at him enthusiastically. Fortunately, he didn't seem to mind being made as muddy as the car. He crouched down and made a fuss of Luna then reached into the car and pulled out a large basket. My heart jumped as I recognised Fiammetta's handiwork.

"Come on in, I'll make you a drink. I'm sorry but I don't know your name. Your Grandmother always called you her grandson."

"Gianni." He replied, and then added with a grin "She wasn't very good with names, always said they were impossible to

228

remember so she made up a kind of secret code, used descriptions for everyone." Gianni slipped off his boots in the hallway in spite of my reassuring him not to bother since Luna was leaving a muddy trail anyway. As he followed me down the hall toward the kitchen he said,

"She liked you. Called you *Ragazza* but I always thought she meant more than just girl, it was almost as if she thought of you as her girl, her daughter. She wasn't always so kind though." I shot him a look and we both laughed. I could imagine all too well some of the caustic assessments that she would have made.

Gianni accepted a coffee and sat down at the kitchen table, placing the basket in the middle. When I put his coffee in front of him he pushed the basket across the table to me and nodded at it.

"That is what she asked me to bring to you when she was dead. She had it all packed the last time I went up to see her. That was Friday. I didn't go up on Saturday because I went for a pizza with some friends and on Sunday you found her." He looked suddenly sad and vulnerable beneath the cocky assurance of youth and I wanted to say something that would help him but it was a struggle to find the right words.

"She was very proud of you. She spoke about you with such warmth." At my words Gianni raised his eyes to meet mine and I saw tears swimming there that he was barely holding back

"I will miss her." I said quietly. The boy nodded, swallowed and then in a strained voice said,

"People thought that she was strange but they didn't know her. She was just different. She had a way of looking right inside you and accepting you the way you really are. I think that most people find it hard to be understood in that way. They want to keep up their defences, make other people believe in the persona that they have created, not what they really are. That is why Nonna unsettled people."

I nodded, thinking that his assessment of people showed his intelligence and sensitivity.

229

"Did you know that Nonna once wanted to be a teacher?" he asked. "She studied in Arezzo but when she tried to get a job at the local school, people said that she would not be a good example for the children. They already thought that she was strange, because she spent all her time either studying or traipsing around in the woods and in those days a woman did not behave like that. They all thought she was lucky to find a man to marry her but she was very beautiful, or so my grandfather used to say. He could never understand why she chose him instead of going off to work in the city but she said that she needed to be here, in these woods. When he died she caused a scandal by insisting on moving into that house out in the forest, but she was much happier there."

When Gianni mentioned the house in the woods I suddenly remembered Fiammetta's animals and asked him about them. He reassured me that they had all been taken care of. The sheep had been given away to a local farmer. The rabbits had not been so lucky.

"The rabbits were good." The boy grinned, rubbing his stomach appreciatively and I thought that Fiammetta would have approved of this thoroughly practical end.

"We couldn't find the cats though," Gianni continued, with a frown. "They must have run off. They were pretty wild anyway though so I expect they can fend for themselves."

Gianni shrugged and sipped his coffee then looked at me appraisingly, and said,

"You have her kind of eyes but yours are gentler. She could be really bloody-minded, when she wanted." He laughed, finished his coffee and stood up. I walked him back to the door. He pulled his boots on, hampered by Luna who had taken a fancy to him and was trying to help by chewing the laces undone as soon as he tied them.

This time I kept hold of Luna's collar and we watched him walk away down the muddy path. I felt a sudden overwhelming pang of sadness for him; half man, half boy still. I could feel his pain, his guilt at not having gone to see Fiammetta on the Saturday night, his regret at having lost the one person who understood him without judging him. I also knew that this feeling was not all my own imagination. There was a presence alongside me and I knew that I was seeing Gianni through Fiammetta's eyes. As if to prove that I was not imagining it Luna suddenly stopped struggling against my grip and sat at my feet, head turned to one side as if listening to an unheard command.

A faint scent of resin floated in the air and when I called out to the boy, my voice sounded as though it came from far away.

"Gianni." He stopped, turned to face me.

"She has not gone, you know. She told me that death is not an end, just the start of something new. If you need her, for any reason, go to the cypress and think about her and you will find the answers you need. When you need her, she will be there. " I saw a hint of fear flutter across Gianni's face as I started to speak but then it faded and instead I saw a new respect form in his bright eyes.

"I was right. You are very like her. Thank you." Then he grinned and opened the car. I shut my door and leant back against it. Luna looked quizzically at me. She came and butted her head against my knees and I fondled her ears, wondering how to react to this new capacity of trance-like speech, rendered in perfect Italian. There was no doubt in my mind that Fiammetta had been speaking through me. I was surprised that I had not found it frightening but very natural. Pondering this rather disconcerting legacy I went to see what else Fiammetta had left for me.

The basket was covered in an old tea-towel. Inside were packets and jars, all neatly labelled in what I now knew was Fiammetta's handwriting. She had studied to be a teacher. That explained the cultured remarks that she habitually hid beneath her rough, countrywoman's speech. I opened one packet labelled *Camomile* and breathed deeply, remembering her laughing eyes when she had told me I needed some, to make me calm. How long ago that seemed now. Alongside the carefully dried herbs and tisanes were jars of honey and bottles of oils. I opened a bottle marked *For aches and pains - massage a small amount over the area* and the strong aroma of ginger and some other herb that I couldn't identify made my eyes water.

I was still studying these treasures when Joe came back in from his workshop. He left his boots by the door and padded up to me, nuzzling my neck and looking over my shoulder at the table littered with sachets and potions full of marvellous scents. As I explained about Fiammetta leaving me her medicinal herbs, Joe rummaged in the basket and it was he who found the diaries at the very bottom.

There were three notebooks with the same lined paper she had used to write the note when she sent me the camomile. I flicked carefully through the pages. They were mostly covered in detailed sketches of plants. Alongside each sketch she had written notes in black ink; lists of medicinal uses and recipes. In the margins, written in pencil, in a shaky hand that indicated a more recent addition, were lines that seemed to have been written especially for me.

Tall men tend to suffer from backache. Try this when he starts to moan.

Give this to Lucia when she has a sore throat. Try to explain that if she could shut up for half a minute now and then she wouldn't have such trouble with her throat. She never would listen to me!

This promised to be a very entertaining read. I surveyed my legacy spread across the table and closed the book with a smile

WINTER

The Realization

Winter, season of inner growth and hidden mystery. Suddenly, with no warning, winter tightens its icy grip on the land; a cold, remorseless embrace that will endure for months. Winter has a terrible, stern beauty. In the linearity of bare branches and frosted furrow, the true shape of things is unveiled. Muddy brown earth is sealed with a shimmering coat of frost. The wind sears like white heat. Ridges of mud crack, blades of grass snap. When all else has faded and died away only the bare outline is left, like webs of dark branches against white sky. Nature, stripped of its bright adornments, is starkly skeletal and what is left is the essential core. Then another transformation as soft snowflakes swirl around me, wrapping me up along with the rest of the world.

Under the snow's cold blanket all is isolated. It is hard to recognise my world in the rounded, crystal perfection.

While other trees lower their heavy boughs to form tunnels that spring back when touched with a shuddering flurry of white, I am unbending. The snow that wraps me is the first to slip away in the pale winter sun. Under the cold glittering starkness of the winter world, life lies in wait. In the dark womb of the earth the hidden mystery of life is quickening. Snow sculpts the landscape into pregnant curves and, when the spring eventually brings the thaw, that same snow will melt deep into the earth, nourishing, swelling, easing new life to the surface.

22

Now there is a transmutation, from the fecundity of autumn's slow decay to the austere sincerity of winter. The first frost bleaches the colourful leaves that cover the land. Trees, plants, fields, all are stark skeletons. The life forms that can do so retreat, hibernate or withdraw. Animals scurry forth in the bleak afternoons when the world is at its warmest and their hunger drives them from their refuge, to unearth a seed from the hard soil or scavenge among the frugal supply of winter food.
My winter song is of the purity of snow, the severity of icy winds, the quiet spaces that are revealed in nature's most extreme contrast.
In the enormous silence of this waiting time the girl undergoes her own meditative retreat. She reads the words that the old one left and stretches out with her mind and spirit to grasp the healing skills that are growing within her.

Autumn dragged on. The trees slowly changed colour; startling flashes of fire along the tree line fading to dull brown. The leaves seemed reluctant to fall, stubbornly clinging to branches as the wind tugged viciously and the rain streamed off them. The rain, which had started at the funeral, continued intermittently for the next couple of weeks and the ground was completely sodden. I walked less and less, feet squelching and sticking in mud, hair plastered to my scalp. Luna also showed a remarked reluctance to going out. After a few days of rain, she set off on our daily walk with her tail between her legs and at the end of the driveway, sat down and refused to go any further. As soon as she got back into the kitchen and had suffered me drying her paws and rubbing her fur down, she stretched out by the radiator and stayed there for the rest of the day. She also demonstrated an amazing bladder control. She managed to limit her essential outdoor excursions to a maximum of four a day. When she could wait no longer she would reluctantly nudge us and lead us to the back door. When we opened it for her, she would hesitate there, nose sniffing the damp air, as if deciding whether her trip was truly necessary, before gingerly stepping across the grass, choosing the driest spot beneath the nearest tree and then racing back to the house in relief.

Joe was very busy. He had several commissions to finish for the shop in Arezzo and he spent most of the day in his workshop, appearing only for a brief lunch break. That gave me the personal time that I needed but it was nice to have someone else to think of when I prepared lunch and Joe repaid the effort in full, since he nearly always cooked dinner himself.

For the first time in my life I was living the life of a couple. We saw friends occasionally but were happiest when we were alone together. We went out sometimes in the evenings, exploring the local restaurants and at weekends Joe took me sightseeing. Together we explored the various cities and towns in the area. At this time of year, many villages had their own small festivals, most of which were named for what they considered their culinary specialties. Joe loved these events where he could eat his fill of such varied delicacies as cannellini beans and sausages, spare ribs and steak cooked over wood fires, rabbit done in every imaginable way and even tripe. This last dish turned my stomach but Joe declared it delicious.

Lots of things seemed to make me feel a bit queasy at the moment, which I put down to my different eating habits. Joe was such a good cook that I found it hard to eat as frugally as I had when cooking for myself. I did not often feel like coffee either but had developed a craving for hot chocolate. All this, added to the lack of daily walks was not helping my waistline but Joe did not seem to notice and I reassured myself that I would get back into my good habits when the spring came around again.

There was nothing nicer than sitting by the fire that Joe lit every morning with one of Fiammetta's notebooks on my knee, a mug of chocolate and a couple of biscuits. The notebooks were fascinating. I read them slowly, smiling to myself at her sharp asides and barbed remarks. I followed her recipes, used herbs when cooking, mixed oils and brewed simple remedies. When Joe and I felt a cold coming on I dosed us with Fiammetta's myrtle syrup and by the next day our symptoms were gone. I used the oil that Fiammetta had said was good for backache one day when Joe was suffering in silence. I got him to lie down on the bed while I massaged him. He made the most remarkable recovery and after that, I was always very suspicious when he complained of backache, especially when his statement was accompanied by a lively twinkle in his eyes.

Joe's place felt more and more like home to me. I accumulated things at the various fairs and towns we visited, knickknacks really but they helped me to stamp my own personality on the house. I bought some beautiful copper pans for the kitchen and Joe hung them from the beam above the worktop where they glowed prettily when the sun managed to fight through the clouds. I did not think they would ever be used but they were lovely to look at. I also indulged in delicately handcrafted bed linens and soft furnishings, which added a feminine touch to Joe's rather Spartan décor. He encouraged me to do what I wanted and even hung a painting that I had done, of the cypress at sunset, in the lounge. He seemed genuinely pleased with the changes I wrought and I came to realize that he did not see it as an invasion of his territory but rather an expression of my permanence in his life.

Nature seemed to be encouraging our love. As the days shortened, we spent long dark evenings in front of the fire, pulling up two armchairs and toasting simple food over the glowing embers, cuddling and making plans as we gazed at the flickering flames. Occasionally Joe opened a bottle of wine. He swore that roasted chestnuts simply could not be swallowed without a glass of good red wine and he was right, they were delicious. Unfortunately, I felt queasy when I drank wine too and could usually only manage a few sips. After the first time when I mentioned my stomach upset Joe avoided things that he knew were likely to upset me and he began making me a mug of hot camomile every evening before we went to bed. I felt fine most of the time but decided that if I did not feel better in a couple of weeks I would have to see a doctor. When I was not queasy, my appetite seemed to have increased but maybe it was just that the food was so good eaten in front of the fire. The simplest things cooked there tasted different; thick slices of country bread toasted then rubbed with a clove of garlic and drizzled with the new extra-virgin olive oil that Pietro gave us or slightly charred chestnuts that burnt our fingers as we tore into them greedily. Luna was crazy about chestnuts too and she would stand guard on the pile that Joe put to one side for her, drooling and quivering with anticipation, until they were cool enough for her to eat.

I searched Fiammetta's notebooks for a mention of chestnuts and found a long entry that spanned several pages. As always when reading the notes, it seemed as though the old woman was in the room with me. It would not have seemed strange if I had read the words *Ciao Raggazza* at the top of the page.

Used for just about everything, chestnuts were the staple food for the mountain people in the old days. They would be roasted or boiled in soups and sauces. When dried they were ground into flour, to make gnocchi or a sweet flat bread with raisins, rosemary and pine nuts. Try the dried ones – you can suck them for ages and they give you the minerals and vitamins that you need. Good for convalescence and general weakness, especially after flu. Gargle with an infusion made from the leaves for pharyngitis. Leaves are good for the hair too – they give a shine to brown hair and help cure dandruff.

As I read on I thought that I heard a dry chuckle behind me as if Fiammetta was reading over my shoulder. I knew that it was just my imagination but the thought of her presence was comforting and made me smile.

We frequently woke to thick fog, which would linger until midday. I felt sort of muffled, wrapped up in the warmth of the house, sheltered from the inclement weather that rattled the shutters and beat upon the windows. On days when the rain held off, limiting itself to an ominous threat in smoky cloud-mountains that rolled above our heads, I managed to convince Luna to go for a walk. She soon overcame her squeamishness, bounding off ahead, slipping and skidding through the muddy lanes and bouncing delightedly in every puddle we came too. Each time we walked down to my old place my heart would lift when I saw the cypress, although the house no longer felt like home. It was freezing inside and I never lingered long. There was no central heating and I would have been miserable there once the summer had ended. Soon the postman began delivering the few bank statements and official letters that I got to Joe's house, even though I had not notified the post office of my change of address and after that there was no reason to enter the house at all. I still walked that way though, to be with the cypress.

I saw everything so clearly in the shadow of the cypress. With its rough, damp bark beneath my fingers I absorbed the elements, became part of them. The raw participation with nature was exhilarating. As the wind tugged wildly at clothes and branches and cold drizzle soaked into me, I often found myself transfixed by some moment of breathtaking beauty and would stand still, straining with my whole being to assimilate it.

At such times, the sullen, rain-sodden countryside would be transformed and I would live that moment with heartbreaking poignancy: a single ray of sunshine penetrating the gloom, turning all that it touched to burnished brass and gold: the power of an ominous, smudged-charcoal sky lying across the tawny hills: cloudscapes formed by patches of baby blue among curling wraiths of cloud. It was a time of shadows and sudden contrasts, of dark sombre beauty suddenly illuminated by the power of the rarely seen sun.

On our shopping trip one day the supermarket was full of Halloween novelty items and chrysanthemums, which Joe said were traditional flowers for All Saints Day, a national holiday when Italians visited their family graves. Where we lived was too remote for us to have any children playing trick or treat but the thought of childhood celebrations made me think about Guy Fawkes and Joe of Thanksgiving. We decided to throw a big party in the middle of November to combine all the various festivals.

It was too wet for a bonfire but I found some fiery coloured leaves and hung them around the house as decorations and Joe bought some indoor fireworks. Joe cooked a huge turkey dinner with all the trimmings and we served it buffet style with everyone taking turns for a proper seat or perched precariously on chair-arms to eat. After the meal we organized a few games such as bobbing for apples and passing the orange under the chin. I thought I would die laughing as I watched Pietro trying to bend enough to be able to pass his orange down to Rita and judging from the happy faces as everyone left, the party was a great success.

Joe was rarely bad tempered. The man I had once judged by his dark, enigmatic gaze to be cool and distant was in fact gentle, warm and fun loving. There were the odd moments when his temper flared up, like when his chisel slipped and ruined a carving or when the toaster broke and he tried to mend it without success while mumbling Italian imprecations under his breath. However his temper was never aimed at me and was quick to pass. I was constantly discovering different facets of him and he of me, as we opened up to each other more and more.

On the first of December I discovered that Joe had a touching, childlike love of Christmas. He came down to breakfast with a huge box that he had fetched from the attic and insisted that we put up the Christmas decorations. I watched as he wrestled with a slightly tatty old fake tree, straightening out each branch carefully.

"I can't have a real one, it would be bald well before Christmas" he joked. Then he checked the tree lights, patiently changing bulbs until the whole long strand worked properly. Christmas had not really been celebrated after my father's death. In later years I had usually gone out with Becky on Christmas Eve where we would exchange small gifts. On Christmas day itself I used to cook a small piece of turkey and stuff myself with pudding and mince pies while watching whatever the television had dusted off to show that year. Now, hanging baubles and wrapping tinsel, I felt the joy of Christmas for the first time since I had been a small child.

When we had finished decorating it, the tree was transformed. As the evening closed in Joe turned the tree lights on and then came over to wrap his arms around me. A warm kind of magic pulsed to the beat of the twinkling lights and I understood what it felt like to be part of a family.

Stored in a separate box was a nativity scene that Joe had carved years before. There was a stable and crib, three wise men, several shepherds and their sheep, cows and horses and of course Mary, Joseph and the baby Jesus. Simple but exquisite. As Joe set it all up, in a corner by the hearth, he explained that every Italian family took great pride in their *presepe* and that each day the wise men, who were journeying from afar, should be moved one step closer to the stable and that, on Christmas Eve, Mary and Joseph could be placed inside and finally baby Jesus would be laid in his bed of straw on Christmas morning. Luna kept away from the nativity scene which surprised me until Joe picked up one of the wise men and showed me teeth marks that Luna had made when she was a puppy. She had been thoroughly told off and now avoided the presepe corner.

Later on that month Joe had to go to Arezzo to take the pieces of furniture that he had made to the shop there. I decided to go with him and do some Christmas shopping while he was busy. We set off after breakfast, leaving Luna with her usual bone-chew. For the first time I felt the grip of winter on the land. Frost glinted and sparkled across the fields, turning the rutted mud in the road to furrows of white. Pale grass by the path crunched beneath my boots, the blades silvered and brittle. As Joe drove slowly down the lane, avoiding icy puddles where he could, I gazed across the olive groves towards the distant mountains. It had snowed there during the night and the peaks looked as if they had been dredged with icing sugar. The contrast between the dark, undulating waves of cloud and the silvery ground was dramatic. The majesty of this land was a constant thrill.

As we drove past the cypress I reached out to it with my mind and my heart beat faster. I could still feel my head bump against the headrest and the jerky vibrations of the jeep through my body but at the same time I swirled free and, for the first time since Fiammetta's death, I soared towards the tree, spiralled through its frosted branches and upward into the glowering sky. The cypress made no attempt to hold me back this time. I was not trying to follow a departing soul; there was no danger.

From above, the ground was a glittering patchwork of icy hues and the dark green of the cypress a defiant exclamation mark. I soared higher, buffeted by gelid winds, drawn into the centre of the dark cloud mass. My body did not feel the cold. I was aware of the jeep's belaboured heater blasting air on my legs and Joe humming under his breath, but at the same time, I saw the cold. The cloud had a heart of ice, a roaring maelstrom of raw fury. I shuddered as the power raged around me and I absorbed its awesome energy.

"Annie?" I came back to myself at the sound of Joe's voice. Currents of ice still shuddered within me but I was safe here, with Joe's big hand enveloping my knee. He was searching my face for the source of the distance he had felt opening between us. I flashed him a grin and saw him relax back against his seat.

"If you don't keep your eyes on the road, we will never make it to Arezzo.""

"The road isn't as interesting to look at," he teased back then pulled the jeep to the side of the road and stopped.

"Where did you go?" he asked. His eyes were concerned. He cupped my chin with one hand, drew his thumb gently across my lips. I pointed vaguely upward.

"I went to the cypress," I said. It was so good to have someone who cared about me, who noticed every small change in me and with whom I could open up completely. Joe might not understand my relationship with the cypress; I did not understand it myself

242

really; but he was willing to try and was there for me when I needed him. My feelings for him must have shown in my face because he smiled and leant across to kiss me gently. As he put the jeep back in gear and pulled onto the road again I bent forward, looked up at the sky overhead once more and asked,

"Have you got the chains in the back?"

"Somewhere, under all the furniture but I think it is too soon for snow."

I laughed and shook my head.

"Believe me, there is snow up there." I assured him, slipping my own hand across to rest on his thigh as we drove. Under my fingers was power of a different sort, strength in the subtle clenching of his muscles as he changed gear. I smiled to myself at the solidity of his being there for me.

In Arezzo I left Joe unloading the furniture from the jeep. He had a special delivery permit that allowed him to drive into the centre of the old town, along the steep, narrow streets that were closed to ordinary traffic. The shop was at the top of the town, just behind the Piazza Grande where, in summer, earth was packed down over the cobbled stones for the famous jousting tournament. I wandered along the narrow lanes, heading downhill towards the boutiques and department stores where I hoped to find gifts for Joe and a glamorous outfit for myself for the New Year's Eve party at the manor that Lucia and Pietro had invited us to. These back lanes belonged to antique shops and small bistros. The smell of garlic frying, as lunch was prepared behind the shuttered facades, made my stomach rumble. I window-shopped, enjoying the old oil paintings, burnished brass lamps and delicate jewellery evocating another time.

Half way down the street I came across a different kind of shop, brightly lit and displaying an eclectic selection of knickknacks. It seemed like the kind of place where I might find some novelty gifts to fill a stocking for Joe, so I went in. The shop smelt of incense and damp and was far bigger than it had seemed from outside, long and narrow with an amazing array of small gift

243

items. I nodded a greeting to the shop assistant by the till who had looked up from her crossword puzzle book when I came in. She nodded back, a gesture that set into motion various adornments. A green scarf that tied back her hair wafted in the air, long earrings swayed and a collection of bangles and beads clattered together.

I wandered through the shop and stopped to search through baskets of gemstones, enjoying the feel of their polished surfaces against my fingers. Behind the gem baskets were larger stones; exquisite caves of jagged amethyst, highly polished slices of rock crystal and balls of tiger's eye. A piece of obsidian caught my eye. I picked it up, surprised at the weight of it. Its uncut surfaces were dark and glassy and reflected the ceiling lights in a way that reminded me strongly of Joe's eyes. A soft, slightly breathless voice spoke behind me, making me start and tighten my grip on the rock.

"Obsidian is a natural glass, formed by rapidly cooling magma." I turned to look at the shop assistant, who smiled hesitantly.

I felt a shock of recognition run through me, although I knew I had never seen her before in my life. She was not much older than me but she looked it, with the dried out skin of a starved and nervous body. There was a hollow look in her eyes, a loneliness that no amount of gaudy accessories could hide. I had an urge to touch the thin skin on her hand, lend her some of the new-found strength within myself. Instead I returned her smile and drew her into conversation about the stones and other items in her shop. She was eager to talk and share her new-age beliefs with me. Obsidian, she explained, flaked easily and so had been used by early people to make weapons and tools.

"It is a stone that offers great protection and black is a colour that helps us find grace in silence and inner peace."

For me the stone symbolised Joe, his enormous strength, his air of protection, his comfortable silences and glittering soul. I decided to buy it as a gift for him, knowing that he would

244

appreciate it as a natural sculpture and imagining it on the fireplace, reflecting the flames as they danced.

The woman led me on, pointing out items that she thought might interest me, unaware that she herself was the object of my thoughts. A faint scent of resin blew in the air and I knew that my intuition about the woman was right. Her loneliness was eroding her inside, sapping her appetite and making her susceptible to all kinds of nervous ailments. Her movements were jerky and she seemed both desperately keen to talk and frightened of saying too much.

On a sign above a rack of greetings cards was a word I did not know, *onomastico*. I asked her what it meant and she explained that it was the saint for whom a person was named. She went to the desk and delved beneath the cash register for a tatty book. Flicking through the pages she found the entry she wanted and said,

"For example, today is 21st December. It is the shortest day of the year, by the way and the first day of winter."

"It certainly feels like it too, it is freezing out."

"So if you were born on this day and your parents were very religious, you would be called after St Temistocle." She looked up, saw the repressed laughter in my eyes and began to giggle. I joined in. The thought of calling a tiny baby Temistocle seemed absurd. The woman visibly relaxed and went so far as to tell me that her name was Settimia.

"I was the seventh child and my parents had run out of ideas by then." She said with a self-depreciating smile. She asked mine and then looked up Ann in her book of saint's birthdays. I found out that my onomastico would be on 26th July, the day of St Anne and St Joachim. I asked about Joe.

"That is an easy one," Settimia replied. "San Giuseppe is father's day, 20th March." She looked up at me and laughed in her breathless way.

"Just think what a connection. You are Anne, after the mother of Mary and you have found a Joseph, who was Mary's husband and the father of Jesus."

Settimia gift-wrapped the obsidian for me along with a pretty crystal star that I had seen and wanted to hang above Joe's nativity scene. As I watched her the scent of cypress grew stronger until finally I felt compelled to reach across the table and take hold of her hands as she put the finishing touches to a ribbon curl. I don't know who was more shocked at the touch but maybe for her, used to slightly eccentric clientele, it was less because she nodded and let her hands relax in mine, saying,

"Oh, so you are a healer, I wondered if you were."

I could not reply. Ripples of emotions that were not my own were flowing through my hands and arms, making me tremble. I felt like crying as Settimia's emotions flooded through me and I closed my eyes, breathed deeply of the resinous air and concentrated on sending my own warmth and strength flowing back into her. When I had finished I broke the connection and looked at her. Her cheeks were flushed and there was a spark in her eyes that had not been there before.

I left the shop with her quiet words of thanks ringing in my ears and walked down the hill towards the brightly lit centre in a kind of a trance. I expected to feel drained but instead it seemed as if I had a new energy tingling and rushing through my veins. I had never felt like this before and knew that until my connection with the cypress I would not have been able to harness whatever force it was that had come to me back in the shop. It was a good feeling, like having an extra sense that allowed me to see deeper inside people than I had been able to, or maybe wanted to, before. I remembered Fiammetta and how her eyes had seemed to see deep into my soul whenever we met, how she had seemed to understand me and know what I needed to help me heal. There had also been the moment of clairvoyance when I had been saying goodbye to Gianni and had seemed to speak with Fiammetta's voice. I wondered wryly whether her herbs and note books had been the only legacy that she had left me.

I reached the centre of town and began to browse among the boutiques, all the time aware of the thrill within me. Everything seemed so bright against a darkening sky. I found some more gifts for Joe in the small department store; a green jumper to replace his holey old favourite and a pair of warm gloves. In a corner just off the main high street I got him a handmade leather wallet and belt, knowing that they would appeal to the craftsman in him. I loved the Italian way of gift-wrapping things for you in the shop. They made up the most exquisite parcels and even if Joe tried to peep inside the bags, he would not be able to tell what I had bought for him.

I walked back down the hill, past the theatre towards the main piazza where I had arranged to meet Joe. There were Christmas stalls set up in the piazza and all the food of the fair was on offer; wafer thin, aniseed tasting *brigidini*; nougat and nut brittle; striped, marshmallow walking canes and multicoloured jelly sweets. Other stalls displayed ornaments and rhinestone jewellery, a wide assortment of clothes and novelties. I bought a wedge of nut brittle for Joe, a squeaky toy for Luna then checked my watch. I still had half an hour before meeting Joe and there was a shop just across the road that I remembered from an earlier trip to Arezzo, where I might find my outfit for the New Year's Eve party.

My dream outfit was displayed in the shop window. A long, velvet, jacket in deep burgundy that reflected the shop lights in a soft red glow. I took it into the changing room along with black velvet trousers but to my chagrin I could not get the trousers done up at the waist. The shop-assistant tried to sooth me by saying that they were a model that were cut small and complimenting me on how good I looked but, for the first time in ages, I did not feel comfortable in clothes. I looked at my reflection, trying to be objective. Trousers in the next size up did fit, but only just. I turned sideways to see how they looked at the back and pulled a face at my reflection. Did my face look more rounded too? The shop assistant had not been lying though when she said I looked good. Being in love showed, my eyes were bright and happy and my lips were ready to smile. I told the assistant that I would take the lot then dashed to meet Joe.

I had been more than half an hour. Joe was waiting in the piazza, eating brigidini from a long packet that already looked half empty. I rushed across the road to him, flushed from the warmth of the boutique changing room and the struggle that had taken place within it.

Joe looked at me and all the carrier bags that I was laden down with and his lips twitched. He suppressed the grin and took the bags from me.

"You are late."

"Sorry, I got carried away."

"So I see," he began to laugh "You must have bought up the whole town." Joe looked up and jerked his chin, unable to gesture with his hands full of bags.

"You were right about the snow," he said.

I looked up too. A few small snowflakes drifted down. One brushed my cheek, a cool, soft tickle on my flushed skin.

"Come on, I'm starving. Did you get something for the party?" Joe asked, heading across the piazza. The brigidini had obviously given him an appetite.

"Yes but I had to get a bigger size than usual." I replied mournfully "Being in love with you is bad for me. You eat like a horse and never put on any weight and I get tempted too much." Joe stopped. He wrapped his arms round me, banging the bags together and looked down.

"You look just right to me," he told me with a gentle smile.

Frail snowflakes shivered in the air around us. His eyes shone like the obsidian I had bought for him, offering strength, protection and peace. Love shone there too, a warmth that no stone can possess. I let him comfort me. Snow landed on my nose and speckled Joe's dark hair. As we walked on it began to settle between the cobbled stones in the narrow side streets. Joe's heat spread through me from the fingers I had tucked into the curve of his elbow. The noise and bustle of the city seemed muffled by the snow. There was that secretive quality in the air that snow always creates, as it mutes all sound and allows you to hear your own heart beat more clearly. I tilted my head up to the sky, relying on Joe to guide me and caught snowflakes on my tongue. Joe laughed.

"Do I have to carry all the bags and steer you too?" he grumbled then grinned to show that he was teasing.

"Try it," I said, letting another snowflake melt in my mouth. Joe dumped the bags on the ground and turned his own head up to the sky and we laughed like children at our first taste of winter.

23

The winter air that swirls in icy breaths around me, or rips in furious gusts through my branches, holds the whispers of old friends. The connection between us is unsevered by time, undiminished by death.
It is easy to focus on their song, the song of life that the old ones croon to me as they circle through the air. .
This music that I live within; whose strains once drew me through the dark earth and into the light, whose percussion drummed in my sap as I grew ever upward and whose melodies twine around me and the surrounding world in harmonious riffs; is the sound of the constant spiralling movement of life. Growth finishes in death, which passes in turn to rebirth and a new existence.

One morning we had visitors. As I opened the door to let Luna out I saw a bundle on the doorstep. Luna bristled and stopped abruptly, staring as the bundle moved and separated into two furry shapes. Fiammetta's cats stretched slowly, arching their backs simultaneously. They were both the same size now, one black and one tabby. After Fiammetta's death, they had disappeared into the forest. They had obviously not had any trouble hunting for food because their coats gleamed healthily and they looked well fed. Luna retreated into the kitchen as first one cat and then the other stalked across the doorstep and rubbed themselves around my ankles. Luna barked once. The cats turned their heads to look at her. The black one sat down, slid smooth claws from its paws and, keeping its gaze firmly on the dog, licked them with a small pink tongue. The tabby sauntered up to the dog that towered over it and then walked underneath her, its tail brushing the fur of her tummy. Luna gave up pretending to be fierce and galloped out into the garden.

The cats rubbed around me once more and then went into the lounge and settled themselves by the fire. I smiled at the thought that Fiammetta's familiars had come home. Wild they might be but a warm fireside to curl in front of in winter was preferable to the rigors of the forest.

Fiammetta was constantly in my head. Her presence had been growing stronger since her death, which was alternately comforting and unsettling. Since the first time that I had felt her in my mind, when her grandson had brought me the basket of herbs and her note books, I had been aware many times that she was hovering behind my own thoughts. At times, when I was with Lucia, listening to her chatter away, I could almost hear Fiammetta's hiss of irritation in my ear whilst, when Pietro and Joe were working together last week, trying to mend the generator that heated Joe's workshop, I had felt Fiammetta's amused affection added to my own. Sometimes, like the experience in the shop in Arezzo, my clairvoyant experiences were clearly a free flowing connection with the cypress but most of the time I felt the old woman first. I was getting quite used to the sensation and accepted it as proof that, as Fiammetta had said, her death had been merely a transition from one state to another.

My religious beliefs were rather vague. I had gone to the local Protestant church and Sunday school as a child but when my mother's depression had begun I had stopped. I had developed a dislike of any creed that laid down rules on how one ought to live. Since coming here my spiritual side had taken on an importance that had been missing before. The cypress had taught me that life was not one-dimensional and had allowed my mind to open up so that I could sense life, as it flowed around me, through nature's constantly shifting seasons. I liked the idea of death being nothing more than another step forward within the universal spirit.

Right now, as I sat by the fire trying to read, Fiammetta's busy thoughts kept intruding. The cats lay on one side of the rug in front of me and Luna slept on the other side. The animals had decided to pay no heed to each other and were getting on in a surprisingly peaceful way. I reached for my hot chocolate and sipped it, shifting my slippered feet slightly on the hearth to make my ankles more comfortable.

If you leave your feet there too long, you will get chilblains, came the voice in my head. I sighed, turned the page and stared at the words written there, hoping she would leave me alone. The chocolate was delicious and I played with the idea of going to the kitchen for a biscuit to dunk in it. I had been trying to diet and was being quite good really but had not lost any weight yet.

You need to eat properly, look after yourself girl. Chocolate is good, in small quantities but you don't need a biscuit.

Fiammetta as my conscience was downright annoying and I told her so, hoping that Joe would not come in and find me talking to myself.

"Go away Fiammetta, you are bothering me." I snapped, grumpily. I heard a distinct chuckle and then blessed peace folded round me again as the old woman took herself off elsewhere. I checked the clock and saw that it was nearly lunch time. Joe was in the workshop, making something mysterious that he would not allow me to see, so I presumed that it was something for me, for Christmas. Now that the generator was working properly again he was spending a lot of time out there but I knew that his stomach would not let him miss lunch so I had better start cooking something. I would do something light because Rita, Luca and Giulia were coming for dinner that evening and Joe was planning to roast spare ribs and sausages over the fire.

I almost tripped over Luna as I pushed back the armchair. As my feet touched the ground, the heat that had accumulated there shot through the soles of my slippers and made me hop around madly, narrowly avoiding Luna's paws. She looked up at me quizzically as I jumped around. The cats each opened one eye briefly, then ignored me. Deciding it was a new game Luna stretched lazily and then pranced around me a few times. Fiammetta had been right about not leaving my feet too long on the hearth I thought darkly.

252

As I filled a pan with water for pasta I looked out of the kitchen window. The light snowfall had mostly melted away but some still remained in the shady corners of the garden. There was a rim of frost and ice highlighting the lake but the path and road had turned sludgy brown and Luna had made muddy trails all across the lawn.

Pietro's winter garden was looking good. I found it comforting to know that if we ever did get snowed in up here we would have a good choice of vegetables to pull up. The sky was grey, clouds hugging the tree line and masking the mountains. More snow was forecast but for now was holding off.

The workshop door opened and Joe came out. The wind caught his hair and flipped it across his face, like a sleek, black wing. He turned his back on me to shove the bolt across the door then hitched his jacket collar up against the bitter cold as he crossed the lawn to the house. He looked up and saw me at the window. A slow smile curled his lips and crinkled his eyes and I felt a tremor of desire at the sight of him.

I met him at the kitchen door, waited until he had kicked off his boots and closed the door behind him and then slid my arms round his waist. I breathed in the scent of wood shaving and varnish as I stood on tip-toe and kissed his neck. His skin was cold. A pulse drummed steadily beneath my lips. Joe caught my head between his big hands and turned my face up. His eyes were black, the pupils huge and almost lost in the smoky dark that surrounded them.

"This is what I call a proper welcome," he murmured, letting his lips touch mine softly. Pushing aside the collar of the old brushed-cotton shirt of his that I was wearing he laid slow kisses along my collar bone. My back arched at his touch. His hands slipped under my shirt and along my spine. The rough calluses on his fingers scratched slightly. I pressed against him, resenting the clothes that separated our bodies and smiled as I heard him groan. All thoughts of lunch had disappeared completely. We swayed clumsily down the hallway and up the stairs struggling out of our clothes as we went, while trying not to loosen our grip on each

253

other. As we groped through the doorway of our bedroom I was horrified to hear an appreciative cackle and a voice in my head say,

I told you that you had chosen well, ragazza.

I glared into thin air over Joe's shoulder and sent Fiammetta a telepathic message to get lost, with all my might. Then I kicked the door shut and giggled as Joe picked me up and threw me across the bed.

It was mid afternoon by the time we were finishing our snack in front of the fire. Joe cracked walnuts and passed them to me to pack inside the dried figs that we had bought to replace the ones that I had picked in the summer with Fiammetta, which we had finished long before they had a chance to dry properly. I bit into a fig and smiled to taste the sweetness of the summer sun concentrated there. Luna was aquiver, every pore concentrated on Joe's movements. After roasted chestnuts, walnuts were her favourite winter treat. Occasionally Joe would hold out a small piece of nut and she would take it from his fingers with great delicacy.

The phone rang and Joe went to the hallway to answer it. I heard him say hello to Luca but the rest of the conversation was muffled by the thick stone walls of the house. I had not felt Fiammetta's presence since I had shut her out of the bedroom earlier but now, as Joe's low voice murmured in reply to something Luca had said, I felt a warmth behind me and smelt the scent of resin that I associated with the cypress. My head began to ache suddenly and I shivered, in spite of the fire. I tried to shake my head to clear it but, almost as if cold hands were pressing into my temples, I could not move.

Don't fight it, Ragazza. Learn to listen with your soul, to trust in your instincts. Fiammetta's words reverberated around my head and at the same time I caught a whiff of lavender beneath the scent of the cypress, as if the old woman's spirit was rubbing lavender into my forehead to ease the pressure there. I forced myself to take a deep breath and tried to focus on the images that were coming to me. I gazed into the flames that leapt along the blackened bark of a log in the fireplace, until the flickering brightness seemed to melt away. As if I were looking at the sun through closed eyelids, all I could see was a glowing, throbbing light but then, as I gave myself up more completely and the resinous perfume became overpowering, a grainy image began to form.

Slowly the image became clearer, a sketchy outline at first that then clarified itself into Rita. She was pushing herself upright, using the railing of her outside staircase for support. Her face was contorted in pain and she was clutching her side. I thought she was going to fall again and tried to call out to her but she just looked straight through me and the only sound I heard was the sputtering crackle of a log moving on the fire. Rita slumped against the house wall, propping herself against it as she shuffled up the stairs, one agonising step at a time.

Another heady burst of cypress scent and I felt myself flowing through the air towards Rita, hesitate an instant and then slide beneath her grasping fingers and into her body. I was aware of the different textures of skin and flesh, sinew and muscle and the constant hot pulse of her blood. I saw the frail curve of white rib bones and then, protruding towards the vibrating lung sack, a jagged piece of broken bone.

I came back to myself with a jolt and found Joe, sitting on the hearth peering at me as his fingers felt the pulse in my wrist.

"Do you feel dizzy?" he asked. I shook my head, then, before he could carry on with his diagnosis, I interrupted him.

"Joe, I am fine. It was just the cypress, there is nothing wrong with me at all. The problem is Rita, she is hurt. We have to get down there. I think she will need to go to the hospital."

"I know, Luca just phoned to tell me. He said she had a fall and bruised herself a bit and she will not be coming here tonight. He and Giulia were still planning to come though. He did not think it was anything to worry about, Annie."

I made an angry noise worthy of Fiammetta at this. I really liked Luca but he hardly noticed his mother at all. She cooked and cleaned and ran the house around him and he, with spectacular disregard, took everything that she did for him for granted.

I told Joe what I had seen in my vision. His expression grew grim as I described the jagged sliver of rib bone.

"That doesn't sound good," he admitted. "Let's drive down and have a look at Rita," he decided, suddenly the professional doctor and I was glad that he, at least, would know what to do if Rita had hurt herself as badly as I believed. I felt a little shaky now and my heart was racing with a mixture of adrenalin from the vision and fear for Rita. Joe's medical background was an added bonus. I found myself calming slowly as this reassuring thought occurred.

Luca answered the door at Joe's knock. He looked surprised but pleased to see us and welcomed us in, calling out to Rita as he led us into their formal front room. I had expected to find Rita lying in bed but she was perched at her usual seat by the window, employed in the fiddly business of assembling the links of a gold chain, as if it was a normal day. The only sign that she gave, of there being something wrong with her, was the fact that she did not leap up and offer to make us drink. I began to wonder whether I had been mistaken. Maybe my vision had been nothing more than imagination.

Joe crossed over to Rita and bent to kiss her cheeks. She put her hand on his arm and started to push herself up but he stopped her and crouched down by her chair. As he began to question her quietly I was overwhelmed once again by his kindness.

"Oh, Joe, I am such a silly old woman. There is nothing wrong with me. I just slipped on the stairs when I was bringing up the wood earlier. I must have a bit of a bruise but I am fine."

"You should let Luca bring the wood up for you." I said heatedly. Luca flashed me a look of utter surprise but then shrugged and grinned sheepishly. I smiled in spite of myself. Rita had spoilt her children so much that they never thought to do jobs for her. Maybe that would change a bit now. I had the idea that Rita was going to be forced to rest for a while.

256

While Rita explained about the steps being slippery with frost, Joe was gently probing her side. She broke off her story and sucked her breath in sharply as he touched her. When he pressed his fingers again she yelped and turned white. Luca moved over to his mother, looking concerned for the first time. Rita grabbed hold of his hand and squeezed hard, trembling now.

"That hurts Joe. Stop please, it hurts," she begged and her eyes filled with tears. Joe looked up at Luca,

"We need to get your mother to the hospital. I think she has a broken rib and I don't know how close it is to her lungs." he said, shooting me a look of complicity. Rita tried to object but by now Luca was looking really worried and he and Joe overrode her protests. I fetched her coat while Joe helped Rita to stand. We draped it over her shoulders because it was too painful for her to lift her arms, then Joe and Luca half carried her down to Luca's car and settled her inside. Joe decided to go with them to the hospital and gave me the keys to the jeep. I leaned into the car, took Rita's hand in mine and kissed her cheek.

"You will be fine," I assured her. Joe looked at me and I smiled weakly. I felt relief surge through me, as if I knew that Rita was going to be all right now. Joe held my gaze as Luca drove off and for the first time in ages I could not read his expression but thought I had detected a certain guarded perplexity there.

I drove the jeep home slowly. It took me a while to get used to the gears and the size of the vehicle but I was pleasantly pleased by the ease with which I could manoeuvre through the muddy potholes. At the cypress I stopped. I wound down the window and the wind tore in immediately. The late afternoon light was dulled by dense, white clouds that almost covered the pale blue sky and this time I did not need to soar up among them to sense the snow. The air was so cold against my cheek that it seemed to burn and I could smell ice in its limpidness.

Maybe it was a trick of the light but as I sat there gazing through the open window, it seemed as though small tendrils of cloud drifted down through the gloaming, wrapping themselves around the cypress, mirroring its tall curves. I heard a hauntingly beautiful sound, like spectral voices raised in song. Listening to the song of the cypress, I remembered how it had called me from my bed, in what I had thought to be a dream, the night before my mother's funeral. That seemed so long ago now, part of another life that I could barely recall. Then, as I had drawn near, the song had lost its clarity but now I felt as if I were a part of the harmony. I watched the ghostly shapes swirl around the cypress and let my mind slide free from my body. Moving toward the tree, I smoothly joined the misty tendrils as they stretched out, until they wrapped the cypress like a veil.

The song was in me. I was a small, elemental chord within the music and was aware of myself; my essence and its infinitesimal yet real significance in the universe. Linked with the mist, I spiralled upward, lost in the eternal dance of the spirit. In a fork between branches, a movement caught my attention and I slowed, focusing on the shape that hovered there. The vaporous, white form shimmered like dandelion fluff and shook with the rhythm of mirth and, as I studied it, a sudden glimpse of sky seen through the tight-knit foliage flashed like two, twinkling, blue eyes.

"Fiammetta" I breathed, then began to laugh with her, at the sheer beauty of life and the graceful freedom of our soul's mesmeric dance.

24

We meet in dreams, when the edges of reality are blurred by time and she sees the world through my eyes.
She stretches herself to assimilate the ancient wisdom, to explore the force of connection between all things in nature.
Once common knowledge, this sense of belonging has been lost so completely throughout the generations that those few who can tap into the universal spirit and use its force are now looked at askance, revered or feared.
Since my first sight of her in spring I have watched the girl grow and shed her pain. I have shared her fears and heightened her joys. She knows who she is now, and is where she wants to be.

Joe phoned around 6 pm to say that Rita was fine. She had been operated on and was still sleeping off the anaesthetic, so Luca was going to bring Joe home, collect some things for his mother and then go back to be with her. She was being kept in hospital for a few days, for which I was glad, because only enforced rest like that would be capable of keeping her from trying to do everything she usually did at home.

"What did the doctor say about the broken rib?" I asked. There was such a long pause before Joe replied that I wondered if the connection had been broken.

"He said that we were lucky to have brought Rita in when we did. Any small movement could have been enough to push that sliver of bone into her lungs." Joe sounded strained, quite unlike himself and I had a sudden flash of fear so strong that it cramped my guts and made me clutch at my stomach. Up till now, he had seen my bond with the cypress as something innocuous and easily put down to feminine intuition, so he had been understanding and encouragingly matter-of-fact about it with me. Now I realised that he was struggling to assimilate this new depth of affinity that linked me to the cypress.

"See you when you get home." I said quickly and put the phone down. My heart was aching. What if Joe could not cope with my ability to see the world from the cypress's viewpoint, its intuitive empathy, its absolute disregard for the confines of time and space; what if he decided that he could not live with someone like that?

I moved to the window. It was almost dark already but, before my breath misted the cold glass, I saw that it was snowing. I called Luna, suddenly desperate to be outside, immersed in the miracle of the snowfall and to throw off my fears. The night air was icy, so cold that it made me breathless. Luna galloped around the lawn while I stood still, eyes closed, feeling the dry snowflakes whisper against my cheeks and eyelids. I stood until the cold had penetrated me completely, as a kind of penance maybe. I knew that I could not turn my back on my new sense of reality, could not withdraw from the cypress, even if Joe were to ask me to. As much as I loved him, to abandon the visionary realm that I had discovered would be to refute part of my own soul and, now that I knew myself so deeply, I could not deny any part of myself for someone else.

Finally, I went back into the house. Luna had got tired of the cold long before me and had returned to the warm spot in from of the fire, where the cats lay. I went upstairs and ran myself a hot bath then, still shivering, undressed and lowered myself into the scented water. I heard a car draw up, then the front door bang and Luna's enthusiastic greeting. I kept silent. I was so scared of how Joe would behave that I did not want to see him, wanted to hold on to the belief that he loved me and nothing could alter that, for as long as I could.

I heard Joe's steady footsteps on the stairs then a light knock on the bathroom door. He did not wait for me to respond, opening the door at the same time as he knocked. As he walked in, the room seemed to shrink, condensed by his sheer size. I searched his face for traces of the carefully guarded look I had seen as he drove off with Luca to take Rita to hospital. Instead, I saw the familiar warm grin that I loved. He sat on the side of the bath, raised one eyebrow playfully and swirled the bubbles with his hand.

"Room in there for me?" he asked. I laughed. There was absolutely no room for him but he stripped off and got in facing me anyway, knees and shoulders staying well clear of the bubbles. He took my foot and gently rubbed my toes and I felt as if he was massaging away my fears.

"I thought that you might think I was too weird, having visions and talking to trees and ghosts." I said, my voice defensive and full of heavy sarcasm, aimed at myself. Joe looked up from my toes and studied me carefully before he replied. Usually I loved the way that he weighed every word before speaking but tonight I wished that he would hurry to condemn or reassure me. Finally, his lips curled slightly and his eyes crinkled in a pensive half-smile.

"Annie, you have a rare gift, honey. You saved Rita's life tonight. I cannot claim to understand how, or know exactly what it is that enables you to tap into these kind of psychic undercurrents but, whatever it is, is part of you." He pulled my legs until I was sitting astride him and kissed me, long and hard.

"I love you," I told him, when he let me come up for air and then slithered around on top of him, oblivious of the water that splashed out of the tub, knowing only that Joe still loved me and all was well with my world.

The next day we woke to 30cm of snow. It was piled up on the balcony railing, even balancing impossibly on the washing line strung between the outbuildings. It weighed down the limbs of the trees around the lake and along the entrance to the woods, creating a magical new landscape of ice tunnels and grottoes. It was not a barren world though but one of magical extremes. There were signs of life in the tracks that birds and small animals left in the snow, which Luna sniffed at with delight when we let her out.

There were only a few days left before Christmas. Joe eyed the snow and decided that the jeep would be able to negotiate the drive today but if we had any more then we would be snowed in, so he decided to go to Arezzo after lunch with his last lot of commissions for the shop and promised to drop off our Christmas presents for everyone in Montalino too, since there was no way that my little car would be able to get through the layer of snow that had transformed the countryside and almost hidden the road.

While I watched him, from the warmth of the lounge, as he carried pieces of furniture and wrapped carvings from his workshop to the jeep, I searched the air for some hint of Fiammetta but had no sense of her nearby. Since my glimpse of her in the misty swirls around the cypress, Fiammetta's presence in the house had not been so constant, or at least not as obvious and there had been no more disturbing conversations in my ear. I almost missed her mischievous intrusions on my thoughts.

After our shared bath last night, Joe and I had talked well into the night and I had unloaded all my fears and doubts onto him. I had told him, in as much detail as I could, about how it felt to be connected to the cypress and about how Fiammetta still hovered in my subconscious. We had lain in bed and Joe had held me close, wrapping his strong arms around me with a touching gentleness. He had been unable to offer any rational explanation for the strange phenomena that I was undergoing but, by the time I had finished unburdening myself, I had felt closer to him than I ever had.

Afterwards I had dreamt about the cypress again but I had no longer felt as if I were being called to it, instead it was as if I had become a part of the massive tree. In my dream I had moved leisurely, like cold, slowly-rising sap. I had felt as though I was caught within the rhythm of a giant's deep and steady breathing and when I woke I had been filled with a deep sense of serenity and latent power.

Joe finished loading the jeep and turned to wave at me. Luna tried to climb into the jeep with him but he grabbed her collar and turned her round, then to cheer her up he spent a few minutes throwing snowballs for her, scooping snow from the roof of the jeep. I laughed so hard that I had tears in my eyes as I watched Luna's look of utter bewilderment each time one of those tempting-looking white balls broke into icy pieces in her mouth. I took pity on her as Joe finally drove off.

"Luna - walkies!" I shouted and she barked loudly in appreciation. I quickly dressed in warm layers, pulled on my thick boots and picked up the dog's lead then locked up and set off, intending to take a walk up to the manor to say hello to Lucia and fill her in on what had happened to Rita.

Today, the sky was a clear azure with not a single cloud to mar its perfection. It was as if yesterday's winter-white sky had never been. The snow glinted in the pale sunlight and transformed the landscape into a gently undulating, silver sea. I cut across the field to the woods behind the house and, by the time I had made it to the footpath that skirted the hunting reserve, had decided not to continue on to the manor house. What would normally have been a nice afternoon stroll had become an army assault course.

The snow was not really deep but it was enough to hinder my progress and I had to keep negotiating the uneven ground full of dips and drifts, where the snow had piled up unexpectedly, causing me to sink almost to my knees. Luna leapt around like a bounding deer and I admired her energy. It was so beautiful to be out here though that I could not bear to turn back straight away. The snow crunched beneath my boots and sparkled on the low-bent boughs of saplings, spider's webs glowed like cotton bolls waiting to be picked and scales of lichen clung reptile-like to exposed bark. As I looked up, the sky was criss-crossed with skeletal, white limbs. I touched a branch that bent like a bow across the path and gasped in surprise as it pinged back up, releasing its snowy weight in a shower that covered me. I laughed joyfully as I brushed away the icy particles from my clothes.

I stopped for a moment and looked across the fields to our home. How I loved living here. I was so relieved that Joe seemed able to accept me as I was, even though just who I was seemed to have changed enormously since he had met me. Today there was yet another change. Up till now I had accepted the thrall of the cypress and Fiammetta's influence in my life, taking what they gave as a gift without trying to manipulate life for myself. Today however, with the world stripped to its bare truth by winter and enhanced by the purity of snow, I thrilled to the new power within me and had the urge to test it. I knew that I could move at will within my mind. If I wanted to explore the nature of an icicle or a cloud I need only reach for them to become one with them. I had moved just as easily to penetrate Rita's body. The distance had meant nothing. Now I wondered exactly how far or deep I could go. Instinctively I raised my arms to my side, palms facing upwards. I could feel the power of the universe pressing into them and I tingled with unspoken need.

Only then did I become aware that the sounds of the day had changed. The frosty quiet, occasionally broken by snow falling from the branches and the snap of ice, had taken on a muffled quality as if I was dreaming. A movement to my right made me turn my head in a kind of slow motion and my eyes gradually focused on the flickering shapes that had drawn my attention.

There was not merely one image swirling against the backdrop of white but many indistinct shapes, which moved in and out of focus as I concentrated on them. I smelt the cypress then and felt reassured by its presence. As its strength enfolded me I saw a vision of it, superimposed on the confused images, the frosting of snow on its wind-driven side glowing like the sheen of a sword blade. Then the cypress slowly faded into the background and the images ran on, like a grainy old cine film flickering across the snow. The more power I pulled from the universe the clearer the images became until I could make out people moving. From their clothing they seemed to come from many different eras without any sense of continuity. They walked singly or in groups, travelled in all seasons, in all weathers. They were unaware of me and of each other, occasionally walking across the same spot simultaneously without noticing each other. As if from a great distance snatches of conversation echoed in my head in modern and archaic Italian.

Time, I realised. I was looking through time itself, not to anything of great import, no great battles or earth-shattering events, merely the actions that this particular place had witnessed. I concentrated on slowing down the flood of images as I adjusted to seeing in this unusual way. One of the images, a young soldier in Second World War uniform stopped so close to me that I wondered if he had seen me but he was just patting his pockets for his cigarettes. He cupped his hand around a match to shield it from the wind that blew in his time alone and exhaled in my face but I could not smell the smoke and he was as oblivious to my presence as they all were. Something touched my leg and I lost my concentration. The images blurred then vanished. Luna's tail bumped against my leg again bringing me fully back to the present.

"Hello girl" I murmured, my voice sounding a little shaky. The experience had been intense and I felt a little tired and very cold but otherwise fine. Judging from the light it was early evening. I had no idea how long I had been swimming in the boundaries of time. It had seemed to be a matter of minutes but must have been at least an hour. No wonder I was cold and Luna must be too. Keeping a tight hold of her lead to keep myself anchored in the present I set off for home revelling in the power that coursed through my veins.

The rest of the evening passed in a kind of a daze. Every now and then my mind would return to the episode in the woods and I would relive the thrill of the force that I had conjured up. The cypress must see life in that way I thought, as a series of moments in time. I felt almost invincible, as if I had received some precious ability to protect myself and help others.

I was so engrossed in these sensations that it was not until the early evening that I began to wonder why Joe was so late coming home. I stoked up the fire and put the guard in front of it again then wandered into the kitchen and peered into the fridge, wondering what to make for dinner. The cats weaved in and out of my legs. Luna joined them and three hopeful, whiskery faces stared up at me. I laughed and set about getting some food for them. If we were all getting hungry then Joe was going to be starving when he got in. *Pasta e fagioli*, I decided. The hearty winter soup made with cannelini beans was just what I fancied and it was one of Joe's favourite dishes. I started chopping onions, garlic and bacon then fried them in olive oil. I opened a can of beans, drained it, mashed half, and then added the lot to the pan, covered it with water and left it to simmer. I glanced at the clock.

It was almost 7 pm and for the first time I began to worry about Joe. With all the snow he might have had an accident or got stuck in a snowdrift. I checked the shelf where we recharged our mobile phones. Sure enough, he had left his phone to charge when he went out. I shook my head equally amused and irritated. I opened the kitchen door, shivering in the icy draught that swept over the threshold and stared into the darkness, hoping for some sign of Joe, the glow of his headlights in the distance or the sound of an engine. There was nothing, just the sigh of new snow as it fell.

When I heard the jeep crunching up the drive half an hour later, my body began to relax and I hummed to myself, anticipating Joe's pleasure when he smelt the soup that was bubbling thickly on the stove.

The door opened and Luna bounded over to greet Joe. When he straightened up from petting the dog and I saw his face properly, I was shocked. I had never seen him look so angry. He crossed the kitchen in three huge strides and I had to force myself not to flinch as he grasped my shoulders and pulled me to him, almost suffocating me with the strength of his embrace. I returned the bear hug he gave me and then eased away from him.

"What's happened" I asked as I watched him kick off his shoes and shrug out of his damp coat.

"Here, come and sit down and tell me about it" I coaxed, giving the soup a stir.

"Ok. Something smells good." Joe said pulling out a chair and leaning back in it, the tension beginning to leave him gradually. He shot me a calculating look and rubbed a hand over the stubble on his chin then said,

"Annie, you sure do make life complicated. I'm not sure whether to tell you what happened or not."

"You better had or I will torture it out of you!" I teased, waving the wooden spoon at him and was rewarded by his the first smile of the evening.

"I stopped off in the bar for a drink with Luca before coming home and there was the usual crowd of old guys there, talking politics and putting the world to rights. Then someone cracked a joke saying that I should be careful, taking up with a witch. Everyone was nodding and murmuring about you being the new witch of the woods and nonsense like that."

I snorted with laughter at that and Joe stopped his tale and looked at me as if surprised at my reaction.

"You don't mind?" he asked and I shook my head.

"How did that rumour get started?" I wondered, finding the situation quite funny but touched that Joe had felt angry on my behalf.

"It seems that Rita told some of her visitors in hospital that you were responsible for saving her life and so the latest village rumour is that you have some kind of second sight or something."

I shook my head.

"So then what happened?"

"I told them they were all *coglione*." I burst out laughing at this uncustomary rudeness and got up to wrap my arms around Joe.

"My hero" I said kissing him gently. I was sorry that people were talking about me and even sorrier that Joe would have to put up with their nonsense but I thought we were both strong enough to withstand a bit of gossip. People would lose interest in me soon enough and hopefully accept me for what I was.

I sat on Joe's knee and began to talk about my own experiences that afternoon, trying to make sense of the time-warped images I

267

had witnessed. I was waxing lyrical, quite carried away in my description when Joe's stomach rumbled loudly and I broke free of his embrace with a laugh and ran to stir the soup pan. It was sticking but not burnt and the smell that wafted from it made my own stomach rumble in unison with Joe's. I added a little more water and dropped in a couple of handfuls of small, ditalini pasta. Joe set the table and opened a bottle of red wine. He poured two glasses and handed me one as I stood, stirring the soup. I sipped it and raised my head to find him studying me intently. He raised his glass to mine in a toast and said quietly,

"To the new witch."

25

Nothing is as it seems. What at first appears uniformly white is gradually revealed in icy shades of silver, rose, violet and blue; a mantle of great beauty that hides beneath it the promise of life.
The girl and I are as one, able to voyage together in the flux between the ethereal realm and human reality. The man who loves her is patient, allowing her all the freedom of soul that she needs, in order to bind her to him completely. He sees many things that she has yet to see, caught up as she still is in her journey of exploration. He continues to hold her with all the tenderness he possesses and waits, with winter, for her to awake from her inner journey and discover what lies within her.

The snow continued sporadically over the next few days, cutting us off from the rest of the world. In our isolation, Joe and I turned to each other, consolidating our closeness. Between snowfalls, the sky remained a flat, white expanse that the sun scarcely penetrated, even at midday. The scent of winter was elusive; cool, clean purity. In the deep trails that Luna wore through it each day, the snow was packed down to an icy layer as hard as diamonds. The days were now as bitter as the nights and, apart from moments of snowball fun with Luna, we stayed inside, close to the fire.

Watching the feathery snow fall beyond the window was a constant source of fascination. We talked for hours, sitting in the old armchairs, watching flames tremble across smouldering logs, with the soft crackle of the fire in the background. Occasionally there was an answering crack from outside as ice split on the lake or a build up of snow fell from the roof but otherwise the land was quiet, muted. This outer winter-world of chaste restraint was a perfect foil to the warmth and passion that filled our home. We made love often, lazing in the warmth of our bed for hours in the morning and going to bed early each night

Night fell early over the land and I found it oddly comforting, like being held in a safe, womblike embrace, while the firelight and bright Christmas decorations put vibrant colour back into our home and softened the stern beauty of winter. As I lay in Joe's arms at night, listening as his breathing slowed to the rhythm of sleep, I considered this kind of enforced hibernation to be profoundly necessary, a time to pare everything down to bare essentials so that we could examine our lives in minute detail.

With a well-stocked freezer and rows of sturdy black cabbage hidden beneath the snow in the garden, I was confident that we had enough food to keep even Joe happy while we were snowed in. We had bought a turkey and frozen it weeks before and Joe had insisted on buying several of every type of Italian Christmas delicacies for me to try. At the time I had thought the supplies exaggerated but now I was very glad of the abundance. To my relief I was no longer suffering from the sensation of queasiness that had gripped me recently and, with all the Christmas goods to choose from, it was easy to eat too much. I found to my chagrin that I adored the sticky sweet *Panforte* and was quite unable to resist it. My diet was going to hell but Joe laughed at me when I told him this and insisted that I looked perfect the way I was. In the end I let go and just enjoyed the treats. The only small regret that I had, as we woke up on Christmas morning, was that I would not be able to indulge in my favourite, Christmas Pudding, this year. When I confessed this hankering to Joe at breakfast, he surprised me by reaching to the top of the kitchen cupboard and producing a small, foil-wrapped basin.

"I saw it in the delicatessens in Arezzo and wondered if you would like it," he told me, laughing at my expression of delight.

The phone began to ring then and continued all morning as our various neighbours called to wish us Merry Christmas. I answered the phone most often because Joe had taken charge in the kitchen, happily whistling to himself as he peeled potatoes and basted the turkey.

"Pronto," I said, picking up the phone for the umpteenth time. I smiled when I heard Rita's voice. She was glad to be home from the hospital but fed up because her family had rallied around and were making a concerted effort to stop her from doing too much and she was suffering from being forced to stay still.

"Luca is cooking," Rita told me, sounding so horrified that I had to laugh. She joined in, then said,

"I have a house full of children and grandchildren and am being spoilt rotten." In an undertone she added, "I hate to think what a state my kitchen will be in, Ann and I am sure that Luca did not put enough chicken livers in the meat sauce."

"It sounds as if he is doing a great job." I placated her and was glad when she changed the subject and thanked me for the Christmas present that Joe had left for her.

I had spent ages trying to decide what to get for Rita. I had not wanted to embarrass her with anything excessive but at the same time had wanted to give her something special, knowing that she could never afford even small luxuries for herself. Lucia and Pietro had been easy to buy for, some unusual flower bulbs that I had ordered by catalogue for him and an extravagant box of chocolates for her. Joe had chosen a music CD for Luca and in the end, I had settled on a hand-painted silk scarf for Rita. I had paid a small fortune for it in a boutique in Montevarchi but the delicate pattern of dusky pink roses and the lush coolness of the silk between my fingers had been just perfect.

"Thank you Ann," Rita effused, "It is too beautiful to wear." I could suddenly imagine her folding the scarf up and putting it in a drawer to be taken out and admired every now and then but never worn, so I quickly assured her that it was inexpensive, just a small token.

"You could wear it on New Year's Eve, to the party at the manor," I suggested, wondering as I said it if we would be able to get there or if we would still be snowbound then.

"Yes, I will and I will give you your gift then." Rita sounded quite excited at the idea of wearing something pretty to the party and I smiled, glad that she had swallowed my bit of subterfuge.

"You know," she continued "I have never got into the habit of exchanging gifts at Christmas. That is why I did not have your present ready when Joe came the other day. When I was a girl Christmas was a purely religious day and us children had to wait until *Befana* for our presents." She must have sensed that I was confused and began to explain.

"Befana is an old woman, a kind of white-witch who comes on the night of the Epiphany." She hesitated for a fraction too long after saying the word *witch* and I knew that she was thinking about the latest village gossip. She cleared her throat and continued,

"On 6th January she brings presents for children who have been good and coal for those who have been bad. Father Christmas didn't exist in Italy in those days. Sometimes I was given coal too but it was only the pretend, sugary type, thank goodness," she laughed. "There is an old proverb which says that Befana comes and takes all the festivities away and then there are no more celebrations until Carnival." I heard a commotion in the background and Rita said,

"I have to go Ann. Luca does not know how much pasta to cook for all of us and he will use the wrong pan if I do not sort him out." I said goodbye and put the phone down with a grin, thinking how very happy Rita had sounded to be needed.

In our kitchen, Joe had everything well under control. He grinned at me and indicated the oven,

"Everything is in there, now we can have a small break. Come and sit by the fire. I want to give you my present," he said taking my hand and pulling me down the hallway.

"I thought we had agreed to do the presents after lunch," I protested half-heartedly. Actually I could not wait to see Joe's face as he unwrapped the things that I had chosen for him. He had already opened one ages ago, the crystal star that I had bought in Arezzo. I had wanted it to shine above the stable in the *presepe* for

272

as long as possible. That morning Joe had unwrapped a smiling baby Jesus, the final piece of his nativity scene. When he had laid him in the manger, the star had swirled above the baby's head like a primeval mobile.

I allowed Joe to drag me into the lounge and sit me in an armchair. I closed my eyes when he asked me to and listened with amusement to loud bumping, scuffling noises as he fetched my surprise. When I was finally allowed to open my eyes, on the floor in front of me was the largest gift-wrapped present imaginable. Joe had used several different types of paper to cover a long, tubular shape that was about 2 metres long. At one end he had fastened a big red bow. I laughed, getting down on my hands and knees and beginning to rip away the paper. As soon as I touched it, I guessed what it was but kept Joe laughing with a running commentary of improbable, tubular things.

"It's a giant tube of toothpaste."

"No."

"Then it's a huge rolling pin - the world's biggest fountain-pen – a certificate for learning to cook the enormous meals that you need." Joe shook his head in mock solemnity. I grinned at him, loving the way his hair flopped over his forehead and caught the glow from the fire. He was wearing another of his tatty old sweaters. I hoped that he would like the one I had bought him and wear that instead, at least when we went out. While I hesitated, examining the strong planes of his face he raised an eyebrow at me, a gesture that I adored. I smiled, holding his gaze for a long moment then started on another section of the paper patchwork.

Finally, all the paper was off and I unrolled the carpet that I had seen and fallen in love with recently but which, at the time, I had decided was something that I did not really need. I was a little surprised because I had been convinced that Joe had been making something for me in the workshop since he had been so secretive and shooed me away from there whenever I went out to visit him. I wondered what he had been doing.

273

Joe helped me to shift the carpet into place in front of the fireplace. Brightly patterned in warm shades of red and orange, the carpet added intensity to the room and complimented the fire blazing nearby. I remembered saying to Joe, when I had first seen it, that it looked exactly the way that a magic carpet should look.

"Come for a ride?" Joe asked, grinning cheekily up at me as he sank cross-legged in the centre of the carpet.

"Why not," I replied, plonking myself opposite him so that our jean-clad knees touched. Only then did I see the small tissue-paper package tied to the tassels at one corner of the carpet. Joe detached it and handed it to me, leaning over for a lingering kiss before letting it go. I took my time on this present, knowing instinctively that it contained something special. Inside the flimsy layer of tissue lay a pair of aquamarine and platinum earrings. I slipped them through my ears. They hung almost to my jaw-line and as I swung my head I could feel them dance coolly against my cheek.

"They are the exact colour of your eyes." Joe told me.

"How romantic!" I teased, sliding closer so that I could kiss him, then pulling away.

"My turn," I said, starting to get up and fetch his presents but Joe would not let me go. He held me back and kissed me softly where the earrings swayed.

"Later," he murmured. It was easy to be persuaded. I stretched out on the carpet, pulling him to me. He shrugged off his sweater and I slid my fingers into the neck of his shirt, smoothing his chest as I undid it, pressing kisses onto the soft skin beneath each button.

A buzzer sounded in the kitchen. Joe looked at me in disbelief and we both started to giggle. If he hadn't put the timer on, our lunch would have undoubtedly been burnt. Joe moved reluctantly, standing up and then holding out his hand to pull me to my feet. Before he could go to sort out the roast, I stopped him, pressing my hips against him and nuzzling the bare expanse of chest that I had uncovered.

"Later," I reassured him.

26

The girl has moved slowly through the bars of her own mind-built cage to find true freedom of the soul.
People fear what they do not know, scorn that which they cannot understand and, though they want to believe in the idealistic concept of liberty, they fear it too. Those with more open minds will turn to the girl for advice; others will judge her by their own self-restrictions.
I sense that the man from the house by the lake is troubled by my presence now. I will wait for him, as once I waited for the girl.
Let him come; ask of me what he will, unburden his heart;
I will try to ease his cares.

I heard a car pull into the drive as I was pouring out our morning coffee. Joe was still dressing, I could hear him lumbering around upstairs. He was probably searching for his socks again. Luna and he played a rather sweet game in the mornings, where she would gently pick up some article of clothing that Joe had put out on the chair and then run off with it while his back was turned. Her favourite items were socks and she was very good at hiding them, usually dropping them in some obscure corner, so that when Joe finally found them they would have accumulated a layer of dog hair and dust.

The snow had begun to thaw just after Christmas and now, as the end of the year approached, the roads were fairly clear. Thinking that the car probably belonged to the postman, I wandered around the side of the house to greet him, warming my hands on my mug of coffee as I went.

It was not the postman after all but a family that I did not recognise: a boy with a tear-stained face, his belligerent looking father and his mother, who saw me first and gave me a hesitantly hopeful smile. The others looked up when I called out to them, with varying degrees of trepidation in their expressions. I heard the boy ask, with childish disregard for good manners, if I were the witch. His mother hushed him quickly and the father moved, somewhat protectively in front of them. I smiled as pleasantly as I could, noticing for the first time the small bundle that the little boy was holding awkwardly in his arms.

"Can I help you?" I asked. The father cleared his mouth and tugged at his coat lapels before answering. *Tedious man* the thought flashed through my brain, making me grin: it was exactly the kind of thought that Fiammetta would have expressed out loud. Before his father could make up his mind how to address me, the boy, whom I judged to be about eight or nine, staggered forward, indicating the bundle with his chin,

"This is Rex." He informed me. I saw a whiskery-brown snout move amid the cover.

"Hello Rex. What is wrong with you?" I asked, addressing the animal. The boy laughed,

"He can't answer you. He is only a dog."

"Well, maybe you can tell me instead. What is your name?"

"Samuele"

"Ok, Samuele, come on inside, where it is a bit warmer and you can explain everything to me."

At that moment Joe opened the front door to see what was happening. He was fully dressed, so he must have recovered his socks. Luna dashed over to greet the strangers. She leapt up at the boy, almost knocking him over in her desire to smell his bundle. Joe called her back in a tone he rarely used and she slunk to his side, ears down and a mournful look in her brown eyes. The cats obviously thought that two dogs in their home was too much and stalked, disdainfully, down the drive, heading for the woods.

We all trooped through to the kitchen. Samuele's father tried to take Rex from the boy, who stubbornly clutched his bundle tighter and earned himself an irritated glare.

"Put Rex there, on the table, Samuele," I said, restraining myself from trying to help. It was obviously very important to the child that he be the one to take care of his dog. Once on the table and unwrapped from its tatty blanket, the dog was revealed as a small, brown and white mongrel. He eyed me dolefully as I approached, panting heavily but staying still as his young master stroked his back.

"What seems to be wrong with Rex?" I asked.

"He was sick all last night and again this morning and he doesn't want to eat anything." The boy's voice quavered and he bit his lip as more tears threatened. His father broke in impatiently,

"I told him that I would not waste my money on a vet. The dog is old, he has to get used to the idea that it will die soon."

A huge tear slid down Samuele's cheek and plopped noiselessly onto the table. Rex struggled to his feet and licked the boy's face. The dog certainly did look old and rather moth-eaten but, as I ran my fingers gently over his wiry fur, I did not get the sensation that there was any serious problem.

Samuele's mother moved to put a protective arm around his shoulders and spoke for the first time.

"I am sorry to bother you," I waved away her excuses with a smile, which she returned, looking suddenly prettier and less harried.

"People have been talking about you in the village. They say that you have the same skills with the wild creatures as Fiammetta did."

"Did you know Fiammetta?" I asked, intrigued by the idea that I was being associated with her and expected to take over the role of local healer.

"Not really, but I went to school with her son, when she still lived in the village and I remember that if anyone found an injured animal they always took it to her."

I turned my attention back to Rex. As I concentrated, my mind cleared slowly, until I was aware of nothing and no person, just the small, shivering dog. I could feel numerous small aches that were caused by nothing more than age and a sensation of nausea and cramps in its stomach. I had a strong suspicion that Rex would live for another few years yet, as long as his loving master did not give him the kind of rich treats that he had gorged on over the Christmas break.

"Samuele, has Rex been eating things that he doesn't usually?" I asked. His face flushed and he nodded.

"Well, I am sure that he loved them but they gave him an upset tummy. Don't worry, he will be fine." Samuele rewarded me with a beatific smile at the verdict but his father looked disgruntled, as if I had somehow cheated him. I examined the dog again, trying hard not to show my amusement, as I imagined the kind of caustic remark that Fiammetta would have fired at the man. I crossed the kitchen and took a small bottle from my herb cupboard. I half filled it with tap water, carefully checking its exact level and then rummaged in the cupboard until I found the packet that I wanted. Fiammetta had written on the folded paper *Nepetella – good for stomach disorders.* I unfolded the packet, took a small pinch of dried wild mint and dribbled it slowly into the bottle. As I did so, I kept up a running commentary about the herb and its properties in English, hoping that I was giving the impression of a wise woman at work, muttering incantations as I prepared my remedy.

"What on earth am I doing, I must be out of my mind," I intoned solemnly as I screwed the lid on the bottle, careful not to catch Joe's eye. He had moved to stand behind the others, and his shoulders were shaking with suppressed mirth. After I had shaken the medicine well, I handed it to Samuele, with strict instructions on how the medicine should be administered: half a teaspoon added to Rex's dinner once a day until he was fully recovered and absolutely no treats or it would ruin the effect. Samuele did not object this time when his father picked up Rex and carried him to the car. I took the boy aside for a moment while his parents settled the dog on the back seat.

"You know," I told him, "It is true that Rex is old but, with all the love and care that you give him, I am sure that he will live a long and very happy life." Samuele flashed me a smile and climbed into the backseat to cuddle up to the dog. Joe and I watched until the car was out of sight before we broke down. We laughed until we cried and I felt so weak that I had to hold on to Joe to keep from falling.

"I can tell that this house is going to be transformed into a menagerie." Joe said ruefully. "I can already imagine people coming to drop off unwanted kittens and lame dogs."

"I hope not," I replied, wiping my watering eyes.

"You were not there when they arrived so you did not hear him, but the little boy actually asked his mother if I was a witch!" I grinned up at Joe, but was surprised to glimpse a frown crease his brow before he turned away from me and walked back to the house. He obviously had not got over his anger at the way people were talking about me yet.

The rest of the day was uneventful. We walked in the afternoon, enjoying the brightness of the sun, even though it offered little warmth and the ground beneath our feet was still frozen hard. Knowing that we would probably be expected to eat huge amounts at Lucia and Pietro's New Year's Eve party the following day, we settled for a simple evening meal of cheese and bread, toasted over the fire. I was preoccupied with plans for the party. I had my outfit, which I could not wait to wear, but I had a head full of girly beauty preparations and the difficult choices of what jewellery and underwear to wear with it and so I failed to notice that Joe was withdrawn. It was only when we were in bed and I was unable to sleep because of his restlessness, that I realised he had been unusually quiet all day.

In the end I slept fitfully, aware of Joe as he shifted frequently, tugging the covers and murmuring in his sleep. The next morning we were both quiet at breakfast, smothering yawns and drinking more coffee than usual. When I asked Joe what had disturbed him in the night he shrugged and said he had no idea but I noticed that he avoided my eye. He wasn't hungry for once and after a small bowl of cereal he rose, kissed my cheek and went off to his workshop. Luna chose to accompany Joe rather than stay with me in the warmth of the kitchen, as if she too thought there was something unusual about him. I wondered if he was maybe catching a cold and took down Fiammetta's note books to search for her cold remedies. I took the books into the lounge and threw a log on the fire but I could not settle properly. Mid morning I decided to check on Joe and see if he fancied a coffee break. I dressed warmly intending to take Luna for a walk if Joe did not want to be interrupted. As soon as I got out of the house I sensed that something was different. I could hear no sounds coming from the shed and when I pulled the door open I was not surprised to see the workshop empty. It was so unusual for him to go off without warning me though that I was worried about him.

I closed my eyes and waited for the scent of wood shavings and varnish to fade as I sought out the cypress. I would use our connection to soar over the valley until I could see where Joe and Luna were. They could not be far because the jeep had still been parked in its usual spot when I had come out of the house. However, as soon as I sensed the cypress I knew that there was no need to stretch beyond my body in order to find Joe because the cypress could see him crossing the field towards it.

For a few seconds I hesitated, not sure whether to intrude or not since Joe had obviously not wanted me to know where he was going but then concern overcame all else. I hurried through the ploughed remains of the sunflower field, slipping on the ice in my haste. My breath showed in white, dragon-like exhalations until I buried my mouth in my scarf and began to breath the icy air in through my nose. The path and road themselves were relatively clear but the fields were still white, strangely swollen and distorted where no one had trampled the snow. A sudden change in the vibrations of energy linking me to the cypress told me that Joe had reached it. Shortly after, when I was close enough to see the tall spire of the cypress I stopped. There was a movement ahead and Luna trotted up to join me. I patted her, hesitating about how much closer to go. The cypress looked almost black against the background of snow. It had shrugged off the small amount of snow that had settled on it before Christmas and was once more impregnable.

It was strange to see Joe standing so close to the cypress, looking up into the thick branches that rose above him. I edged forward as Joe put out his hand, touching the trunk almost gingerly, as if wary of receiving some kind of shock. He must be remembering what I had told him I felt whenever I touched the tree. He stood still for a while, face intense with concentration. When he opened his eyes again they burned with anger and frustration. He withdrew his hand and hung his head then, so suddenly that I jumped, he raised it again with a roar and hit the bark with his fist.

"Why?" he yelled, "Why do I feel nothing. What is it you want from her? Why won't you leave her alone?" I felt the most enormous surge of sympathy flood through me. I reached out to the cypress with my mind. He loves me, he is worried about me, I thought and felt the tree's response of impartial compassion.

"I don't understand," Joe's voice was quieter again, almost a whisper. "Please, let me feel something. I want to look after her. I used to think there was a simple explanation for this whole strange situation but there isn't. How can I know that you are not harming her?" He shrugged then and laughed bitterly, walking away.

"I am an idiot," he said. "There is nothing here, it is all in Annie's head."

My God, I thought, Joe thinks I am crazy, that I'm having hallucinations, suffering from delusions. As I thought it, some small part of my mind stopped and examined the idea dispassionately. Maybe that was the answer. Maybe I was having some kind of breakdown. I turned this unpleasant thought over in my mind, but then I straightened my shoulders and dismissed it. I heard a soft cackle of amusement and sensed Fiammetta's presence strongly for the first time in ages. Then I felt a sudden surge of energy emanate from the cypress and shudder in the air around it.

281

Joe jerked and stumbled back a step. He had felt it too, I realised. He straightened up and moved back to stand where he had been before. He reached out his hand again but this time with resolution. I saw his upturned face, saw the expression of wonder spread across it and I felt the cypress as it communicated with him.

The song was a quiet one, like a gentle lullaby, sung for an infant. It sung of strength and patience, of combating fear with love and finding freedom in the gesture of setting free. The music strummed the space between us all, like a delicate air on the vibrating chords of the breeze. Joe turned his head and looked straight at me so that I knew that he had felt my presence linked with the cypress's. I quickly crossed the distance between us and took his hand, placing my other on the cypress's cold bark.

"Forgive me, Annie. I was scared of what I couldn't understand."

"It's ok," I reassured him, squeezing his fingers. They were icy. I noticed that the knuckles on the hand that splayed wide across the trunk were scraped and bleeding, the blood seeping down over the tears of resin. The cypress crooned on softly as I broke the connection. I took off my scarf, wound it around Joe's hand then kissed him tenderly. We walked away from the cypress to where Luna sat waiting for us. I slipped my arm around Joe's waist as we walked and looked up at him. He held my gaze then smiled slightly.

"It is peaceful. It's a really peaceful feeling, isn't it?" he said, questioningly. I nodded. Joe squeezed me tight.

I did not know how long Joe had been nursing his worries about me but I could tell that they had been eradicated by his own gentle contact with the tree's energy. I thought myself incredibly lucky to have the love of this man, who had enough courage to challenge his deeply rooted beliefs. He had gone out with the intention of challenging whatever it was that had a hold on me, of negotiating with something that he did not really believe could exist.

282

There was so much in this world yet to be discovered, so much potential in our human bodies that remained unused. I had concluded long before that the force I felt with the cypress was one of these mysterious, undeveloped resources and that it was intrinsically benevolent. I had become so used to the power that I no longer found it perplexing but for Joe, as each new aspect manifested itself, it must have seemed highly disturbing.

When the house came into sight; mellow stone framed in crisp white, the two cats waiting on the doorstep like unmatched bookends; I looked up at Joe. He tightened his grip on my hand for an instant, all the force of his love concentrated in that touch. Luna streaked ahead and nudged the cats, who surged up and rubbed along her. They had long since overcome their initial state of cold war and now more often than not all slept curled around each other by the smouldering embers of the fire. How lucky I was I thought, squeezing Joe's hand back as I sent a message of gratitude to the cypress before it relinquished its hold on us.

27

The air in winter has a uniquely candid quality. The sky is often so bright that it hurts to gaze upon it. Each breath of ice burns like fire, purifying the soul with its crisp innocence. At this time of year, when all is reduced to its very essence, I feel the force of life most strongly. The absence of distractions in the landscape allows me to focus on the inner beauty of the world, revealed in all its stark honesty.

There is also a secrecy about winter that I relish. Beneath its icy mantle, the earth holds life in its dark womb, nurturing it patiently as it waits for spring. The mystery of life is hidden by swollen drifts of snow, like the soft flesh of a pregnant woman's curves.

Winter bestows a threefold gift, of protection, mystery and hope.

Coming out of the steamy bathroom, I almost collided with Joe, who had already showered and dressed. I stepped back to appraise him and let out a long slow whistle of approval.

"Hey, you stole my line!" Joe laughed, sliding his dark eyes over me as I stood, wrapped in a bath towel, on the landing. I shooed him away and he clattered down the stairs, the heels of his polished black shoes echoing on the tiles.

To keep warm, I pulled on an old tracksuit while I dried my hair and put on my make-up. My outfit lay on the bed where I had put it earlier and the soft velvet caught the light and reflected it warmly. I smudged charcoal eye-shadow along the upper corners of my lids and added black mascara, then counterbalanced the sultry look with a pale shimmer of lip-gloss. I slipped the aquamarine earrings that Joe had given me through my lobes and swung my head to see them dance. I smiled, thinking that, after so long without make-up, I looked like a different person tonight and it was fun to dress up occasionally.

My happy mood ended when I pulled on the black evening trousers. I had such a struggle to do the button up on them and yet, I had bought a larger size than usual. I grimaced and shrugged into the jacket. Its smooth, long lines concealed my tummy and the wine colour really suited me but my happiness of a few minutes ago had fled.

Just then Luna reappeared, damp sock clamped in her jaws, claws clicking and skidding on the floor tiles as she swerved through the doorway. Seeing me, she forgot about the sock game and decided that my velvet outfit needed a good covering of dog hairs to finish it off. By the time I had finished pushing her away, avoiding wild sweeps of tail and tongue, I was laughing again and said a silent thanks to Luna for snapping me out of my female sulk. I scratched her silky ears the way she liked as she calmed down a bit then straightened up and noticed Joe leaning in the doorway watching us. I had not heard him come back upstairs with the noise Luna was making.

The corridor at his back was dark, as were his clothes, so that his face stood out in stark relief. With one dark eyebrow lifted in amusement, the sleek hair flopping across his forehead, he looked like a 1950's movie star; urbane sophistication gilding a rugged frame. As he pushed himself away from the wall and moved decisively towards me, the look in his eye reflected the sudden desire that swept through me.

Needless to say, we were late for the party. Lucia had been given permission to use the manor's big hall for the evening and light spilled from the large arched windows and into the courtyard, already full of cars by the time we arrived. Joe pulled the jeep to a halt near the horse-chestnut tree. How long ago that first glimpse of him, as he'd stood beneath the tree in all its springtime glory, seemed now.

Joe opened my door for me and tactfully helped me out. I had almost twisted my ankle in the new high-heeled shoes when we had left home. Reminding myself to walk like a lady tonight, I held his arm gratefully as we crossed the cobbles where someone, probably Pietro, had been hard at work, shovelling away the slush.

Joe pushed the great oak doors open and ushered me in. I had been in the big hall many times but only when it was empty; an echoing, vaulted room that held the chill of winter even during the summer heat. Now a blast of warm air greeted me and chased away the shivers brought on by the brittle night. I loosened my coat and looked around. Lucia had been busy. The hall was bedecked with boughs of fir and holly. Mistletoe was hung strategically over the apex of every arch and a long table had been prepared in the middle of the room, covered in white linen and crystal that reflected the light from the many candles spaced along the table and around the room.

Lucia herself bustled over to greet us, shouting for Pietro to come and take our coats. Her face was flushed from the warmth and the excitement of playing hostess. She folded me into her arms in a big hug then held me away from her and looked me over approvingly. She led me over to the fire to warm up, asking me where I had got my jacket.

"Such a colour would suit me I am sure, and so soft!" I looked back at Joe and returned his grin.

Rita was seated in splendour by the fire on an upright chair borrowed from the table. She looked much better and I was touched to notice that she wore the scarf I had given her for Christmas around her neck. Big logs blazed in a fireplace built wide enough to seat people around its inner hearth. Above the mantelpiece hung the heraldic coat of arms of the manor's owners. Other such mementoes hung on walls around the hall, crossed lances, shields and a few hunting trophies with sad, dull eyes gazing over the guests heads. As always with Lucia I was able to relax and let her do most of the talking. She had a lot to tell us about; the preparations for the dinner, the complicated menu, the small panic when she had realised that Pietro had forgotten to buy more cheese and a final discussion of the seating plan. Rita nodded or shook her head in response to the running commentary and I followed her gestures, only partially concentrating on what Lucia was saying.

Luca was not there. The party had promised to be too tame for him so he had taken Giulia to Florence, for a night of street parties and an open-air concert. The hall was full of people though. A lot of them I knew or recognised from the village but there were also quite a few of Lucia's relatives whom I had never met. There was also a bunch of small children dashing around and shouting to each other. I smiled at the behaviour of the adults. Apart from the odd benevolent pat on the head or brushing down and setting upright again of an unsteady toddler, they ignored the children completely.

The warmth in the hall was as much due to the crowd as to the fire and I was pleasantly surprised. My memories of the place had made me worry about being underdressed before leaving home. Now I unbuttoned the jacket and would have taken it off if I had not felt the tightness of the top underneath. I would save my dignity and leave the jacket on.

Firelight flickered on Rita's face and the glow made her look quite young. She smiled at me, a mischievous look of complicity that went unnoticed by our hostess as she continued her monologue. A log rolled out from the fire, sending small sparks flying upward. I saw a pair of tongs on the hearth and bent to pick them up and roll the smouldering wood back onto the fire. Swirls of smoke curled around the blackened log, tendrils reaching upward, seeking the gaping maw of the chimney. As I jabbed the thick log with the tongs and set it rolling back to the fire, the smoke seemed for an instant, to draw together and form an unmistakable image. The smoke became a halo of white hair around a ghostly face, mocking eyes surprisingly gentle as they found my own. Then the smoke dissolved and spun away into the chimney and the starry night beyond.

"Fiammetta!" I must have said her name aloud but neither Lucia nor Rita had heard my exact words and I managed to cover up by mumbling something about the heat as I straightened up.

287

Lucia left us to hurry things up in the kitchen and I took her place by Rita's side, facing the fire so that I could more easily study the flames, while asking Rita about her Christmas. In spite of watching carefully, I saw no more signs of Fiammetta and I gradually turned my attention back to the room. Fiammetta's presence in my life had been less frequent recently. However, for whatever reason she had chosen to visit me now, startling me in her inimitable way, I was glad to feel her closeness as the old year, which had brought so many changes in my life, slipped imperceptibly into the next.

Lucia had really gone overboard with the food for the party. Sitting between Joe and Rita, I was introduced to a typical Italian festive dinner, the kind Joe dreamt about but which had me full by the second course and wondering how I could politely refuse something. Since there was no Luna under my chair to help me out, I picked my way though small portions of each course and let Joe finish off whatever he liked most. Glancing at his slim frame one would think he ate sparingly. My clothes had been tight before I came and now were digging in uncomfortably. I grimaced as Lucia leant over the table and urged me finish my pasta in Tuscan ragu.

I had relished the warm crostini with dark meat sauce that had been our antipasto along with various sliced cold meats. The ravioli in meat broth that followed had been delicious. The pasta with ragu now heaped on my plate was one of my favourite dishes but I had heard Lucia and Rita discussing the menu earlier and knew what was still to come: *bollito*, mixed cuts of meat boiled with carrots and potatoes and served with fresh mayonnaise, then a selection of meat roasted on a spit and served with roast potatoes and a winter salad and finally a selection of all the traditional Italian Christmas cakes and sweets.

Joe reached over, kissed my cheek and dug his fork into my pasta. His own plate was empty already. I glanced at Rita, who was involved in a deep conversation with one of Lucia's relatives about a trip she had taken recently, organised by the church, to see the various *presepe* in Rome. It was, she said the only trip she had ever been on, apart from a yearly pilgrimage when she was younger to the sanctuary San Francesco at La Verna. For some reason Rita's request of small portions had been granted whilst mine had been ignored. Maybe there was something to be said for all that piety.

Joe offered me some more wine but I shook my head. I was still toying with my first glass. In fact I was feeling rather strange. The heat of the crowded room, the rich scents of the food and wine and the flickering candlelight and smoke from the table decorations were making me feel light-headed. I reached for my water. Lucia had placed thick, white candles along the big table, decorated with holly berries and cypress fronds. The small flame from the nearest candle danced in the air, quivering as laughter shifted the air. A thin thread of smoke shimmered up toward the vaulted ceiling.

Plates were cleared away and the bollito appeared. Rita turned to me and asked about my Christmas. I picked at the food and chatted until the roast was brought out. Pietro handed me the salad.

"See, the tiny heart of the black cabbage goes well in a salad," he said, picking out a leaf to show me.

Finally, out came the cakes and the sweet vinsanto and the room smelt of icing sugar and sweet wine.

My head was really spinning now although I had hardly touched my wine. Suddenly Joe seemed too far away. I felt a mixture of concern for myself and embarrassment at the fuss I would cause if I actually fainted. The edges of my vision grew dark, until all I was aware of was the small dancing candle flame near me.

"Fiammetta. Her name meant small flame." I said, but no one replied so I supposed that I had not spoken aloud. As I thought her name, though, I became aware of the old woman's spirit near me and felt comforted. I felt as if her arms were wrapped around me holding me up. A waft of her lavender scent counteracted the clammy, sick heat that gripped me. For a moment I leant my head back to rest on her shoulder. The candle in front of me glowed brighter whilst the rest of the room grew dark until the flame danced alone.

Seconds passed and I heard Fiammetta murmur that it was time to see clearly, to open my mind. The flame before me drew upwards in a sudden draught and became cypress shaped; red at the base, like the colour of the blood moon; golden like the moon-sheen on Joe's hair as he had pushed me down into the cold stone in the hollow. In a kind of delirium I remembered that night. Joe's heat invading me. The red moon that hung low in the night. Blood moon, no monthly blood, flame bulging, smooth curves of pregnant snowdrifts. I knew.

As the realisation hit me, I blacked out completely and when I came back to my senses Joe's arm was holding me up and Fiammetta had gone.

"Are you ok?" Joe's voice was soft, his eyes gentle. I struggled to sit straight and he released me and passed me a glass of water.

"Don't worry; you were only out for a fraction of a second. I don't think anyone else noticed," he reassured me. "The room is very warm; I expect it just got to you."

I nodded and swallowed the cool water.

The vision had gone and with it the feeling of weakness but I was left shaken and with a desperate need to be alone, to assimilate my newfound knowledge. I forced myself to sit still for a few minutes until Joe was no longer worried about me and had turned his attention to Pietro who was talking about his plans to buy a new tractor.

With a quick murmured excuse in Joe's ear, about needing some fresh air, I slipped out of the big hall, found my coat under a pile of others left on the entrance hall table and stepped outside. After the warmth indoors the night clasped around me, iron cold, squeezing my lungs like a vice. I tucked my head down into my collar and warmed my breath as I stepped gingerly over the cobbles and the icy sharp sludge piled at the edge of the grass verge. I made my way towards the low wall of the viewpoint, heels catching on the sprawling roots of the horse chestnut beneath the snow. Looking behind I saw the strange footprints the marred the pristine beauty of the lawn, a tiny hole where my heel dug deep and the smudged hollow of the pointed toe. The darkness of the night was softened by mellow light that poured from the arched windows of the hall, painting honey-coloured stripes on the snow. Above, the stars shone in a moonless sky with fervent brightness.

By the time I reached the wall, my feet were wet and freezing but the rest of me had acclimatised somewhat and I felt fairly warm with my coat wrapped tightly around me. This was what I had needed, solitude and time to ponder what my vision in the flames had revealed. I had no doubt about the truth of the revelation. What amazed me was how I could have been unaware of my state until now.

I was pregnant with Joe's child, conceived that night in the magical hollow in the woods. I supposed that there had been so much happening in my life, so many changes, that I had not thought about the possibility of being pregnant. Now it all seemed ridiculously clear; the nausea, dislike for certain foods and cravings for others, my sudden revulsion for coffee and wine and my thickening waistline. I had been seeing so clearly through the eyes of the cypress, aware of other people's needs and fears. I had been connected to this world and the next, had even, fleetingly, seen through time, but I had been unable to see the new life that lay within me. Now Fiammetta's presence tonight made sense. She had been telling me that it was time to wake up to myself. With her countrywoman's practicality she had brought me back down to earth, steadied me and made me look inward.

I was seized by an emotion far bigger than anything I had ever felt before. My hands inside my deep coat pockets curved around my stomach with a sense of fierce protection and overwhelming love.

My eyes blurred with joy. The valley, from the towns and villages in the centre to the small mountain hamlets, was strung with festive lights like an upside-down sky that merged with the starry firmament and I felt giddy, as though I was floating in the night. It was hard to see where civilisation ended and the vast universe began.

Strong hands gripped my shoulders and I was anchored in reality once more. I had not heard Joe coming but I had expected it. I leant back on him, drawing extra warmth from his embrace and let the silence rest whilst I sought the right words to tell him what I had just discovered. From inside the hall came a sudden crescendo of noise as people rose from the table and raised their glasses to toast the New Year. Far off, down in Montalino, bells chimed midnight. From the valley, a rocket shot skywards and burst into stars over our heads. Soon everyone was outside and the silence of a perfect night exploded. Lucia was urging Pietro to set off the rockets they had planned. As everyone poured from the big hall, laughter and light spilled from the huge doors. Someone spotted Joe and me and whistled. Lucia called out something about young love. Then the doors closed behind them again and they forgot about us as Pietro's firework display began.

I was about to speak when Joe slid his arms down my side and then folded them gently over my own which were clasped protectively around my belly. He kissed my hair, whispering,

"Happy New Year Annie," and I realised that there was no reason to tell Joe anything – he already knew.

28

Stark, unyielding, severe and austere; words that people use to describe winter, which they also use for me.
They are right, in part. I do belong to a different world, one so alien that it must perforce seem disturbing. I look across this snowy world of transparency and refracted light but see also into the contrasting dark chasms of shadows. Beneath the surface, I feel the constant throb that rises from its core. Death, with its icy scythe, grips winter's hand tightly, but beneath the frozen ground is the pregnant hope of spring.
To leave the surface and look beyond, is to discover life's most precious secrets. All is continual. Life circles us and forms the music of life. Stand still and listen with me if you will.

The floor was freezing beneath my bare feet as I padded softly across the dark bedroom, groped my clothes from the chair by the window and quietly left the room. Joe's breathing remained slow and steady.

In the bathroom, the sudden light was too bright for comfort. I splashed cold water on my face then pulled on my clothes. I felt my way downstairs, not turning on the light because Joe deserved his sleep but wary of Luna who was bound to be waiting for me somewhere along the way. As I reached the bottom step, her warm head butted my legs and I bent down to scratch her ears. Fortunately, she kept quiet, even when I pulled on my boots and took my coat from the hook, although her tail beat a frenzied tattoo against the wall at the thought of this unexpectedly early walk.

Before I left the house, I could not resist looking into the lounge. On the carpet by the hearth was the sturdy wooden crib, which Joe had given me the previous night when we had got home from the party. Joe had made it strong but carved delicate woodland scenes around the sides and into the headboard. The crib was what he had been working on for me before Christmas, because he had already understood that I was pregnant. When I had asked him why he had not said anything to me, he had smiled and kissed me gently, saying that he had wanted me to discover the truth in my own time. His happiness had been so obvious that I wondered how he had managed to hide it from me.

The snow crunched satisfyingly underfoot as I crossed the garden, heading for the lake. Dawn's subtle pallet changed infinitesimally slowly. Luna bounded across the garden, leaping out of the snow like a deer but the cats were just two streaks of shadow as they slipped beneath the dangling willow branches ahead of me.

From afar, the lake lay like a smooth grey stone, reflecting the colourless expanse above. However, once I drew nearer, the trees and undergrowth that rimmed it cast deeper shadows, so that it looked like a huge eye, silvered by dawn. In the half-light I cast no shadow. The faint mist of condensation as I breathed was a spectral emanation flowing down and around me. I had never felt so alive, all my energy concentrated deep within, to the new life that quickened there.

After Joe had given me the crib, we had talked until the early hours, making plans, discussing our child. Then I had lain awake, fingers curved around the swell of my belly even after he had fallen asleep. I had been unable to stop my thoughts and had finally decided that I would not rest until I had shared my happiness with the cypress.

I pulled my coat closer at the neck and shoved my hands back into its pockets. The cold air was so pure and silent. It was too early for birdsong and there was no wind, just a faint note vibrating in the silence. I stretched out my mind and found the cypress immediately. The note changed and expanded into a gentle song and I sent my elation flooding out to form a harmony. At once, I was with the cypress, held in its strong branches.

Of course my news was no surprise to the cypress. I lay back in its branches, rocked by the soft breeze that the dawn had conjured up and watched the sky lighten as a warm pink tinge spread slowly through the grey. The unseen ghosts, the tree's dryads, hummed a different melody to herald the day and harmonise with the birds that began to sing as the sun rose slowly.

I was aware of my real body standing by the lake but the sensation of union with the cypress felt just as real. I smiled as I remembered my early hesitant attempts of communion; the way it had felt the first time I had allowed my soul to swoop and swerve within the wind, fall like rain and seep softly below the surface of the world; my recent exploration of the boundaries of time.

Stretching out I flowed up into the pale sky, higher and higher, exhilaration rushing through my veins. A thin layer of cloud hung below me, undulating like ripples of sand near the shore. As I watched, the clouds shifted. A small section curled up and separated and I was looking into Fiammetta's laughing blue eyes, her hair a wild mass of seething cloud.

I grinned at her as she swooped up towards me. She rubbed her gnarled hand tenderly across my belly.

"Want to see for yourself, Ragazza," she asked with a grin. I nodded and took her hand.

As she blended into the air, I heard her wild chuckle and felt the same delight spread through me, as together we plunged into the universe and slipped, invisibly through time. I felt as if I were swimming in cloud, slowly moving its vapours aside with one transparent hand while still aware of the rough warmth of Fiammetta's grip on my other side. When Fiammetta let go, the abrupt cold that replaced her presence by my side brought me up short.

The clouds parted and below me I could see our house. For a moment, I thought that only a few minutes had passed and that the reddish glow on the old stone house was caused by the sunrise. Then I realised that the light was different, the deeper, fiery red of sunset and the air, which had been so brittle and cold earlier that morning, now wrapped me in a sultry cocoon. I drifted down, seeking Fiammetta's shape and saw her cotton-cloud hair bob above the trees by the lake. Drawing nearer I stopped suddenly, struck by the curious experience of seeing myself in the flesh whilst being present in my mind form.

My other-self stood on the bank by the lake. Joe stood behind her, arms wrapped around her in such a familiar pose that I felt a wave of love sweep over me. I wondered if this was past or future that I was glimpsing, as I watched their shadows stretch out across the lake like a dark flame. Then, behind them, a movement caught my eye and I drifted forward.

Playing in the dry earth near the lake was a small child. My daughter, I thought, and in an instant, I was beside her. Her hair was as sleek and dark as her father's but as she raised her face and stared straight at me, her eyes were mine. She smiled a bright, glorious smile and said,

"Hello Mummy."

Behind me my future-self turned slightly and replied,

"Hi sweetie."

"Are you getting hungry, love?" Joe asked and both of me laughed at the inevitability of his question.

"A bit," said the child.

"You two are always hungry. We'll go in, in a minute, Ok?"

"Ok Mummy."

All the time she had been talking to her parents, the child had been looking at me and now her gaze flickered behind me and she laughed. Turning my head, I saw Fiammetta pulling faces and waving at the girl.

Do you know her? I asked silently. The child nodded and her silent reply was as clear to me as her spoken voice had been,

Of course Mummy. She is the flower fairy.

Fiammetta snorted with glee at the description and the girl grinned at her. It was obvious that they were well acquainted with each other. The sunset reflected in red glints in her shiny hair and her pale blue eyes were bold and fearless. She was a mixture of

Joe and myself and at the same time uniquely herself. I knew that I had never been that confident. Young as she was she had a look of daring and self-assurance.

The child bent her head and continued with what she had been doing before we had disturbed her. I felt Fiammetta at my side as we both watched the child, drawing with a stick in the dry ground. Her chubby, baby fingers held the stick a little clumsily but the drawing was clearly recognisable. She was drawing the cypress,

Do you know the cypress too?

She smiled up at me from beneath dark lashes.

He is my friend. Mummy takes me to see him when we go for a walk. Sometimes he sings me to sleep and he is always waiting for me when I shut my eyes.

As she spoke, she did shut her eyes and suddenly music welled around us, born on a warm breeze. Annie by the lake turned her head and smiled as if suddenly aware of our presence but Joe felt nothing.

The child opened her eyes again but the music stayed with us. As if it was already a well-established ritual, all three of us reached out to touch the drawing of the cypress. I was incredibly moved by the sight of our three hands. The child's real hand was small and soft. Fiammetta's and mine were ghostly images, my skin smooth and white; hers, dark and gnarled with age.

Such power already, in one so young. Fiammetta breathed.

Our fingers touched and the link between us; future, past and present; surged strongly, as we slipped into the song that the cypress was gently crooning. Separate but joined, the power of the universe strummed the air and, around us, the world spun slowly to the omnipresent song of the cypress.

I sing my song through time, as the old souls weave their circles in the air.
I sing the song of life.
I sing the song of love.
I sing of the absence of boundaries and of the tearing down of barriers, so
that the soul may grow strong.
I sing for all to hear, although few choose to do so.
Pause a while in your busy life when next you pass me by.
Listen to your heart as you shelter in my shade and, if it pleases you,
sing with me for a while.

Tonia Parronchi was born and grew up in England where she
obtained a degree in English Literature. She then worked in the
travel industry and in fashion before moving to Italy in 1990.
She now lives in Tuscany with her husband Guido, their son
James and their adorable dog, Stella.

toniahall121@gmail.com
www.toniaparronchi.com

Author Photograph by Guido Parronchi